Buying In

Buying In

LAURA HEMPHILL

New Harvest
Houghton Mifflin Harcourt
BOSTON • NEW YORK

www.hmhbooks.com

Library of Congress Cataloging-in-Publication Data
Hemphill, Laura, date.
Buying in / Laura Hemphill.
pages cm
ISBN 978-0-544-11457-9 (hardback)
1. Women capitalists and financiers — Fiction. 2. Consolidation and
merger of corporations — Fiction. 3. Wall Street (New York, N.Y.) — Fiction.
4. Global Financial Crisis, 2008–2009 — Fiction. I. Title.
PS3608.E4885B89 2013
813'.6 — dc23
2013001718

Printed in the United States of America
DOC 10 9 8 7 6 5 4 3 2 1

To my husband

1

Wednesday, October 10, 2007

Sophie Landgraf

IF ANYONE FOUND HER HERE, she'd be fired. It was 2 A.M., and Sophie was crouched under a desk, sweat collecting under her collar, ankles wobbling over four-inch heels. The footsteps in the hall were getting closer. She stared at the nickel-gray carpet and prayed that whoever was out there would turn around, march past the senior bankers' offices, and disappear.

Moments ago Sophie had been weaving through the honeycomb of empty cubicles and blinking computer screens, struggling to balance the printouts propped against her hip, teetering on the heels that almost allowed her to look the men she worked with in the eye. She'd planned to leave the merger analysis for Ethan Pearce, her boss, and run home to get some sleep, but as she rounded the corner, she noticed Sinclair's open door. The dark open slice, no more than an inch, invited her to reconsider. It seemed to say, *It's 2 A.M. No one's here. Who's to know?*

Sophie couldn't help peeking through the glass wall. Sinclair's desk glowed with the ambient light from Times Square, begging her to take another look inside its drawers, just for a second. Her reflection hovered on the glass door: suit a safe shade of navy, red hair pulled back tightly enough to give her a dull ache at the temples, entire appearance carefully constructed to be as unobjectionable as the maritime photographs lining Sterling's halls. Being careful wasn't getting her anywhere.

The door swung open with her nudge. Pictures rested on Sinclair's modular shelves: his young daughter grooming a mare, his wife perched outside a thatched bungalow that looked too perfect to be real. She hoped she'd find something new in Sinclair's desk, her favorite for late-night explorations — she deserved to get something out of being the last person on the floor to leave.

She slid open the top drawer. Only the familiar bow tie, *Zagat's*, blister pack of antianthrax pills, June's Harvard alumni magazine, and a half-eaten bar of Toblerone. She felt a delicious squeeze around her heart when she saw something strange stuffed between the files in Sinclair's bottom drawer. She fished out an envelope, puckered and creased, "1997" scrawled across its flap. Inside were broken seashells, smooth and white as bone.

Sophie was holding a shell to the light when she heard footsteps in the hall. She jammed the envelope back into the drawer and dove under the desk, banging her head. The footsteps were getting louder. Bile crept up her throat. Please let it be the sweet Romanian cleaning lady who once showed Sophie pictures of her son. Anyone but a banker. Let whoever was out there pass her by, and she'd never explore ever again — she promised.

A shadow swept across the carpet. The elongated form stretched all the way to the windows. No vacuum. No wheeled trashcan. Perfect posture. It must be a banker.

The steps grew softer but Sophie didn't dare breathe, waiting, listening for any sound beyond the buzz of Sinclair's computer tower. It wasn't until she heard the distant ding of the elevator that she closed her eyes in thanks. She was safe.

$$$

As Sophie knocked on Ethan Pearce's door the next afternoon, every muscle from her fingers to her neck tightened into a single, stressed-out mass. The other analysts said she was lucky to be working for the most profitable managing director in their group, but honestly, Ethan scared her. It was perfectly obvious he thought everyone around him was an idiot. He wasn't bad-looking — thick dark hair, commanding square jaw, skin that always looked wind-burned even though with the hours he worked, he couldn't possibly spend much time outside. He was in better shape at forty than most of the twenty-two-year-olds she knew. But his dark eyes had a cold-ness, like he was assessing her worth.

Ethan hardly looked up as Sophie slid into the chair beside Vasu Mehta. No *thanks for staying until three last night*, no *nice work on the presentation*, and definitely no *sorry it took me until almost 5 P.M. to actually look at it*. Ethan slashed red pen across the analysis like it had somehow offended him. It was nineteen hours before Ethan's lunch meeting with the CEO of AlumiCorp, his prize client. In a week, the set of strategic alternatives the managing director planned to present at the meeting had mushroomed from five to fourteen; the stack of pages before him was now over an inch thick. If the meeting were delayed a day or two, Sophie was pretty sure fourteen would become thirty, the work expanding to fill every last possible second.

Sophie looked over to Vasu, hoping for a smile, a thumbs-up, anything encouraging. Vasu's shrug confirmed what she'd already suspected: she wouldn't be seeing her boyfriend, Will, for the sixth night in a row, and Vasu wouldn't be tucking his daughter into bed. Vasu was a vice president — a midlevel — and her direct superior, but as far as she could see, the only difference between them was that he got to go home before she did.

Ethan laid his pen in perfect parallel to the edge of the desk. The other bankers decorated their identical modular desks with construction-paper Father's Day cards, photos of themselves in scuba gear. Not Ethan. Not a single picture. Nothing on the walls. Ethan's desktop was empty except for a Sterling & Sons mug holding pencils sharpened to a stiletto-thin point. One peek inside his top drawer had been enough for Sophie. Swimming goggles, nail clippers, a Ferragamo tie wound into a tidy coil, and packets of Gulden's Spicy Brown Mustard. Nothing that compared to Ira Blumenstein's gold tooth, Kenneth Yang's Darth Vader lollipop, or Rich Angstrom's Magic 8 Ball.

Ethan swiveled his chair to face his floor-to-ceiling window. He pointed twenty-six stories down, to the twin spires stretching over Fifth Avenue. "We should've held this meeting at St. Pat's. Then maybe we'd have a prayer."

Sophie could never tell if Ethan was joking or criticizing — other disadvantage of being new. Vasu raised a finger, and Sophie knew what was coming.

"We could add a split-off of the Midwest, no?" Vasu asked.

"Can't hurt," Ethan said. "Anything that brings in fees."

AlumiCorp was their best shot at booking business before year-end, or so Ethan reminded them pretty much constantly. Which was why, in the four months Sophie had worked at Sterling, she'd pulled more all-nighters than she had in four years at Yale. It wasn't enough that she'd spent her entire Sunday modeling a merger between AlumiCorp and Millennium Can — on Monday, Ethan made her add a deal with Safe-Tee Tube. This past week, she'd modeled mergers between AlumiCorp and the rest of the top ten aluminum manufacturers. Correction: every one of the top ten except Roll-Rite. Now that she thought about it, why weren't they including Roll-Rite? Should she suggest it?

Her first month at Sterling, Sophie had taken it upon herself to wordsmith Ethan's talking points so they would read more smoothly, confusing *alumina* and *aluminum* in the process. As

Ethan reviewed her changes, he'd said, "Analysts should be seen and not heard, unless they're right. You might've read every book in the library of whatever Ivy League school you went to, but in this business, you need to become an expert in the real world. Until you know the client's business as well as the client does, please, do us all a favor and keep your mouth shut."

Now, watching Ethan eviscerate the AlumiCorp presentation, Sophie could hear her mother: if you don't treat yourself with respect, no one else will either. She cleared her throat. "I wonder." Her voice sounded hoarse. "Maybe it would make sense to add a merger with Roll-Rite?"

Ethan squinted at her in a way that Sophie remembered perfectly from the girls who'd tied ribbons around their ponytails in middle school, who'd scanned Sophie up and down with an irritation that said, *we both know how badly you need me and you're , very lucky that I'm barely tolerating you right now.*

"You must be kidding," Ethan said flatly.

She could feel the heat under her cheeks. She wondered why no one had ever told her that after college graduation, she might never feel smart or capable again.

Ethan slid his markup across the table. "Finish the presentations by 5 A.M. Leave them here. I'll pick them up before my flight. I want both of you at your desks, queued up, 8 A.M. In case we need to run any analysis on the fly." Ethan rose, fastening the top button of his suit jacket with a quick flick of his thumb and index finger: they were dismissed.

Vasu held the door for Sophie, stooping like he didn't want to offend Ethan by towering over him. When they were out of Ethan's earshot, Vasu said, "AlumiCorp's and Roll-Rite's Midwest operations, they're the worst in the industry. Too many plants, not enough demand. Combine a $9 billion wreck with a $5 billion wreck . . . Well, that's a full-on disaster, isn't it?"

"So basically I had the stupidest idea ever."

Vasu shrugged with noncommittal patience she imagined he'd

perfected on his six-year-old. Sophie got the sense that that was exactly how he thought of her — as a child who asked too many questions. He pulled a pack of Parliaments from his pants pocket and headed toward the elevators.

The problem with Sterling was that after you made a complete fool of yourself, there was nowhere to hide. The offices, the cubicles, the conference rooms — everything was transparent, designed to remind you that your productivity was being carefully monitored. Sophie and the other entry-level analysts were cloistered in cubicles at the center of the floor, where they could be watched from any direction.

If her quadmate, Jordanne, weren't downstairs at a Credit Committee meeting, they could've ducked out to the Starbucks across the street, and Jordanne would have told Sophie that she shouldn't let it get to her because Ethan Pearce was notorious for being a jerk and he'd probably forgotten the whole thing already. Sophie's mother would have thought it suspect that in a group of thirty, there were only two women, both analysts, the lowest of the low. Her mother would have said it was absolutely inexcusable that of all the empty desks on the twenty-sixth floor, the powers that be had seated Sophie and Jordanne alone in a quad by themselves, as if they needed to be quarantined. Sophie couldn't have been more grateful. Like Jordanne said, "Girls have to help each other out."

Sophie dropped into the chair that still sprouted the short, dark hairs of its last owner, reminding her that her desk was on loan, until she'd proved she could live up to it. Rows of tiny holes dotted the carpet, an axis on which her cubicle could be reconfigured or eliminated entirely. Her first week at the bank, Sophie had dreamt that her cubicle kept shrinking smaller and smaller until her entire life fit inside a four-inch square.

Sophie's boyfriend, Will, had given her a ficus bush for her desk, which she refused to bring to Sterling because it would have made her stick out — there weren't any plants on the floor, only two enormous vases by the elevator that were refilled each week with colossal stalks of Hawaiian torch ginger, dogwood branches that were taller than she was. The most Sophie dared was to tape a few pictures to the thin strip of Plexiglas that couldn't be seen from the hall: Will atop Mount Frissell, dark curls wayward from the climb, feet planted wide in a way that made his wiry frame seem solid and confident. The latest nursery-school portrait of her godson, Bryce, a freckled, cowlicked kid who'd be five next week, the same age Sophie had been when she'd met his mother, Kim. Her last family snapshot, the three of them on Yale's Old Campus the day her parents had come down for her eighteenth birthday. At the moment the camera snapped, she'd been secretly furious at her mother for telling her roommate about the waste-burning generator they'd just installed on the Western Massachusetts sheep farm where Sophie's parents had homesteaded since the seventies. Sophie had been extremely careful to give her roommate the impression that her parents were actually normal.

First things first: Sophie texted Will to let him know she wouldn't make it to Trivial Dispute that night. It would take until at least midnight to make Ethan's changes, not to mention getting the books printed and bound — cutting it awfully close if she was going to get the presentations to Ethan by 5 A.M. She needed to refuel.

Sophie searched for her nail polish, pushing aside the Ziploc bag of perfume samples in her bottom drawer and carefully lifting the scarf she'd knit with the last of her mother's yarn. She tucked the bottle into the sleeve of her suit. The ladies' room was empty, as usual. Perched on the cool lid inside the handicap stall, Sophie painted a fresh coat of red over her chipped nails.

$$$

At 4 A.M., the beeping of her BlackBerry broke Sophie's nap. In the moment before she became fully awake, she reached for Will's chest. Her hand met cold plastic. She bolted upright, hitting her head on the underside of her desk. She peered around the trashcan to make sure the floor was empty before she crawled out — no one could know she'd snuck in a few hours' sleep. Strewn across her desk were a half-eaten container of massaman curry, Ethan's edits, and four empty cans of Diet Coke. The guys in production would be finished with the presentations by now.

The elevator opened to forty copy machines clicking in mechanized counterpoint. Men stooped over the copiers, glowing blue lines moving across their faces as the machines read another page. The presentations were spiral bound in maroon, the covers embossed with the Sterling stag. She'd thought Vasu was joking the first time he'd told her to flip through each page and check for smudges and mistakes. "Trust me," he said, "all shit flows downhill."

The twenty-sixth floor was silent except for the whir of an occasional computer: perfect conditions for exploring. Sophie was tempted to revisit the seashells in Sinclair's bottom drawer. Her mother used to say that most wrongs were the result of human weakness, not calculation. Sophie owed it to herself to be stronger. Straight to Ethan's office to drop off the AlumiCorp presentations.

Inside the dark room, music played, so soft and eerie that Sophie thought she might have imagined it. As Sophie set the AlumiCorp books on her boss's desk, she saw a silhouette, statuesque against the midtown skyline. Ethan stared out the window, soldier straight.

Sophie braced herself for a reprimand. "I'm sorry, Ethan. I didn't know—"

He raised his hand and held it there until the recording tapered into silence. Ethan turned from the window. His mouth twitched into, not a smile exactly, but the memory of one. "Sibelius."

Si-be-li-us. The word, the music—both sounded like *loneliness.* Sophie didn't know what Sibelius was, but if she'd learned anything since arriving at Sterling, it was to keep quiet about things she didn't know. She'd look it up later.

"Leave the books on the desk." Ethan turned back to the skyscrapers framed in his window.

The door clicked close behind her.

Sophie was dropping her BlackBerry into her coat pocket when Ethan strode past her cubicle, a Sterling gym bag slung over his shoulder. He raised his hand in good-bye, his eyes not meeting hers. In the months she'd worked with him, this Sibelius was the first hint of any interior life.

Her elevator descended through two dozen Sterling fiefdoms, one stacked on top of the other. Nearly ten thousand employees worked in this building — more than lived in Stockton, the town where she'd grown up. Not to mention Sterling's back offices in Jersey City, its satellites in Houston, Chicago, and Menlo Park, or London, Zurich, Beijing, Doha . . . Pretty easy to feel insignificant in this place.

Sophie's heels clicked across the cool marble of the Sterling lobby. Outside, wind whistled down the concrete. The lights of Times Square pulsed on quiet sidewalks, ticket stubs and napkin scraps strewn at her feet. Sophie was not a young woman who stood out in a crowd, and had it been a few hours later, she would have been lost in thickets of businessmen slamming shoulders with tourists, but for now, it was just her. She stared up — neck craned, head back, mouth open to the stock prices crawling around Sterling, the stag mounted above the skyscraper's entrance, the first ten dark stories containing the trading floors, the next ten of asset management and legal, to the floors that held the investment banking groups, where a few windows were still checkered with the Oz-green glow of fluorescent lights. No matter how hard you worked, someone else worked harder.

The guy driving the town car woke Sophie when they reached Eighty-Fifth and Amsterdam. A garbage truck crept down the block, its flashing lights and steady beep an unwelcome reminder of the alarm that would wake her in a few hours. The hallway of Sophie's apartment building smelled like her mother's beef stew. How anyone could afford to live on the Upper West Side and get home in time to make dinner, she had no idea. She would never let her father know that she paid fifteen hundred a month — half her paycheck — for an apartment the size of a two-car garage. When she signed on with Sterling, he'd called her a Stepford sleepwalker. If she wasn't going to convince him that she hadn't sold out, she at least wanted him to believe that Sterling bought her a comfortable existence.

Honestly, her apartment looked better in the dark. She'd moved in the first of July and spent Independence Day painting the walls a shade of yellow that the hardware store had called butter but that turned out more like canary. She'd considered changing it until Will joked that if she actually spent any time at home, she might get a sunburn. After that, she refused to change it on principle. The walls were still bare, but when she had a few more paychecks and some free time, she planned to fill them with art deco travel posters — "Fly Pan Am to Panama," "Sail Jewel Steamship to Japan" — places she'd never seen, but would like to, one day.

She flicked on the light. Will yanked a pillow across his eyes.

"Sorry!" she whispered. She'd thought he was staying at his place in Williamsburg. He was curled into a spoon, waiting for her. She knew from the way the comforter was balled up that her side of the bed would already be warm. It was as though he'd known she needed him here tonight even though she hadn't known it herself. He pulled the pillow back an inch, eyes barely visible, the right corner of his lip pulling into the same smile it had two weeks into her freshman year when she'd explained that she was sorry she was so nervous but he had to understand that she'd only ever kissed two or four guys depending on whether you counted dares, which Will, a junior, found adorable.

"I'm up, I'm up." He propped himself on his elbows, skin pulled taut across his narrow chest. His hair fell in dark waves just past his chin, his aquiline nose so fine and delicate that Sophie sometimes thought he'd make a better-looking girl than she did. "What time is it?"

"Five. I'm trying this new thing where I spend as little time in daylight as possible. I want to see whether it's actually possible to turn into a mole."

She stepped out of her heels, pressing her arches into the floor, stretching them out. She didn't waste time taking off her suit, crawling beside him and resting her head against his neck, the fit perfect after four years of practice. She took a deep breath and let it out. Will smelled of warm wood chips, cozy sweaters, and clear winter skies, of places she wished she could be.

"Bad day?" He kissed the tips of her fingers, nail polish picked clean off.

"So I'm not just neurotic, I'm predictable. Great." She said this sarcastically, though secretly she liked being known. "How was pub trivia?"

"We lost. The deciding question: How many of the Seven Wonders of the World are still standing?"

"One — the Pyramid of Giza."

"Show-off." He grinned. "So tomorrow's that big pitch?"

"Finally."

"Does that mean they'll let you go tomorrow night?"

"I'm all yours."

His eyebrows lifted in a skeptical way that he really should know kind of irritated her. She knew she hadn't exactly been the best girlfriend since starting at Sterling, but he didn't need to rub it in.

By the time she'd hung up her suit and set her BlackBerry on the radiator she pretended was a nightstand, Will was asleep. When she'd moved to New York in July, reuniting them after two years of long distance, he'd follow her to the sink when she was getting ready for bed, his arms wrapped around her waist, kissing the back of her neck.

Will had taped a note to her bathroom mirror: *package on counter*. Teeth brushed and face washed, Sophie used her BlackBerry as a flashlight so she wouldn't wake Will. The small cardboard box took up half the kitchen counter. Her father hadn't skimped on the packing tape. Sophie sifted through Styrofoam peanuts for the yin-yang her father had made from a repurposed hubcap. Printed on the back of a form letter from *The Nation* was a note:

Dear Ms. Serena Silver,
Thank you for your purchase of *Balance*. Please visit recyclingchuck.com to see the latest additions to my work. I appreciate your continued support.
Sincerely,
Chuck Landgraf

Her elaborate ruse — alias, post office box, money orders — had been fun at first, but now she only tolerated it because her father never would have accepted financial help outright. As a kid, she hadn't been aware of money problems, but in retrospect, her parents' insistence that they didn't believe in things like orthodontists, vacations, or cell phones should have been a tip-off. Their small sheep farm had always been more of a political statement than an actual business. Four years ago, when Sophie's mother died, her father sold the sheep, sold the barn, and retreated into the shed behind their house where he made sculptures from scrap metal. He'd never said he was tight on cash, but it didn't take a genius to figure out that without the shearing money coming in, "Serena Silver" needed to start an art collection.

Sophie had hated her name when she was little — it was too dogmatic, too her mother. Sophie, wisdom. Tracy, warlike. Jan Landgraf wanted her daughter to fight and fight smart. When, at age eight, Sophie said she wanted a peaceful name like Serena or Olivia, her mother's face puckered. "Those women die of consumption while waiting for white knights." Sophie could only imagine how livid her mother would have been if she'd known that her daughter's initials were the same as Sterling's ticker on the New York Stock Exchange.

Sophie tried to stack the sculpture in her closet, on top of the others, but she'd run out of space. She settled on the kitchen cabinet, which was empty except for two bars of her favorite dark chocolate and the marsala Will had used to cook dinner for their anniversary, a meal they'd gamely pretended was a Tuscan picnic, spreading a blanket across her floor. Sophie was a decent cook, but the most she'd done in this kitchen was burn toast. Hunching over the two-burner stove wouldn't have appealed to Sophie even if she actually had time to eat at home.

She pulled her laptop from under the bed and Googled "Sibelius." Wikipedia said that the Finnish composer's Sixth Symphony reminded Sibelius of the scent of first snow. That was exactly how Sophie would describe the piece she'd heard in Ethan's office: still, cold, solitary. Sophie yawned and closed her eyes against the computer's soft glow.

2

Thursday, October 11, 2007

Jake Hutchinson

SOMETIMES HUTCH WONDERED if bankers tried to look like parodies of themselves. As Hutch shook Ethan Pearce's hand in the lobby of the Cincinnati Hilton, he couldn't help noticing Pearce's nails: better buffed than the '68 Ford Mustang that Hutch polished with Turtle Wax and baby-blanket shammies every Sunday. No guy should have nails that neat. Pearce was the sort of man who would be at home in the Hamptons, sipping rosé. The sort who'd never drink PBR or set foot inside a one-room cabin like the one on Haskin Lake where Hutch had gone for twenty-three years, since he was a plant engineer at AlumiCorp's Chambersburg rolling mill.

A real lunch might be the best part of this meeting. Hutch's wife, Trish, kept him on a low-fat, low-taste diet, though his cholesterol was 180, he jogged two and a half miles most mornings, and his doc had pronounced him fit as a fiddle at forty-eight. Once, Trish snuck up behind him and wrapped a measuring tape around his gut because she'd read that excess girth was a risk factor for heart disease. They'd be married twenty-six years come January and it was the best decision of his life, but sometimes, Trish made Hutch question his sanity. Last Tuesday he came home to an itty-bitty piece of salmon and steamed broccoli, starving from listening to his forecasting team predict that this might be the first time in his four-year tenure as CEO that AlumiCorp didn't post a profit. Hutch left the dinner table hungry and went on a rampage, pulling open cupboards, looking for the chocolate he was sure Trish hid for herself.

The hostess laid two menus on their table. Hutch hadn't even sat down, and Ethan Pearce jumped right in. "Technicals suggest downward pressure on the equity markets . . ."

For a minute, Hutch thought Pearce might try to restart the equity offering Hutch had squelched earlier that year, but he didn't. Smart man. Hutch hated how bankers thought they came up with the ideas. Bankers were a necessary inconvenience, like jockstraps. If Hutch could've financed AlumiCorp's transactions without relying on the investment banks, he would've, in a heartbeat.

" . . . and we've noticed investor appetite for highly leveraged names . . ."

Come on, *speak English*. Either Wall Street–speak was designed to keep out the riffraff, or bankers didn't understand financial concepts well enough to put them plainly.

Hutch waved over a tuxedoed waiter and ordered coffee, black. Hutch was only willing to sit through these pitches because he owed Pearce for the credit line Sterling had granted them last spring. He and Pearce understood each other: pay for play. The arrangement wasn't official, but the next time AlumiCorp did a deal, they'd need to hire bankers, and Hutch would rather throw the business to Ethan Pearce than to that smarmy Mike Bennett at Goldman.

"The market isn't giving AlumiCorp full credit for your cost-cutting initiatives . . ."

Hutch tuned out Pearce and scanned the menu, settling on a cheeseburger, potato casserole, and lemonade. Hutch motioned for Pearce to hand over one of the presentations. Heavy as a brick. The table of contents alone was three pages long: Optimizing the Midwest Operations, Restructuring Alternatives, Merger Opportunities, Asset Sales, Project Financing Options . . . Some poor sap at Sterling had run AlumiCorp six ways from Sunday.

"We've prepared an analysis of a spin-off of AlumiCorp's Midwest assets."

The Midwest: Hutch's Vietnam. Every day, another defeat — a lost order for heavy-gauge foil, a beverage company playing hardball on a contract renewal. The surplus of smelters and rolling mills in the Midwest meant customers constantly threatened to take their orders elsewhere, driving down AlumiCorp's prices and everyone else's. Pulling out of the region was not an option. AlumiCorp was a Midwestern company, and it'd stand by its Midwestern assets. The company had weathered rough patches before, but those crises were before Hutch was CEO. Now that the future of a century-old company was in his hands, the pressures felt different. They felt personal.

Hutch didn't have to look at Pearce's numbers to know that without the drag from the Midwest, AlumiCorp would look pretty darn good. But a Cincinnati-based company letting go of assets in its own backyard? They might as well run up the white flag and beg some private equity shop to buy them, fire half of AlumiCorp's employees, salvage what they could, and leave the rest for scrap. Not on his watch.

Hutch held up a hand. "Spin off the Midwest. I'm not convinced that'd maximize shareholder value."

"All right," Pearce said. "If you look on page twenty-two . . ."

Hutch's pride would never let him consider Pearce's next idea, a merger with Midwest Metals, whose hostile takeover attempt on AlumiCorp back in '96 nearly cost Hutch his job and his dignity.

The waitress arrived with Hutch's coffee and Pearce's macchiato. Hutch seized Ethan's presentation by its maroon binding and off-loaded both copies onto the waitress.

"Could you toss those for us, hon?"

He leaned back in his seat, squared his shoulders, and said, "Give me your best shot."

Sophie Landgraf

Sophie hurried to her ringing phone later that afternoon, hoping Ethan was calling with news of the AlumiCorp pitch. It was Kim again — Sophie owed her about five phone calls and a dozen IMs. She glanced at her monitor, a pop-up reminding her that the Industrial Group's weekly status meeting started in five minutes. Sophie wanted to tell her friend about the weird thing she'd seen in Ethan's office last night. Even more, she wanted to tell Kim not to worry, she was definitely going to make it to Stockton for Bryce's fifth birthday party on Friday — the four-hour bus ride was nothing. But there was zero chance she'd make it to the party, and if she answered the phone right then, she'd be late for the meeting. She'd call Kim later.

All thirty members of the Industrial Group had gathered in the conference room, save Ethan. The senior bankers sat in maroon leather chairs circling an oak conference table. Vasu and the other midlevels occupied the ladder-back chairs along the windowed wall. The second- and third-year analysts perched on the credenza at the head of the conference table. Jordanne Terney and Ned Donnigan, the other first-year analysts, leaned against the inner glass wall.

Sophie had learned the hard way that Jordanne's first name

wasn't pronounced like the country and her last name didn't rhyme with "gurney." She was Zhor-*dah*-nah Tair-*nae* of Hong Kong and Lisbon by way of Le Rosey, the elite Swiss boarding school, and Wharton undergrad — she was, like her accent, from everywhere and nowhere. Jordanne's aristocratic cheekbones came from British baronets on her father's side, and her dark hair and exacting, almond-shaped eyes came from her mother, Portugal's former minister of finance. Jordanne was an NCAA-ranked sabrist, she carried an American Express Platinum Card, and next to her monitor sat a dog-eared Excel textbook she called the Bible. Sophie owned four suits that she'd purchased at the outlet mall, but Jordanne had a seemingly endless wardrobe with grosgrain trim and flounced sleeves in shades like Byzantine blue. Just standing next to Jordanne made Sophie feel like the world would take her seriously. Donnigan, on the other hand, took nothing seriously, including himself.

Donnigan leaned over to Sophie. "You look like shit. Another late one?"

"Don't listen to him," Jordanne said.

Sophie shrugged. She'd decided to tolerate Donnigan after he'd stood up for her a few weeks ago. The new associate from Chemicals had walked past the assistants' desks in front of Sophie's quad, passed the visiting Donnigan, and asked Sophie to photocopy some binders. Donnigan saw what was going on before Sophie did. "She's no assistant — she's an *analyst,* fuckwit."

Jordanne whispered, "You can have some of my NoDoz."

Sophie held out her shaking hands. "I think if I have more caffeine, I might blast off."

Sophie turned her attention to the conference table. Grant Sinclair, the head of the Industrial Group, had chosen the race-car cufflinks today. He rotated his collection, never wearing the same pair in a given week. The golden stags' heads were Sophie's favorite. The race cars ornamented a pink shirt. With his periwinkle tie, matching pocket square, banker belly, and shiny scalp, Sinclair looked like an Easter egg on legs. Now that she thought about it, the seashells she'd found in Sinclair's desk last night were just about the only things associated with him that weren't the color of sherbet.

Sinclair cleared his throat. "Success is elusive this year, isn't it? I have a meeting with Safe-Tee on Tuesday — they're holding a bake-off to finance the old S.T. Corp assets. And I'm taking Ball & Bearing to dinner tonight. We may have to take down a block of their credit facility."

Sinclair turned to Ira Blumenstein, a managing director whose forehead was creased with an impossible number of frown lines. The second years said he'd thrown a binder at an associate once. In Blumenstein's middle drawer, there was a box that contained paper clips and a gold tooth. Sophie couldn't help wondering whether he'd knocked it out of some poor analyst's mouth and saved it as a trophy.

"Ira," Sinclair asked, "what's on your plate?"

"Midwest Metals. Monday. New high-yield issue."

"Anyone else?" Sinclair asked. "That's it? At least one of us is focused on fees. Ethan's pitching AlumiCorp on strategic ops as we speak."

Fees: the magic word. Fees funded bonuses for Sterling's senior bankers, and Sophie hoped some of that bounty would find its way into her bonus that summer. The rest of the bankers would get their bonuses the day before Christmas, but analysts didn't receive theirs until July, a year after they started. Her bonus might be a pittance to the Grant Sinclairs and Ethan Pearces of the world, but to Sophie, who graduated Yale seventy thousand in debt, it would be no joke.

"We should all be out in front of the client. In this business environment . . ." Sinclair leaned back, lifted his glasses, and pressed his thumb and forefinger against his eyelids. "Might as well just say it. Our group's twenty million behind budget."

Grumbles rippled through the room. Jordanne caught Sophie's eye and winced. Did that mean bonuses would be cut? That some of them would be reassigned? Fired?

"We're the worst performing group in the Investment Banking Division," Sinclair continued. "This isn't Hollywood, folks — no one likes an underdog. The powers that be will only tolerate a lagging group for so long."

The men around the table bowed their heads.

Sinclair surveyed the room. "Who's working with Ethan on AlumiCorp. Vasu? And —?"

Sophie raised a finger.

"Give it all you've got," Sinclair said. "I shouldn't have to tell you all other deals take a backseat to this one. AlumiCorp's our best bet for booking some solid fees before year-end."

Sinclair stood and everyone else followed. Sophie caught up with Vasu, whose dark head bobbed in a distinctive rhythm that made it seem like his life had a soundtrack. "Any chance you've heard about the AlumiCorp meeting?" she asked.

"Radio silence." His hand fiddled in his pocket. After two months working under Vasu, Sophie had gotten used to the antsiness that prefigured his cigarette breaks. "Let's catch up in a few. I'll swing by." Vasu loped toward the elevators, hunching in the way of the very tall.

If the AlumiCorp meeting fell flat, the week Sophie had spent on the analysis would only add a few more maroon-bound inches to her rapidly growing stack of PowerPoint presentations: the tower of going nowhere. When she took the job at Sterling, Sophie pictured herself leading meetings where millions of dollars were volleyed back and forth, like they were nothing. Sophie wasn't leading meetings; she wasn't even invited to them. Not exactly what she'd pictured when the Morgan Stanley recruiter told her, "Nowhere but Wall Street can a twenty-two-year-old get so much responsibility."

Her senior year of college, Sophie had attended a career fair at the Payne Whitney Gym. Half her classmates were falling over themselves trying to work at an investment bank. She figured they must know something she didn't. The Lehman Brothers recruiter was enthusiastic when Sophie mentioned she was an applied math major. The recruiter told her an entry-level analyst earned a salary of $55,000 and a bonus that might bring the total to $100,000 — more than four times what her parents used to make from their Corriedales.

She called Will, who'd then been in New York almost two years.

"Seriously? Banking?" he'd asked. "You know, you could reconsider med school."

"Too late."

"Postbac premed programs aren't as bad as you think. You could do one in New York. With me."

There were certain things she couldn't say out loud, like how after her mother died, Sophie knew she'd resent patients who lived.

"Banking jobs are in New York too," Sophie said. "And it's good experience, right? They're like grad school, except they pay you."

"What about a nonprofit or something? You don't have to sell out to come to the city."

"My dad's not exactly going to pay my rent, not that I'd let him." In her head, it had sounded less judgmental.

"Supplement. My parents supplement."

NPR called Will a production assistant, but at $400 a month, he was basically a glorified intern. He managed $1100 in rent with his parents' help, but OK — "supplement." Will seemed happy enough with his life in the city, where Netflix was an indulgence and a two-dollar falafel a nice meal out, but if Sophie was going to move to New York, she wanted to party at Capitale and Cain and Lollipop, like her classmates who'd gone to Andover and Chapin. She wanted to try foie gras and uni. She wanted to drink cocktails with egg whites. Otherwise, what was the point? If she was going to sit at home and play Trivial Pursuit, she might as well move back to Stockton and have a cozy, monotonous existence, like her father and Kim. To do New York her way, she'd have to pull a decent salary, which meant she had to be a consultant or a banker.

"Don't worry," she said. "It's just a job. You have to buy in before you can sell out, right?"

Jordanne walked into their quad, toothpaste and toothbrush in hand. Jordanne brushed her teeth about thirty times a day — Sophie had counted once. Jordanne brought in a new tube of Crest each Monday, which she kept in her bottom drawer next to five bottles of Tums, a box of strawberry Pocky, and a Mason Pearson brush.

"What do you want for lunch?" Jordanne asked.

Officially, they took turns running downstairs to the cafeteria, but unofficially, Jordanne made their food runs because AlumiCorp kept Sophie tied to her desk.

Sophie grabbed her BlackBerry. "I'll come with you."

"Don't you have that meeting with Nancy Cho?"

The Sterling women's network had assigned Cho, one of three senior women in the division, as Sophie's mentor. "She canceled again."

Jordanne's BlackBerry buzzed. As she clicked through the email, her eyes screwed into two tiny, miserable pits.

"Sinclair?" Sophie asked.

"My mom. Letting me know that her friend's son at Credit Suisse is already working on a live deal. How sweet of her to remind me that I'm not good enough."

"Don't let her get to you. You're doing great." When Sophie was little, she'd wanted a mother like Jordanne's, one who took grades seriously instead of insisting that all that mattered was to learn.

Jordanne jammed the elevator button. "Do you know what she said when I didn't get the job at Blackstone? 'For some women, there's nothing wrong with being a wife and mother.'"

"Sometimes I think the reason you have parents is to show you a way not to live your life."

When Jordanne thought hard about something, her lips pushed out like a fish. "Where were you when I didn't get into Harvard?"

They weaved around the salad bar, the pasta station, the grill. Jordanne grabbed a tuna-fish sandwich that would stink up their quad for the rest of the day, as usual. It was the only thing wrong with Jordanne.

"Up to anything tonight?" Jordanne asked.

"Reuniting with my long-lost boyfriend. *If* I manage to stay awake."

"Where's Prince Charming taking you?"

Sophie played with the plastic wrap around her turkey sandwich. "We haven't decided yet." Sophie wasn't about to tell Jordanne, who had views about whether Nobu or Masa had better toro, that tonight, Sophie would be taking Will to the Crocodile Lounge, where beers cost four dollars and there was free pizza after 10 P.M. She wouldn't have been her mother's daughter if she hadn't appreciated that this was a step forward for feminism, but it wasn't ideal — not because of the money, which Sophie was fine with. She missed the way in college Will had taken her to the film society to see a Swedish movie she'd never even heard of, or to a wine and cheese night that was infinitely more fun than the predictable sophomore dorm parties she would have gone to on her own.

"Want to come to Lollipop?" Jordanne asked. "I'm dying to meet Will."

It might be the best offer a friend had made since Kim had somehow convinced Natalie Tibirski, who basically hadn't known Sophie existed, to invite Sophie to her lake house after prom. At Lollipop, she, Jordanne, and Will would sip lavender-infused cocktails. Jordanne would run into people she knew from the summer she'd worked in the Athens office of her father's shipping business and would introduce Sophie as her best friend from Sterling. Will would impress them with stories about the up-and-coming French director his radio show had interviewed last week. Yes, Sophie had promised Will that she'd be all his tonight, but he'd have to understand that an invitation to Lollipop was the sort of thing you didn't pass up.

"Do you think we'll get in?" Bouncers had it out for Will — they saw straight into his duct-taped wallet: ten dollars, a MetroCard, and an old Yale ID whose date Will doctored with nail-polish remover every year to get student discounts.

"The manager's a friend from Saint-Tropez." Jordanne held the elevator for Sophie. "So you'll come?"

Sophie tried to sound casual. "Sure."

Jordanne dropped her sandwich and vitaminwater onto her desk. "Question." She jutted her pointy chin at the spreadsheet open on her screen. "Does this look better in currency format, or in accounting?"

Jordanne's spreadsheet was perfectly formatted: inputs coded in blue, links in green, outputs in black.

"What you've got looks great," Sophie said.

"You sure this one isn't better?"

Sophie had majored in applied math, not applied bullshit, and honestly, she didn't see the difference between the two options. Sophie knew there was plenty of room for her and Jordanne to both succeed at Sterling, but looking at the perfectly aligned decimal points on Jordanne's spreadsheet, Sophie couldn't help but be reminded that as far as the managing directors were concerned, she and Jordanne were direct competitors. Sophie had a feeling she wasn't the favorite.

Before starting at Sterling, Sophie had never built a financial model, the analyses that projected a corporation's fiscal future. She saw her first model during training and found it simplistic yet frustrating: put one formula in the wrong place and the whole thing fell apart. In the last four months, Sophie had learned to suture Excel cell to Excel cell, making spreadsheets come alive by pumping numbers through their veins, coaxing them to spit out probability-weighted outcomes, capital ratios, and sensitivity measures. But Sophie hadn't inherited her father's talent for beautifying the ordinary — her spreadsheets weren't pretty. Jordanne's models were sleek machines with shiny macros and state-of-the-art formatting. Sophie's models produced the same results, but they looked like crap. She told herself the numbers were what counted, not the way they were dressed up.

"Really, I think what you've got looks good," Sophie said.

Jordanne wrinkled her nose.

"So you think it's OK to ask Vasu about finding Ethan in his office last night?" Sophie asked.

"Why not? Vasu's about as nice as VPs get."

The analysts dealt with Vasu more often than they'd like — besides being a vice president, Vasu was the air-traffic controller in charge of tasking the analysts. He was the one who'd forwarded them an email from Ethan that August: *I need a warm body to jam over the weekend for an AlumiCorp pitch on Monday.* It was Labor Day weekend, Jordanne was already in East Hampton, and the others were reluctant to forfeit the end of summer, but Sophie leapt at the chance. AlumiCorp had consumed her life ever since.

Sophie double-checked that no one was watching before she opened the fire door to the stairwell. If she called Kim from her cubicle, everyone within a forty-foot radius would know she wasn't working. Sophie envied Jordanne, who spoke to her mother in Portuguese and her father in French, so their colleagues couldn't tell what she was saying. Sophie's steps echoed against the metal stairs. She was careful not to look over the edge of the railing into the twenty-six-floor spiral.

"Hey!" Kim said. "It's so good to hear from you!"

Sophie had almost forgotten how chipper people could be outside Sterling. For a moment she wanted so badly to be sitting on Kim's couch in Stockton, where people actually thought she was smart. "Tell me everything! What have you been up to?"

"Up to? Oh, you know."

Kim was never evasive, unless . . . "You had a hot date last night, didn't you?"

"Maybe. Maybe definitely."

"Tell me! Who's the guy?"

"This new teacher at Bryce's school."

"First date?"

Kim paused. "Fourth."

"Oh." Sophie owed Kim a couple of calls, but had it really been that long? Before Sterling, she and Kim had talked on the phone almost every day, Sophie calling between classes, Kim during breaks at the hospital where she worked as a pediatric nurse. "I am the worst. I'm so sorry — everything's been nonstop at work and I guess I just lost track of time."

"How does anyone there have a life?"

"Actually, I don't think they do."

"Conrad called today. He's officially not coming to the party. Don't know why I'm surprised."

"I'm sorry." In retrospect, it seemed ridiculous that Sophie had been insanely jealous when Kim had started dating Conrad their junior year of high school. Kim had told him she was pregnant three weeks before prom, and it took about five minutes for Conrad to dump her. It was Sophie who rushed Kim to the hospital after her water broke at the North Adams MoviePlex. It was Sophie whose hand Kim squeezed so hard Sophie thought it might break. It was Sophie who cut Bryce's umbilical cord twenty-six hours later. Last year, when Will had floated the idea that he and Sophie live together when she started at Sterling, she'd cited Kim as evidence that under no circumstances would she even consider getting married or doing anything that looked even remotely like it until she was thirty-five, at least.

"Bryce keeps asking if you'll be there," Kim said. "What should I . . ."

Sophie stared at the stairs overhead and wished she had a different answer. "Work is kind of ridiculous — Friday nights, I don't get off work until at least six thirty, and then it's four hours on the bus . . ."

"We'll hold off on the cake until you get here — I'll show a movie or something. You sure you can't duck out a few hours early, just this once?"

"I'm really sorry. I'll make it up to Bryce. I promise."

"Oh," Kim said, dejected.

"Dynamic duo?" It had sounded better in high school, when it had seemed possible that Kim's looks combined with Sophie's brains could actually make them unstoppable.

A clatter sounded in the background. "The munchkin. I should go."

Sophie was weighing potential outfits for Lollipop when the smell of tobacco wafted into the quad. Vasu must be coming. Sophie pulled the AlumiCorp model onto her screen just as she heard steps behind her.

"You know," he said, "it wouldn't hurt to take a crack at those new tables in the merger analysis while you're sitting on the runway."

"Sure, Vasu. I'll get on it."

"I'll loop you in when I hear from Pearce."

He turned to walk away. Jordanne was talking on the phone in Portuguese. Sophie caught her eye and Jordanne nodded vigorously, telling Sophie to go ahead and ask Vasu about Ethan and Sibelius.

"Hey, Vasu?" She lowered her voice. "Pearce was in his office at four this morning when I dropped off the books."

Vasu scratched the back of his neck.

"For someone as senior as he is, the guy sure cranks pretty hard," she said.

Vasu squinted at her.

"It was kind of strange," she said.

"Pearce is a machine. All the good ones are. And they expect the people under them to be the same."

"But at 4 A.M.? Isn't that a little weird?"

"What's weird about working hard?"

$$$

Sophie checked her BlackBerry at the corner of Little West Twelfth and Washington later that evening. Still no word from Ethan. On the far side of the cobblestoned street, at the entrance to Lollipop, satiny scales flashed along a black line, phones glowing green for a moment before snapping shut. She could already tell from the number of gold stilettos that Lollipop was going to be infinitely cooler than Toad's, where Yale undergrads went dancing on Saturdays. She wondered if inside there would be people dancing in cages suspended from the ceiling — Jordanne had told her about a place like that in Moscow.

Will leaned against a brick wall, one hand resting in the pocket of worn jeans. He wore his usual elbow-patched corduroy jacket and scuffed leather sneakers, admittedly underdressed, but one of the many things she loved about Will was that he was the same person wherever he went, that it was something you could count on. As Will kissed her, she wrapped his arms around her shoulders, asking him to squeeze her tighter.

"You smell nice," he said.

She couldn't remember which of the perfume samples she'd grabbed from her stockpile. She burrowed into his shoulder and he scratched her scalp the same way he had night after night for months after her mother died, when her father was so depressed that it felt like she'd lost both her parents, when Will was the only stable thing.

"Two hours, tops," she said. "Then we'll go to Annabelle's thing. I promise."

He shrugged just as he had last fall, when she'd said she really wanted to come to Delaware with him for the holidays, but she couldn't leave her father alone. She knew he thought places like Lollipop were soulless — in Will's book, something qualified as interesting only if it wasn't mainstream. But Sophie had no desire to wear her individuality like a weapon; contrarianism for its own sake was just as mindless as conformity.

"I can't wait for you to meet Jordanne," she said. Making friends in New York wasn't as easy as freshman year, when she'd constantly met new people, admittedly mainly through Will, who had a knack for amassing friends. Making connections from scratch wasn't a muscle she'd ever had to develop, and she didn't really know where to start. She told herself that one real friend, especially one like Jordanne, was better than a handful of sort-of friends.

"Mitsuko's bringing her new guy to Annabelle's tonight," Will said.

"The chef?"

"Jonas was two guys ago." He wrapped his fingers around her fist, the same way her father used to hold her hand. "This one's the law student?"

"Oh. Right." She and Mitsuko had hung out two or three times a week in college, but when you didn't see someone, the second-hand news all kind of blended together. "What's Annabelle's theme tonight?"

"Rocktoberfest. Marcos found these lederhosen at Housing Works that he wanted to use."

Will's friends used to party in Annabelle's dorm room and now partied in Annabelle's tiny Hell's Kitchen apartment — always with a new theme, always with the same Franzia boxed wine. Since moving to New York, Sophie had only made it to July's Tour de Franzia, held the week before she'd started at Sterling. She'd worn spandex that almost looked like bicycle gear and raced from the box of Sunset Blush on Annabelle's windowsill to the Fruity Red Sangria on the kitchen counter. Honestly, she couldn't see why, after two years in New York, Will's friends didn't move on. In college, when buy-

ing her own alcohol was enough to give her a rush, Sophie had arrived at Franzia nights at 10 on the dot and stayed until Annabelle
brought out the late-night nachos, but that was New Haven, where
there weren't places like Lollipop.

A lacquered hand squeezed Sophie's shoulder. "Hellllooo!" Jordanne kissed her on both cheeks. Next to Jordanne's breezy, elec-
tric-blue dress, Sophie's sequined top felt about as subtle as a disco
ball.

"And this must be the famous Will." Jordanne stepped back, taking him in. Her eyes paused on the scuffed leather sneakers. "Aren't
you adorable."

Will looked vaguely amused, which on the Will scale was roughly
equivalent to suffering through one of the performances Mitsuko's
improv class gave at Upright Citizens Brigade. Sophie had expected
him to jump in as he had with Kim three years ago, complimenting
the decals she'd put up in the nursery and asking remarkably in-
formed questions about Bryce's sleep schedule, but maybe it wasn't
fair to hope that he and Jordanne would hit it off right from the
start.

"Have you seen Donnigan?" Jordanne asked.

"You invited *Donnigan?*"

Jordanne shrugged. "Ran into him on my way out of the office.
There he is — I'll grab him."

This was supposed to be their night, the three of them. Will and
Jordanne were supposed to be laughing over how his boss had
cleaned out the entire box of Nips Will kept on his desk. Will was
supposed to ask whether everyone who worked at Sterling was as
great as Sophie and Jordanne. Having Donnigan with them would
ruin it.

Donnigan made his way through the crowd, coat collar flipped
up to his ears. During analyst training, Sophie had trouble dis-
tinguishing Donnigan from the rest of the new analysts. They all
clipped their hair to the same close crop, they had white-shirt days
and blue-shirt days, eerily in sync. She'd only been able to tell Don-

nigan apart by his prominent chin, two silver dollars separated by a deep cleft. The only interesting thing she'd found while exploring his cubicle was the Wolverine action figure he kept in his bottom desk drawer, which she'd lost any curiosity about after he'd waved it around in broad daylight and said that they both had lots to learn from Wolverine: he had this ability to endure absurd amounts of punishment.

Donnigan extended a hand to Will, shoulders pushed back, chin in the air. "You must be the Mrs."

Will cocked his head, possibly running an inventory of all the times Sophie had complained about Donnigan.

Jordanne steered the four of them toward the sausage-armed bouncer. She laid two fingers on the bouncer's bicep and smiled. "François put me on the list — Jordanne Terney?"

The bouncer inspected his clipboard. "*You're* on here. But . . ."

Sophie tried not to appear anxious as the bouncer scanned her up and down. Will looked like he didn't care, which he probably didn't. Donnigan puffed out his chest an extra inch.

Jordanne whispered in the bouncer's ear and slipped something into his hand.

"Two-bottle minimum," he said.

Jordanne smiled. "Of course."

The bouncer unclipped the velvet rope.

Sophie kissed Will, thankful he'd been game to join her here. Bass pummeled her chest as they walked through a too-bright tunnel into the black box of the club. She had her boyfriend on one arm, her new best friend on the other, and for a second, everything was perfect. Inside, sleek women swirled around the dance floor, men's white shirts glowing blue in the club's light. There weren't any cages hanging from the ceiling, but that was fine — except for the fact that Jordanne and Will weren't already best friends, Lollipop was everything she'd hoped for.

A brunette in a cling-wrap dress led the four of them to a table in the corner where the light was bright enough to see the edge of foundation at the woman's jawline. Jordanne talked her way into a banquette at the edge of the dance floor. Sophie had never gotten a table at a club before — sitting so low to the ground made everyone look like a better dancer. The strobe flashed over men in collared shirts who could have been Donnigan's stunt double, women whose bodies must be their jobs. Compared to the other girls at Yale, Sophie had been reasonably decent looking, but here at Lollipop, let's face it, she was average, at best. She nestled closer to Will's shoulder. She'd never been a jealous girlfriend, or at least she'd never been jealous with Will, the only guy she'd dated, but she'd also never been somewhere like this.

Sophie tried not to look too shocked when she saw that the cheapest item on the menu was a 750 mL bottle of Absolut, for $150. She'd never paid more than twenty-five dollars for a bottle of booze, and now they were supposed to buy *two?* She snapped the menu shut so Will wouldn't learn that tonight would cost more than Annabelle's annual Franzia budget.

The cocktail waitress shouted something over the music about starting a tab.

"Step right up, folks." Donnigan said. "It's time for credit-card roulette."

Sophie stared at his open palm. No way she could afford to gamble over what she guessed would be a $450 drink order, but what was the alternative? She avoided Will's eyes as she presented Donnigan her Visa, gesturing that it was for both her and Will. She waited for Donnigan to joke about how Sophie must also buy Will's dresses, but it was Jordanne who squinted for a split second. Sophie pretended not to notice.

Donnigan shuffled the credit cards and presented a fan of plastic and glinting holograms to the waitress. Her fingers fluttered over the cards and plucked an American Express. Sophie took a deep breath and let it out.

"Thanks for the drinks, Donnigan."

Donnigan's gaze followed the swing of the waitress's hips as she sashayed off.

"What do you think of that one?" he asked Will.

"Not my type." Will put an arm around Sophie. Jordanne gave Sophie a tiny thumbs-up. "You?"

Donnigan cocked his head, considering this for a moment. "Nah. That dress is a magic trick. It hides her dirty secret. She's got a foopa."

"A what?" Sophie asked.

"A FUPA. A fat upper pussy area. A gunt."

Jordanne rolled her eyes. Will stared at Donnigan — he said that looking someone in the eye after they said something awful was the best retort. Sophie felt the same way she had when she was little and a sex scene came on television: so embarrassed that she wanted to get up and move around. She settled for checking her BlackBerry instead.

"Charming, Donnigan," Jordanne said. "Lots of dates lately?"

"Yes, actually."

"Any of them willing to go on date number two?"

"I believe in portfolio diversification. You gotta tolerate some volatility in your holdings if you want to win big." Donnigan turned to Will. "So. Tell us something interesting. What did you do with yourself today?"

Will inched away from Sophie — he liked to have space when he was collecting his thoughts. "Mostly I was booking hotels for an interview my boss is doing in Minneapolis ... Oh, this is great: I was on hold with Delta and they were playing that awful music so I put them on speaker and then Johann Jalneke walked in for his interview and pounded me on the shoulder and said, 'Don't let them break you.' "

"Jannigan?" Donnigan asked.

"Jalneke. The German director?" Will said this with the same earnestness he had her freshman year, when she hadn't known about the semisecret waffle iron in the back of the dining hall where Will toasted a chocolate and banana sandwich when dessert wasn't so great. He had this amazing knack for discovering gems that everyone else overlooked. "Have you seen *The First Game? Stone Skipping?*"

Jordanne was craning her neck toward the dance floor. Sophie rubbed Will's knee, hoping he'd take the hint and move on.

"Well, I guess the other interesting thing today was that I found out my colleague's pregnant."

"Mindy?" Sophie asked. "She told you?"

"Extremely educated guess — I saw her eat bread."

Jordanne laughed, possibly in recognition.

Will smiled at Donnigan. "I can't blame her for being a little neurotic when guys out there can be such dicks."

Donnigan seemed to actually enjoy this. "Don't think I know any of those guys."

Will grinned. "Neither do I."

Sophie was getting worried that Donnigan might retaliate when the cocktail waitress returned with their drinks.

Jordanne proposed a toast. "To . . ."

"To liberal guilt," Donnigan said.

Will clinked Donnigan's glass. Sophie swallowed her shot quickly so she wouldn't taste the burn. Definitely better than Franzia.

Jordanne perked up when the music changed. "This was our anthem the summer I was in St. Barth's." She grabbed Sophie's hand. "Come on, let's dance."

Donnigan led the way, shoulders thrust back, lower lip pushed forward. Jordanne swayed, languid and lovely. Sophie bopped tentatively. Jordanne beckoned Sophie over with an index finger, sliding her leg between Sophie's and pressing their hip bones together. Donnigan hooted. Sophie caught Will's eye, hoping he wouldn't hate Jordanne for it. Her mother used to say that the way you knew someone was really smart was that they made you feel smart when you talked with them. Dancing with Jordanne made Sophie feel like a good dancer. Jordanne was soon spun into the arms of a bronzed man with a popped collar, leaving Sophie as self-conscious as she'd been at the end of Mitsuko's dorm parties, when the drinks wore off and it became painfully clear it was just five of them dancing in a room.

Sophie tugged Will back to their banquette. She made sure Donnigan wasn't watching before wrapping her ankle around Will's leg and kissing him, enjoying the fact that they were surrounded by all these single people who were trying to find exactly what they had.

"Sorry about Donnigan," she said. "I didn't know he was coming."

"You know, I want to think that underneath it all he doesn't actually think those things."

She slid her hands around his waist. "Don't you love Jordanne?"

"She's nice."

"Nice." Will had said the freshman-year roommate who ate Sophie's granola bars and sexiled her for ten hours straight was nice. "Come on, what do you actually think?"

Will considered for a moment. "Did you see that look she gave when you put down your card for both of us?"

"What look?" Sophie lied.

"It just seems like money is awfully important to her."

"So what?" At least Jordanne understood what Sophie's mother never had: money mattered.

"So nothing. Just saying."

"She doesn't need the money. Sterling, I mean. Her dad thinks she should just travel for a year, but she wants to prove to her mom that she's smarter than she is."

Will didn't look convinced.

Sophie scanned the dance floor for her friend, who'd moved on to another guy. "Doesn't she look amazing?"

Will bit his lip, which meant he was about to say something a little mean. "More like a praying mantis."

Sophie's BlackBerry buzzed. She rolled her eyes, so Will wouldn't make a comment about her checking it for the millionth time. Ethan wrote:

To: Mehta, Vasu; Landgraf, Sophie T
cc: Sinclair, Grant
From: Pearce, Ethan
Re: ACorp follow-up
productive meeting. want to show Hutchinson #s on a merger with roll-rite.
pls run merger analysis tonight. want to get provisional #s to the company before COB fri.
tx
EP

She looked out at the couples on the dance floor, the DJ swaying in his booth, everybody getting warmed up for an epic night out.

Will leaned over her shoulder. "Something bad?"

"That big pitch, there's follow-up. Ethan says it's urgent."

"That means you're working tomorrow?"

"It means I'm working tonight. I have to run home and change."

The cocktail waitress appeared with a fresh bucket of ice. Sophie stopped her before she refilled their drinks.

"So no Annabelle's." He had to shout because the music had just gotten louder, like it wanted to rub it in that she was leaving just as things were getting good.

"I'm sorry. We should've gone there first."

He raised a skeptical eyebrow.

"It's not like I planned it this way." At the same time, now that she knew she was only going to get in thirty minutes of fun, she was thankful it had been at Lollipop, not the Franzia Rocktoberfest. "I know you're cutting me slack. I know I've been a little distracted lately."

"A little."

"I'm sorry we haven't gotten enough time together. It can only get better, right?"

Will laughed. She ducked under his arm so it rested around her shoulders. She'd drop him off at Annabelle's on her way uptown, as a peace offering.

Sophie hunched in the fluorescent light of her cubicle an hour later, rereading Ethan's email. A merger between AlumiCorp and Roll-Rite? The same combination Ethan had reamed her for suggesting? The stupidest idea ever? Why was Ethan pushing it now, and why didn't he acknowledge that it had been her idea in the first place?

Sophie flew down the hall and yanked open Ethan's top drawer. Swimming goggles, mustard packets. He owed her something new for dragging her back into the office. AlumiCorp annual reports. Blank legal pads. Sophie checked his computer's CD tray, hoping for the recording of the Sibelius she'd heard last night — empty. And she'd thought there might be something to this man.

She returned to her cubicle only more frustrated than when she'd left. Sophie looped her mousey scarf around her shoulders, letting the familiar warmth loosen her lungs. The lumpy beige wool wasn't exactly pretty, which was why she only wore it at the office when she was sure no one would see.

Before Sophie was born, her parents had left Boston with her mother's small inheritance and bought a fourteen-acre home-stead in the Berkshires. The way her mother told the story, they'd planned a sheep farm from the start, but best Sophie could tell, what actually happened was that her mother had bought a dozen Corriedales because she felt bad for a local struggling to put his daughter through college. Her mother named the sheep after her favorite philosophers — Rousseau, Sartre, Marx. Her parents sold the wool that spring, but under no circumstances would they send an animal to the slaughter. They should have realized this would make the flock grow pretty quickly, but they didn't, and soon the Landgrafs were in the sheep business by default. Her mother had to hire someone to do the birthing and shearing, but she always held back a portion of each June's wool to spin her own yarn, a scratchy, grayish thick gauge that no one else wanted.

Four years ago, during Sophie's freshman year of college, a neighbor from Stockton called Sophie's dorm room to tell her there'd been an accident. Her mother didn't suffer. Her father wasn't handling it too well so they'd taken him to the hospital — how soon could she get home? Alone in her parents' house the night after the funeral, Sophie saw a skein of the yarn her mother had loved sitting on the kitchen windowsill. Her mother had tried to teach her how to knit when she was seven and Sophie had hated it, but at that moment, the brush of wool across her palm, the mathematical repetition of knit one, purl two comforted her.

A month later, her father closed the farm. Sophie sat in her dorm room, unable to study, wishing she could go back to a home that didn't exist anymore. She unraveled the sweater and knitted a vest. After that, a poncho. But with each incarnation, the yarn's magic seemed to dissipate, and Sophie had let it be for almost a year now. Usually, wearing the scarf was comfort enough.

The cursor blinked on her blank spreadsheet, reminding her of what lay ahead, thankless and never ending. She'd finally gotten to Lollipop only to have to leave within an hour. She'd disappointed Will. She was going to let down Kim and Bryce. It was 1 A.M., she had at least six hours' work ahead of her, and she hadn't had a good night's sleep in weeks, let alone a night off.

For the first time since moving to New York, Sophie wished she were at home, hiking Mount Greylock with her father, playing Botticelli after dinner, sitting on Kim's couch with a mug of chamomile tea — even sleeping under the log cabin quilt her mother had made, which she hadn't even considered taking with her to college but now wished she'd brought to New York. She picked at her nail polish. What if she said she had a doctor's appointment tomorrow afternoon and headed straight to Port Authority to catch the bus? If they didn't hit traffic, she'd be home in time to see Bryce blow out the candles. She'd have to leave Stockton before dawn to be back in the office Saturday morning, but it was doable. Barely.

Ethan Pearce

A foreign-exchange trader once told Ethan that the Japanese had sixteen ways of saying "no" without actually using the word. After seventeen years in banking, he was sure CEOs had more. Ethan went into any pitch prepared to hear at least four, and Hutchinson hadn't disappointed him. "I'm not convinced that'd maximize shareholder value." (No.) "Look, I need to focus on running the company we've already got." (No.) "My board doesn't have the appetite for that transaction." (No.) The secret to client management wasn't handling the "nos"— you hardly noticed those after a while. The secret was catching the "maybes."

The "maybe" that launched the Century Can split-off was the CEO's remark that a cheese course privileged variety at the expense of quality. The "maybe" that started the Relia-Run restructuring was a bad joke six years ago at Avery Fisher Hall. Ethan had gotten tickets to the New York Phil: fourth row, dead center, a four-hundred-dollar dent in his client entertainment budget. By the time the orchestra had finished the obligatory symphony and the soloist swept on stage for the concerto, Dick Honigarden must have lobbed at least six "nos." The violinist was a teeny little thing, the kind of woman you knew would complain that a restaurant was too cold. Pretty in a pale, tubercular sort of way, if you're into that, which Ethan usually wasn't. But her focus. If the guys who worked for Ethan had half of it, they wouldn't have lost Callahan Cement's secondary offering to Goldman. He remembered thinking, she should bottle that and sell it. By the end of the first movement, Ethan knew: Camille Marin, concert violinist, was going to have a drink with him. During her curtain call, Dick Honigarden leaned over and said, "A woman like that makes me want to throw out what I've got and start over." Ethan pounced. "At home, or at Relia-Run?" Dick shrugged: the "maybe" that netted Sterling $22 million in fees. Dick apologized for the joke when Ethan married Camille. He apologized again after she was gone.

You had to catch the "maybe" and then you had to force that door wide open. You couldn't expect anyone to hand you an invitation — not in business, not in life. The summer after Ethan's sophomore year at UNC, his mother wanted him to come home to High Point and work at the Coggin lamp factory. Ethan took a less lucrative job with Sag Harbor Rod & Reel in Long Island. He didn't care about fishing or Long Island but he cared about money, especially the kind of money that flocked to the Hamptons every summer. One afternoon, Noah Sterling came in for some swim shads, and Ethan told him that someone had caught a shortnose sturgeon over at Noyack Bay. Noah Sterling explained that shortnose sturgeon were his particular passion. "I know, sir," Ethan said. "I make a point of knowing what my customers want and how to get it for them." Ethan got his first gig, a clerk on Sterling & Sons' foreign exchange floor. As far as Ethan knew, no one had ever caught a shortnose sturgeon in Noyack Bay.

Jake Hutchinson's "maybe" marked the first time Ethan nearly failed to force that door open. The lunch began the usual way: with the "nos." Ethan and his team had prepared a hundred odd pages and fourteen strategic alternatives — Vasu was good like that, you gave him a rough idea of what you needed and he worked wonders, like a magic little elf. Hutchinson flipped through the ideas impatiently, launching a flurry of "nos" with a *Leave It to Beaver* grin that Ethan wanted to believe was a front. But then Hutchinson fixed his eyes on you — *straight* on you, like he'd never hidden anything in his life, never doubted the goodness of human nature, not even his own — and Ethan almost believed the guy was for real.

Hutchinson speared a wedge of potato casserole and asked,

"Ever been to Pamela's Diner, in Pittsburgh? Best potatoes in the USA."

Ethan didn't doubt that Hutchinson was literally talking about potatoes. That was the thing about "maybes": the client didn't know he was tipping you off. Hutchinson shifting the conversation to Pittsburgh after rejecting fourteen transactions pointed Ethan to Roll-Rite, the Pittsburgh-based aluminum manufacturer. Ethan heard the opening loud and clear, but for the first time in his seventeen-year career, he hesitated. A merger between AlumiCorp and Roll-Rite was such a ludicrous idea that just yesterday Ethan had laid into his analyst for floating it.

Thank god Ethan came to his senses. As Hutchinson drowned his plate in ketchup, Ethan asked, "Ever consider a deal with our friends in Pittsburgh?"

Hutchinson looked up from his burger.

There it was: the "maybe." And Ethan had almost let it slip away. He was so furious with himself that as soon as lunch ended, he headed straight to the Cincinnati Hilton's fitness center and forked over a hundred and fifty bucks for a day pass and exercise gear. Ethan swam when he wanted to clear his head, ran when he needed to think something through. Today's stupidity called for both.

Ethan programmed the treadmill for a comfortable seven-minute mile. What was Hutchinson thinking? AlumiCorp and Roll-Rite were too similar — in their footprints, their business lines, and their struggles. The bulk of both companies' operations were in the Midwest, where business was abysmal. Roll-Rite's international assets in India, Indonesia, and Brazil were the biggest differentiators, but they were worth little more than the debt Roll-Rite had saddled them with, if that. Neither company would turn a profit any time soon.

Mergers are like marriages: only one spouse can be depressed. If Ethan were AlumiCorp's CEO, he'd go for Midwest Metals — AlumiCorp's extensive footprint in aluminum refining and Midwest Metals' enviable bauxite mines would be natural strategic complements. But the client wanted what he wanted, and Ethan wasn't complaining: an AlumiCorp–Roll-Rite deal would create the biggest aluminum merger in history and earn Sterling a $112 million payday.

It was just the sort of blockbuster deal Ethan needed to break his way into the next level. Every time he tried to secure capital for his clients, he butted up against Sinclair. It infuriated Ethan that Sinclair — fifty-something, a dinosaur in banking years — didn't have the grace to retire. If Ethan landed a corporate merger and the fat fees that came with it, he'd be in a position to insist the higher-ups oust Sinclair and make him group head. If they didn't, he'd be marketable enough for a rival bank to buy him out of his Sterling stock.

Ethan increased the treadmill's speed to match his mood. When he brought in $112 million in fees, Sterling would have to cough up eight figures for his bonus. It didn't embarrass Ethan that he wanted a summer home in East Hampton and a winter villa in Trancoso. Vacations to shoot rare game in Kenya and heli-ski in the Chugach. A chauffeur and a personal chef. Season tickets to the Met and the Mets. All of it. Everything Sinclair had had since the day he was born.

Ethan swapped running shorts for a swimsuit. The Roll-Rite idea was a long shot. Even if the deal kept Hutchinson's interest, which Ethan doubted, there were too many chances for a merger to fall apart, for those fees to disappear. The odds didn't matter. What mattered was that he beat them.

3

Friday, October 12, 2007

Vasu Mehta

VASU STRODE INTO SOPHIE'S CUBICLE at 8 A.M. the day after the pitch, prepared for the worst. Analysts were a liability their first year — everything they touched had to be checked twice. Best case, they did no harm. Sophie had not proved to be the best case. Her hair was disheveled and a waste cloth hung around her neck. Why Americans dressed like beggars, he would never understand. Her desk rivaled the Delhi streets where he had grown up — granola-bar wrappers, a browning banana peel, soggy coffee cups. Seeing her struggle on full display was not reassuring. He could only imagine the mess she had made of the AlumiCorp–Roll-Rite merger analysis.

"Are we there yet?" Vasu asked.

She stuffed her rag into a drawer.

"It's close."

"Let's take a look."

"Should we wait until I've checked it? I wouldn't want to waste your time."

He respected that—you stayed up all night, you wanted to make sure the work was perfect.

"You have it under control?" he asked.

He could not tell whether her frantic nod was evidence of panic or exhaustion coupled with a steady drip of caffeine.

"You are sure?"

"Positive."

"Hurry then. No time to waste."

Pearce had been very clear: Hutchinson must have the numbers by close of business. Close of business at Sterling meant before you went home—midnight, 5 A.M., no matter—but for Sterling's clients, it meant five on the dot, precisely.

"I'm on it, Vasu. Don't worry."

He fingered the Parliaments in his trouser pocket. Seven years ago, when he started at Sterling, he might have had sympathy for someone as clearly overwhelmed as Sophie, but underneath her insecurity he sensed a deep-seated faith in the world's fairness, like the rest of the bankers who had started after 9/11. Vasu did not need to be reminded that optimism had been a stranger to him for years now.

When Vasu and Aditi moved to Tribeca in the summer of 2001, they were sure they had the ticket: his job as a first-year associate in Sterling's Investment Banking Division. They hoped—stupidly—that Aditi would find a job like the one she had left at the biochemistry lab in Delhi. Everything would fall into place. How Vasu had laughed when, humbled but hopeful after his first day at Sterling, he came home to empty cans of paint and a speckled robin's egg of a wife.

Two months later, he was in his office on Liberty Street, opposite the World Trade Center, on the phone with his mother-in-law in Gurgaon. He could hear the BBC playing in the background. When the first plane hit, she shouted at Vasu to run. He and Aditi, then nine months pregnant, holed up in their Franklin Street apartment in facemasks, watching the dust and ash rise on their windowsill. Outside, rats ran through the streets.

Lower Manhattan was cordoned off. Sterling rented the entire midtown Marriott and moved all its operations there, four bankers and an assistant sharing each hotel room. The beds were moved out but the headboards remained, floating on the walls, stranded. In the devastation that pervaded those green- and gold-carpeted halls, Sterling's refugees hardly noticed as week after week, more and more were sacked. Mickey Wright, the CEO, told them that Sterling's strength was in its people. He said Wall Street wasn't a physical place, it was a frame of mind. Sterling joined the mass exodus from downtown and purchased a new headquarters just north of Times Square. Vasu and Aditi fled Manhattan for Park Slope, but even Brooklyn did not seem far enough. He still had a job — a miracle. Had he been too cheap to sack? Had they taken pity on an immigrant who would lose his visa? Or perhaps he had just been lucky. He did not know and he could not ask.

Vasu was thirty-six now and felt like fifty. He sensed another downturn brewing — merger activity was slowing and the fixed income market deteriorating. Kenneth Yang, Rich Angstrom, and the other midlevels thought him unduly pessimistic. They reminded him that corporate profits continued to improve, consumer confidence remained robust, and he hoped they were right. As a midlevel with no clients of his own, he would be at the top of the list to be cut in a downturn.

If he were sacked, Aditi would push for them to return to India. She still thought of India as home. She liked the idea of living with his parents and sister in the Delhi house that he had always seen as a beginning, never an end. To Vasu, going back to India was admitting defeat. Going *back*. Retreating. Giving up. In grammar school, he read a passage from Thoreau about a young man gathering materials to build a bridge to the moon. Years later, that same man, middle-aged, used the lumber to build a wooden shed. Vasu accepted that all he would manage was a wooden shed. But if that was all he got — a shed — he wanted it here, in New York. He wanted at least that much.

Vasu stared at Sophie's spreadsheet. "This can't be right."

Sophie pushed back her chair to give him a better view. He could not remember seeing a merger that had such a negative effect on earnings. The numbers told of a disaster in need of fixing, not a deal any CEO in his right mind would ever consider executing. Sophie must have botched the analysis. If they showed bad numbers to Pearce, it would be on him.

"May I drive?" Vasu asked.

He traced the chain of formulas in the model, tapping at his calculator. He audited each assumption, equation, and result twice but failed to find a single mistake. Baffled, he turned to Sophie.

"You are *sure* this is right?" he asked.

She nodded, not quickly enough.

"If Pearce finds anything wrong —"

"It's right," she said, with confidence that, though not entirely sufficient, Vasu judged passable.

He glanced at the clock: 2:30 P.M. It was time.

Vasu laid the printout on Ethan's desk. "Sophie completed the merger analysis. I checked her numbers. I didn't quite believe them at first."

"I expected as much," Ethan said evenly. "There's a reason we haven't put this idea in front of Hutchinson before. But if this is the deal he wants to do . . ."

"We can revisit the assumptions," Vasu said. "These numbers are embarrassing, no?"

"Tinkering would undermine our credibility."

"What can Hutchinson see in this deal?"

Ethan shrugged. "There's no accounting for taste. If I had to guess, I'd go with a cost-cutting story."

True, both companies had bloated workforces. AlumiCorp employed 39,000, and Roll-Rite roughly 31,000: in each case, about twenty-five percent more than they needed. A merger could be a means for streamlining — closing plants, downsizing the workforce. But Hutchinson did not need a merger to lay off workers. He could fire employees anytime he wanted — without paying the double-digit premium Roll-Rite would want for their stock.

"Send this to me and I'll get it to Hutchinson," Ethan said. "We'll revisit assumptions at his say-so — he needs to feel like he's in control of this thing."

Whatever Vasu's reservations about the deal, he hoped he was wrong. He needed this. It was just his luck that merger activity had slowed so soon after he became a vice president, the midlevel fat Sterling loved to trim. He had fought to be involved with as many clients as he could, and now he was working with Pearce on AlumiCorp, Blumenstein on Midwest Metals, and Sinclair on Ball & Bearing. He hoped one of those assignments would lead to a proper transaction with fees that would justify keeping him around until business picked up.

He was not the only one at risk — surely Sophie had figured that out. Last fall, when Sterling had extended offers for her analyst class, business had been robust. Since then, deal flow had waned, and now the bank was overstaffed. They would not let dead weight stay around for long.

"I have a feeling about this one," Ethan said. "You two are on deck until we hear back from Hutchinson. In the meantime, if you think of any analysis that supports doing this merger, I want you to run with it." Ethan turned to his computer. "Shoot this over so I can get it to Hutchinson before he takes off for the weekend."

On their way back to her desk, Sophie asked, "I wonder what he meant, on deck?"

"The acceptable response time to an email has been reduced from ten minutes to two minutes."

Sophie laughed. She was even more naïve than he had thought.

"I'm not kidding. Send the numbers to Ethan."

"Is it still OK if I go to that doctor's appointment this afternoon?"

She avoided his eyes, which made him suspicious. Perhaps she had a doctor's appointment, or perhaps she had correctly intuited that this was the only acceptable reason to leave the office during business hours. If Sophie was under a personal obligation, he did not care to know. The question was whether, with only so many "doctor's appointments" a banker could attend, Sophie chose this one. "You can't postpone it?"

"It's sort of important."

The rest of the day should be quiet — tomorrow was when he really needed her. "Don't take your eyes off your BlackBerry until we hear back from Hutchinson. Nothing is more important than this deal right now."

He did not tell Sophie how doubtful he was that the deal would succeed; nothing was worse than an unmotivated analyst. He used to think that of all the Industrial Group's clients, AlumiCorp was his best shot. Earlier that year, AlumiCorp had engaged Sterling to raise equity to fund capital improvements in their Midwest plants. Vasu had worked around the clock for seven months, until the deal fell apart. In the end, Sterling only got paid their expenses.

He could not get outside quickly enough. On the corner, he lit a cigarette, a Snickers wrapper and Splenda packets at his feet. On the Delhi streets near where he grew up, the West side threw their trash on the East side's curb, and the East tossed theirs on the West's. Cows loped by the side of the road, chewing plastic bags, *paan* wrappers, whatever else people threw out. A constant cycle of filth, a serpent eating its own tail. He wished he could be there now.

Vasu's mother had gone into the hospital over the summer. AlumiCorp's equity deal was busy then, and Vasu could not get away. He told himself his mother would understand. Eight years his parents had worked in Saudi Arabia, leaving Vasu and his sister in his grandparents' care. Physicians were better paid in the Middle East, and the extra money allowed Vasu to attend Cornell. They had hoped a US education would put their only son in line for a position at a proper firm, like Sterling. Never would his mother have wanted him to jeopardize his job.

Aditi wanted to go to Delhi, to be there with his family, even if he had to stay here for work. She said she would take their six-year-old with her, but Vasu did not want cancer to be what Meera remembered about her grandmother. Besides, his sister, Dipti, was there to help their father and care for their mother. So Vasu and Aditi stayed in New York, waiting for news. After three weeks and countless cigarettes, he got the call from Dipti: it was time. He needed to come. AlumiCorp's equity deal was at a boiling point — Sterling was taking the offering to market the following week. It damn near killed Vasu to go to Pearce and Sinclair and explain that he needed to take time off, and it could not wait. They were as gracious as he could have expected, and his family went to India for two weeks.

Except his mother hung on, and Vasu returned to New York, to wait. In his two-week absence, the AlumiCorp equity deal had fallen apart. The market indications were not as favorable as AlumiCorp's CEO had hoped, and Hutchinson pulled back, saying maybe they would give it another shot later that month, which never happened. Sometimes, Vasu wondered whether he could have saved the deal if he had not gone to India.

He used to think his sacrifices would earn him a break one day — working on a blowout merger, getting top bonus. That was a rookie mistake. The sacrifices were a ticket to play the game. They did not get you any closer to winning.

Sophie Landgraf

Sophie raced up the Port Authority escalator two stairs at a time. One more minute and she'd miss her bus. She pushed past a couple carrying Macy's bags, a man holding the hand of a little girl with butterfly face paint. How did they manage to hang out in the middle of a weekday afternoon — didn't they have jobs?

Will was waiting for her outside the gate.

He kissed her hello. "FYI, your bus is late."

She bent over her knees, trying to catch her breath. "I think I need to go to the gym."

"There's time to change."

"I'm OK." She kind of liked the idea of Kim and her father seeing her in her suit, an independent professional. "You remembered the present?"

He raised the Sterling duffel bag that he'd packed according to her instructions, since she hadn't made it home the night before. "There's some granola bars in there too."

"Oh my god, you're the best." She gulped her coffee.

"Are you sure you want more caffeine? You seem on edge."

"Of course I'm on edge. I just lied to my boss."

"I still don't see why you can't tell them the truth — it's three thirty on a Friday, it's not that big a deal to leave a few hours early. And when are you getting back tomorrow? Like 9 A.M.?"

She took a deep breath and told herself not to remind him that she'd already explained this about a million times. "At school, career services actually warns you that in banking interviews, you're going to be asked a question like, 'You have a pitch tomorrow and it's your grandmother's ninetieth birthday, what do you do?' The trick is not to hesitate when you answer that you stay at the office. No way they'd let me go."

"At least you can nap on the bus."

She shook her head. "It's business hours, and they think I'm at the doctor."

The hiss of brakes at the gate announced the bus's arrival.

"You sure you don't want to come?" she asked.

"I tried to get someone to switch shifts for Housing Works — no dice."

Will handed her the ticket, eyes fixed on the tremor in her hands. He grabbed her coffee cup and tossed it into the trash. It took her a second to catch up — it wasn't like him to tell her what was best for her. He was down the hall before she could say anything. The bus driver was already collecting tickets. She watched Will's sloped shoulders disappear into the crowd and got on board.

Sophie settled into a window seat, wishing the bus would hurry up and get on the road. Her father would be waiting for her at the station, so at least they could catch up for twenty minutes on the drive to Kim's. The visit wouldn't be nearly as long as she'd like, but if the bus didn't hit traffic, she'd get to see Bryce blow out the candles. She'd get to drink tea with Kim after the kids started their movie. And tonight, she'd sleep under her log cabin quilt.

When Sophie was seven, her mother had taken her to the Round Robin Thrift Store to pick out fabric for a quilt. Sophie chose blue rosebuds and white daisies. Her mother asked if Sophie was sure she wanted flowers and pastels like all the other girls — didn't she want something that was just hers? Maybe yellow elephants and bright blue paisley? This was around the same time that her mother had said the names kids were calling Sophie at school might sound like insults, but they were really compliments: nerd, stubborn. It was the first time Sophie remembered not believing her mother. She stuck with the rosebuds. When her mother stitched the quilt, she backed it with the elephants, just in case Sophie changed her mind. Her mother had this way of making it seem like she was letting Sophie make her own choices even when she wasn't.

Sophie scanned the strip mall as the bus pulled into the parking lot — Dollar General, China Fun, Tim Horton's, Supercuts. She spotted her father, copper beard bright against his barn coat, bouncing on tiptoe, waving in giant arcs. She was pretty sure he couldn't see her through the tinted window but she waved back anyway.

He lifted her off the ground with his hug, like she'd disappear if he didn't squeeze hard enough. His neck smelled overwhelmingly of peppermint — Bengay. He must be working on another oversized sculpture, lifting pieces that were too big for him. Her father liked to think he didn't have limits.

He stepped back to take in her suit. "Look at you."

"You hate it?" She worried he saw in her the grandfather she'd never met but had heard plenty about, an insurance executive who died of a heart attack at forty-five — because the human body wasn't meant to work that much, her parents said.

"You're still in there, right?"

She nodded.

"Then you look great."

She looped her arm in his as they walked to the rusted-out 1987 Civic.

"Hungry?" Her father ducked to peer over the dashboard as they pulled out of the strip mall. "We could stop at Wendy's on the way."

"I'm really hoping to see Bryce open presents."

They passed the Donut Kitchen where Kim had worked in high school. Kim used to stockpile stale donuts that Sophie would chuck out the window of Kim's Taurus at the couples parked along the Housatonic River.

"You hiking a lot?" her father asked. In college, Sophie had saved up her stories of hiking Mount Tom or Mount Frissell with Will so she'd have one to dole out each time she called her father. Her mother had been the one who was interested in things like whether Sophie should take Dante in Translation or Tolstoy and Dostoevsky to satisfy her distribution requirement. "Found any good trails down there?"

"Not yet." She hadn't been hiking since June, the last time she'd been in Stockton, but there were certain things she didn't say to her father unless she was prepared to listen to a twenty-minute lecture: she was coming down with a cold, she'd bought something that cost more than twenty dollars, she'd turned on the heat when it was not below freezing. "Have you been up Mount Greylock since the leaves turned?"

"Tuesday. Unbelievable. You know it's not going to be the same — the Lyndqvists, the ones who own the land next to the trailhead? They sold to a developer — condos, summer homes. We're trying to slow down their permits, but you just know they've got the town council in their pocket."

The Civic shuddered as he pulled onto the highway, begging to be shifted into fifth gear: Sophie's fault. The day she got her learner's permit, he'd taken her to the parking lot behind Dollar General and sat patiently while she stalled out and restarted the car, over and over. When she finally got the car to drive in first gear an hour later, he bounced on his seat, clapping as he explained that next she should put in the clutch and pull up on the gearshift. Sophie took his instructions to "pull up" too literally: the handle of the gearshift detached in her hand, dangling exposed wires, all of which thankfully remained connected except the one for fifth gear. Her father refused to have it fixed — he said he liked knowing that his only child wouldn't be able to drive over forty miles an hour.

"How's my man Will?" he asked. Her father was Will's most adoring fan. She and Will joked about how much easier their lives would be if they traded parents; Will's parents — accountant, lawyer — made no secret of wishing he was more practical.

"He's good. He's hoping his boss might let him do his first interview soon."

"What are you guys doing for fun?"

"We went to this outdoor dancing thing at Lincoln Center." They'd done so only once, months ago, before she'd started at Sterling, but it was the sort of thing her father would want to hear. "And Annabelle has people over a lot."

It looked like her answer was enough for him. She'd forgotten this part of being home, how she had to cut herself into tiny, easy-to-swallow bites.

"You guys have a good thing going," he said.

Sophie wondered whether her mother would have agreed. When Sophie had gushed to her mother about Will two weeks after they'd started dating, her mother encouraged her to taste all the wines before buying a bottle, which of course made Sophie decide that she was going to stay with Will for the foreseeable future, just to prove her mother wrong. The accident was three weeks later — her mother never met him.

"And the neighborhood's turning out OK?" he asked. "It's a good thing you have a doorman. I read an article about a woman getting attacked in her entryway — those apartment buildings, anyone can walk right in."

"The Upper West is great." Based on the ten minutes she spent getting to and from the subway on her way to work. "It's really safe. Lots of families, strollers and stuff."

They pulled into the center of town, a crossroads with Berkshire Savings and Food Lion on one side, IHOP on the other. They passed the public library where during middle school, Sophie had renewed a calculus textbook so many times that Mrs. Mastrick had finally given it to her.

"About tomorrow," Sophie said. "I need to catch the 5 A.M. bus. I'm going to set like four alarms, but if —"

"You seem tired." His lips stretched tight, the same look she remembered from grade school, when he'd said he knew she wanted a sister but sometimes you just don't get what you want. "You really should get some sleep."

"I'll sleep on the bus. I should be in the kitchen by the time you get up." Her father was always up an hour before dawn. "But if I'm not, please, *please* wake me up."

A Spider-Man cutout and balloons were taped to the front door of Kim's tidy Cape Cod.

"Sure you can't stay through the weekend at least?" he asked. "Tomorrow's supposed to be beautiful — we could hike Mount Greylock — you could see the view one last time before the developers wreck it." It was the same way he'd said during her senior year in high school that Amherst and Williams were such great schools, and they were so close.

"I'll come again soon. I promise."

Sophie rang Kim's doorbell for a full minute before letting herself in. She followed the squeals through the hall and into the basement, ducking to avoid crepe-paper streamers. Downstairs, moms who looked vaguely familiar bustled around a folding table, trash bags open to receive pizza crusts and slices of cake licked clean of frosting. Kids zipped across the carpet, playing tag, others tossing Velcro balls at a felt spider's web tacked against the wall. No one looked up.

Kim knelt in the corner, applying a SpongeBob Band-Aid to a kid's arm, her honey-blonde hair falling in front of her face. She wore jeans Sophie recognized from high school and an aqua T-shirt that would've made Sophie look like an eight-year-old. Kim had the kind of body that looked amazing in just about anything. Donnigan had seen a picture of her on Sophie's Facebook page and said that Kim looked like a rare bird — you couldn't decide whether to watch her fly, or shoot her and mount her on your wall.

Sophie tapped her friend on the shoulder. Kim gave her the same cockeyed smile she had their first day of kindergarten, when the fact that their last names were next to each other on the class list was enough to make them best friends.

"You made it!" Kim hugged her so tight she lost her breath.

"What did I miss?"

"One allergy scare — he's fine. One bite on the arm — also fine. And the ten Tylenol I've popped in like the past hour."

"AuntSophieAuntSophieAuntSophiiiieee!" Bryce whizzed over, brown hair sticking out from under his Spider-Man mask, his squat little body colliding into Sophie's leg with surprising strength.

"Happy Birthday, Bry!" Sophie knelt for a hug.

He'd lost a front tooth since she'd seen him last. "I'm five and three-quarters."

"Five and three days," Kim corrected.

"Aunt Sophie, are you going to sleep over? Jesús and Minna and Tyrell and Jack are going to sleep over."

Sophie looked to Kim, who mouthed something Sophie couldn't decode. "I'll be here until you guys go to sleep, definitely." Kim gave her a thumbs-up.

"Is that for me?" Bryce pointed at the festooned package peeking out of Sophie's bag.

"Bryce!" Kim whispered to Sophie, "We're working on manners."

Bryce was already making short work of the lizard wrapping paper Will had picked out. "Harry Potter!"

"Cool!" He added "thank you" at Kim's prompt and wrapped his hand around Sophie's index finger. "Come on, let's play Spider-Man ball."

After four rounds, Sophie had yet to hit the center of the spider's web. The little girl in fairy wings who'd joined them wasn't much better. The girl's mother appeared, kneeling to tie the little girl's shoe, the woman's shirt riding up in the back to reveal a butterfly tattoo.

It took Sophie a minute to place Dolores Carson. Dolores wore a fleece not unlike the one she used to wear after volleyball practice, when Sophie would pass her after mathlete meetings and Dolores wouldn't say hello back, making Sophie think that being around other people could make you feel more alone. The last Sophie had heard, Dolores was working at Shady Pines Nursing Home along with the rest of Sophie's high school classmates, which shouldn't have made Sophie happy but did.

"Dolores — hi!" Her voice came out high and squeaky.

"Oh my god, Sophie Landgraf? Wow, you're dressed up."

Not changing had definitely been the right decision. "I came straight from work."

"Oh yeah, Kim mentioned you worked at a bank now. My cousin's a teller at Citi."

When she'd come home during breaks from college, it had been the same way: all schools that weren't Berkshire Community were created equal. "That's great."

Sophie couldn't help inspecting Dolores's nails. The tiny, trim ovals had been caked with dirt and blood the last time Sophie had seen Dolores, five years ago now. It was Sophie's fourth call after joining the Stockton volunteer ambulance corps on her seventeenth birthday, back when she'd planned to go to med school. Her pager had squawked around 3 A.M.: a car had skidded off Deer Hill Road into a forty-foot ravine. As the ambulance raced to the scene, Sophie's crew chief told her that they got called to that spot at least once a year, that Sophie should be prepared, the ravine was studded with rocks. They pulled up beside the flares, where a young woman in a shock blanket was leaning against the hood of a police car. Sophie started a body scan just like she'd been taught but she couldn't get past the woman's nails, broken and bloody from climbing up the side of the ravine. It wasn't until Sophie slipped the blood pressure cuff over those fingernails that Sophie recognized Dolores, who had a million friends and hair that flipped perfectly, who basically had everything. Sophie's crew chief performed the exam and Sophie checked boxes on the call sheet — no loss of consciousness, no head trauma, no spidering of the windshield — Dolores was *lucky.*

At her mother's funeral, Sophie couldn't stop thinking about Dolores. A drunk girl had skidded off the road and flipped four times before landing at the bottom of a forty-foot ravine, and she'd survived. Her mother must have safely passed the spot where Dolores crashed hundreds of times. Then one day, at three in the afternoon, her mother was driving down Route 7 just like she did every Tuesday, and a fawn wandered onto the road. She swerved. The car flipped. The roof crumpled against asphalt, her fate decided as instantly as the flip of a coin.

Sophie boxed the extra bags of party favors, temporary tattoos, and stick-to-the-wall snakes that Kim said every parent would throw out in about two days. The kids were tangled together on top of sleeping bags, watching *Peter Pan*. Kim and Sophie disappeared into the kitchen they'd sponge-painted together three years ago, and Kim put on a pot of coffee.

"So what's it like?" Kim asked. "You guys must be so thrilled to be back in the same place."

"Will's great. He's exactly the same. I can't imagine being in New York without him — I'd be so lost." Sophie sank into a wooden chair. "So how was the hot date with the teacher?"

Kim stared at her fingers, just like she had their sophomore year, when Kim said Tyler Engel had asked her out, but don't worry, she said no, she wouldn't do that to Sophie. "Turns out he forgot to mention that he's married. Grade A asshole."

"I'm so sorry! What a creep."

Kim slid the sugar bowl in front of Sophie. "How's your Grade A asshole boss?"

"I'm still working on not hyperventilating when I go into Ethan's office." Just admitting that out loud made her feel so much better.

"The doctors used to scare me too. You'll get used to it."

She hoped Kim was right. "I'm just so unbelievably behind Jordanne and Donnigan — they actually know what they're doing."

Kim set a mug in front of Sophie and flopped into the chair, sliding down the seat until her face was level with the table. "It's so you to say you're behind when you're not."

"I think this time it's pretty clear that I'm objectively behind."

A little girl in snowflake pajamas pattered in. How people had the time to have kids, Sophie had no idea.

Kim sent the girl off with a juice box. "I think you said you were behind before you aced your first college midterm. You'll be running that bank in two years."

"It's different this time. High school and college, there's this two-dimensional path to follow. But it's like, at graduation, someone hit the reset button and now the world's 4-D and no one tells you anything about the rules except that they're totally different and you have to start all over again."

Kim folded her arms. "And while you figure out the rules you get to live in New York and get paid a billion dollars. I'll bet the minute you walk out your door, there's more guys on one block than there are in this whole county."

With anyone else, Sophie would've felt guilty for complaining when she basically had the best job a twenty-two-year-old could get, but one of the many things Sophie loved about Kim was that no matter what you told her, she wouldn't judge you for a second. "Want to know how many times I've had a night off in the past month? Twice. New York's amazing, but I hardly get to enjoy it, and in the meantime I live in a city were no one has your back, where if you didn't make rent you'd basically end up in a gutter."

"I've got your back. Will's got your back."

"In theory." Sophie got up to pour herself a second cup of coffee. He'd always had her back in college, when what she needed was for him to help her fall to sleep at night, to remind her that she wasn't alone in the world, but in New York, at Sterling, it wasn't that simple. Practically speaking, Will didn't even have his own back—his parents did—how could he have hers?

Kim held out a dish of M&M's. "Your dad."

"Same." Sophie picked out the green ones. "Did I tell you about the associate in my group who was in Mississippi during Katrina? Sterling actually sent a helicopter to get him out."

Kim pressed her lips in that way Sophie remembered perfectly from high school, when she was about to say that for someone who got a perfect score on her SATs, Sophie could sure be dense.

"What?"

Kim's eyes scrunched up, like she was apologizing in advance. "I just wonder ... I'll bet you wouldn't feel this way if your mom hadn't ... you know."

Sophie picked at her nail polish. She'd dwelled on what-ifs too much that first year after the funeral. If her mother were here, she would have told Sophie to stop feeling sorry for herself and focus on what she's got.

"I'm sorry," Sophie said. "I'm blabbing. This is what happens when you spend zero time with anybody except your colleagues. Tell me everything. What are you up to this weekend?"

"Actually? I have this amazing plan for tomorrow night."

"Yeah?" Sophie pulled her knees to her chest.

"I have this cologne that smells like boy—jasmine or some-thing—but it's basically bottled BO. I'm going to spritz it on a T-shirt and cuddle with it."

"Stop."

"Let me know if you want to trade."

Vasu Mehta

Early Saturday morning, Vasu inched out from under Aditi's arm and retrieved his BlackBerry from his nightstand. Damn. Hutchin-son still had not replied to the Roll-Rite numbers from the night before.

Meera knelt on the hall rug with her crayons and sketchpad. Tall and spindly for her six years, Meera had a seriousness of purpose that he admired and encouraged, but he was not sure about her new habit of lying in wait outside the bedroom or right next to the front door, locations that gave her the best negotiating leverage. Her instinct showed an incipient talent for business, but the fact that she had to angle to get his attention also saddened him.

"Want to draw, Papa?"

He knelt as she flipped to a fresh page.

"You can do the grass," she said.

She selected Spring Green and laid it across his outstretched palms with a regal nod. Her crayons were organized with Cornflower, Spring Green, Maize, Orchid — her favorites — at the top left of the box and Maroon and Tan at the bottom right. Bittersweet was bandaged with masking tape he had helped her apply. Robin Egg Blue was not there. He had stepped on it in the dark one morning. He could not save it.

"Papa, can we go to Coney Island today? After Hindi school?"

Meera had been asking to go for months, ever since her classmates told her about the beach and the ice cream. Meera wanted nothing more than to be like the other girls. He did not object to it, as Aditi did, insisting Meera enroll in *kathak* rather than ballet. In fact, he approved.

"We'll talk about it when your mummy is up, OK?"

As he drew grass along the bottom of the page, Vasu recalled Ethan's directive: come up with any analysis that would support doing this merger, and run with it. He still did not have a single worthwhile idea. If he went into the office, he would stare at the glass wall just as he had stared at the ceiling last night, unable to sleep. Was that a proper reason to miss a day with his family?

No matter how you ran the AlumiCorp–Roll-Rite numbers, they were a disaster. Drawing further attention to them could only dissuade Hutchinson from proceeding with the deal. Vasu watched Meera, bent over her picture — three stick figures, a sun that took up half the page. Which gave him an idea: what if he showed a visual instead of financial analysis? Vasu's fingers fidgeted inside his pocket as he tried to catch an idea just out of reach. Its edges, he could see, but the rest was hidden. There were too many distractions here at home. He could not think clearly.

"Can you explain your picture to me?" he asked.

"This is you and me and Mummy and we're at Coney Island and we're eating cotton candy and then we're going to ride the Ferris wheel and get ice cream and it's going to be really fun."

The drawing was the world as Meera wanted it to be. *That* was what he needed to show Hutchinson: the world as he wished it, rather than the world as it was. Vasu told himself to concentrate. What was Hutchinson's bridge to the moon? He knew the CEO hated Midwest Metals. What if they showed Hutchinson how, together, AlumiCorp merged with Roll-Rite could rival Midwest Metals?

Must they go to Coney Island today? Better they go in December, after annual performance reviews were in, no? Then he would be able to give Meera the day she wanted. It would be worth the wait. They would have hot dogs and crinkle fries at Nathan's. They would eat ice cream. Even if it was snowing, they would eat ice cream.

He shot Sophie an email: *Meet me in the office this A.M. See you in 45.*

Meera was absorbed in her sketch pad when Aditi swished into the room, the pink tunic of her *salwar kameez* fluttering behind her. She gave him a thumbs-up followed by a thumbs-down, asking whether he was free to go to Coney Island. Vasu shook his head, bringing his hands to his chest and miming climbing a ladder, their code for going into the office. Aditi pursed her lips.

Vasu leaned over to kiss Meera good-bye. "I have to go to work, *beti*. We'll go to Coney Island another weekend, OK?"

"You always say that."

It alarmed Vasu that she sounded resigned rather than disappointed. Meera presented him with the page from her sketchbook.

"For me?" he asked, though he was the recipient of at least five such pictures each week. "*Achchaa,* how beautiful. I have a special place to hang it."

"Time to get ready for Hindi school, Meera," Aditi said.

Meera tore off down the hall.

Aditi shot him a look that cut through all his enthusiasm for the new AlumiCorp idea.

"Yes," he said. "I *had* thought I might be able to go. But I'm doing this for you and Meera, cent percent."

She knelt to pick up the crayons. "I'll take her on my own."

"You cannot wait for me?" He knelt to help her. "Please."

He wrapped his arm around her as they filed the crayons according to Meera's system of favorites.

The regular weekend crowd had gathered on the twenty-sixth floor: analysts, associates, a midlevel or two, all in khakis and polo shirts. Sinclair's stocking feet rested on his desk, the paper spread across his lap. The floor smelled of bacon. By Sunday evening, the trash would be overflowing with plastic takeout containers.

Vasu could not believe Sophie's desk was empty — particularly after the speech Pearce had given them Friday afternoon. Even if she had not yet intuited the risk of layoffs among her ranks, surely she understood that the two-year analyst program was a protracted audition. She should be *living* in her cubicle.

Jordanne Terney sat at her desk opposite Sophie's, finger holding her place in a ragged textbook. Vasu's grammar school in India had idolized British literature. His schoolmates favored *Great Expectations*, but Vasu preferred *The Great Gatsby*. When he met Jordanne, he thought of Daisy Buchanan — her voice was full of money.

"Have you seen her?" Vasu asked. He fired off an email to Sophie: *need you in office at once.*

"I haven't," Jordanne said. "Is there something I can help with?"

"No, no. That's quite all right."

Ten minutes later, Sophie still had not replied to his email. He shot her a second note: *to be clear, this is urgent.* He paced down the hall to check her cubicle a second time.

"Vasu," Jordanne asked, "are you sure I can't lend you a hand? I'm happy to."

Vasu considered. Unlike Sophie, Jordanne made sure the dollar signs on a spreadsheet were meticulously aligned: a junior who inspired trust. Sophie was smart enough, but intelligence was not as important in an analyst as perfect attention to detail. Jordanne's offer tempted Vasu, but AlumiCorp was Sophie's deal. You did not circumvent staffing assignments unless absolutely necessary.

Vasu called her BlackBerry. "Sophie, call me as soon as you get this. Better yet, get here ASAP."

Sophie Landgraf

It was 10:27 A.M. and Sophie's bus was only now passing Waterbury — Vasu was going to kill her. She'd woken up at seven thirty that morning to find all three of the alarm clocks she'd set for four thirty unplugged. Her father refused to admit it was sabotage.

"I wanted to let you sleep," he'd said as they'd raced to the station. "You got in so late last night."

"Do you know how late I'm going to be for work?"

"You're running on empty. Don't the people you work for see that?"

"What they'll see is that I'm not doing my job."

She told herself that if she said anything more, she'd only be giving him anti-Sterling ammunition that he'd use against her later, but the number-one thing that drove her crazy about her father was that he prided himself on being open-minded when really he didn't allow room for any view but his own, that in this way he was the most rigid person she'd ever known, except her mother. He'd never worked a desk job, never worked for anyone other than himself — how could he be so sure he knew best about something he'd never experienced?

She barely caught the 8 A.M. A mile out of Stockton, she realized she'd forgotten the log cabin quilt, the least of her problems. She wished Will were here, so he could scratch her scalp and calm her down. He'd been unbelievably patient, listening to her freak out for thirty minutes, even though he thought it was really simple, she should just fess up.

How could she possibly respond to Vasu? She was a terrible liar — if she returned his voicemail, he'd know she wasn't telling the truth. She could email him and claim a family emergency, which if you thought about it, this almost was, but then he'd ask her about it when she got to the office, and her blush would give her away. Maybe Will was right: she should just tell Vasu the truth.

Her BlackBerry buzzed again. She was about to turn it off until she saw it was Jordanne.

"Are you OK?" Jordanne asked.

If Jordanne knew something was wrong, it must be even worse than she'd thought.

"Vasu's on the warpath. I was going to get your doorman to pound on your door if you didn't pick up. I'm trying to cover for you, but you need to get here fast."

Sophie stared out the window at the Burger King and Vac'n Tackle that weren't passing quickly enough. "Can other people on the floor hear you?"

"I'm in the stairwell."

"I'm on my way back to the city. I went home last night. It's a long story — I overslept. I'll be in the office in an hour and a half. Two, tops. I'm thinking I should just explain that to Vasu."

"Are you insane? No way you can tell him that. As soon as you get into Manhattan, check yourself into the emergency room."

"Emergency room?"

The woman next to Sophie shushed her.

"Seriously," Sophie whispered. "What should I do?"

"I am serious. Don't you remember what Kenneth Yang told us? About Blumenstein throwing a binder at an associate for being late during the *transit strike?*"

Jordanne was right. Vasu would get her fired. She couldn't quite breathe. "Any other ideas?"

"You got pickpocketed and had to ID the guy at the station?"

"I can't lie to save my life."

"OK, then, keep it simple. Tell the truth — you overslept — just leave out the part about going to Massachusetts."

Why hadn't she thought of that? "Will that work?"

"Vasu will be pissed, but you'll live to bank another day. You're driving?"

"Yeah." She wasn't about to tell Jordanne, who took cabs to work instead of the subway, that she was on a Bonanza bus.

"Just wait to email him until you're twenty minutes away from the office. The last thing you want is to say you'll be right there and then get stuck for two hours on the Cross Bronx. And make sure that when you see Vasu, there aren't any binders within arm's reach."

After Jordanne hung up, Sophie closed her eyes and counted Pillai primes, to calm herself down. *23, 29, 59, 61, 67, 71, 79, 83, 109, 137 . . .* 137 minutes until she got fired.

As soon as she got off the elevator on the twenty-sixth floor, Sophie could feel the eyes sneaking looks at her through the glass. Everybody must know that she'd screwed up. Donnigan didn't meet her gaze. Jordanne shot her a weak smile. Rich Angstrom didn't even pretend not to stare as she raced to Vasu's office.

Sophie clutched her bag to her chest, shielding herself, praying that Vasu wouldn't be able to tell that she hadn't just overslept. She was wearing yesterday's suit, which probably smelled like the beef patty that the woman sitting next to her on the bus had been eating. She'd considered running home to change, but that would've meant getting here another hour later. Her duffel bag was downstairs with the security guard and for a second she wished she'd left it on the bus, so there wouldn't be any evidence of her lie anywhere even close to Vasu.

Vasu waved her inside his office with a flick of his fingers that said he couldn't wait to get rid of her. "Close the door."

"The alarm clock — I'm so sorry —"

"I'm not going to insult you by reminding you what it means to be on call." She'd never seen him like this. His arms were crossed, and the fingers of his right hand kept opening and closing into a fist.

"It won't happen again." If he was this mad because he thought she'd overslept, she didn't even want to think about where she would have been if she'd told him she'd left town. Thank god for Jordanne. She couldn't believe she'd even considered confessing.

"Do you know what would happen if you did this to Pearce or Blumenstein? You'd be cleaning out your desk right now."

Sophie couldn't get a full breath.

"Take a seat. We have work to do."

"Have you heard from Hutchinson?"

"No."

If they hadn't heard from Hutchinson, why the urgency?

"Hutchinson hasn't said no. Yet. Which is why we're here. What do you do if a fish won't bite?" He tore a page from his legal pad. "You throw him more bait. We're going to send him a map."

"Not a model?" It came out so fast — she shouldn't have opened her mouth. She should be nodding at everything he said. She grabbed a notepad from her bag and jotted a note, to show him how diligent she was.

"You have to understand how the client thinks. Showing a CEO a map with the combined operations of two companies is like showing Napoleon a map of his empire combined with Russia."

Sophie didn't remind Vasu that Napoleon's troops died in Russia, that the campaign was Napoleon's downfall.

"We need to show him how his empire can be expanded."

"Empire?"

"We'll call the pages 'expanded footprint.' Hutchinson will see how this merger will make his operations dwarf his competitors, Midwest Metals in particular. Hutchinson *hates* Midwest Metals."

Sophie preferred to believe that the CEO of a multibillion-dollar corporation made strategic decisions based on numbers, not pictures.

"What's the problem?" Vasu asked.

She capped her pen. "No problem. I'll get right on it."

Jake Hutchinson

Hutch spotted a familiar face among a cluster of men inside the Hannibal smelter. Why Pete Gasiewski, AlumiCorp's Chief Financial Officer, had asked to accompany Hutch on his regular Monday morning site visit, Hutch had no idea. Pete had hardly looked up from his BlackBerry the whole time. This smelter was one of the easier trips, just over the Kentucky border, a two-hour drive from Cincinnati.

Hutch had trouble remembering the names of lawyers, accountants, and bankers, but a man in a hardhat, Hutch never forgot. Three years ago, Kareem Nickens had given Hutch his first tour of the Hannibal plant. If memory served, Kareem had two daughters, his wife was from Paducah, he drove a used Ford F-150, and he loved the Cardinals. Hutch shouted hello over the roar of machinery.

This was where Hutch belonged: in work boots and spats, jumpsuit and protective apron, hardhat and visor. Hutch surveyed the tidy pot line, five rows of thirty-two pots, each taller than a grown man. Inside the carbon-lined steel vessels, alumina was dissolved in a cryolite bath and fed an electrical current that separated the oxygen from the aluminum, so the molten metal could be tapped and cast into ingots, a process AlumiCorp had perfected over the past century. His company sure made him proud.

As Hutch headed to the holding furnace, Pete Gasiewski handed him a manila folder. Now he understood why Pete had wanted to come on this trip. Pete wasn't a hands-on kind of guy— there must be something he wanted to talk about privately. Fine. Hutch tucked the file under his arm. You didn't tour a smelter that employed 512 men with your head buried in paperwork. The whole point was to put the numbers aside and show the employees they were more than a line item on a staffing report.

Which reminded him. They'd better head back to Cincinnati if he was going to make his meeting with the head of human resources. He caught Pete's eye and tapped his wrist.

As their driver headed north on I-75, Pete Gasiewski snapped his gum, filling the backseat with the smell of sticky-sweet orange. The CFO had lost 150 pounds a few years ago and now lived on Diet Dr Pepper and Trident Tropical Twist. The sound of Pete's chewing was driving him nuts.

Hutch studied the sales roster that Pete had slipped him inside the smelter. "We lost U-Drink?"

"Switched to Ohio Aluminum. Ohio dropped their pricing another five points."

"What's Ohio trying to do, start a race to the bottom?" Gravity had kicked in, pulling down the Midwest even faster than he'd thought possible. His board would have his neck. "Heaven help us."

When Hutch got his first job at AlumiCorp right out of Penn State, his father, a roofing contractor, approved. "They're a good company. They'll take care of you." A few years after Hutch got promoted to plant manager, his father had his first stroke. The next one, right after Hutch became CEO, took him for good. That was 2004. Since then, they'd gotten on the wrong side of alumina prices, labor and electricity costs kept going on up, and AlumiCorp's Midwest operations had been in the red for so long, Hutch was getting used to losing money. Hutch had hoped seeing his father deteriorate was an experience he'd never have to revisit. But here he was, watching his company slide, and frankly, it was hard not to jump to the obvious conclusion: the final stroke.

Merry, Hutch's assistant of twelve years, sprang from her desk as soon as he walked into the office. "Trish called, she says it's not urgent." She matched his brisk pace, back straight and steps clipped, just like her army husband.

Hutch's office housed a conference table and a private bathroom, but it was furnished with the same wood-laminate desk and swivel chairs his employees used.

"Klaus Kuczma," Merry said. "And Gene Marson called twice. Do you want me to get him on the line?"

Hutch squeezed his eyes shut. The last thing he wanted was to talk to a member of his board, let alone Gene Marson, who was set on hanging him for problems that were bigger than either of them. At last week's board meeting, Marson had announced that if AlumiCorp's stock price lost any more ground, they would reexamine Hutch's leadership at year end. That was what concerned the board — the stock price, not the reasons behind it. Never mind that the stock price was falling because of an anemic bottom line. Never mind that the bottom line was anemic because the Midwest assets were losing more money every day — which Hutch could've fixed if only the board would authorize the layoffs necessary to stop the bleeding. The board was so scared of the press they refused to lay off a single man. Of course Hutch wanted to avoid layoffs. A man's job was his dignity, and you didn't jeopardize that unless it was absolutely necessary. But it was: absolutely necessary. AlumiCorp was sinking fast, and if a few weren't sacrificed, they'd all go down. Schwarzkopf said it best: *you always know the right thing to do. The hard part is doing it.*

"Thanks, Merry. I'll call Gene Marson later."

"Here's tomorrow's meeting schedule. And Ethan Pearce at Sterling sent this over," she said, laying a folder before him. On top of the last folder, Merry placed two golden capsules, Hutch's morning dose of fish oil, as prescribed by Trish.

A quick glance at the day's itinerary and he turned to the folder from Sterling. Two sets of follow-up materials in forty-eight hours — aggressive, even for Ethan Pearce. Business must be slow at Sterling. The first set of numbers had been such a joke, he'd thrown them straight into the trash. But this . . . One page, nice and simple. No bullshit financial projections, no convoluted banker metrics, not a single number. Just two maps. The domestic operations of Midwest Metals in one, AlumiCorp and Roll-Rite combined in the other, a dot marking each smelter, refinery, and rolling mill. The smattering on the AlumiCorp–Roll-Rite map stretched from coast to coast, as impressive as Midwest Metals.

Hutch focused on the cluster ringing Pittsburgh, Roll-Rite's headquarters. Hutch imagined a dot marking the site of the three-room house where he'd grown up, which was demolished years ago to make way for the parking lot of the Pak 'n Save. He imagined a dot marking the high school goalpost where he'd earned a scholarship to Penn State. He imagined a dot marking Olbinski's, where he'd taken Trish Jaskula on their second date because she said the haluski was just like her grandma's. The two of them had sat in that vinyl booth for six hours despite her father's insistence that Trish shouldn't waste her time with a no-good piece of white trash. Nobody in Pittsburgh had thought Hutch was good for anything but football. He leaned back in his chair. He could picture the articles that would run in the *Pittsburgh Post-Gazette: Cincinnati-based AlumiCorp, headed by Pittsburgh native Jake Hutchinson, acquires local company, Roll-Rite.*

Merry knocked. She carried a glass of water and a jumbo chocolate chip muffin even though Trish had made her swear not to let him eat junk.

"Bless your heart," he said, making short work of the muffin. "Can you get Ethan Pearce on the phone for me?"

Hutch pressed his thumb over a few crumbs scattered on his desktop. He was licking them off when Merry buzzed to say she had Ethan Pearce on the line.

Pearce answered a little too loudly. "Jake, good to hear from you. What did you think of the materials we sent over?"

"Tell you the truth, I've been preoccupied with bigger problems."

"The Midwest," Pearce volunteered.

Hutch knew Pearce would take his lack of a denial as confirmation.

"Actually," Pearce said, "we may have a way to solve your Midwest problem within the context of the larger transaction."

"The larger transaction? The larger transaction looks like crap."

For once, Pearce was silent.

"Look. You know as well as I do, there's no way I can sell my board on those numbers."

"I'm confident our team will find additional sources of value," Pearce said.

"Such as . . ."

"Off the top of my head, I'd say rationalization of the work force, for one."

Layoffs.

"Optimizing facilities."

Optimization, a word easier on the eyes than *shutting down* or *closing.*

"And the merger will give you air cover to rightsize the Midwest operations."

He couldn't argue with that.

Hutch considered. Not much harm in letting Sterling go at it. With Pearce pushing this deal so hard, the bankers would do the initial work for free. Hutch could wait to see what Pearce's team came up with before committing and signing an engagement letter. Until then, he wouldn't have to pay a cent.

"All right. Have your guys go ahead and kick the tires."

Pearce didn't skip a beat. "We'll get going. We'll find a way to turn around the Midwest."

4

Wednesday, November 14, 2007

Sophie Landgraf

SOPHIE HAD SPENT HALF of the month since the Alumi-Corp pitch shuttling between her cubicle and Vasu's office. It used to annoy her that he called to tell her to swing by when he just as easily could have come by himself, but it also made her nervous when he suddenly appeared in her cubicle, especially after the dress-down he'd given her about being on call last month. It was better for them both if she just went to him.

She knocked on his glass door. "You wanted to see me?"

Vasu was the most chipper she'd seen him. "Hutchinson liked the second merger scenario — this deal might go live."

Live? She'd be the only first-year analyst in their group on a deal that would actually bring in fees. She hoped Jordanne wouldn't be too jealous.

"Clear your calendar. These things are unpredictable."

No Thanksgiving hike with her father up Mount Greylock. No

sleepover with Kim and Bryce. Canceled plans were the norm at banks like Sterling—she'd expected this when she signed on. But now, watching her trip to Stockton evaporate, she considered what remained—her, here, on her own—and she had to admit that it wasn't very much.

Vasu stared at her, forehead creased, waiting.

She mustered the enthusiasm she knew he expected of her. "Live! This is great."

"From now on, under no circumstances are we to mention AlumiCorp or Roll-Rite by name. Confidentiality. We're calling the deal Project Steelers."

She nodded.

"This is important: Hutch will only consider signing our engagement letter if he likes what we come up with on the synergies."

Sophie wasn't sure what exactly synergies were, but she'd perfected her ability to project blank competence over the past few months, and she did so now. "How will we estimate the synergies, exactly?"

"Combine one bloated manufacturing company with another bloated manufacturing company, cut out any bloat that overlaps, and while they're under the knife, shave off whatever else needs to be shaved. Simple, no? Reduce overhead to make the new company a lean, profitable machine."

People's jobs were the synergies. Closing plants, cutting jobs, saving costs as a result of the merger. "Synergies" sounded like such an innocuous word.

Vasu grabbed his notepad and scribbled circles and boxes. "We need to make lots of maps with the AlumiCorp and Roll-Rite smelters."

Sophie studied the scribbles. "More maps? Not numbers? Shouldn't we build a model?" Maps couldn't be the right way to make a decision about who would lose their jobs and who wouldn't. Sophie preferred to rely on the rationality of Excel: input numbers, enter formulas, link them together, run the model, and accept its objective conclusion. Unlike people, numbers didn't have motives. They just had answers.

Her reluctance must have shown, because Vasu said, "Aren't you here to learn how business leaders think? Here's a lesson we all need to learn: the days of the benevolent employer are over. If AlumiCorp runs unprofitable plants, the factories will get closed one way or another — they'll be taken over by someone else, or they'll go bankrupt. Better for it to happen when the company's still viable and the pension fund hasn't been wiped out in a bankruptcy, no?"

Her mother used to say that capitalism pitted people against each other. Which, of course, it did. What Sophie had never understood was, if you're living in a capitalist society, if it's really every man for himself, why wouldn't you align yourself with the fiscally fit?

"We need to get the synergies maps to Hutchinson *today*," Vasu said. "I want them on my desk by 4 P.M. Then Hutchinson will get us a list of plants to put on the block, and we'll build your synergies model."

Vasu swiveled his chair to face his computer, and Sophie hurried back to her cubicle and did as she was told.

Jordanne was halfway through her tuna sandwich, a finger holding her place in the Excel Bible. "What did Vasu want?"

"Um, AlumiCorp went live." She tried not to sound too excited, so she wouldn't rub it in — the pitches that Jordanne was doing for Safe-Tee Tube weren't going anywhere.

Jordanne's mouth opened into a dark little oval. "Live? Oh my god."

Sophie waited for her to say that she deserved it, that she'd worked so hard and it had finally paid off. Jordanne studied her sandwich for a moment and tossed it into the trash.

"Do you want anything from Starbucks?" Sophie asked. Jordanne zipped across the street at least four times a day because she said the Sterling coffee tasted like crayon. "Cappuccino? Some of those chocolate grahams?"

Jordanne's finger traced a line in the Excel Bible. "I'm good."

Sophie took her seat. She could see Jordanne through the glass, her mouth working like a fish. Jordanne sprang from her chair and disappeared down the hall, toothpaste in hand.

A few hours later, Sophie was editing the map, making sure the dot representing Roll-Rite's rolling mill in Paris, Ohio, was correctly sized to correspond with its production volume. Donnigan sauntered into the quad.

"AlumiCorp still running you ragged?" he asked.

Sophie pointed to the map.

"Then I guess you don't want to come with me and my friends to Vegas this weekend."

It was kind of difficult to be grateful to be working on a live deal when Jordanne and Donnigan got to have fun and she was stuck with this stupid map.

Plastic creaked as Jordanne swiveled her chair to face them. "You should go to Dubai. Grosvenor House is unreal."

"Nah," Donnigan said. "In Vegas, we can hire strippers to play paintball with us."

Sophie had gotten so used to Donnigan's quips, she hardly noticed them anymore.

Jordanne rolled her eyes. "Do you know what? You're full of shit."

"Aren't we all, really? We're like snowflakes — no two of us full of shit in the same way."

"Hey snowflake," Sophie said. "Any idea how to resize this dot on my map?" She hadn't wanted to bother Jordanne.

Donnigan was leaning over her monitor when an envelope icon popped up onto her screen. It was a message from Greg, a friend from analyst training:

To: Landgraf, Sophie T
From: Liden, Greg
Re: Challenge?
    hey soph—
any chance you can ref for the Challenge today? starts in 10. we
need a non-energy group ref, and i put in a good word for you w/
Backenroth. it's yours if you want it.
    g

"You sly minx," Donnigan said. "How'd you score that one?"

Sophie started an email to Greg saying that she was tied up.

"I'm not going to let you do that," Donnigan said. "I'll be lucky if I get a clear view from the hall, and you're passing up a chance to be right there in the middle?"

Of course she wanted to go to the Challenge, but there was the map. Donnigan was right, though, she wasn't going to get a chance to ref again. And hadn't she just been thinking that Donnigan and Jordanne were the only ones having fun? Here was her chance. Besides, if you thought about it, taking a quick break might make her more efficient. "Hey Jordanne? Are you going?"

Jordanne twirled around, pink pashmina draped perfectly over her shoulders. "Sinclair's waiting on this PowerPoint."

"Do you mind pinging me if Vasu comes by for me?"

One corner of Jordanne's lips curled up. "Sure."

Sophie emailed Greg to say she was in. Donnigan pounded her fist and walked off.

That summer, each of the groups in Sterling's Investment Banking Division had pitched the new recruits in their Jersey City training classroom. The men of the Energy Group explained that their Houston oilmen clients wanted their bankers like tanned cowhide: tough, yet pliable. Sophie had thought the comparison was an exaggeration until she heard that the head of the group had once been gored by a bull. Sophie had no interest in joining the Energy

Group—it was strange enough to be one of eleven women in her analyst class of 110. She didn't need to sign on with a group of men who prided themselves on having testosterone oozing out of their eyeballs.

Sophie was certain she'd made the right decision when, months later, one of the second-year analysts regaled her with tales of the Energy Group's Guns and Beer Night. They started the evening at a shooting gallery, firing .22s at targets with Goldman's logo stuck to the bull's-eyes. Then the guys—and they were all guys—gorged on grass-fed beef and Guinness at Tribeca Steakhouse. When the steaks were done, a managing director passed around Ziplocs for each man's wedding ring, which were safeguarded by an analyst while the group went dancing at Le Petit Trianon.

The Energy Group wouldn't have wanted her anyway. They were known for recruiting Texans, football players, and fraternity presidents. Once they had their pledges, they hazed them. Years ago, the Energy Group had devised the Challenge as a test for new recruits, and it proved to be such a success that they now held it every few months.

"So who's playing?" she asked Greg. They were hurrying to the conference room that doubled as the arena.

"Mitch, Joe, and Akash," Greg said. "The place is packed. The guys are saying Mitch's going to set a new record. He was first-string running back at UVA."

Greg led Sophie through the scrum of bankers clogging the hallway. Donnigan was camped out with a few other analysts from their training class. Ethan leaned against the door, scrolling through his BlackBerry, the last person Sophie had expected to see. Except for his morning swim, she hadn't known him to ever step away from his desk. She tried to catch his eye but he seemed to look right through her.

Inside the conference room, the Energy Group was packed shoulder to shoulder. The air had the soggy locker-room smell of sweat and rivalry. Greg signaled to Backenroth, head of the Energy Group and officiant of the Challenge. "Here's our third ref."

She could tell from the whispers that she wasn't what they'd been expecting. She could almost hear her mother. "Come on, straighten up. Someone who looks at her feet and bats her eyelashes is asking to be walked all over." She straightened her shoulders and strode to the conference table at the center of the room. On its surface, Twix lay next to bags of Lay's. Boxes of Sno-Caps topped mountains of Mounds bars. Shiny packages of Cheetos, honey-roasted peanuts, PowerBars, Snickers, Skittles, M&M's, and Caramellos shone on the polished oak. Sophie couldn't wait to tell Will about this.

The other ref was an owlish man who was probably a midlevel in the Energy Group. He told her not to worry, there hadn't been a close call in years. Backenroth cleared his throat and brought the room to order, and Sophie tried not to stare at the white scar curving from his chin to his cheekbone.

"Welcome all to the twenty-second Vending Machine Challenge!" Backenroth waited for the crowd's cheers to taper off. "The Challenge is more than a test of digestion. It's a test of determination and grit." He turned to Mitch, Joe, and Akash, who stood behind the piles of snacks. "Today, three volunteers will vie for the title of Challenge Champion by consuming the contents of an entire vending machine. There will be the delights of the salty snacks. There will be the joy of milk chocolate in its smooth candy shell. But there will also be items that are tougher to swallow: the beef jerky, the PowerBar, the pack of gum, the pork rinds. Not to mention the real differentiator: the Cup O'Noodles. May today's contestants be strong of will and iron of stomach. Contenders, take your places —"

The three analysts leaned over the table and rolled up their sleeves, hands hovering over the packages. Sophie grabbed the ceremonial stapler and passed it to Backenroth, who raised it into the air and fired. "Eat!"

Sophie couldn't believe Jordanne was missing this.

"Come on, Mitch!"

"Go Cavaliers!"

The bankers behind Sophie edged forward, gaming for a better view, squeezing her against the edge of the conference table. The trio attacked the first set of obstacles: the salty snacks.

"Eat!"

"Eat!"

Mitch tore into a bag of Lay's, tipped his head back and funneled the contents into his mouth. He chomped on the chips, spraying crumbs as he glowered at Joe, who had finished his Cheetos and was moving on to the honey-roasted peanuts. If any small part of Sophie had wished that the Energy Group had recruited her, she was cured.

"Mitch and Joe, tied at the end of the first obstacle," Backenroth announced.

"Akash! Hurry up with those Cheetos!"

The lead pair moved on to the candies. Sophie was rooting for Akash, still stuck on the salty snacks, but she kept it to herself. Like Sinclair said, no one at Sterling liked an underdog.

"Where are your balls, Akash?"

"Yeah Mitch, that's it — you're killing them!"

As Joe ripped open the bag of Skittles, it exploded, launching a rainbow into the air, candies painting an arc as they fell, pellets pinging against polished oak and dribbling to rest inches from Sophie. Joe scrambled to gather the Skittles and stuff them into his mouth. By the time he'd recovered from his misstep, Mitch had already polished off the M&M's and the Mounds bar, and was starting on the Snickers. Sophie silently cheered Akash, still three obstacles behind.

"Our leader's concluded the candies course, up two," Backenroth shouted.

Mitch sank his teeth into the PowerBar and paused for the first time. Streams of peanut spittle sluiced down his chin. Sophie didn't even want to think about what her mother would have said if she were here.

"Don't slow down!"

"Power through that PowerBar!"

Mitch slowed to a halt. A bead of sweat hung above his eyebrow. He was panting, his chest rising in shallow gasps. For a split second, Sophie worried he was having an allergic reaction, like the boy their ambulance had rushed to after he'd been stung by a bee. Mitch clutched his stomach, and Sophie came to her senses.

"Come on, Joe!"

"Here's your chance! Take him!"

Joe raced through his bag of M&M's, candies clicking against his teeth as he poured them into his open mouth. Mitch's face was flushing purple.

"Don't lose your nerve, Mitch!"

Mitch clapped his hands over his mouth, eyes darting around the room. Sophie recoiled as Mitch barreled past Joe, made a line drive through the crowd, and spewed the contents of packages one through nineteen into the garbage can. Sophie buried her nose in the crook of her elbow. All she could think of was the monster hangover she'd had after the Winter Olympics party at the SAΣ house her freshman year. Will had to sneak her saltines and Gatorade from the dining hall for two whole days.

"Not so tough, are we?"

"Nasty!"

"Foul!" Joe jumped up and down, shaking the empty bag of M&M's.

"Time out!" Backenroth said. "Refs, let's huddle."

Sophie slid reluctantly under one of Backenroth's extended arms, praying the two other refs would know what to do.

"We need to throw Mitch out," Backenroth said.

The other referee shook his head. "He ate the goods. It's fair. The rules are to eat everything, not to retain it."

Backenroth pointed at the trashcan. "This contest is about digesting shit. We can't allow this."

The pair turned to Sophie. She was going to have to actually do something? In front of all these people? She scanned the crowd for Ethan, who was nowhere in sight. If Ethan were in her position, would he side with Backenroth, the more senior of the two refs? What were the odds that she'd be the deciding factor in this Challenge? Near zero, probably, but here she was, one hundred percent stuck. Her best bet was to do as she had years ago, when her parents were split over buying a gun to protect the sheep from coyotes: reject both sides and offer a new solution.

"We should have Mitch keep going," she said. "If Joe and Akash throw up too, they'll all be even. If not, we disqualify Mitch — conduct unbecoming, right?"

Backenroth clapped his hands. "Fair is fair."

The midlevel referee nodded. "Deal."

Sophie took a deep breath and let it out.

Backenroth turned to the crowd. "Contestants, resume the match!"

Sophie couldn't have been more thrilled when the crowd focused on the contestants, focused on anyone but her. Mitch wiped his face and slunk back to the table, clearly disappointed with himself. He tackled the last PowerBar, the beef jerky, and the gum with renewed zeal. When he'd polished off the Cup O'Noodles — the last obstacle — he leaned back, shamefaced. The crowd ignored Akash, who was still plodding through the candies, and homed in on Joe.

"Sprint! Sprint!"

Joe slowed down when he reached the PowerBar. He consumed the jerky and the gum, unfazed. He peeled back the lid of the Cup O'Noodles, sneezing just once, the powdered broth and flecks of freeze-dried carrot rising in a mushroom cloud over the plastic container.

"Swallow that shit down!"

Joe slammed the plastic cup on the table and pumped his fist. The crowd cheered.

Backenroth extended his hand to Sophie. "I don't believe we've met. Ben Backenroth."

It took Sophie a second to catch up. "Sophie Landgraf. First-year analyst, Industrials."

"Thank you for your assistance in this matter. Keep up the good work."

Vasu Mehta

It never failed. When a deal went live, the infighting began. Jordanne sat opposite his desk, squinting with the focus of a sharp-shooter, right on schedule.

"That's not how it works, Jordanne. We all have our turns." His stock line — to the analysts, to his daughter. "AlumiCorp is Sophie's."

"Are you sure she really wants it though?" Her lips worked silently. "Maybe now that she's back from the Challenge, you could —"

Vasu leaned closer to make sure he had heard correctly. The *Challenge?*

"Oh, I was sure she'd run it by you."

Jordanne knew perfectly well that Sophie had done no such thing.

"Please forget I ever said anything."

He punched Sophie's extension into his speakerphone as Jordanne swanned out of his office. "My office. Now."

Vasu cursed himself for staffing Sophie on AlumiCorp. Two months ago, when Ethan asked for someone to help on AlumiCorp, how could Vasu have foreseen that the assignment would become the multibillion-dollar merger that came along only once in a banker's lifetime? If he had known, he never would have brought on someone as green as Sophie. She was agreeable enough, but clearly her priorities were out of whack. Someone needed to teach her how to comport herself inside an office, and Vasu had neither the time nor the patience. He already had one child. American twenty-two-year-olds needed a primer on how to be an adult — Jordanne could write the chapter on self-preservation.

"What were you thinking?" he asked when Sophie sauntered into his office.

"Excuse me?"

"I give you a time-sensitive deliverable for a deal that could go live and you go off to watch the *Challenge?*"

"I —"

"Do you realize what AlumiCorp is? Do you realize it's our group's best shot? *Your* best shot?"

"Of course, I —"

"Must I lecture you on the sanctity of the deal?"

"I wasn't blowing off the assignment," she said, her voice wavering. "You said to get it to you by four. I'll have it to you by two."

"You'd better."

She rose, avoiding his eyes. *Achchaa,* she was quite upset. Better she hear it from him than from someone higher up, no? For both their sakes. His analyst behaving improperly would reflect as poorly on him as it would on her.

Vasu hurried down the hall to Ethan's office. Vasu caught his eye through the glass, and Ethan pointed to his speakerphone and held up his index finger: hold on a minute. Vasu leaned against Ethan's secretary's desk and asked who Ethan was on the phone with. She mouthed, "Hutchinson."

Ethan must be trying to convince Hutchinson to sign the engagement letter. Vasu had chosen a bad time to swing by. He was about to make himself scarce when Ethan waved him inside. Ethan straightened into the hypererect posture Vasu knew Ethan adopted when he wanted to hide weakness. Hutchinson must have refused him.

"I apologize," Vasu said. "It wasn't right, barging in like this. I'll get on your calendar for this afternoon."

Ethan crossed his arms: spit it out.

"I think we should discuss AlumiCorp staffing."

Ethan's head twisted an inch to the side: why are you bothering me with this?

"I have concerns about Sophie Landgraf."

"Is she making mistakes with the numbers?" Ethan asked.

"The numbers are fine. But I'm not sure she has the proper dedication."

Ethan raised his index finger in the air and drew two tight circles: get on with it.

"I gave her an assignment — the synergies map you and I discussed — and rather than going at it full steam, she went off to the Challenge."

"I know."

"Jordanne Terney is smart, and she has an excellent attitude. I'm inclined to . . . Wait, you were *there?*"

Ethan nodded curtly. "She did well. One of —"

"Excuse me, she was *in* the Challenge?"

"She reffed. One of the contestants upchucked. Pathetic. Sophie brought reason to the ref's ruling — even Backenroth was impressed."

Vasu wondered if Sophie knew how difficult it was to get Backenroth to notice you. To get Ethan to notice you.

"If you're saying the numbers are fine . . ." Ethan looked to Vasu for confirmation.

"They are."

"Then we'll keep her for now. We've got a big push coming. Hutchinson and I just spoke — he wants the synergies analysis by the Monday after Thanksgiving. Someone new won't get up to speed in time."

Ethan swiveled to his computer, dismissing him. The first two years Vasu worked at Sterling, Ethan had bungled his name. He was Vishnu one week, Vikram the next. Ethan would never have vouched for him if a superior had expressed doubts about his professionalism. Vasu closed the door behind him and leaned against its glass, silently cursing Ethan.

Ethan Pearce

The cat, Clara Schumann, scurried into the foyer of Ethan's Tribeca penthouse as soon as his keys hit the Danish modern table. Clara flung herself against his ankle and purred. Clara had been Camille's cat. Ethan hadn't wanted to keep her — he was mildly allergic, had never cared for cats, and was hardly ever home. He'd considered a cat kennel, but here they were, three years later, resigned and resentful as a couple who'd been married fifty years.

Clara had gotten fur all over the legs of his chalk-stripe Brioni suit. He left it in the hamper for his housekeeper, a dour woman who kept the apartment immaculate, left his dry cleaning in his cedar-lined closet, brought in Pellegrino and OrganiCat Raw Cat Food, and most importantly, was gone by the time he came home.

Ethan was feeding Clara when his BlackBerry buzzed with Sinclair's call.

"Any movement with Hutchinson on the engagement letter?" Sinclair asked. Their group head had been beating that drum all week.

"No dice." Ethan freshened Clara's water.

"You did everything you could, I hope."

"We've been through this before. If I push too hard, Hutchinson's going to think we want this more than he does. He needs to think it's his idea." Everyone in their division knew the Industrial Group was behind budget. Sinclair needed the $112 million in fees that AlumiCorp would pay if the merger went through — that was nothing new, but Sinclair pushing him this hard on the engagement letter was, and it made Ethan suspicious. "Is there something going on that I should know about?"

"If there are any more levers you can use with Hutchinson, I want you to pull them."

Sinclair's nonresponse was answer enough: something was definitely up. Perhaps their division head had finally decided to revisit the Industrial Group's leadership in light of its paltry revenue production, which could only benefit Ethan, who'd been the group's top earner for six years running. All the more reason not to hurry the engagement letter and help Sinclair's case.

"Remind Hutchinson of all the free work you did on the equity issue last summer, on the project financing —"

"I'm telling you, Grant, he's not ready."

"We need that letter signed."

"And I need cartilage in my knee, but what I've got is bone on bone."

"Let's both try to think of something," Sinclair said. "We need to throw every punch we've got on this one."

With Sinclair's soft, girlish hands, Ethan doubted Sinclair had ever gotten into a real fight. Sterling had a reputation as one of the scrappier banks — more of a Lehman or a Bear Stearns than a Goldman or a Morgan Stanley — but as far as Ethan was concerned, none of the bankers in the bulge-bracket firms, the Ivy League of Wall Street, had one ounce of grit. Grit was what drove him as a third-year associate to tour smelters and rolling mills, to study metallurgy textbooks until he'd mastered every inch of the aluminum supply chain. Grit was what drove him to cold-call Aaron Lockhardt, the old CEO of AlumiCorp, and force a meeting. Little Prince Sinclair had been trying to poach AlumiCorp from Morgan Stanley for years, but it was Ethan, the state-school kid from High Point, North Carolina, the son of an assembly-line worker, who bagged the suckers.

Clara dashed down the hall to the bedroom wing, and Ethan followed. She hovered expectantly outside the room Ethan avoided whenever possible. She probably thought Camille was still inside.

He'd given Camille that room the first year they were married, as a Christmas present. She hated having anyone listen to her practice — she said, *it's like knowing they've seen you naked and remember every last lump.* It was on those grounds that she'd refused to move in with him before they were married. While she was in Vienna on tour, Ethan had turned the guest room into a studio. He'd had soundproofing installed. Contractors ripped up the carpeting and replaced it with parquet, to improve the acoustics. When he unveiled the room, Camille leapt onto him, legs wrapped so tightly around his waist he could scarcely breathe.

Ethan knelt before the studio door and scratched Clara behind the ears, her favorite spot. He liked to think that Clara wasn't unhappy with him. Camille wouldn't even let Clara listen to her practice. The cat would sit in the hall, poised beside the doorjamb, just as she did now. Camille would crack open the door and sing *meine liebe Clara* to the tune of the fourth movement from the Brahms C Minor String Quartet. He'd asked her about that piece once. She said something vague about how it was the composer's homage to the love of his life, Clara, the widow of Brahms's friend, Robert Schumann. Ethan didn't see how she could know that — string quartets didn't have words, right? *Never mind*, she said. *You don't understand.*

After Camille was gone, his mother ignored his insistence that he wanted to be alone. She flew up from High Point and filled the apartment with oppressive, oniony soup smells — neither Camille nor Ethan cooked — and stuffed the freezer with Tupperware. She removed the soundproof panels and framed concert flyers from the Room, changing it back to the study of Ethan's bachelor days. It was four months before she returned to the High Point house Ethan had grown up in, a squat two bedroom whose back clapboards had never, as far as Ethan remembered, been painted. Soon after, he'd hired her the best home-health aides money could buy.

She was buried in High Point, on a double plot she'd purchased herself. That had been a surprise — Ethan's father had left when Ethan was two, and never once had his mother given any inkling that she particularly cared. Sometimes Ethan wondered whether his mother had meant the other plot not for Ethan's father, but for him.

Ethan had no intention of going back to High Point, living or dead — he'd erased that part of his life as completely as he'd erased his drawl. Camille had told him once that Antonín Dvořák, the Czech composer, had produced his greatest works during his three years in New York, when he was miserable and aching to return to his homeland. Ethan didn't get it. A place of origin should be nothing more than a stake in the sand, the thing to beat. If you were homesick, it was because you hadn't succeeded in creating your world yet.

5

Saturday, November 17, 2007

Sophie Landgraf

OUTSIDE, NORMAL PEOPLE were spending the weekend before Thanksgiving stocking up on canned pumpkin and frozen piecrusts. Sophie was spending her Saturday with the Steelers synergies analysis. She'd already sunk twelve hours checking her model but still, the results didn't make sense. She'd read and reread the relevant sections in Jordanne's Excel Bible, but she still couldn't figure out what she'd done wrong. She wished Jordanne weren't in Greenwich, taking advantage of a rare Saturday off. Jordanne would have fixed it.

Sophie was pecking at her calculator when Vasu called for the millionth time.

"How are the numbers coming along?" he asked.

Pretty slowly didn't seem the wisest answer. "Working on them as we speak."

"When will you have something to show me?"

She couldn't show Vasu the model as it was. Ever since the Challenge, he'd been waiting for her to mess something up.

"I'll get it to you as soon as I can, Vasu. I'm working on it."

"Well, work on it faster. Ethan wants to send it to Hutchinson ASAP — by the Monday after Thanksgiving, at the absolute latest."

Nine days from now — not nearly enough time.

"Sophie, neither of us can afford a mistake on this one. Send me an update before you leave tomorrow." He hung up.

Sophie tugged her mousey scarf tighter around her shoulders. *Neither of us can afford a mistake on this one.* Vasu was going to have her fired. Sterling wasn't going to take care of her anymore. She was going to have to get four part-time jobs and live on ramen and Franzia, like Annabelle.

She could almost hear her mother: *Take a deep breath. You have a way of letting your imagination get the best of you.* When Sophie was five or six, she'd make herself stay awake at night because she was positive that a fanged creature would attack her the moment she fell asleep. Their house was torture for a kid who was scared of the dark — it creaked and sighed with the slightest breath of wind. One night, she thought she heard a sheep crying. She ran into her parents' room and crawled into the warm space between them. They listened, but the wailing had stopped.

"You're a big girl now, Sophie," her mother told her. "You need to learn to stay in your own room."

"But it *was* crying. Really. I heard it."

Her mother took her back into her room and pretended to check each corner for monsters. The next morning, they found tufts of bloody wool on the grass. A few feet before the tree line, an ear. A lamb named Derrida was missing. At breakfast, she overheard her parents whispering about a coyote. After that, Sophie lay awake, imagining wet jaws opening wide.

"Here's what we'll do," her mother said. "When you get scared, knock on the wall behind your bed. I'll knock back, and you'll know I'm close by, OK?"

It worked — her mother's knock had broken up the dark.

Sophie closed out of the model on her screen. Maybe that was the answer: she needed to turn on the light. Pretending that she could handle this wasn't working. It was time to ask for help.

Jordanne wasn't answering her phone. There was only one other option.

"Hey, Donnigan." She punched the speed ball punching bag hanging in his quad. "Can I ask a favor?"

"What, you forget your Xanax this morning?" He stared at her hands. She hadn't realized she was picking the polish off her thumbnail.

Maybe this wasn't the best idea. She didn't know if she could trust Donnigan, but besides Jordanne, of all the people in the Industrial Group, she mistrusted him the least. Even her mother would have to agree there was a perverse fairness in the way he picked on everyone equally.

"It's the Project Steelers synergies model," she said. "I've hit a wall. I was wondering —"

He smiled. "You're asking me to fix your shit?"

"Not fix it, just take a look. Vasu's —"

"Let's see what we can do."

She pulled up the spreadsheet on his computer, but he cut her off before she could lead him through the model's calculations. "Give yourself some credit. You laid it out nice and clear." He shook out his arms. "Step back and watch me work my magic."

She couldn't just sit there and watch him uncover her mistakes. "I'll grab you some animal crackers." For once, there wasn't a half-finished bag sitting on his desk.

She took the long way to the vending machine so she'd walk along the south wall, where the lights of Times Square pulsed in the distance, reminding her that outside, people were actually having fun. Mitsuko's improv show was probably about to start. Will and Annabelle would be grabbing beers before they sat down.

Donnigan ripped open the bag of animal crackers and funneled them into his mouth. "Your numbers are good," he said, his mouth full.

"But the result doesn't make sense."

He offered her the Grey Goose he kept in his bottom drawer. "Here. Try this."

She took a shallow sip but still coughed.

"You've got a clear case of GIGO. You feed garbage in, you get garbage out. The model's built right, but I'll bet one of your assumptions is off."

Great. How was she supposed to figure out which one? "So now what?"

He shrugged. "You think I understand the aluminum business? Vasu will tell you what's wrong."

That wasn't the answer Sophie had been hoping for. She couldn't let Vasu fix her mistakes — the model she showed him had to be perfect.

"Look," Donnigan said, glancing at his BlackBerry. "I'm supposed to be meeting some guys."

"Oh! Sorry. Thanks for taking a look. I seriously appreciate it."

"Want to come with? It's this fashion-meets-finance happy hour."

"Sorry, what?"

"Men in finance, women in fashion, lots of drinks —"

"That actually exists?" she asked.

"Yep." He grinned. "It'd be pretty funny to watch you confuse the hell out of everyone. You could bring Mr. Liberal Guilt."

She *wished* she could be out with Will tonight. "I think I have a date with my cubicle."

He pounded her fist and walked off.

One of your assumptions is off. How would she figure out which one was the culprit when she'd never even seen the aluminum refineries and smelters she was supposed to model? Vasu would know what was wrong, Donnigan was right about that, but asking Vasu would only give him another reason to question her performance. This wasn't like college, where if you knocked on your professor's door during office hours, he'd smile at your curiosity and massage his temples for a moment, affirming the complexity of your confusion. You had to hide your weaknesses until you had none — she knew that now. It was like Ethan had said during her first month at Sterling: *Until you know the client's business as well as the client does, please, do us all a favor and keep your mouth shut.* Ethan would know what was wrong with her model, but he was out of the question for the same reason as Vasu. Or was he? What if she concealed the reason she was asking? Vasu would see right through it, but Ethan was far enough removed from the model that if she phrased it right . . .

The idea of asking Ethan for anything was enough to tense every muscle in her body. *You're kidding,* Ethan would say, squinting in that way that seemed to say, remind me who hired you, because he needs to be fired. Still, Ethan was her best shot. Her only shot. She tiptoed to the corner of the floor. Ethan's light was on — he was still here.

She tried calling Jordanne again, still no answer. Sophie sealed herself in the ladies' room, hands braced against the sink, steeling herself. The key was under no circumstances to let Ethan know she needed anything. He was the sort of man who was offended by human weakness. She'd have to seem confident, casual.

She hovered outside Ethan's door, telling herself that fear was not a helpful emotion. He sat at his desk, shoulders stiff right angles, square hands squeezing a pencil sharpened to a stiletto-thin point. Maybe this was a mistake. She was about to hurry back to her cubicle when he looked up, the crease in his brow reproaching her for interrupting him. She was stuck.

"Ethan? I'm sorry to bother you —"

His lips pressed into a thin, impatient line.

"Could you maybe recommend a primer on the aluminum industry?" Her voice sounded hoarse. "I want to get up to speed on the technical side of the business. I thought you might have an idea about where to start."

Ethan's nose twitched like he smelled sour milk.

"Interesting way to spend a Saturday night," he said.

In her script, this was where she'd hoped he'd give her what she'd asked for. She didn't trust herself to improvise, so she said what Ethan had once told her, "I want to know the business as well as the client does."

He scanned her up and down. She felt about as inadequate as she had in middle school, when Natalie Tibirski said all the seats at her lunch table were taken, and Kim had to intervene on Sophie's behalf.

He pointed to the volumes on his top shelf: *Midwest Metals 2007 Investor Day, The State of Smelting, Mining and Refining Aluminum, Soderberg v. Prebake, Bauxite 101.* "How much do you want?"

"I'll take anything you'll give me."

Sophie could barely carry the stack he handed her, but she pretended she could handle it until she was out of his view.

$$$

By Sunday morning, Sophie had already found four mistakes in her analysis, and she'd only made it through half of the materials Ethan loaned her. *Four.* Donnigan was right: garbage in, garbage out. She'd been about *this close* to disaster. And now she'd have to crank nonstop to fix the model before the deadline. Jordanne was talking on the phone in Portuguese and the noise was driving Sophie crazy, but she kept it to herself because she knew that talking to her mom stressed out Jordanne enough.

A chat window appeared on her screen:

Kim2003: hey—saw chuck @ the store.
Kim2003: he had 4 boxes of bisquick. hope u r hungry
Kim2003: b and i can't wait 2 see u!!!!!
SophieLand: not going 2 make it.
Kim2003: delaware with will?
SophieLand: i wish. work.
Kim2003: they won't let u off 4 TGIVING?!?!?!
SophieLand: i'm scared 2 tell dad.
Kim2003: yeah, good luck w that

She should've called home before now but she'd been so caught up in the synergies analysis, she'd completely forgotten. Her father must already be stowing biscuits in the freezer so they wouldn't waste their time together cooking, which meant he'd be that much more disappointed when she told him there was no way she'd make it home. She'd resigned herself to this, and a small part of her was relieved to be saved another lonely holiday with her father, which of course only made her feel that much more guilty.

She slipped into the stairwell to call him.

"Soph!"

Sophie could see him sitting at the kitchen table, winding the black cord of their old rotary phone around his finger — alone.

"Perfect timing," he said. "I can't decide: pumpkin, apple, or pecan. Or all three? What —"

"Listen, Dad, I have some news you're not going to like."

"Something wrong?"

"Everything's fine." Better just spit it out. "I'm not going to make it home for Thanksgiving."

"What do you —"

"Work's going crazy, there's this really big project . . ." Her voice echoed throughout the stairwell, thin and hollow. She was going about this all wrong. "I really want to, but I can't get away right now."

"You can't get away? What does that even mean? Have they chained you to your desk?"

"I can't," she said. "I was thinking —"

"You mean you won't."

"I was thinking," she said. "Why don't you come here? I'll be working some of the time, but we could —"

"I already started cooking — the bird's in the brine, I put up the cranberry sauce, the baked apples. You should see the freezer."

"Thanksgiving in New York could be fun!" She was trying to sound chipper but it came off as frantic. "We could go to the parade. Remember when we used to watch —"

"I don't understand why you can't take off just two days."

She took a deep breath. "Please come."

"Me and cities, we don't mix."

They both knew this was true.

"You know," he said, "the first Thanksgiving your mother and I spent on the farm, the oven broke. We did the turkey on the grill," he said. "Your mother, she stayed out in the cold, basting the bird with her mittens on. Nothing stopped her, your mother."

He'd told Sophie that story a million times — after she'd hiked Mount Greylock despite the downpour, after she'd finally explained sine and cosine in a way that Eriqua, the middle schooler she'd tutored, actually understood — when her father was applauding her, not reproaching her.

"I'm really sorry, Dad."

"Yeah, well." He said this like he was used to being the victim, like he'd never unplugged an alarm or done anything other than being perfectly supportive of his daughter.

"I know Kim would be thrilled for you to join her —"

"Kim's sweet. But she's not you." He sighed. "I'll be fine. Don't worry about me."

Once her father shifted into passive-aggressive mode, she'd lost. "I really —"

"You're young. You should live your life."

"Dad —"

"It's late," he said. "I should let you go."

Sophie squeezed her eyes shut, wishing that her father was more like Jordanne's mother, who understood that your twenties were for working as hard as you possibly could.

Positive she couldn't feel any more inadequate, she returned to her cubicle only to find Vasu perched on her desk, staring her down.

"Whenever I come by your cubicle, it's empty. Why is that?"

It was part of her master plan to disappoint everyone. Jordanne stared at her lap, pretending not to hear Sophie being dressed down.

Vasu cocked his head. "How's the synergies model coming?"

"Under control." The model was about the only thing that was.

He picked up the copy of *Soderberg v. Prebake* lying open on her desk. "Pleasure reading?"

"You could say that, yeah."

"So when will you have something for me?"

"Saturday?"

He shook his head. "Not soon enough. Ethan's worked up — he wants this out. Hutchinson needs to sign the engagement letter."

"Friday?"

"Thursday." Thanksgiving. "Close of business." He dropped the aluminum primer on her desk with a thud.

Vasu Mehta

Vasu would never understand why Sinclair always ordered a buffet for the morning he delivered performance reviews. Perhaps a first-year analyst would make the mistake of helping himself to a scone instead of gathering intelligence, but the analysts would not receive their reviews until the summer. Every year, the platters of bagels, muffins, fruit salad, and Danish resting on Sinclair's credenza remained untouched.

Sinclair focused on something behind Vasu's head. "We have some reservations about your performance."

"Reservations?" In seven years, Vasu had received only glowing reviews about his work ethic, his initiative, his attention to detail. "What about?"

"There are concerns that you're spending too much time spinning your wheels and not enough time moving the ball forward. We think you could be more effective."

"What in particular are you asking me to improve?"

"There's always more to do, more to contribute. We want to see you giving 110 percent."

They were papering the record, it was the only explanation. They did not want to look entirely capricious when they skimped on his bonus next month — or worse, fired him. "How specifically is my performance not satisfactory?"

"Everyone here is driven, committed, smart. That's a given. Those who distinguish themselves go above and beyond."

Vasu knew he was good at his job, and he knew Sinclair knew it, which meant uncertain business conditions were to blame. And if business conditions were uncertain, a midlevel like him with no clients of his own was definitely at the top of the list to be sacked. Vasu had predicted a round of layoffs so many times that Rich Angstrom and the rest of the midlevels called him Chicken Little, but this was it, he was certain. All he asked was that they wait until year-end to fire him, so he could collect one last bonus.

Sinclair rambled on, and Vasu could not help but blame himself. In years past he had diversified his risk, making sure to get in front of Sinclair, Blumenstein, and Pearce as often as possible. These past three months, he had been spending all his time on AlumiCorp, thinking that working on a live deal that might bring in $112 million in fees would be enough to buy him another year at

Sterling. He had lost sight of the fact that Ethan Pearce protected no one.

"Is there anything I can do to improve my situation?" Vasu asked. "Any projects that could use an extra hand? I'm happy to take on whatever would help the group."

Sinclair scratched his chin. "You could write up your impressions of the new analysts. I suspect that while you've been staffing them, you've gotten to know them better than anyone else."

Sinclair never expressed interest in analysts — further proof that something was amiss. "Anything else?"

Sinclair closed his file. The meeting was over.

Vasu's hands flew to his Parliaments as soon as he was out the door. He could not tell Aditi. Not yet. Tonight she would ask him how work had been, and it would be easy enough to say that work was work. The difficult part would come in two days, when they drove to her cousin's in Edison for Thanksgiving. He already knew what would happen. When Radhika Auntie served the *mohanthal*, Mahesh Uncle would hint that his grandson had not yet found a job. Aditi would say that perhaps Vasu could put in a good word for him at Sterling, and Vasu would agree, even though the last thing he should be doing right now was asking favors. On the drive home, Aditi would say how wonderful it was to be with family — when they were in India, she had taken that for granted. That moment would be the real test. He would want so badly to tell her that there was a very large chance they would return to India sooner than he had planned, but if he did, she would begin to hope. That, he could not bear.

Sophie Landgraf

Sophie waited inside the Starbucks across the street from Sterling, watching her BlackBerry. Nancy Cho, an MD in the Healthcare Group and the mentor Sterling's women's network had assigned

Sophie, had not yet written to cancel, as she had their first four meetings. If Nancy bailed, that would be fine — Sophie had her work cut out for her on the Steelers deal. But she wasn't about to cancel on Cho, one of three senior women in Sterling's Investment Banking Division and, according to Jordanne, by far the most impressive.

"Sophie?" Nancy extended her hand, squeezing Sophie's fingers so hard they hurt.

Cho carried a quilted Chanel bag that matched her ballet flats. Her shoulder-length black hair showed the slightest bit of gray at the roots. She wasn't exactly pretty, but her discus-thrower's jaw screamed "don't mess with me," and her shell-pink nails were as smooth as plastic. Sophie's nails looked more like an impressionist painting: only with distance did the layers of red blend into something pleasing.

The café was packed, every table taken by office workers and tourists, but Nancy persuaded a pair of women studying a map that it was time to move on, in New York you don't just camp out when other people are waiting for seats.

Nancy set her BlackBerry on the edge of the table. "Sophie, what can I do for you?"

Sophie had expected someone like her mother, who spewed advice unbidden — she hadn't realized her mentor would want a pitch. Unprepared, Sophie asked what she had at banking interviews, when she had nothing left to say.

"Could you tell me a little bit about how you got here?"

Cho sipped her cappuccino. "Started on the stock exchange. Sugar futures. Terrible gig, but it made me sharpen my claws. Stanford for B-school, landed a seat at Sterling. Fought my way up, and here we are. What else?"

"The managing director I work for. What can I do to impress him?"

"Who's your MD?"

"Ethan Pearce."

"Ah. The tragic widower."

"What?" Sophie shouted so loudly that the family next to her stopped their conversation. How had she possibly missed that? She'd combed through Ethan's desk. His office was so unbelievably unexciting that she'd been absolutely positive it could only belong to someone with zero personal life. "What happened to his wife?"

Nancy glanced at her BlackBerry. "What can you do to impress your MD ... Do you know your Excel shortcuts? Standing behind an analyst, watching him fly through a spreadsheet without a mouse — *that's* impressive. What else?"

What Sophie really wanted to know was what Ethan's wife was like. How could anyone not be scared to death of that man, let alone put up with the hours he worked? She wondered how often his wife had guilt-tripped him the way Sophie's father had for not coming home for Thanksgiving. "What do you do when people in your life give you a hard time about how much you work?"

Nancy smiled wryly. "The ones worth having take you as is."

"I hadn't really thought about it that way."

"Look." Cho leaned across the table. "If you're going to do this — really do this — you can't let anyone get in your way. You can't have doubters on your team."

Sophie winced.

"The sooner you sharpen those claws, the better. I've got a 9 A.M. with the lawyers." Cho rose and gripped Sophie's hand. "Good luck."

$$$

Sophie repeated Nancy Cho's words like a prayer as she slaved over the Steelers' synergies analysis. *The ones worth having take you as is.* She repeated them on Monday afternoon as she rerouted the switches in her spreadsheet. She repeated them on Wednesday evening as she triple-checked her results on her calculator. She repeated them on Thursday morning as she stood at the conference-room window, watching the Spider-Man, Kermit, and Hello Kitty balloons crawl downtown, so much tinier than they'd seemed when she'd watched the Thanksgiving parade with her mother on their ancient, wood-grained TV.

Will called from Delaware at four, just like he'd said he would. "How are you holding up?"

"I think I might have found this great new macro for my model." She could hear kids squealing in the background.

"How's your sister?" she asked. "Did you tell her I say hi?"

"They're wrapping you up some of that cranberry bread you like."

"I love Leah." She wondered if her father had baked the pies he'd told her about. "My dad's still not picking up the phone. I wish he'd finally get an answering machine."

Will didn't say anything.

"What?"

"Maybe just because you're OK with not having a life doesn't mean he's OK with it."

Will too? Her spreadsheet glowed, so many formulas to fix, so much that needed to get done. Were they really going to have this conversation now? "I'm sorry, OK? I'm sorry we don't have enough time together. I'm doing the best I can."

"I know you are. It's just . . ."

"Remember what it was like when you graduated? When you went backpacking for two whole months?" And she'd been *fine* with it?

"That was different."

"How is it different?"

"It just is."

Will's steadiness was one of the many things she loved about him, but it had a way of making their lives unbelievably difficult when anything changed. "So we don't automatically run in parallel anymore. So it's not like college. We just have to work at it, that's all."

"So work at it. That's all I'm asking."

She dropped her head onto her desk. Didn't he see how hard she was trying? "It's not fair to expect me to have everything perfect right from day one. There's an adjustment period."

"Sophie, it's been five months. And nothing's adjusting."

After they hung up, Sophie stared at her screen for twenty minutes before she admitted that she couldn't concentrate. She watched and rewatched the YouTube clip Donnigan had sent her that morning with a note to hang tough: a monkey hugging a puppy, leathery fingers picking something out of the puppy's fur, making it look like it was so easy to be with someone who was different from you, like taking care of someone was this simple thing that you were born knowing exactly how to do.

It took her four more hours to audit the model backwards and forwards, cross-checking her assumptions with the textbooks Ethan had loaned her. Certain the model was as right as she could make it, she sent it to Vasu. It was time to collect her prize.

She rode the elevator to the twenty-ninth floor, where Nancy Cho and the rest of the Healthcare Group had their offices. It was Sophie's first time on twenty-nine, but she found her way easily — the floor was a carbon copy of Sophie's own. She made a thorough sweep of the halls before turning the cool handle of Cho's door. The office smelled of Chanel No. 5. Photos crowded the desk: Cho next to a racing bike, Cho on the ski slopes, Cho in marathon gear. In a desk drawer, Sophie found a membership card to the New-York Historical Society, still affixed to the welcome letter; a bottle of women's multivitamins; a hairbrush; two packages of control-top stockings; and a tube of Christian Dior lipstick in a bright red called Blood Diamond.

Sophie uncapped the lipstick, which was honed to a perfect scoop. She applied a coat, careful to preserve the sculpted edge. It tasted like a grape Jolly Rancher. She knew she should put it back, but the slick, bullet-shaped tube fit so perfectly in her palm. Nancy Cho must have dozens of tubes of her favorite shades lined up in a tidy row in her medicine cabinet. Surely Nancy wouldn't miss this one. Sophie dropped the lipstick into her pocket.

She was about to close the drawer when she noticed a printout of a dating service questionnaire among Nancy's Post-its and legal pads. "What are you looking for?" the questionnaire asked. "Age?" *35–70,* Nancy had written. "Profession?" *Any.* "Religious Affiliation?" *Any.* "Height?" *Any.* And under "Other," Nancy had written, *Must have a passport and a library card.*

Sophie resolved to cool it on the office explorations for a while. There were some things she didn't want to know.

$$$

Sophie's quad reeked of tuna fish even though Jordanne hadn't been in since Wednesday — the trash guys hadn't worked the holiday either. It was the Friday after Thanksgiving and Sophie was about to get a third cup of coffee when her phone rang.

"Let's get this over with," Vasu said.

She applied two coats of Blood Diamond lipstick before heading to Vasu's office.

"How was your Thanksgiving?" she asked.

"Better than yours, I imagine," he said, with a sympathetic smile that she hadn't expected.

Vasu pecked at his calculator, reviewing her work.

"Looks like you're ready for the Soap Box Derby." He leaned forward, lowering his voice though she was pretty sure they were the only two people on the floor. "Want some free advice? Give this deal everything you've got. And stay near Pearce. It's always wise to align yourself with a senior guy who's a machine."

A machine. Now that Sophie knew about Ethan's wife, it made so much more sense why he worked so hard. After her mother died, Sophie had avoided her dorm room at all costs because if she spent more than two minutes alone there, she wouldn't come out for days. After class, she'd go straight to the library, Koffee Too, her professor's office hours, Will's suite — anything to remind her that there was a world outside her head.

She wondered how much Vasu knew about Ethan's wife's death. "Has Ethan always been that way?"

Vasu thrust a stack of printouts into her arms. "How do you think he got to where he is?"

Ethan Pearce

Ethan waited for Hutchinson in the lobby of the Omaha Hilton, the epicenter of the annual Metals Industry Consortium Conference. Investors, bankers, and lobbyists were milling around the coffee service, chatting, but Ethan had no interest in networking. He was here because one look at Hutchinson's face would tell him whether the Roll-Rite merger would move forward. Hutchinson was supposed to have met him here ten minutes ago. Ethan had a feeling Hutchinson liked making him wait.

The lobby looked like a high school science fair — stalls plastered with posters, each manned by a competent-looking suit ready to hand out marketing brochures: *Energy Efficiency and the Bayer Process, How Steel Nanotechnology Can Reduce the Weight of Our Cars.* The svelte head of Millennium Can investor relations smiled at him from behind one such booth. She had wheat-colored hair and a Midwestern athleticism Ethan found attractive. He returned her smile with noncommittal amusement. He had no intention of becoming attached to any woman again; at conferences like this, it was easy to meet women who understood that.

The last conference he'd attended, Sterling's High Yield boondoggle in Taos, opened with a Western-themed casino night. As Ethan entered a ballroom ringed by poker tables and craps, he was greeted by cowgirls in daisy dukes and checkered bikini tops. Inside, a cowgirl rode a mechanical bull, one arm grasping the saddle horn, the other thrown behind her head. She winked at him. After a few rounds of Texas Hold 'em, he called her bet. The sex was as forgettable as she was.

When Camille performed, her eyes grew heavy lidded in what equally could have been pleasure or pain. She held herself still on the stage, shoulders flung back and sternum lifted, proud as a swan. A thin blue vein trailed between the bones of her clavicle and up the side of her pale throat. He'd always hoped to elicit that look from her in bed: fragile and formidable at once.

"Ethan," Hutchinson said, pulling him into a pungent hallway where kitchen staff wheeled carts of discarded buffet dishes. Hutchinson looked breathless and a little sick. "We need to talk."

"Good to see you, Jake. What did you think of—"

"What the heck is going on?"

"Pardon?"

Hutchinson leaned in close. "Roll-Rite and Midwest."

"Wait—what?"

"They're having dinner together as we speak. With your colleague Grant Sinclair."

"This is news to me, Jake." What the hell was Sinclair doing? The management of Roll-Rite and Midwest Metals having dinner together at a conference like this would only get people talking merger. There had to be a reason for all this. Sinclair might be lazy, but he wasn't stupid.

"No way I'm letting Midwest Metals poach my prize."

Hutchinson's mouth was pressed into an angry little line, irrational as a child, which had to be Sinclair's intention. Everyone in the industry knew that Hutchinson had hated Midwest Metals ever since '96, when Midwest launched a hostile on AlumiCorp that almost cost Hutchinson his job and his credibility. That was the thing about the aluminum industry: same old feuds, same old friendships. Sinclair had correctly predicted that if Jake Hutchinson thought Midwest was going after Roll-Rite, he'd fight that much harder to get Roll-Rite for himself. Ethan couldn't imagine how Sinclair had gotten Midwest to play along, and he didn't care.

Hutchinson rubbed his hands together. "I'm gonna get to Carbonell, quick. Your team better hurry up."

"Don't worry — we'll fix this." Sinclair had handed him the magic bullet. Their group head had some fight left in him after all. "We'll do whatever it takes. Of course, we'll need you to sign the engagement letter."

"Done. Send it to Merry. Let's get this thing moving."

Ethan clapped Hutchinson on the shoulder. "Now how about that drink?"

6

Tuesday, December 18, 2007

Sophie Landgraf

SOPHIE THREW HER weight against the door of Redeye
Steakhouse. Inside, the Industrial Group holiday party was
already in full swing. The smell of melting cheese and cinna-
mon filled the restaurant. Ira Blumenstein and Kenneth Yang hovered next to a zinc bar decorated with pine garlands and Scottish
plaid, the slim brunette on Blumenstein's arm smiling patiently as
she sipped a glass of champagne. Grant Sinclair, Rich Angstrom,
and their wives chatted as they waited on the long queue for the
coat check, each couple fitted so tightly together and pressed so
close to the next that there was, it seemed, no place for Sophie.

Before walking the two blocks to the restaurant, Sophie had
stretched over the sink in the Sterling ladies' room to dab concealer
on her forehead and apply two coats of Blood Diamond lipstick.
It had been no use — looking around, she felt like a second-class
citizen. The wives were pressed, blown out, powdered, like they'd

been beamed in straight from the salon. After six months working with the Sterling men, Sophie still found their ways alien, but of the people here, she felt more kinship with the men than the women. Even if Sophie had their airbrushed makeup, suspiciously unscuffed shoes, and filmy dresses, she'd never be what they were: professionally pretty. Sophie hadn't felt this inferior since high school, but now she couldn't rely on her impending escape to college.

Sophie didn't feel up to facing the scrutiny of those women, so she followed the smell of baked Brie to the buffet. A plateau of crab claws and oysters towered over runny cheeses, salmon rillettes, sirloin sliders, platters of sushi, goat cheese tartlets, tuna tartare, and sides of marbled beef quivering on carving boards. A chocolate fountain announced the desserts: mousse in silver goblets, diamond-cut pecan bars, stag-shaped sugar cookies, maroon macarons, miniature tartlets — raspberry and lemon and chocolate, each the size of a silver dollar. The chocolate ones were topped with a candy coin with "STL" stenciled in gold: chocolate with her name on it. It didn't get much better than that.

Sophie was washing down a tartlet with a glass of merlot when Donnigan tapped her on the shoulder.

"Where's Mr. Liberal Guilt?"

"*Will* is tied up tonight."

Will was at a poetry slam. When she'd invited him to the party, he'd wrinkled his nose and said that he liked her better off duty. She'd only let that go because she wasn't sure she wanted him to come anyway. When she'd met Will, she'd instantly been drawn to his threadbare corduroys and inexhaustible idealism — they'd reminded her of home. She still loved that about him, but she wasn't sure the Sterling guys would, and she didn't want to have to spend the party worrying whether everybody was getting along.

"Isn't it weird seeing everyone here with their wives?" Sophie asked.

"I bumped into Blumenstein at the bar and he smiled at me for what I swear was the first time since I started — only because his wife was there, no doubt."

"It's like running into your kindergarten teacher at the grocery store and getting really confused because you thought she lived in the school closet."

Donnigan grinned. "You were an even bigger dork than I'd thought."

Jordanne appeared in a gray silk dress so simple and elegant that Sophie wished she'd thought to change out of her suit. Jordanne handed Sophie a glass of champagne. "They're hoarding the good stuff behind the bar. I hear this is nothing compared to last year's party — Cipriani, Cristal."

Donnigan shrugged. "Free drinks are free drinks."

Jordanne looped her arm in Sophie's, steering them away from Donnigan. "What do you think of Sinclair's wife's face lift?"

"She had a face lift?" It was the first time either of them had seen Charlotte Sinclair.

"See the way her earlobe is a little too attached to her jaw? Dead giveaway. So are you holding up OK?"

"Just." All week, the Sterling team had raced to prepare for Hutchinson's meeting tomorrow with Roll-Rite's CEO, the first real test of their deal. Ethan had ordered Sophie to run numbers for every possible scenario. "But I finished everything before I left the office. For the next few days, I'm free as a bird. Will's on cloud nine."

"Where will you guys celebrate? Anywhere good?"

"There's this neighborhood place we like." Sophie spared Jordanne the details of the Peruvian rotisserie place where the two of them could share a roast chicken and pisco sours for twenty-five dollars. And she definitely wasn't going to mention Annabelle's Twelve Days of Franzia, which she'd promised to come to that weekend.

"Guess where Antonio took me last night."

Last weekend, it had been a farm-to-table restaurant an hour outside the city where before dinner, Jordanne had fed the sheep, which Sophie had trouble not finding ridiculous.

"Le B."

"Oh my god — he took you to Le Bernadin?" Wasn't dinner there like two hundred dollars? "How was it?"

"Yummy. But I was the only one in the whole restaurant wearing a color."

In some ways, Jordanne was even harder to impress than Ethan. "Have you seen Ethan, by the way?" Sophie asked. "I'm super curious whether he brought a date."

"Wait a second." Jordanne whispered, "You're not interested in him, are you?"

"Of course not."

"That could get messy, you know." Jordanne's cockeyed smile seemed to say that she hoped it would.

"It's nothing like *that*." What kind of girlfriend did Jordanne think she was? And besides, Ethan was her *boss*. "I mean, I admire him, how could I not? But really, that's it." She didn't know how to tell Jordanne that she was way out of line. "I should say hi to Vasu. I'll find you later, OK?"

Sophie waded past Sinclair and his wife, whose elongated ears, now that Sophie knew what to look for, looked suspiciously like a pixie's. Kenneth Yang's girlfriend was squinting like she'd drunk too much. Mrs. Blumenstein was talking to Donnigan and laughing — with him or at him, unclear. Sophie found Vasu by the cheese plate.

"Did you finish everything for the face-to-face?" Vasu asked.

"Done and done."

Vasu introduced Sophie to his wife, who wore an easy smile, a simple black sheath, and low heels. Aditi's thin fingers flew to touch her earrings in a self-conscious way that Sophie found endearing. She looked nothing like the other wives in the restaurant — she looked normal — and Sophie liked her immediately.

"I've heard so much about you," Aditi said to Sophie.

"Likewise," Sophie said, though this wasn't true. It occurred to

Sophie that she must see more of Vasu than Aditi did. Sophie knew nothing about Vasu's wife and she cast about for somewhere to begin. "Are you in finance too?"

"Oh, no. In India, I was a biochemist. After I got my PhD, I worked in a lab doing DNA sequencing. But that was a long time ago — almost ten years, before Meera was born."

"Oh — I didn't realize — you look so young." And Vasu cranks as hard as a twenty-two-year-old.

"I'll take that as a compliment," Aditi said.

Vasu attempted a smile, but he looked pained more than anything. Vasu always looked stressed, but today he seemed even worse than usual. Maybe he was worried about the face-to-face.

"Have you seen Ethan?"

"Not yet," Vasu said. "But now that you've reminded me, any interest in more free advice? When you see Pearce, it wouldn't hurt to thank him for a great first season at Sterling. Tell him how much you're looking forward to 2008."

Vasu's strange advice combined with his pained smile made her worried. "Is everything OK?"

"Looking grateful goes a long way. We both need to stay on Pearce's good side."

"OK. I will."

A waiter approached with a tray of gougères.

"I'm going to check in with the babysitter," Aditi said. "Pleasure to meet you, Sophie." They headed to the door.

The crowd had separated by rank, the senior guys congregating near the bar, looking bored, the junior guys hovering near the buffet, looking drunk. Ethan was arguing with a bartender. It seemed he was without a date after all. Why had she been so scared of him? He might not go out of his way to put anyone at ease, but he'd been perfectly reasonable when she'd asked to borrow his primers. It was probably her own fault that she'd been so easily intimidated.

"Unbelievable," Ethan said as she slid up beside him. "Next year, they're going to have us buy our own drinks."

"I brought you an extra copy of the Steelers materials for the meeting tomorrow." She pulled an envelope from her bag. "I didn't know if you were going back to the office."

"Perfect."

She remembered what Vasu had said. "Thank you for such a great first year. I've learned so much. I'm really looking forward to 2008."

"Let's hope Steelers brings us something to celebrate this Christmas."

Grant Sinclair cut in, belly ballooning over the cinch of his belt. "Ethan, might I have a word?"

Sophie wasn't sure whether she was supposed to excuse herself. She split the difference, turning to the bartender and asking for another glass of champagne.

"I'm not going to be able to join you in Cincinnati," Sinclair said.

"Really?" Ethan asked.

Even with her back to Ethan, Sophie could imagine his condescending smirk.

"Firm business," Sinclair said flatly.

"Is there another live deal happening that I don't know about?"

She probably wasn't supposed to hear this. Maybe she should go find Donnigan. She turned to leave, champagne in hand, only to find herself face-to-face with Ethan. His arms were folded, his head cocked in a one-eyed squint. He was looking at her — not his usual one-second glance but really, actually looking at her.

"What's your schedule tomorrow, Sophie?"

"All Steelers, whatever you guys need." She was getting better at not hesitating with answers like that.

"You haven't been to a client meeting yet, have you?"

She shook her head.

"You've been reading up on the business, might as well put it to use. Want to come to Cincinnati?"

He wasn't actually inviting her to the face-to-face, was he?

"Hutchinson's expecting two of us. Why don't you take his place?"

It took her a second to catch up. "Wow. Thank you for thinking of me — I'd love to."

"Good. Make your travel arrangements."

She couldn't wait to tell Will.

Vasu Mehta

Vasu handed Aditi a plate with the few vegetarian items he had scavenged from the buffet.

"Are you sure everything's all right?" she asked. "You've been sulking all evening."

"I'm tired, nothing more." So far, he had managed not to tell Aditi about his rotten review and he was not about to tell her now. "These parties get more dreadful each year."

"We've put in a good show. We can leave whenever you want."

"You're right. Of course you're right."

Ira Blumenstein was right next to them — Vasu could not avoid saying hello. Besides, perhaps there was a project for Blumenstein's favorite client that might encourage Blumenstein to protect him.

"Ira, how's everything with Midwest Metals?"

Blumenstein popped a wedge of cheese into his mouth. "Haven't heard from them since Sinclair's stunt. They trusted me because I didn't do that slick banker crap."

Vasu did not understand but did not say so.

Blumenstein turned and complimented Charlotte Sinclair on her earrings.

Midwest Metals. Sinclair's stunt. Blumenstein must mean the dinner Midwest Metals had had with Roll-Rite. Sinclair must have asked Blumenstein to deliver Midwest Metals, so Hutchinson would sign the engagement letter, so there would be at least one deal in the group budget before the higher-ups decided how many in their group would be laid off. Blumenstein would only have burned his best client if Sinclair had threatened him: *there will be plenty of graves to fill at year-end, Ira — you can take your pick.* A tremor started in Vasu's hands. If Blumenstein was that scared, Vasu had every reason to be terrified.

"Let's get out of here," he whispered to Aditi.

"Why don't we get dessert?" She slipped into her coat. "Cupcakes? Magnolia's close by. They whip the frosting for hours."

Vasu looked at the tops of his shoes.

"We have a sitter, Meera's doing fine." She hooked her arm in his. "We deserve some fun, no?"

"I'm tired, Aditi. It's been a long week."

"*Achchaa,* when was the last time we went out, just the two of us?" she asked.

He did not want to be with anyone right now. All he wanted was to go home, go to sleep, and forget about work for six hours.

As they left Redeye Steakhouse, a hand tugged at his coat. Sophie smiled so wide she bared a swath of bright pink gums. Her manic look frightened him. She covered her BlackBerry's speaker with one hand and said, "Ethan asked me to go tomorrow," punctuating this with a series of little hops. "I'm booking my flight."

Vasu's hand clenched Aditi's — too hard, perhaps, because she yanked it away. Sophie waved a frantic good-bye, pointing to her BlackBerry.

"She's a strange one, no?" Aditi whispered, steering him to the corner.

He fell a few steps behind her and pulled out his cigarettes. His lighter did not catch on the first four tries. By the time it finally did, his hands had been overtaken by a tremor. He hoped Aditi would not see.

A bell jingled as they entered a mint-green storefront with cupcakes stacked in the window like a castle, snowy white roofs and pink turrets.

"Can we get the cupcakes to go?" Vasu asked. "Big day tomorrow."

Aditi paused, running her fingers over her earrings, weighing the cost of insisting. "What would you like?"

He pointed at a cupcake with a candy carrot on its top. Aditi chose one for herself and one for Meera—pink icing and white sprinkles. The man behind the counter boxed them and placed a mint-green sticker over the flap that said "how sweet it is."

When they were finally in a cab, Aditi did not lean against his shoulder as she usually did but slid to the opposite door and placed the box of cupcakes between them. Vasu could tell she was disappointed, but if he engaged her, he would not be able to avoid discussing his miserable review. He closed his eyes.

Vasu's buzzing BlackBerry woke him moments later. He must have dozed off. The cables of the Brooklyn Bridge were netted across the cab window. Aditi faced away from him, toward the water. He stroked her arm, a peace offering, but she did not move. He gave up and checked his email. Sophie wrote:

To: Pearce, Ethan
Cc: Mehta, Vasu
From: Landgraf, Sophie T
Re: steelers
This is to confirm I've made travel arrangements for tomorrow's meeting. STL

How could Ethan invite Sophie rather than him? Vasu might not be in a position to remind Ethan of his proper place, but he could certainly remind Sophie. He rattled off a reply:

To: Landgraf, Sophie T
From: Mehta, Vasu
Re: Re: steelers
S—pls print me a copy of all backup for steelers mtg and leave on my desk before u go. safe travels. V

Vasu unhooked his seat belt and slid across the sticky leather seat until his and Aditi's shoulders touched. By the time they pulled up to their apartment building, his head was resting on her lap. They walked inside, arm in arm. As he unlocked the front door, he remembered the box of cupcakes they had left in the cab.

Sophie Landgraf

It was almost midnight when Sophie swiped back into Sterling. She tossed her BlackBerry across her desk harder than she'd meant to. It clattered against the Plexiglas wall of her cubicle. She checked its screen, scolding herself. She hadn't broken it. She unlocked her computer and pulled up the Steelers materials Vasu was too lazy to print for himself.

Twenty minutes, two reams of paper, and a printer jam later, Sophie heaved the thick stack of analysis onto Vasu's chair. For a second, when Ethan invited her to the face-to-face, it had seemed like they'd seen how hard she'd been working and decided that she should finally get her due. She'd gotten to enjoy it for all of two minutes before Vasu reminded her that she was nothing more than a trained monkey: print this, rerun this, build this. She was never going to win here, was she?

Sophie inspected the crayon drawing hanging above Vasu's desk, wanting to find fault with the three blue stick figures in a field of giant red flowers. The sun filled half the sky, an alternate universe where everything was brighter, where hard work paid off. She'd given the bank five months, twenty-two weekends, nineteen all-nighters, dozens of canceled date nights, Thanksgiving, and still Vasu expected her to jump whenever he snapped his fingers. Sterling just took and took — no "good job," no gold star, no vacation, no "thank you," no nothing. They owed her. Big time.

Coins jangled as she opened Vasu's top drawer. She scanned the familiar schedule from the Kathak Dance School in Jackson Heights, a jar of hot mango pickles, matchboxes, a business card for a doctor in Delhi, and a lumpy clay bowl holding loose change. She deserved better than this. She deserved something new.

Steelers presentations filled the next drawer, a tidy row of labeled bindings. Sophie was about to move on when she noticed the manila folders wedged in front of the presentations. Those hadn't been there the last time she'd looked. She teased the folder an inch out of the stack, her pulse accelerating as she read the label: *Donnigan, Ned*. Was Vasu taking notes on them? Or were these his staffing files? She pulled out the other new folders — *Terney, Jordanne* and *Landgraf, Sophie*. She must have found their performance reviews.

Last month, human resources had asked her to submit the names of her reviewers. Sophie's choices were easy — she hadn't really worked with anyone besides Ethan and Vasu. At the last minute, she'd added Jordanne, which she knew was a stretch since they were both analysts and they'd only worked together for a few weeks right after they started, but Jordanne would write her a good review, and she needed all the help she could get. The three had filled out report cards that Sophie was never supposed to see, evaluations the Sterling powers that be would use to decide her bonus that summer. Even then, when human resources sat them down one by one and told them how they could improve, the analysts wouldn't see their actual reviews, they'd only hear abstract takeaways that cloaked the identity of the reviewer who'd written them. And now all that was separating her from her reviews was a thin manila folder.

She should close the drawer and forget what she'd seen — looking at her performance reviews was practically treason. She could hear her mother: most wrongs are the result of human weakness, not calculation. The problem was that she *was* weak. She'd spent the past five months trying to hide this truth from Ethan and Vasu, yet another reason why she needed to know what they'd said about her.

She peered through Vasu's glass wall. Screensavers glowed on monitors, printers idled, the floor quiet. She slid her file out of Vasu's drawer, yanked the Steelers printouts over it, clutched the stack to her chest, and raced down the hall to the ladies' room. She tried not to look at the mirrors, her hunched reflection so pathetic, so guilty. She sealed herself inside the safety of the handicap stall. Perched on the edge of the stainless steel lid, she opened the file:

Reviewer: Vasu Mehta
Reviewer Title: Vice President
Analyst: Sophie Landgraf
Analyst Class: 2007
Rating (5=Outstanding, 4=Strong Performer, 3=Meets Expectations, 2=Reservations, 1=Serious Concerns): 4
Comments:
Sophie's work product is reasonably good for a first-year analyst. She puts in long hours, generally with a positive attitude. Sophie earns her keep as a member of the Industrial Group.

She'd hoped Vasu would be a little more enthusiastic, but it was no secret that he found everyone lacking, including himself. Maybe lukewarm praise was the best she could expect from him. She hurried on — she shouldn't waste time:

Reviewer: Ben Backenroth
Reviewer Title: Managing Director
Analyst: Sophie Landgraf
Analyst Class: 2007
Rating (5=Outstanding, 4=Strong Performer, 3=Meets Expectations, 2=Reservations, 1=Serious Concerns): 5
Comments:
Ms. Landgraf is a stellar analyst. Her intelligence and grit make her truly stand apart from her peers. Sterling would do well to give this young woman as much rope as she wants to hang herself with.

That was a pleasant surprise. Backenroth must have volunteered to review her after the Vending Machine Challenge. It didn't seem fair that the fifteen minutes she'd spent as a referee carried as much weight as the months she'd slaved away on Steelers, but she wasn't about to argue with an error in her favor. She turned the page:

Reviewer: Ethan Pearce
Reviewer Title: Managing Director
Analyst: Sophie Landgraf
Analyst Class: 2007
Review requested; none on file.

Sophie curled tighter over the folder. Ethan had invited her to Cincinnati, but he hadn't bothered to fill out her review? Had he just forgotten? Maybe he'd been planning to write a bad review but decided to do her a favor and not write one at all. Thank goodness for Backenroth. She flipped the page:

Reviewer: Jordanne Terney
Reviewer Title: Analyst
Analyst: Sophie Landgraf
Analyst Class: 2007
Rating (5=Outstanding, 4=Strong Performer, 3=Meets Expectations, 2=Reservations, 1=Serious Concerns): 1
Comments:
Sterling should be aware of some of the indiscretions I have seen Sophie commit during our time as quadmates. Sophie travels out of town despite being on call and lies to her superiors about it. Sophie sleeps at her desk, takes numerous personal calls, and is frequently late for work. I cannot imagine Sterling condones such behavior.

Her body folded in on itself, chin to chest, chest to knees. It didn't make any sense. Just three hours ago, Jordanne had been fawning over her, bringing her drinks, checking in on how she was doing with so little sleep. Sophie read the review four times, wanting so badly to find something that she was missing, but there was no doubt. Her one friend in New York. The holiday party, their Starbucks run that afternoon, the sandwich Jordanne had gotten her for lunch — the whole time, she'd written this? Jordanne had told her to lie to Vasu the day she went to Stockton, and then she used it to sabotage her? It embarrassed Sophie how easily she'd been manipulated. Had Jordanne been planning this since their first day, when she'd told Sophie that girls have to help each other out?

Why had Jordanne done this? Everyone knew that Jordanne was better at her job than Sophie. Jordanne had *everything*. Sophie closed the file. Jordanne didn't have a live deal. That had to be it. This was all because of AlumiCorp.

Sophie wanted to believe that it hadn't been Jordanne's idea, that her crazy competitive mother had told her to do it, that Jordanne had protested, but you could only blame parents so much.

Sophie dragged herself back to Vasu's office. She wished she'd never opened up her file. Two hours ago, she'd thought she had a friend. Two hours ago, Ethan had invited her to Cincinnati and she'd thought she was actually worth something. She slid her file back into Vasu's drawer. She was done exploring. For real.

Will was asleep on top of the covers when Sophie got home, head hanging back, neck soft. He didn't know how right he'd been when he'd said that Jordanne looked like a praying mantis. If she told him what she'd found, would he say that he wasn't surprised? Or maybe he'd say that as mad as she was, as hurt as she was, it wasn't exactly fair to get all self-righteous when she hadn't had any right to see her file in the first place. It was like her mother used to say: the things you do wrong have a funny way of coming back to bite you. The worst part was that she couldn't let anyone at Sterling know that she'd seen her file — especially Jordanne. She couldn't put Jordanne in her place.

She rested her cheek in the hollow below Will's collarbone. She wished she could undo everything that had happened after she'd left the holiday party. If she'd had just a tiny bit more willpower, she'd still be riding high on Ethan's invitation to Cincinnati. That was what she should be concentrating on: her first triumph at Sterling.

Will's shoulder twitched underneath her.

"Guess what?" she whispered. "This really amazing thing happened."

He flicked on the light.

"Ethan asked me to come to the big meeting tomorrow." Saying it out loud almost made it seem like it was all that mattered.

"Oh." He yawned.

"I think he asked me because I borrowed those aluminum primers." That was basically the first thing she'd done right. Maybe she should be getting in front of him more often. Maybe Cincinnati was just the first step.

"I thought you hated him."

"He's not exactly warm and fuzzy, which is totally understandable, if you think about it. Do you realize how much he's got on his plate? And he's been through so much — the poor guy lost his wife. It's amazing that he got past that — I mean, he's the most successful banker in our group." She would kill to be half as good.

He raised an eyebrow. "Do you have Stockholm syndrome or something?"

"OK, Mr. I Got an A in Abnormal Psych." If he was giving her a hard time about the good news, she didn't want to even think about what he'd say if she told him about Jordanne's review. Maybe she should keep the whole thing to herself.

"I'm just saying. So you don't think Ethan's self-absorbed?"

Jordanne was the one who was self-absorbed. "No."

"And you haven't been the slightest bit self-absorbed lately."

"Well, maybe just a little, but —"

"Just a little? OK. Tell me this. When was the last time you asked me about my day?"

She considered. Surely she'd asked sometime last week . . .

"October. Two months ago."

"Oh my god." Was she really that awful? "I'm so sorry. I know I haven't been the best lately. I know I've been canceling plans and stuff."

He squinted at the ceiling. "That's not even the point. Even on the two times a month we're alone together for five minutes, your head is somewhere else. You're so caught up in Sterling, it's like you've forgotten the rest of us actually exist."

Someone who bought her father's sculptures couldn't be *that* bad, could she? "I'm sorry. Really. I'll be better."

"I've never understood why your normalness is your least favorite part of yourself."

"Normalness?"

He fell back onto the pillow. "Never mind."

She resolved to be better, starting right that second. "So how was your day? Tell me all about it."

"Jamal's going to let me do my first interview," he said softly.

"Oh my god!" She wrapped her arms around him. "I'm so happy for you! Your first interview! What's it for?"

"Gunnar Sonnenborn's new film. The one I told you about, the incest thing with Quinn Claridge?"

"When can I hear it?"

"Unclear. I'm doing the spot the day after tomorrow. There's an after-party for the film that night, if you want to come." He said it like she wouldn't want to.

"Are you kidding?" She slid her arms around his waist. "You know I want to come."

"I know you well enough to know you'll say that and then something will come up."

"Nothing will stop me. I'll be there."

Will turned out the light. He inched over to the other side of the mattress, turning his back to her.

She was doing her best, but her best wasn't good enough. She couldn't help thinking back to the time her sophomore year when they'd almost broken up. Her father was still a mess then and Kim was overwhelmed with a two-year-old and nursing school. Will was the only remotely stable thing in her life and she couldn't get enough of him. She remembered begging Will to please skip developmental psych just that once, to please stay with her just a little bit longer, and he'd said, *I'm giving as much as I can, Soph, but there's a limit.* At the time, she hadn't understood what he meant.

$$$

Sophie had assumed that when Ethan asked her to come to the face-to-face, he'd meant actually sitting in on the face-to-face. Instead, she and Ethan were camped out in a conference room four floors down from the suite where Hutchinson and Carbonell were meeting. Ethan was stationed at the opposite end of the table — basically, as far away from Sophie as possible. He was talking into his BlackBerry in a voice that filled the whole room, like she wasn't even there.

Sophie tried to focus on the spreadsheet open on the laptop that Sterling had loaned her for the trip. She didn't understand why juniors were so eager to come to client meetings when as far as she could see, they were no different from Sterling, right down to the fluorescent lights and gray carpet. So far the only difference was that she'd had to get up three hours earlier than usual to make their flight.

She peeked over her laptop, trying not to look like she was watching Ethan. He leaned back in his chair, confident, telling whoever was on the other end of the phone that Sinclair was kidding himself if he thought Safe-Tee Tube would ever pull the trigger on that deal. Maybe Ethan really was self-absorbed, like Will had said, or maybe he was just lonely. He didn't seem to have any actual friends at Sterling — he was openly hostile with Sinclair and Blumenstein, sometimes even with Vasu. Maybe Sinclair had betrayed Ethan the way Jordanne had betrayed her.

When Ethan got off the phone, she cleared her throat. "May I ask you something?"

Ethan nodded, possibly at her, possibly at his inbox.

"How do you know who to trust at Sterling?"

"Trust?" He said this like it was a four-letter word.

"Is it only the people who aren't the same level as you, who aren't your competitors? Or . . ."

He pointed his pen at her like it was a weapon. "Trust no one. If you haven't figured out exactly how someone is trying to screw you, you've already played right into his hand."

Was she the only person who'd been stupid enough to believe all that stuff they'd said in training about banking being a team sport?

Ethan scrolled through his BlackBerry. She stole a glance at the crisp crease of his chalk-stripe suit, his perfectly pressed pink shirt. Did men actually buy themselves pink shirts? His wife had probably gotten it for him — before. She wondered if Ethan used to tell his wife about how Sinclair or Blumenstein was trying to poach his clients. She wondered if his wife made him a gin and tonic and told him not to listen to those jerks — she believed in him.

What did Will expect her to do, dig a hole inside herself and bury everything that happened with Sterling, with Jordanne, with Ethan? The strange thing was, if you'd asked her a year ago, she would've said Will was beyond supportive. Her sophomore year, after she'd aced Linear Systems, he'd borrowed a car and whisked her off to hike Mount Frissell. It had been so much easier in college, when they'd both wanted the same thing: to graduate with honors, to blow off steam on Thursday nights when classes were done, to sleep until at least noon on Sundays. Maybe it wasn't so surprising that things were more difficult now that their lives had decoupled. Not that Will was the only one to blame — how had she not known about his first interview? Tomorrow, she'd go to Murder Inc., Will's favorite bookstore, and pick out a present to bring to his party.

Ethan looked at his watch.

"Is it normal for these things to take this long?" she asked.

"Short is bad."

There was so much she didn't understand. "Is there anything I should know about Hutchinson before I meet him?"

Ethan squinted at her. "You won't be doing the talking. If he asks you a question directly, by all means, answer, but otherwise . . . Try to seem interested when he talks about his Mustang. You'll see, *it's the same car that Steve McQueen drove in* Bullitt. He says it every time."

"Is it usually like this, us down here, them up there?"

Ethan didn't look up from his laptop. "You know, we don't have to talk."

She tried not to look too flustered and busied herself with her spreadsheet.

Jake Hutchinson

Some CEOs conducted mergers by committee, bringing in management, bankers, lawyers. Not Hutch. He and Bruce Carbonell, Roll-Rite's CEO, were the only people inside the suite at the Cincinnati Hilton. Hutch had banished the bankers so that he and Carbonell could cut to the chase: how much Roll-Rite was worth. Carbonell would take an optimistic view of Roll-Rite's potential so he could jack up the purchase price, then Hutch would talk him down. They both knew this dance.

Hutch double-locked the door to the suite and joined Carbonell by the coffee table.

"How're you thinking about our international assets?" Carbonell asked. He reached a bronzed hand into his leather portfolio and pulled out a monogrammed cigar case. "Cuban?"

Carbonell's forehead crinkled under a shock of white hair that got thicker each time Hutch saw him. The seventy-year-old's vanity made Hutch uncomfortable, but today it also gave him hope, each hair plug a marker of Carbonell's advancing age, of Carbonell's need to secure a succession plan for his company. It'd be convenient for everyone if Hutch took over the reins. Roll-Rite's employees would like having a man like him at the helm — someone who didn't spend half his days in a tanning bed or at the plastic surgeon's.

Hutch plucked a Bolivar Belicoso from Carbonell's cigar case.

"There's plenty of unrealized value in our Asian assets," Carbonell said.

Hutch leaned across the table to accept Carbonell's lighter. Maybe he'd made a tactical error, framing the discussion as one between equals instead of making it crystal clear right from the start that this was his meeting.

"India has a lot of upside," Carbonell said.

Hutch knew from Roll-Rite's earnings calls that the Varanasi and Orissa smelters were going nowhere fast. Carbonell was a decent manager — his main strength as a CEO was keeping investors happy, but still, a decent manager. If there was upside in the India assets, Carbonell would have harvested it. He had some serious gall, talking up those crap smelters. But no one in the industry had ever called Carbonell cautious.

"Look. We both know that any value in India is offset by the liabilities in Brazil." Hutch inspected the portrait on the foil ring of the cigar: Simón Bolívar, the great liberator who unified the fragmented nations of Latin America. He sat up straighter.

"Our situation in Brazil isn't nearly as bad as yours in the Midwest."

It was true — this past month, the Midwest operations had gone from bad to worse. AlumiCorp had been forced to cut prices, or lose customers to the competitors that would. His board had warned him that he needed to come up with a solution before their next meeting in March, or else. (Or else what? Can't stop a runaway truck.)

"Look," Hutch said. "That's the beauty of this deal: a chance to rationalize our assets." The air cover from the merger would let them close the plants they needed to. "Your Midwest assets don't exactly smell like roses, either."

Carbonell clicked his tongue. "Maybe, in different hands . . ."

Hutch didn't like where this was going, but he knew better than to let Carbonell see him getting hot under the collar. Frankly, Hutch had expected a valuation fight, but he wouldn't have thought Carbonell would challenge him on succession. Hutch only wanted to get in bed with Roll-Rite if he could be on top.

"Look, I want what we both want," Hutch said, "the best possible operator to run our business."

Carbonell chuckled. "Of course you do. Let's see what the bankers come up with. This may turn out to be premature."

Hutch nodded. Neither of them had any desire to open up the kimono unless this deal was going somewhere.

Carbonell rose and extended his hand.

Hutch was starving by the time he went to check in with the bankers. Conflict made him hungry. A redhead in a cheap suit sat surrounded by a fort of folders, pecking away at her laptop. She jumped up and presented her hand.

"Sophie Landgraf." Her grip was stronger than Hutch would've expected for a girl with baby fat on her cheeks.

"How'd it go?" Ethan asked calmly.

"The bastard's pushing on succession issues." Hutch grabbed two chocolate chip cookies from a platter, stacked them into a sandwich, and took a giant bite. "Let's talk about it on the road." He wiped the crumbs off his lips with the back of his hand. "I'm starved."

Pearce nodded. "I'll get my things."

Merry had made them a reservation at McCluskey's Steakhouse. Hutch already knew what he'd order: oysters Rockefeller, New York strip, creamed spinach, a slice of caramel cake.

The girl slipped on a red coat with threadbare elbows, the sort of thing you'd expect to see here in Ohio, not on Wall Street. A welcome change from Sterling's usual young men with smug faces, French-cuff shirts, and watches that cost more than his car.

Hutch led the way to the elevator.

"I brought the Mustang," Hutch said.

"Oh, Ethan told me about your car," the girl said.

Hutch turned to her. "It's the same one Steve McQueen drove in *Bullitt,* when he chased those hit men through San Francisco."

Her lipsticked smile revealed a slightly crooked eyetooth. Hutch had spent forty grand so both his daughters, now grown, would have perfect smiles, but he found this girl's imperfect one endearing.

While the valet brought around the Mustang, Hutch called Merry to get his messages. Gene Marson had called again. Gene hadn't left a message and didn't need to — Hutch knew Gene had called to ask whether Hutch knew how low the stock had closed yesterday. *You need to restore investor confidence* now *or we're not going to wait until March to discuss your future at this company.* As if Hutch needed to be reminded this business was eat or be eaten.

The Mustang pulled under the carport.

"I may need to take a call," Hutch said. "Ethan, why don't you drive?" He settled into the passenger seat and tossed Pearce the keys.

"Sorry," Pearce said, pointing at the stick shift.

What kind of man can't drive stick? "Well, shoot."

A chipper voice came from the back seat. "I can drive."

Hutch turned to face the girl. He'd never seen a banker blush before. She reminded Hutch of Alice Hoffmeyer, a girl he sang with in the Lebanon Presbyterian Choir growing up: not a stunner, but sweet-looking. He gestured for her to come on up.

By the time Hutch had left a message for Marson and returned the rest of his calls, they'd already gotten off Route 71 and were zipping past Becker Paint & Hardware and T.K.'s Wings.

"How'd you learn to drive stick?" he asked.

She checked the rearview mirror. "Umm, my father."

He knew it — a daddy's girl. Gwen had been that way when she was little, but at thirteen, both she and Darcy had turned into creatures he couldn't begin to understand. In a few days, Gwen would come home from Wash U in St. Louis for Christmas break. She'd seal herself in her room with her cell phone, yapping away. How had this girl managed to stay so . . . normal?

"Where'd you grow up?"

"Massachusetts."

He wasn't sure what he'd hoped she'd say, but it definitely wasn't the land of the Vineyard and the Kennedys. "Boston?"

"Stockton? Near Pittsfield? My parents had a sheep farm there."

"*You* raised sheep?" How she didn't get eaten alive at Sterling, he had no idea.

"Just watched them sometimes — I was awful at it. I'd sit under a tree with my homework and hardly pay attention."

Humble too. But she'd missed their turn.

"I'm sorry, Mr. Hutchinson." That blush again.

"Aw, you're making me feel old. Call me Hutch."

7

Thursday, December 20, 2007

Ethan Pearce

I N THE EIGHT YEARS ETHAN had known Hutchinson, he'd never once received a thank-you note, let alone one signed "Hutch." The CEO had just emailed: *pleasure seeing you in Cincinnati. Thrilled to have you on the team.* Ethan scrolled through the note twice, trying to make sense of it, until he saw that he'd only been cc'd — the email had been sent to Sophie.

Who would have guessed she had a talent for client management? Ethan applauded his impulse to bring her along. He'd fought not to laugh from the backseat of Hutchinson's Mustang yesterday when she'd launched into that spiel about the relative merits of Corriedales and Merinos and Drysdales, fertility rates and fleece density and which breeds were the most efficient converters of feed into gain. How much of it was true, he didn't know and didn't care. Hutch ate it up, hook, line, and sinker. He'd never seen Hutch as agreeable as over dinner, when he'd insisted that Sophie really must try the caramel cake.

In retrospect, perhaps he shouldn't have declined to review Sophie. He made it a practice to abstain from writing reviews altogether. Writing negative reviews was bad business, and as for positive reviews, Ethan couldn't risk diluting his brand by sponsoring mediocre employees. But Sophie was proving a useful addition to the team. Next review season, he'd consider throwing his weight behind her.

Ethan announced his entrance into the Sterling steam room with a short cough. Sinclair's pale flesh spilled over a slatted wooden bench. Ethan tried not to stare at the small, damp towel fig-leafing Sinclair's lap or the gray hairs sprouting from his nipples, but it was like driving by a traffic accident: Ethan couldn't not look.

"So, do we still have a deal?" Sinclair asked flatly.

"For now. Carbonell's pushing on succession. It's making Hutchinson gun shy." Whorls of steam rose between them. "I suspect it's a bargaining tactic. Not too tough for Carbonell to guess succession will get Hutchinson all emotional."

"All irrational, you mean."

"Exactly."

"So what's Carbonell peddling, valuationwise?"

"The international assets."

"Pretty thin case he's got there, don't you think?"

"Who am I to judge?" Ethan said, with a smile. "The companies are exchanging numbers. We'll see what's there."

The wooden bench groaned as Sinclair shifted his bulk. "Anything else?"

"Hutchinson took a shine to our analyst."

Sinclair raised his head. "You mean . . ." He squinted like he was looking down the barrel of a gun.

"I didn't get that sense." He couldn't imagine any man thinking of

Sophie that way. Besides, he'd seen the way Hutchinson had looked at Camille — she was the sort of woman men stared at in front of their wives, which was half of the fun — and Ethan could safely say it was nothing like the way Hutchinson had looked at Sophie.

"So she's worth keeping around?"

"Probably."

"There's been some squabbling between her and Alistair Terney's kid. Vasu backed Sophie, but I wanted to check with you."

"Grant, I'm not an idiot. You rush the engagement letter, you back out of the face-to-face. What's going on?"

The weariness written across Sinclair's flesh gave Ethan hope that Sinclair was about to announce his retirement.

Sinclair laid a washcloth over his eyes. "All will soon be revealed."

Vasu Mehta

Ethan burst into Vasu's office without knocking. Vasu was hoping for an explanation as to why Ethan had taken Sophie to Cincinnati instead of him, but he should have known better. Ethan never saw the need to explain himself.

"When Roll-Rite sends us their numbers, I want you to dig deep into their international operations," Ethan said. "India, especially. Carbonell's talking up those assets."

"The Indian assets? Really?" Vasu's head snapped back. If he handled this the right way, he might manage a trip home. "The ones near Varanasi, or Orissa?"

"You know them?"

"I know of them."

"Is that where your family is? Vara . . ."

"Varanasi? No, I'm from Delhi — seven, eight hundred kilometers away."

"But you have a feel for the area."

Vasu's head wobbled noncommittally. Americans rarely appreciated that India was not a monolith, that you could sit at a tea shop for five minutes and hear fourteen different languages.

"Do the assets have upside?"

Unlikely. But if Vasu said so, he would never be sent to India to find out. "Cheap labor is always an advantage. But they have operational problems that would never be tolerated here."

"Why hasn't Roll-Rite gotten them in line?"

Vasu shrugged. "Hard to be sure. The numbers suggest room for improvement, but we would need to talk to the plant manager and tour the site to see what's realistic." Meaning: send me there and I can find out.

"There's potential, is that what you're saying?"

"Perhaps."

Vasu's phone buzzed. His friend Raj was calling from the trading floor, an event rare enough that it made Vasu nervous.

"Get it later," Ethan said.

Vasu nodded.

"I want you to go through that international forecast with a fine-tooth comb," Ethan said. "Carbonell's driving a hard bargain. I need you to find anything — I mean anything — we can pitch to Hutchinson as a reason to pay up."

Vasu contained his excitement until Ethan left his office. Roll-Rite's Indian operations at the center of the merger — he could not believe his luck. In seven years at Sterling, he had traveled to Abingdon, Wilmington, Grand Rapids, Bakersfield: places that held no interest for him. The Industrial Group's clients' operations were mainly domestic, and as a result, so was Vasu's business travel. Until now.

Vasu could tell that Ethan hoped close investigation of Roll-Rite's operations would uncover additional value, despite the fact that diligence normally turned up less. Vasu would seize the opportunity: next week, once bonus checks cleared, he would volunteer to personally conduct on-site due diligence of Roll-Rite's Indian assets. What he had told Ethan was true: their operations were a day's journey from his family. But it was also true that he would have to fly through Delhi to get to the smelters. He would be able to visit his mother without appearing to take a vacation — a win-win.

Vasu was about to call Aditi to tell her the news when he saw his voicemail light flashing. Raj, his friend downstairs in mortgage-backed securities, must have left a message. The voicemail crackled with the usual shouts on the trading floor. Raj mumbled: *the ax is out.* Vasu replayed the message, unsure he had heard correctly. There was no doubt. The traders downstairs were being sacked. Soon, the layoffs would curl their way upstairs to the twenty-sixth floor. Vasu desperately needed a smoke. He dashed to the lift, hand shaking as he pressed the down button.

He could not believe he had witnessed an entire Wall Street cycle. Six years ago, when Sterling moved out of the midtown Marriott and into this building, Vasu wanted to believe he was finally safe. Days later, colleagues were called to a conference room one by one, and when they returned to their desks, they were locked out of their computers. You walked by an empty desk and you did not need to ask. You kept your head down and your mouth shut.

Outside, it was freezing. He considered going back for his coat, but the world was coming to an end — what did it matter? A cluster of smokers had stationed themselves along Sterling's right flank, the unofficial smoking lounge. Vasu stopped short of them and stood over the subway vent, where hot air rushed to his feet as a train went by. The crowd was thinner than usual — word must have gotten around, employees afraid of being caught away from their desks. Vasu was not sure which was worse: a superior finding his desk empty, or a superior finding a wreck who could not stop his hands from shaking.

Seven years, and what did he have to show for it? He had saved, sure, but not enough. The size of the nest egg that would make the work seem worthwhile increased exponentially with the time he spent at Sterling, destined to outpace the reality of his savings account. The money could never make up for working on his anniversary for five of the past seven years, for missing the chance to be at his mother's bedside, for years of leaving for work in the dark and returning in the dark, after Meera and Aditi were already asleep.

Vasu had to pull himself together. He headed back into the building, training his gaze on the marble floor, careful not to make eye contact with someone who had just gotten the ax, when a man's eyes darted around like a trapped animal, as he had seen in 2001, when he had not known not to look. When Vasu reached the twenty-sixth floor, he took out his BlackBerry and pretended to scroll through his email all the way to his office, not looking at another soul.

As he entered his office, his phone rang. Had the ax found him already? He raced to his desk. It was only Raj calling from the trading floor, where row after row of open workstations left nowhere to hide.

"How bad is it?" Vasu asked, thankful that up here in investment banking, he could at least hide behind a proper door.

"It started at nine. They shot Tanner, shot Yao — even fired a few analysts."

Vasu sucked in his breath. If they were firing the cheap labor, it must be bad.

"It's trailed off. I think it's over."

"*Achchaa*, I'm glad you're safe," Vasu said.

"You and me both."

"How deep were the cuts?"

"Six on our desk."

Twenty percent: worse than Vasu had expected.

"Hold on . . ." Raj said.

The line went silent.

"Fuck!" Raj said when he returned. "That's Haas calling me in. Gotta run."

Haas. The hangman.

Vasu sucked in his breath as he put down the phone. He considered calling Aditi and letting her calm him with tales of dropping off Meera at school, but surely she would hear the panic in his voice. He did not want to worry her.

Someone tapped on the glass. Sophie whisked into his office, bouncing on her toes.

"Hey, Vasu," she said in an upbeat voice that grated on his nerves. She must not have heard about the layoffs. "I've got a few questions on the follow-up materials for Hutch. Ethan asked me to look into Carbonell's comp package —"

"Could you hold on a moment?" he asked, turning to his computer to type an email to Raj.

To: Naranjan, Raj
From: Mehta, Vasu
Re: sorry we got cut off
call when you resurface

He turned back to Sophie. Her lips were moving but Vasu did not hear the words.

An automated message appeared in his inbox: the email to Raj had bounced back.

"Bear with me, Sophie."

He dialed Raj's extension.

"*You have reached a nonworking number at Sterling & Sons. To reach the operator, please dial zero.*"

He slammed down the receiver.

"You OK, Vasu?"

"Let's catch up later."

The door clicked closed. Vasu stared at his reflection on the glass. He had grown accustomed to the transparency of the walls, the predictability of the Sterling maroon. He did not want to leave it.

Sophie Landgraf

Sophie's mother used to be able to look at a clear sky and predict that a thunderstorm was coming because the air got heavier and harder to breathe. That was exactly how it felt outside Vasu's office: the floor had the appearance of calm but didn't feel calm at all. The second years sat in their Plexiglas cubicles, their backs a little too straight. Rich Angstrom and Kenneth Yang were whispering inside their office, and Rich Angstrom never whispered.

Donnigan was crouched under an empty desk at the back of his cluster. He gestured to the bottle of Grey Goose beside him. "Strengthening my resolve. Firing squad's today."

The anxiety around her slid into focus. "Oh my god."

"Want a nip?"

Sophie was already halfway down the hall. She had to find Ethan. She had to convince him to protect her. She started preparing a speech about how far she'd come since she'd started, about how bad it would look if she disappeared from the AlumiCorp deal right after hitting it off with Hutch. They both knew her stock had risen since the trip to Cincinnati, but would that be enough to make up for the mistakes she'd made her first months at Sterling, to make up for Jordanne's awful review?

Ethan's door was open but he wasn't inside — she was screwed. A blank legal pad and pen waited on his desk, ready for anything. He was her ticket to survival at Sterling, and until last month, she hadn't taken advantage of it because she was *scared?* Why hadn't she spent the past six months convincing Ethan of her worth before it was too late? If she made it to the other side of this mess, her number-one goal would be to keep Ethan happy.

She hurried back to the safety of her cubicle, in case there was some small chance that being at her desk would keep them from forcing her to give it up. Disaster scenarios unfurled themselves.

With two months' severance and five months' job experience, she'd be insolvent and unemployable. She'd have to beg Will to let her stay in the awful one-room Williamsburg apartment he shared with Annabelle's brother. She'd have to promise that things would go back to the way they'd been in college, to lie and swear that Sterling was responsible for the rough patch they'd been going through lately. And then she'd be stuck in the apartment she'd avoided ever since moving to the city, where at night they had to crawl behind the curtain that separated Will's mattress from the rest of the room. Where she woke to the smell of rot from the dumpster behind the building, the stench of spoiled food making her so nauseous that her first conscious thought each morning was always that she'd somehow gotten herself pregnant, a dread she'd carry around with her for the rest of the day. In college, when her low standards were a blessing, she'd been able to pretend that staying at Will's was a bohemian adventure — barely — but now that she'd gotten used to an apartment that was entirely her own, staying with Will would be punishment. But where else would she go if she lost her job?

Sophie sank into her seat. Opposite her cubicle, a miserable associate sat in Sinclair's office, shamefaced. Snowflakes swirled across the floor-to-ceiling window, making the glass walls seem too near, like they were closing in. Sophie considered spreading her scarf over her lap, where it might calm her and was less likely to be seen. It was almost worth the risk. Her hand was on her bottom drawer when Jordanne swept into the quad, smiling and smug. Just two hours ago, Sophie had been dreading seeing Jordanne for the first time since reading the review her "friend" had written, but now Jordanne was the least of her concerns.

"Hey!" Jordanne said in a honeyed voice whose falseness Sophie couldn't believe she hadn't detected immediately. "I heard the face-to-face went well. I'm so excited for you!"

Sophie thanked her flatly and turned to her computer, indicating that their conversation was over. Jordanne didn't seem to know about the layoffs. Sophie liked knowing something Jordanne didn't, a small consolation since she was about to lose her job because of Jordanne.

"You seem off," Jordanne said. "Everything all right?"

"Fine."

Sophie sprang from her chair. She was about *this close* to losing it, and another second with Jordanne would push her over the edge. She was halfway to the ladies' room when Jordanne's phone rang.

"Sure," Jordanne said sweetly. "I'll be right there."

They were firing *Jordanne?* The Wharton grad who quoted her Excel Bible? Sophie had no idea why Jordanne, of all people, would get axed, but she did know this: if Jordanne was getting fired, she was screwed.

Sophie wished she'd taken Donnigan up on that vodka. Her mind whirred faster and faster, pulling her into the orbit of her inevitable firing, reminding her that even if she lived with Will, two months of severance wouldn't last very long. Maybe Annabelle could get her a job at the bar where she worked sometimes, but that wouldn't be enough for her to afford to stay in New York. When her severance checks stopped, she'd have to go back to Stockton, where her father would remind her five times a day that he'd told her so, he'd never understood why she'd gotten mixed up with that awful place. It would be like she'd never left. Merle Lockhardt would lean over the counter at the Donut Kitchen and whisper, *You know, Sophie Landgraf got this fancy scholarship and she thought she was so much better than the rest of us and where did it get her but back here, out of work like half of the town.* Anna Maletz would listen to Sophie the same way she'd listened to Jordie Novak, who hadn't made it as a stand-up comedian: Anna would smile sweetly and whisper behind Sophie's back that at least half the things she said had to be made up. If Sophie was lucky, she'd cobble together a few hours of work tutoring math or the SATs, but it would only be a matter of time before she was putting in an application to be a receptionist at Shady Pines Nursing Home, just like Dolores Carson and the rest of the kids from high school.

She needed to talk to Will. He'd calm her down. If she called him, though, everyone in earshot would know she was freaking out. She didn't care. She was about to dial when she remembered what he'd said two nights ago, after the holiday party: *You're so caught up in Sterling, it's like you've forgotten the rest of us actually exist.* Today was his big day, his first real interview, the Swedish director whose name she could never remember. If she called and told Will what was happening at Sterling, she'd only be proving his point that she'd been hopelessly self-absorbed lately.

Kim answered on the second ring.

"Thank god you're there," Sophie whispered. She could see the back of Jordanne's head through the glass, nodding at Sinclair. "I'm losing my shit."

"Did you and Will —"

"They're firing people." Sophie whispered these last two words so softly that even she could barely hear them.

"Firing? Thank god. I thought someone had died or something. It's going to be OK. You're the smartest person I know. No one's going to fire you."

"Actually they most definitely are. Jordanne's in there already, and I can't explain everything right now, but trust me, I haven't got a chance."

"What's the worst that can happen? You'll find a new job, right?"

She wanted to scream at Kim that she just didn't get it. "Do you realize how few jobs you can get in New York as a twenty-two-year-old that actually cover your rent?"

"Will, Annabelle, Mitsuko . . . they all make it work, right?"

"Because their parents help them. This is all me, and I fucked it up."

"Sophie? Breathe."

Steps sounded behind her. "I've got to go. I'll call you back."

Plastic creaked. Sophie turned to see Jordanne slouched in her chair, shoulders rolled forward. Jordanne squinted at her computer monitor, mouth half open, like her desk was something mysterious and somehow threatening. "I've been sacked."

Sophie picked at her nail polish. She wanted to say, *look what you've done. They don't know how to choose between us — one incompetent analyst, one subversive one — so they're going to fire us both. They'll replace us in about five seconds.* Jordanne would cry for one night in the apartment her parents paid for and what would Sophie do? But Sophie wasn't about to tell Jordanne anything else that could be used against her.

"Sinclair was as nice about it as you could expect," Jordanne said. "He said it was a tough decision, that he knew I was a strong performer. He offered to write me a recommendation."

Sophie hoped Sinclair would do the same for her.

Jordanne reached into her top desk drawer and pulled out her toothbrush and toothpaste, her Excel Bible, her ridiculous Mason Pearson brush, and a bottle of NoDoz that rattled in her shaking hands. She opened and closed the other drawers, staring into them without taking anything.

"Who'd have thought it would be so easy to clear out of here."

Who'd have thought it would be so easy to pretend they were friends.

"Maybe my mom's right. Maybe I'm not cut out for this. Maybe I should just get married and have babies."

Jordanne squinted at something at her feet, lips pressed tight. The hollows under her cheekbones seemed darker. Jordanne really did look like a praying mantis.

Jordanne hugged Sophie, her silk suit cold against Sophie's cheek. Sophie stood stiffly, wishing Jordanne would let go and leave.

"We'll keep in touch, right?" Jordanne asked.

Sophie couldn't quite bring herself to lie. "Good luck."

The elevator dinged, announcing Jordanne's departure.

Sophie stared at the phone that would ring at any second, calling her to the same fate. Her breath grew rapid and shallow. She tried to think of what her mother would say, but for once, she had no idea. She had to calm down. Letting anyone see her losing it was the quickest way to getting fired. She told herself to slow down and count Gaussian primes: *3, 7, 19, 23 . . .*

Sophie had reached 503 when she heard a door swing open.

"Rosalie," she heard Sinclair say to his assistant. "I'm stepping out. I'm reachable on my BlackBerry."

"Are you coming back?" Rosalie asked.

"Not if I can help it."

Sophie pulled her knees to her chest. It was over. She was safe.

Donnigan called moments later.

"Hey," he whispered. "You've got the best seat in the house. Come on — I'm dying over here. Give me an update."

"It's not —"

"The walls have ears, I know. How about I rattle off names, and you say 'accretive' if they already got axed, and 'dilutive' if they haven't."

"Shouldn't it be the other way around?"

"You lay a guy off, you save money: accretive."

"Yeah, I guess you're right. But — it's over. Sinclair left."

"So I'm safe? Hot damn!" He screeched so loudly Sophie yanked the receiver from her ear. Whooping sounded down the hall, an offstage echo.

Sophie hung up and bounded to the stairwell, where she could call Kim without everyone overhearing her. She was halfway to the fire door when Vasu waved through the glass wall, arms frantic windmills, pleading with her to come to his office.

"How bad is it?" he asked. His fingers fiddled in his pants pocket.

"You weren't in on it?"

"Are you kidding? Firing — it's double top secret. *Nobody* knows. *How bad is it?*"

"Sinclair just left. It's over."

Vasu sprang out of his seat and thrust his arms in the air like a runner reaching the finish line. He fell onto her shoulders, hugging her so tight she almost couldn't breathe. *Vasu* had been worried? Vasu who practically lived in his office? Was no one safe here?

"We made it!" he said.

"Why us?"

Vasu shrugged. "That, I couldn't tell you. Sometimes it makes no sense. But being on AlumiCorp probably didn't hurt. Someone needs to keep feeding the beast, no?" Vasu clapped her on the back so hard she almost lost her balance. "But, you know, these things, they can turn like *that*."

$$$

Standing on the sidewalk outside Will's film party, alone and away from Sterling, Sophie's hands shook. She felt like she was floating, the same way she had each time she'd gotten into a car for two years after her mother died. She took a deep breath and straightened her suit. Tonight was about Will and his first interview. Not today's lay-offs. Not Jordanne. Not Ethan. Just her and Will, as they'd been before.

Sophie had gotten so used to Sterling's carbon-colored suits and neutral rugs that when she stepped inside the bar's blood-red walls and found herself surrounded by bright flannel shirts and rainbow-colored silks, she couldn't help feeling kind of on edge. There was even a woman with pink hair. Everybody was asking to be looked at, except Sophie.

At the back of the room, Will was enmeshed in conversation with two skinny-tied men, hand resting comfortably in his pocket, shoulders thrust back. The last time she'd seen him this poised and confident was when he'd led the tutoring training session where they'd met. She waved at him, not sure whether to interrupt.

As Will waded over, a man with a handlebar mustache patted

him hello on the shoulder. A woman in a micro-mini waved at him, and Sophie heard Will shout over the techno that he'd find her in a minute.

"Jamal's going to give my spot a whole *two minutes*," he said. "It's like the industry woke up this morning and finally realized I exist."

That was how she'd felt at the holiday party, when Ethan invited her to the face-to-face — before she learned the truth about Jordanne, before the layoffs. She clasped her hands, to stop them from shaking. "You deserve it."

"Yeah?"

"Yeah. Oh — I got you something." She presented the Swedish crime novel that the woman in the bookstore had said was all the rage in England. "You can't get it here yet."

He looked distracted. "Thanks." He slipped the book into his back pocket.

"So what's Quinn Claridge like?"

"Really great. She has this way of looking at you like you're the most interesting person she's ever met. Want to meet her?"

"Does it matter that I haven't seen the film?"

"Just say you thought she was brilliant."

Quinn Claridge was smaller in real life than Sophie had expected, both shorter and tinier. A miniperson, really. When Will introduced them, Quinn tilted her chin forward and smiled through closed lips, like she smelled something wonderful.

"Your performance was brilliant," Sophie said.

"Thank you."

Quinn seemed to expect more praise, but Sophie wasn't up to pandering. Will jumped in about how the spot would air the next day. Sophie did her best to follow when he started talking about Dutch tilts and shemps, but pretty soon she was just smiling and nodding along. They excused themselves when the actress turned to a middle-aged man who appeared to be wearing pajamas.

"Geez, Soph, you could have tried at least a little," Will whispered sharply.

"Will!" A cat-eyed blonde strutted toward them, arms open wide. Her face screamed *you should know who I am,* but Sophie couldn't quite place her. The woman leaned in to kiss Will on both cheeks.

"Dominique," he said, "this is my girlfriend, Sophie."

"Your boyfriend is my favorite. I could just eat him up." She looped her arm in Will's. "Let's introduce you to some people."

Will looked over his shoulder and mouthed "be back." Dominique pressed her hand against his shoulder, and Sophie wondered if she should be jealous.

She scanned the room for anyone who would meet her gaze. No luck. It had been the same way when the layoffs started — nobody wanted to look her in the eye. A tremor began in her hands and she was floating again when all she wanted was to come back to earth, where she still had a job. She touched the BlackBerry in her pocket, to make sure it was still there.

A tanned man who must spend more time doing his hair than she did bumped against her. Sophie introduced herself. Zander was the agent for Rex Randolph, whose name Sophie could tell she was supposed to recognize.

"You're involved with the film?" he asked.

"No, my boyfriend is sort of a critic." She wished she could take back the "sort of."

He asked what she now knew was the first question you'd get from any person you met in New York. "So what do you do?"

"I work at Sterling? The investment bank?" Saying it out loud made her feel better.

He stared blankly.

"I do corporate advisory work," she said, hoping for a glimmer of recognition.

Zander glanced around the room, unimpressed. He patted her on the shoulder and drifted off into the crowd.

Sophie smiled at one of the men Will had been talking to earlier but he didn't smile back. He was talking to a man in a fedora whose hand fell for emphasis, like he was chopping something, the same way she'd seen Sinclair gesticulate through the glass earlier that day. Sophie crossed her arms, clamping her shaking hands under her armpits. She still didn't understand why she'd made it through the layoffs and not Jordanne. The more she thought about it, the only possible explanation was that Ethan had stuck up for her, because of what had happened at the face-to-face. Thank god for Cincinnati, thank god for Hutch. If the layoffs had happened four days earlier, she'd be unemployed by now.

Sophie felt an arm around her waist.

"You look . . . serious," Will said.

"Oh. It's nothing." She tried to smile. "So how do you feel? Cloud nine?"

He raised an eyebrow. "There's something you're not telling me."

She reminded herself that tonight was all about him. "We'll talk about it another time."

"Spill it." His folded arms told her he meant it.

"There was a round of layoffs at Sterling today."

Will put a hand on her shoulder and steered her to a quiet corner. "Are you . . . did you get . . ." He looked more relieved than afraid.

"Thanks for the vote of confidence. I made it. Jordanne got axed."

"I'm so sorry. I know you guys were close."

"Not that close, it turns out."

"Sorry?"

She hadn't thought before she spoke. "Never mind. Sorry, we can talk about this another time. This is your night."

"My call." He swirled his drink. "You seem really upset — are you sure there's not something else, besides the layoffs?"

"Besides the layoffs?" Didn't he get it? "I came about this close to being unemployed."

She caught just the hint of an eye roll.

"They want you to think it's life or death," Will said, "but really, you don't need them as much as you think you do. If you'd been laid off, you would've been fine. Maybe you would have even been happier."

"You mean homeless."

He closed his eyes for a second. "I miss you."

"Aw, I miss you too."

His lips were full and soft, the outer corners of his eyes drooping slightly, so earnest. She reached out to wrap him in her arms.

He backed away. "No, I mean, I miss you — real, actual you. Not this person who cares about client meetings and live deals and finding the perfect macro to fix her model." He put his hand on her shoulder in a way that could only be patronizing. "Do you know how many times you rolled over to check your BlackBerry last night? Eight. I actually counted. And you were only home for like four hours."

She lifted his hand off her shoulder. She wasn't used to having to defend herself to him. "This is me. Real, actual me." Nancy Cho's words came back to her: *you can't have doubters on your team.* "I came here tonight to support you. Isn't that what we're supposed to do — support each other?"

"So I can't be honest with you."

"I'm saying, if you don't have something nice to say, keep it to yourself."

He stood with his head bowed, scratching the back of his neck. "What I came over to tell you was, Dominique and some people invited me to this thing at someone's apartment in the East Village. They're leaving in a few minutes. Do you want to come?"

"Do you want me to?" She wanted him to say that of course he did, that he knew things were tense right now but they were going to figure this out the same way they'd figured things out that first year he'd moved to New York, when she'd call him as she was leaving the library at 1 A.M. and he'd already be asleep because he had to get up at seven to get to work in time, when their lives had pulled apart into two distinct things that needed to be synchronized.

"Either way." He glanced over her shoulder.

She didn't know which was worse: if he genuinely didn't care, or if he didn't want her to come but couldn't say so.

"Here," he said. "I'll help you get a cab."

His shoulders were stooped, resigned, nothing like the confident boyfriend she'd seen when she'd walked in. She was starting to think he was better off without her, but that didn't mean it didn't kill her that he thought so too. She took his hand and put it on top of her head. He laughed and gamely gave her scalp a good scratch.

Outside the bar, a guy with about forty piercings pushed past them, cell phone flipped open. A cab pulled around the corner, a lit sign on its roof.

Will shut her inside. He gave a quick wave, hand at his hip.

"Where to?" the cabbie asked.

"Fiftieth and Broadway," she said. She couldn't wait to get back to Sterling.

She looked back to the bar. Will disappeared into an unmarked doorway, a bare light bulb hanging over the entrance, a whole world inside you'd never know was there.

Jake Hutchinson

Hutch brushed the crumbs off his lips with the back of his hand. "Got a call in a few."

Trish's usual expression was a half smile that deepened the dimples he loved. When she was annoyed, like now, the right dimple twitched. Guess she didn't like that he'd scheduled a business call during vacation. A Saturday, no less. But Hutch didn't bite. He rinsed his coffee cup and plate and left them in the sink.

"Who is it this time?" she asked.

"The bankers, what's left of them. It was all over the *Journal* this morning — Sterling laid off a bunch yesterday."

"Hard to feel too badly for bankers."

"We all need good work and a good spouse," he said. He squeezed her soft shoulder, making her giggle. "Even bankers." He kissed the top of her hair. "Better get going."

Hutch retreated to the den. It had been the playroom, when the girls were young. Now, it was a showroom for his model trains. Hutch pulled the phone onto the table that held his Pennsylvania Flyer. He flipped a switch and the train sped along the G-gauge track, past the flashing railroad crossing, over the trestle, past a handful of houses Hutch had built out of twigs, past a man and a woman dancing, sliding along a curved gap in the ground, back and forth. Hutch dialed the number Ethan Pearce had emailed him yesterday and entered his pass code.

"Jake Hutchinson," he said at the beep.

He heard his recorded name repeated back to him seconds later.

"Good morning, Jake." It was Ethan Pearce.

"Morning, Ethan. Who else is on?" he asked, unsure whether any members of the Sterling team had been lost to the layoffs.

"Grant Sinclair here."

"Vasu Mehta." Hutch didn't recognize the lilting voice.

There was a brief silence, and Hutch was surprised by his own disappointment.

"Sophie Landgraf."

"Hi, Sophie," he said, relieved.

"Hi, Hutch."

"So, Jake, we wanted to follow up on what you and I discussed in Cincinnati," Ethan said. "Carbonell rubbed you —"

The Pennsylvania Flyer whistled. The bankers were silent. Made Hutch laugh. He could flush the toilet and the bankers on the phone wouldn't skip a beat.

"Carbonell rubbed you the wrong way, pushing on succession," Ethan continued.

"You can say that again." Hutchinson ran his fingers over the miniature trees he'd saved a few years back from an architectural model of an AlumiCorp office building.

"Everything has its price," Ethan said. "I think, at the right price, we can make the succession issues go away. Sophie, why don't you tell Jake what you found."

"Sure thing," she said. Hutch envied her youthful enthusiasm. "Most of Carbonell's options are out-of-the-money. But if our offer were seventy-two a share, the bulk of Carbonell's options would kick in —"

"Seventy-two? No way." Hutch pinched the bridge of his nose. Gene Marson would have his neck.

"Just a minute, Jake," Ethan said. "I think the market's substantially undervaluing Roll-Rite's assets. Actually, Vasu and I were discussing their Indian operations. Vasu's familiar with the assets, he thinks they have a lot of potential."

"Yes, absolutely," said a lightly accented voice that Hutch assumed belonged to Vasu.

"I don't know," Hutch said. "Seventy-two sounds awfully rich."

"Maybe we'll get there, maybe we won't," Ethan said, "but I'd like a chance to try."

"Grant? You still on?" Hutch asked. Grant Sinclair's bonus wasn't tied to the merger's success like Ethan's was, which was why Hutch had asked that Sinclair be on the call, as a check.

"Hi, Jake." Sinclair's voice echoed. Too lazy to take them off speakerphone.

"What do you think about all this?" Hutch asked.

"What do I really think?" A sigh rattled over the line. "I'd consider playing hardball. Why not —"

Ethan jumped in. "What Grant means is —"

"I'd like to hear from Grant," Hutch said.

Sinclair cleared his throat. "Playing hardball is better than leaving money on the table, isn't it? What's the worst case — Carbonell runs the company? You're a good operator, Jake. With the exit package you'd get from this deal, you'd have the freedom to choose your next project."

Easy for Sinclair to say — Sterling would still earn their fees as long as the merger went through, even if Hutch wasn't at the helm of the new company. But Hutch couldn't walk away from Alumi-Corp. At forty-eight, Hutch was young for a CEO, but he wasn't so young that the idea of starting all over again excited him. He'd spent more than two decades at AlumiCorp. It was just like his model train set: he wanted to sit back and watch it run.

Ethan added, "I'm confident we'll find value to justify —"

"Sophie," Hutch interrupted. "What do you think?"

The line was silent.

"Sophie?" he asked again.

"You've put so much into the company," she said. "I wouldn't let it go without a fight."

None of that banker spin — what a relief. Sophie answered a direct question directly. *Not without a fight.* Girl after his own heart. It'd kill him to hand the reins over to Bruce Carbonell. But would it be the right thing for AlumiCorp?

"Look," Hutch said. "The holidays are coming. Let's take stock. Carbonell's driving a hard bargain. I need to think on whether it's worth proceeding with this deal. You all cool it, enjoy the time off. I'll think this over."

Hutch switched off the Pennsylvania Flyer.

"Of course," Ethan said. "You're the boss."

"We understand each other then. And, gentlemen, I don't like to be troubled over the holidays. Family time."

"Well," Ethan said. "If you need anything — anything at all — you know where to find us."

"I do. Merry Christmas."

8

<hr/>

Monday, December 24, 2007

Sophie Landgraf

OPHIE BOUNCED ON HER TOES as she waited for the elevator. It was four o'clock on Christmas Eve, and in an hour, she'd be on a Bonanza bus, headed to Stockton. She fired off a text to Kim: *getting in late tonite. when do i see u?*

People in the elevator were actually smiling. Sophie rested her Sterling duffel bag on top of her shoes so she'd fit inside. She'd crammed the bag with every AlumiCorp document she might possibly need during her four-day break, and now it was putting her feet to sleep.

"Are you coming back?" someone asked.

Sophie turned to see Nancy Cho jutting her discus-thrower's jaw at the duffel bag. Sophie briefly wondered if Nancy would recognize the Blood Diamond lipstick in the dim light. What were the odds she'd be wearing it when she ran into her elusive mentor?

Sophie tried to sound light. "If they'll have me back, yeah."

Cho nodded approvingly, as though Sophie had passed some test.

They funneled out into the lobby, Cho adjusting the chain of her Chanel purse, Sophie shouldering her hefty load.

"Nancy, do you have a minute? I'd love to ask your advice about something."

Cho looked uncomfortable. "I have an . . . appointment. But if you'll accompany me, I'm happy to chat. It's across the street."

She led Sophie to a row of storefronts with neon signs advertising Tokyo-style Ramen, a cheese slice and a medium soda for $1.99. Sophie thought they were heading for the Punjabi Deli until Nancy opened the door beside the unassuming restaurant and mounted two flights of steep stairs to the Red Rose Nail Salon.

"Nancy! Pick a color?" A diminutive Asian woman gestured to a display of nail polish bottles arranged in tiered circles.

"Hi, Lan! My friend will be joining me today," Cho said.

Sophie had never had a manicure before. The closest thing had been before the high school prom, when she and Kim gave each other French manicures that looked like they'd used Wite-Out. "Oh, I —"

"Don't be silly. Senior guys buy shoe shines for their analysts. Why not a manicure?"

Cho read the label on the back of four different shades of buff before finding the one she wanted. "My mother — hopelessly old-fashioned woman — used to say a wife should never let her husband see what she does to keep her looks. Don't know if it's good advice about husbands, but it is for bankers — they see you primping, they decide you're not serious." She leaned in to whisper. "Let's keep this between us."

"Of course."

Sophie gravitated to the bottles of red nail polish, reconsidered, and picked one of the buff shades Cho had discarded. Lan directed them to adjacent tables where the manicurist set to work removing the chipped red polish from Sophie's nails.

"Square or round?" the woman asked Sophie.

Sophie couldn't imagine what the woman meant, but she didn't want to seem unsophisticated in front of Nancy, so she said, "Round, please."

As the manicurist forced Sophie's hand into a bowl of tepid water, Cho said, "So. Talk to me."

"I'm working on a large corporate M&A deal."

"Perfect opportunity to sharpen your claws. Who's the MD?"

"Ethan Pearce."

Nancy rolled her eyes. "Don't get me wrong. I have no problem with Ethan — I have a problem with the fact that as soon as you say 'widower and MD,' fifty women within a two-block radius swoon. You say 'single woman and MD' . . ." She shrugged. "What can I say? It pisses me off."

Sophie wouldn't have thought Nancy needed sympathy from anybody, let alone her. "My mother used to say the Brontës were responsible for ruining a century's worth of women — all those brooding widowers and meek governesses." If she didn't ask about Ethan's wife now, she might never get another chance. "What happened to his wife, by the way?"

"Sudden illness," Nancy said brusquely. "So, what's the problem with this M&A deal?"

"I worry I'm attracting negative attention."

"From *Ethan?*" Nancy said this like it was impossible that Ethan would ever find Sophie attractive.

"No, nothing like *that.*"

"Then what?"

"The client — he's *nice* to me. He actually wants to know what I think." She told Nancy about how Hutch had interrupted Ethan during a conference call to ask what she thought.

"Good girl." Nancy Cho grinned. "How'd Ethan take it?"

Sophie shrugged. "I said not to give up without a fight, and Ethan smiled this slow, scary smile. But I've been waiting for Sinclair to tear me apart for contradicting him. It's definitely making my VP jealous, and —"

"High-quality problem. You've got the client's ear. Let them be jealous."

She hadn't thought about it that way. The manicurist filing Sophie's nails said something that sounded like, "cuddle cubicle." After staring at her, confused, Sophie nodded, yes, please cut the cuticle.

"Ouch!" Sophie pulled her hand away from the manicurist. It was beading with blood. "I'm worried I'm going to make enemies."

Cho made a frustrated noise, like a car grinding its gears. "This isn't summer camp. You're going to make enemies no matter what. It's an occupational hazard. Besides, who doesn't want a worthy adversary?"

Sophie nodded. "But I don't want to set myself up to be next on the chopping block."

"Showing your teeth — and working tirelessly and flawlessly — is your best insurance. Besides, I doubt we'll see another round of layoffs anytime soon. Anything strike you as awfully convenient about the timing of this one?"

Sophie considered.

"Right before bonus season?"

That hadn't occurred to Sophie. Her bonus would come in July. By announcing the layoffs now, before the rest of the bankers got their bonuses at year-end, Sterling had saved hundreds of millions.

"Does that mean they'll lay off analysts in the spring, before we get paid our bonuses?"

"Maybe. You're never safe. Always make sure you have a sponsor, a senior guy who'll fight for you, if he needs to. Does Ethan Pearce have your back?"

Sophie considered. Ethan had saved her from layoffs, yes, but he also hadn't filled out her review. "I'm not sure."

"If the client trusts you, Ethan will. As long as you leverage that trust the right way: in Sterling's best interests."

It sounded so manipulative.

"Oh, don't go all Pollyanna on me." Nancy directed the manicurist's attention to a hangnail the woman had neglected to correct. "You have the CEO's attention, use it. Most analysts would *kill* to be you."

The manicurist tapped her file against the table and set to work filing Sophie's nails.

Vasu Mehta

Vasu slurped his *pad see ew,* splattering sauce across the printout on his desk. Aditi and Meera were probably sitting down to dinner about now. He would have been with them if he had not had to prepare the analysis of Roll-Rite's Uttar Pradesh and Orissa smelters on his own — Sophie had left for the holidays earlier that day. Perhaps he should not be so tough on her. She had jammed so hard these past few months. He had been wrong to complain about her to Ethan, to try to get her off the deal. He liked to think he had made up for it when Sinclair had asked him whether Jordanne Terney's accusations about Sophie were well-founded.

While he waited for a clean copy to print, he scanned the *Journal* online:

> **Investment Banks Scrutinized in Subprime Scare**
> **By Austin Schjeldahl**
> *With the continued deterioration of the subprime market, invest-*
> *ment banks are being questioned for their sale of high risk*
> *mortgage-backed securities to institutional investors . . .*

A knock sounded on his door.

"Merry Christmas, V." Ned Donnigan waved Vasu's printout. "Hey, something wrong?"

"It's all about subprime these days, isn't it?" He had first heard the term a month ago. "When I was in business school, interviewing with the banks, mortgage-backed securities was the place for quants who wanted to play it safe. Who would have thought it was a casino down there?"

Donnigan shrugged. "That shit's complicated."

Donnigan slid Vasu's printout onto his desk and left.

Vasu closed his browser. No sense delaying his conversation with Ethan any longer. He had promised Aditi.

Last night, he had set the table for the first weeknight dinner he had spent at home for months, and by the time Aditi served the biryani, they were already fighting.

"Vasu, you must go," she said, slapping a steaming bowl in front of him.

Hanging on the dining room wall were photos of his and Aditi's parents: four serious, unsmiling faces staring at him. Five, counting his wife's.

"Taking vacation now is not an option," he said.

"Keysha's going to Disney World for vacation," Meera said. "For four whole days."

Aditi shushed her.

"I'm just not in a good position at work right now."

"Not in a good position?" Aditi asked.

He looked at his daughter, who was tearing pieces of naan and arranging them on the table in the shape of a flower. "They gave me a signal at bonus. I didn't want to worry you." *Bonus* was not the proper word for the year-end check that had been eighty percent of his pay last year. In banking, a bonus was not something extra, it was the center of everything. He knew what his measly bonus meant: he was first in line for the next round of cuts. "I'm on watch."

"I know."

"Wait — you know?"

"Mummy, can I be excused?" Meera asked.

Aditi glared.

"But, Mummy —"

"Hush. Eat your dinner." Aditi turned to Vasu. "*Achchaa,* you came home on bonus day and you didn't want to talk about it. Why wouldn't you, unless it was bad news?"

This amazed him. His secret had been gnawing at him all week. The whole time, she had known.

"Never mind," she said. "That's not important. What's important is that you go while your mother is still here."

"I can't leave now."

"You're telling me they'll *sack* you for going to your dying mother's side?"

"They'll sack me for anything. I can't just hand them an excuse."

He knew from the way she arched her eyebrow that she did not buy it.

"It's not a good time," Vasu said.

"*Not a good time?* Your mother is *dying.* You are going to phone her and tell her to *please,* Mummy, please wait to die until it's more *convenient?*"

Meera slid off her chair and tore out of the room. Aditi did not stop her.

"Of course not," Vasu said. He kneaded his temples. "She wouldn't want me to come if she knew how bad it was here."

"This company in your top-secret deal — it has business in India, no?"

He nodded. He had forgotten that he had told her about Roll-Rite's Indian assets.

"*Achchaa,* you must convince Ethan to send you *now.*"

It was not until he swore he would talk to Pearce the next day, without fail, that she backed off.

Ethan was putting on his coat when Vasu knocked on his office door, analysis in hand.

"Got a minute?" Vasu asked.

"I'm heading out. Let's catch up the day after Christmas."

"It will only take a few minutes of your time," Vasu said, unsure whose ire scared him more, Ethan's or Aditi's.

"After Christmas," Ethan said, striding off down the hall.

Vasu hurried after him. "Trust me — you want to see this."

As Ethan called the lift, Vasu thrust his analysis into Ethan's hands. Ethan scowled at him but glanced at the printout.

"I did a deep dive on Roll-Rite's Indian assets," Vasu said. An optimistic dive.

The lift was packed. Ethan forced his way in. Vasu could only get one foot inside, and when the doors would not close, a pug-faced woman told him to wait for the next one. Vasu pressed against her until she made room.

"If we can get on the ground and figure out why those numbers are down, we may find the Varanasi smelters can produce volumes well in excess of what they have been. It could give Hutchinson the incentive to pay more —"

"Shh!" He gestured to the rest of the people in the elevator. "We don't discuss client matters here. You know that."

The doors opened onto the lobby. Vasu hurried to keep up with Ethan.

Ethan whirled around. "What part of Hutchinson telling us to hold off do you not understand? This deal is on life support. No way am I sending you halfway around the world for a deal that won't exist in a week."

Ethan shot out of the building and into a waiting town car, leaving Vasu standing in the lobby, clutching the analysis in shaking hands.

Sophie Landgraf

When the first chutes of light shot through the blinds on Christmas morning, Sophie snapped awake, positive she'd overslept and was late for work. No street noise, no neighbors' footsteps, no buzzing BlackBerry, just an eerie silence that made her worry that something was wrong. It wasn't until she saw the cracks spidering the ceiling that Sophie remembered she was in her bedroom in Stockton. The cornflower-blue walls were faded everywhere except the spot where a poster of Einstein had hung while she was in high school, when she'd thought that looking at images of smart people would make her smarter. She'd arrived too late last night to notice the vase of freshly cut holly on her nightstand — she hoped she hadn't hurt her father's feelings by not saying anything about it right away.

The room was so cold that Sophie pulled on two layers of old sweats and still she was shivering. She stamped her feet against the chill, wistful for Sterling, where no matter what, the floor was a reliable seventy-three degrees. Her BlackBerry showed no new messages. She couldn't remember waking up without Ethan or Vasu needing her. She would've thought it would be a relief.

She looked out the bare window onto the snow-covered field where the sheep used to graze, onto the barn, whose roof sagged under the weight of snow, her father's peace-sign weather vane no longer there, as if she needed reminding that the barn was now owned by the Schuylers. The wind chimes her father had made from tin-can tops hung silently under the eaves, the metal rusted over. Everything here was so still, so empty. Five years ago, even before she was fully awake, she would have been aware of her mother playing NPR in the kitchen, *Morning Edition* weaving its way up through the floorboards and into her dreams. For a second, Sophie wished she'd gone to Delaware with Will, where the house would echo with his sister's cute kids and his cousins who didn't know what it meant to talk in an inside voice.

Sophie cranked up the thermostat and went to check her father's favorite wing chair. No sign of him — he must be out back working on his sculptures. After her coffee, she'd lure him back inside so she could surprise him with her present. The Landgrafs didn't celebrate Christmas, her mother's idea, their silent protest against the Celebration of Consumerism. No presents, no Christmas dinner, definitely no tree. *How can killing a living thing be festive? What are we, pagans performing a sacrifice?* This year, Sophie was determined to start a new tradition. She was finally on her own, making a good salary, and she wanted to flex her financial muscle.

Sophie's usual two cups of coffee weren't enough to kick her into gear that morning. The cold kitchen tiles and slow hiss of the pipes seemed to say that nobody would care if she crept back into bed. She wasn't tired exactly but something about being here made her drag. Even if she'd just slept for twenty-four hours straight, she'd probably still feel half awake.

She fixed her father a cup of coffee, light and sweet, just how he liked it. The back porch was covered with a distressing amount of newspapers bound in twine. The path between the stacks was so narrow that Sophie had to shimmy sideways to get through, splattering coffee on the snowy steps.

The door to the wooden work shed groaned on its hinges. An army-issue metal cot and a sleeping bag stood beside the door, both new additions. She shielded her eyes from the sparks flying from her father's welding torch.

Her father pulled off his welding helmet. "Up before noon? I don't believe it."

She handed him the coffee, steam curling from the blue enamel cup. Without his helmet, he looked small and tired. His hair had been thinning for years, but the process seemed to have accelerated in her absence and he was now more bald than not.

Sophie studied the collection of metallic spikes at his feet. Six months ago, she would have identified his medium only as metal, but she now knew it was hot-rolled aluminum coil, a product manufactured by companies like AlumiCorp. The bale looked like a giant spool of silver ribbon you could use to wrap a present, shiny and new. Her father used to sculpt only with recycled metal scraps:

hubcaps, bolts, tin roofing, beverage cans, and, once, the rusted hood of a car.

"Is this a new thing, the coil?" she asked.

"Lyle Rufo set it aside." Lyle Rufo was her father's biggest supplier of materials — he ran the town dump. "Can you believe someone threw it away? Only thing I can think of, some construction crew finished a job and didn't want to haul it back." He shook his head. "The waste some people make."

"Want some breakfast?"

"Absolutely." He laid the coffee cup on his worktable, a thick sheet of plywood bolted to two sawhorses.

While her father washed up, Sophie searched the kitchen cupboards for the Bisquick, which were filled not with flour and blueberry jam, as she remembered. One shelf was full of Dinty Moore Beef Stew, another of Bush's Baked Beans, cans stacked three high and five wide. One cabinet contained dozens of empty mason jars, the same ones that used to hold honey from her mother's bees, the waxy comb caught inside like a snowflake.

Sophie was pouring circles of batter into an iron skillet when her father returned. He went straight to the thermostat and turned off the heat.

"I'm kind of freezing," she said.

He reached around her to turn up the flame under the pan. "Then put on a sweater."

She ceded the spatula. "Did you win a lifetime supply of Dinty Moore stew?"

Her father looked up but didn't smile. "It's easy."

Easy and cheap. First the heat, now the food — maybe Serena Silver needed to crank it up a notch.

They sat down, two pancakes on each chipped blue plate. She wondered who Ethan was having breakfast with.

"How's everything going with the Lyndqvist's developers?" she asked. "Any luck with town hall?"

Her father drowned his plate in syrup. "I didn't tell you? Construction's on hold."

"That's great! How'd you guys convince them?"

"We didn't. The developers just said they decided not to break ground quite yet."

That didn't sound so different from what Hutchinson had told them a few days ago. "They're taking stock or something?"

"Guess so."

Her BlackBerry buzzed. As she reached for it, her father set down his knife and fork so loudly it could only be intentional.

"I don't see why you have to check that here."

She slipped the device back into her pocket. It wasn't worth the argument — knowing she had a new message was enough.

"You haven't been here eight hours and already you're someplace else."

This was about Thanksgiving, wasn't it? "Dad, I'm right here."

He rested his chin in his hand and looked off somewhere behind her head, just as he had four years ago when he said he was worried that she hadn't slowed down after the funeral, that she should take a semester off, like there was a right way to grieve.

"Look, Dad. I'm sorry I missed Thanksgiving. Really."

"You know, I was your age when I met your mother. I was walking through Boston Common and there was this woman sitting on a park bench —"

"Looking at the swans." The story was the only remotely normal thing about her parents. Sophie must have asked them to tell it to her about a million times.

"The whole world's open to you when you're twenty-two. If you're open to it."

The world must have been pretty different in the seventies because as far as Sophie could see, banking was just about the only job where a twenty-two-year-old was allowed to do anything besides getting coffee and paper cuts. Will had put in two whole years at NPR and only now was he allowed to do real work. Her father didn't understand how unbelievably lucky she was to work at a place where people actually treated her like an adult.

"Dad." She tried not to sound annoyed—she didn't want to fight—but it drove her crazy when her father insisted that he was an expert on the world even though for the past thirty-five years, he'd lived outside it. "I like my job. I know you don't quite get it, but really, I do."

His chair screeched as he pulled himself closer to her. "But being back home, doesn't it make you remember all the stuff you're missing?"

Home was different, but it definitely wasn't better. She didn't know how to explain that without offending him. "You know how when you go hiking, the first few days, you can smell yourself—your shampoo, your detergent, how you're different from the leaves and the dirt? And then there's a point when you smell the same as what's around you, and you know that when you leave the trail, you'll smell dirty to everyone even though you don't smell dirty to yourself."

He stroked his beard. She wasn't making sense.

"I guess what I'm trying to say is, both places are so different you can't even compare them." And the worst part was moving between them.

Her father folded his napkin into a tiny square. "I just don't see why anyone would work at one of those places unless they're obsessed with money. And your mother and I didn't raise you to be obsessed with money."

"No. You didn't." They raised her to pretend that she lived in a world where money didn't exist.

"It seems like such a waste."

She reached across the table and took his hand. "Dad, I'm doing exactly what you and mom did. I'm living my life on my terms."

He squinted at her a moment, like he was looking for a reason not to believe her. He raised his hands. "All right, all right. I said it, it's done."

Sophie took in a deep breath and let it out. Syrup had congealed on her plate into thin ribbons, reminding her of the present she'd gotten him. She tiptoed into the hall. She'd shipped the package to Kim's house, so her father wouldn't see it when he picked her up at the station. Kim had promised to leave it in the hall closet — it was a well-known fact that her father never locked his front door.

When she returned, her father was washing dishes, his back to her.

"So what do you want to do today?" he asked, drying his hands slowly on a checkered towel.

"I got you something."

He cocked his head when he saw the shiny red paper. Maybe he wouldn't accept the gift. Maybe it seemed like a bribe to him, like she was buying his forgiveness about Thanksgiving. Maybe he thought it was proof that she really was obsessed with money. This had been a mistake. She shouldn't have gotten him anything.

"You didn't have to do that," he said.

She exhaled.

He slipped his finger under the Scotch tape. When he saw the shape of the leather case, he must have known what was inside. His hands hesitated over the clasps. "Wow."

"I tried to get you the same kind."

He'd had a guitar just like this when she was little. She used to lay it across her lap and pluck its strings. One summer, Sophie was playing with it on the front porch steps when Kim biked down the lane and asked if Sophie wanted to go to the brook, where they made rafts from twigs and grass. The next morning, after a night of rain, her mother found the guitar where Sophie had left it, its wood warped, its seams cracked, useless. He never got a new one.

He tuned the guitar, strings sliding into assonance. He strummed a chord and launched into the refrain of "Sunshine Superman," his voice more hoarse than she'd remembered but still lovely.

"I should've gotten you something," he said.

"Don't be silly." She wanted it this way. It made her job seem real, even in Stockton.

"We can go down to Pittsfield tomorrow and pick something out."

Nancy Cho's words returned to her. *You have the CEO's attention, use it.* "Actually, you know what I'd like? Any chance you'd make me a sculpture out of that aluminum coil you've got in the shed?"

He looked so excited that she almost wanted to tell him about the dozens of sculptures that were already sitting in her apartment.

"*Phoenix* — the work in progress — do you want that one?"

She tried to sound spontaneous. "Do you know what would be fun? A sporty car — a Mustang, maybe."

"A Mustang."

She nodded.

"Wouldn't have thought you'd want that."

"I do." If her father knew it was for a CEO, he'd never make it.

He hesitated. "OK. I can do that."

She kissed him on the cheek, averting her eyes. She already knew what she'd write on the card: *Hutch — If anyone can make Roll-Rite's scraps into something worth running, you can. Happy holidays from Sophie Landgraf and the Sterling team.*

Ethan Pearce

Ethan knocked on the door of Camille's sister's house on Christmas Day, wishing he'd had a fourth drink on the train from New York to Boonton. Camille's phantom opened the door, pinched cheeks and wispy hair, a vein across her forehead pulsing pale blue. In the year since he'd seen Marguerite, she'd started to go gray, yet another thing about the Marins that he couldn't help thinking was his fault. She fell on him, skinny arms squeezing his sternum the same way Camille used to each night, as if he'd been away for weeks, not only twelve hours. Every year, he told himself *never again*. And every year, he came back. He'd spend the next six months recovering, and by the fall, he'd once again decide that he owed the Marins at least one day.

He thrust out the gift basket: a bottle of Dom Perignon, truffles, Marguerite's favorite rose-scented macarons, which he'd had shipped from Paris.

"Oh, Ethan, you shouldn't have. You do so much."

Marguerite hung his coat in a creaking armoire — the Marins and their furniture were trapped in nineteenth-century Europe, oppressive and fragile at once. Ethan followed Marguerite down the hallway, past photos of Camille and Marguerite's father, Gustaf Marin, in recital at Wigmore Hall; Gustaf's father with Yehudi Menuhin and Benjamin Britten. A familiar melody rose to meet them, which Ethan's reason told him must be Alphonse, Marguerite's sixteen-year-old, practicing the violin. Still, Ethan hesitated.

"He's discovered the Borodin Quartet," Marguerite said.

Borodin. *As sweet as I can stand,* Camille had said. *Playing the Borodin Quartet is better than falling in love.*

"He should be practicing his Paganini Caprice," Marguerite said. "There's a reason he hasn't yet had his debut."

Camille had thought Alphonse would be lucky to get an orchestra gig, like Marguerite. She'd had a theory that she'd won the Tchaikovsky Competition when Marguerite hadn't even qualified because she felt things more deeply. That was also her excuse for not taking her lithium — it made her play like someone who didn't care.

Marguerite rapped on the door and told Alphonse to join them. The knock brought Ethan to his senses.

"How's Laurent?" he asked.

"We're hoping sales will pick up." A luthier who made and repaired violins in the back of his house, who carved his life in the shape of his wife's — that had been the Marin women's dream. "Then maybe we won't have to ask so much of you."

"It's nothing." Alphonse's music school, the summer festivals, the Goffriller violin, it was the least he could do. "Anything you need."

"It's so good to see you — we missed you at Thanksgiving. You know if you ever want a break from the city, a room with a view . . ."

"I appreciate that." And he had no intention of taking her up on it. Ethan believed in survival by compartmentalization, and it was impossible to compartmentalize away the Marins when he was with them.

"And you? How is work?"

"It's fine." With AlumiCorp falling apart, for once, he had no desire to talk about work.

The wallpapered dining room was set for four, Limoges china and filigreed silver, claw-footed tureens of *gratin dauphinois* and *boeuf en daube*. They must have been waiting for him to begin. Every year he tried to cut it closer, to minimize the living-room chitchat, but maybe he had overcorrected this time.

Laurent appeared in a threadbare jacket and sweater-vest, reeking of cologne, and extended his hand in his usual truce. "Ethan, we're so glad you could make it."

Marguerite lit the candles. Alphonse scurried in, gangly girl arms hugging Ethan from behind. He slipped a thin present onto Ethan's lap before taking his seat.

Marguerite gave the blessing. "On this day we remember those who are no longer with us. Gustaf. Martine. Uncle Yves. Camille. Amen."

Laurent opened the Dom, the pop pitifully soft.

$$$

Ethan pulled out the bottle of Johnnie Walker Blue he'd bought on his way home and tossed the silk-lined gift box into the hallway trash chute. After Camille's death — three years, eight months, and twelve days ago now — he'd gone on a tear. A few nights of losing control were enough to convince him to stop keeping liquor in the house. He couldn't live with the constant reminder of his weakness. But seeing the Marins earned him a one-day exemption.

Inside his apartment, Clara Schumann wound herself around Ethan's ankles. Ethan grabbed a glass from the kitchen and walked down the oak-paneled hall to the last door on the left, the Room, the place he usually avoided. The door stuck, as though it too blamed him. Clara darted through the crack before he could stop her.

Three years, eight months, and twelve days ago, when he walked through this door, the first thing he saw was the curve of Camille's hip. She had narrow hips — everything about Camille was narrow, barely enough — and the way she lay on the floor, facing away from him with one leg rolled forward, her hip took on an uncharacteristic curviness that turned him on. It ashamed him that he'd noticed her hip before the bottle of Nembutal.

At first, he hadn't heard the music. It wasn't until hours later, after he'd shaken her by the shoulders, after he'd realized she wasn't breathing, after he'd shouted for help, that he noticed the Sibelius playing in the background. Once, when they were in bed together, she'd explained to him why she'd picked that piece for her debut: Sibelius had written it decades after giving up on his dream of becoming a concert violinist. The piece was a tribute to the person he wished he'd been. *A farewell,* she'd said. At the time, he hadn't understood. *Never mind,* she'd said, in the frustrated way he'd learned to accept. Camille had always said that recording was her best work. The day she killed herself, the CD must have been on repeat because it was still playing after they took her away.

Ethan poured two fingers of Scotch. His housekeeper kept the Room clean, but even she couldn't prevent it from smelling musty with lack of use. The Scotch's burn yielded to honeyed malt, and Ethan sat looking out the bare windows onto the Hudson, its water gray and unclean. He topped off his glass.

Maybe, if he'd whisked her away from the city, it wouldn't have happened. *I need to go somewhere — anywhere — far away,* she'd said. He was on the verge of promotion then, and AlumiCorp was auctioning off its portfolio of primary aluminum assets. It wasn't a good time. Second-round bids were coming in when Camille told him she was going to Morocco, with or without him. Not for a moment had he thought that a week after her return from Marrakech, he would find her here, crumpled on the floor by the window.

It was Marguerite who went through her things. She gave Camille's clothes to Goodwill. She kept Camille's Tourte bow and sheet music for Alphonse.

A month after she died, he gave Camille's Tom Tyler Stradivarius back to the foundation that had loaned it to her. Then there wasn't much left. The cat. A platinum band engraved *EFP to CAM 6.27.99.* The enormous red mittens Camille had worn October through March, to keep her hands warm enough to play. A few concert programs. A jewelry box containing nothing but a broken violin string wound into a coil, its end fraying, whose significance Ethan had never thought to ask about.

Today was the worst possible timing, his visit with the Marins coinciding with Steelers falling apart, no work to push him forward, plenty to pull him back. Ethan poured himself another glass of Scotch. It didn't taste like anything. He dropped the rest of the bottle into the trash. Enough. Tomorrow he would get a new deal moving.

Sophie Landgraf

Kim placed teacups and a plate of Christmas cookies between them, stars and bells stuck with haphazard gumdrops: the ones Bryce had decorated. Bryce tore into the sponge-painted kitchen, flopping brown bangs, freckles faded with winter. He rolled the toy taxi Sophie had brought him up the leg of the table, making screeching sounds when the car reached the plate of sweets.

"Taxi needs gas," he said, snatching a cookie.

Kim cleaned up the crumbs he'd left in his wake. "I thought the enrichment program after school would give my mom a break, but they were just watching movies — ninety-six dollars a week so my kid can watch movies!"

In the AlumiCorp model, where the order of magnitude was a million dollars, that would be .000096.

"So I pulled him out of that, thank you very much, and pay Mel Marinaccio to come three afternoons a week. You remember Mel, Leslie's mom?"

"Oh yeah." Sophie only had the vaguest recollection of Mrs. M.'s duck boots and mangy dog.

"How are the schools in New York?"

Ira Blumenstein had told her that his sons' middle school had posters everywhere that said "every child is a winner," that it killed him to spend a small fortune so his kids would be told that they didn't even need to try. "Actually, I have no idea. Expensive, I think."

"Everything in New York's expensive, right? But I guess that's OK when you're earning a bazillion dollars."

"Um, not exactly." A $55,000 salary had seemed like winning the lottery before she'd moved to New York. She'd hoped to save tens of thousands of dollars by now, but her $2500 monthly paycheck had to cover $1500 in rent, $450 in student loan payments, $250 in electricity and phone bills, plus food and the subway and "Serena Silver's" art collection ... She had a couple thousand in her checking account, her emergency fund, but that was it. She'd feel better when her bonus check came and she had some real cash in the bank. Objectively, she knew she was in better shape than most, but that was the thing about New York: no matter how much money you had, you were surrounded by people who had so much more.

Bryce tumbled into the room. "Aunt Sophie, come play in my room."

"Sophie and Mommy are visiting, sweetie," Kim said.

Bryce tugged at Sophie's jeans. He must be at least three inches taller since she'd seen him last.

"How about we play Spider-Man after your mom and I chat?" Sophie asked.

"Spider-Man is for dorks."

"Oh . . ." She'd never outgrow being a dork. "Something else then."

"Harry Potter!" Bryce thrust his fist at Sophie.

Sophie fell over, pretending she'd been incapacitated by his spell.

"You're playing it wrong!" Bryce said.

"Bryce," Kim said, "how about you watch Dora while Aunt Sophie and I visit."

Bryce scurried into the living room and sat cross-legged, two feet from the television screen, transfixed.

Kim slid deep into her chair. "I swore I wasn't going to be the kind of mom who plops her kid in front of the tube, but sometimes you just have to take what you need."

"Yeah, Ethan always says you can't wait for someone to hand you an invitation."

"Is he still running you into the ground?"

"Actually, he's been really good to me lately." Yes, he expected a lot, but look at what he'd done for her: kept her safe during the layoffs, gotten her in front of the client. "I mean, can you imagine where I'd be if Ethan wasn't protecting me?"

"You and your protectors."

"Sorry?"

"Never mind."

"I wish I could crack open his brain. He loses his wife. A normal person would shut down. But he harnessed it somehow — it made him stronger."

Kim pressed her lips the way she used to in high school, when she was about to tell Sophie to wake up and look around.

"You don't think it's fascinating?"

Kim's lips stretched into a cockeyed smile. "Admit it. You're hot for him."

"*No.*" Why did everyone assume that if you looked up to your boss, you were in love with him? "In awe of him, maybe. But hot for him?"

"Come on, whenever I talk to you, it's all Ethan. He's totally the center of your universe." Kim got up and closed the door between the kitchen and the living room, where Bryce sat watching television. "You're saying if Will weren't in the picture, you wouldn't go for Ethan?"

Kim snapped a cookie between her front teeth.

"It's like Tyler Engel in high school," Sophie said. "OK, maybe I'm curious. Maybe I have a little crush. But first of all, even if there was no Will, even if Ethan weren't my boss, nothing would ever happen because Ethan would never be interested in me in a million years, and second of all, I'd basically die of embarrassment if he ever found out. It's just mind candy."

"Come on. You were totally obsessed with Tyler Engel." Kim smiled like she knew something Sophie didn't. "Really zero percent chance?"

"Um, he's my boss."

"People fool around with their bosses all the time. You don't think I wouldn't go for Mr. Hot Cancer Doc if he wasn't super married?" Kim's smile fell. "Is Ethan cute?"

"In an intimidating sort of way — he's in such good shape it looks like he could snap you in two."

"Yummm," Kim mumbled, her mouth full.

For a second Sophie wondered how high she'd have to rise at Sterling to be able to afford an apartment big enough to invite Kim and Bryce to live with her.

"You're telling me you've never thought about making out with Ethan," Kim said. "Not once."

"*No.*" But now that Kim had put the idea into her head, how could she not?

"Don't think I'm going to let you off that easy — you realize this is the most excitement I've had in like a year?"

In high school, Sophie had called Kim first thing every Sunday morning to hear about how Mike had taken Kim to the Pittsfield drive-in, or how Kim had gone to a party at Gabby Munsee's house where there were Jell-O shots, or how she'd run into Blake Sloan at the 7-Eleven and he wouldn't stop staring at her boobs. Sophie would keep Kim on the phone for an hour until she knew the story so perfectly it was like it had happened to her.

"Really. I promise. Nothing will ever happen with Ethan."

Kim cocked her head for a moment, as though deciding whether to accept this. "So was Will OK with you not making it down to Delaware this year?"

"Sounds like it. He and his sister's kids are ice skating today." When they'd spoken earlier, it had felt like a conversation she'd have with a grandparent: he'd watched *A Christmas Story* last night, they were planning to go ice skating today, maybe build a gingerbread house. "Honestly I think it's better we have a little break."

"Really? You don't miss him?"

Sophie reached for another cookie. "I feel like I should, but I'm so used to not seeing him, it feels kind of normal."

Kim leaned forward. "You still love him though, yes?"

She studied the cookie, gumdrops scattered and not quite right. "I love him. But I'm not in love with him."

"That always wears off."

"Honestly, it's like I finally have a sibling."

Kim pressed her lips. "Will's pretty great. You know that, right?"

"Yeah, he is great." That might be enough if she lived in a small town like Stockton, where it was almost impossible to meet anyone new. But in New York, starting over was nothing — the city was designed for people reinventing themselves. "But I'm not sure he's right. I'm starting to think that maybe you can't be with someone for real until you've become the person you're becoming."

Kim's eyes squeezed tight, like she was squinting against the wind. "The person you're becoming? I thought the whole thing about being twenty-two was that you're finally done with that stuff.

For better or worse, I know I'm always going to be five foot four and have hair that frizzes when it's humid and have this weirdo aversion to mayonnaise."

"Really? You feel finished?"

Kim cocked her head. "You don't?"

When she was younger, Sophie would have thought that by the time she was twenty-two, her life would be a stable, complete thing. But now that she was here, there was still so much to do. "Maybe it's a New York thing. It's like there are all these possible yous out there wandering the streets."

"I thought pickpockets and rapists wandered the streets."

Kim sounded like her father.

"Kidding! Oh my god, I *wish* I lived in New York. Maybe I can come down in the summer, when my mom can take —" Kim jerked her head toward Bryce, who'd crept back into the kitchen with his toy taxi.

"Yes! I'd love that." How she'd get off work, she had no idea.

"I can't wait to see your big, fancy New York apartment."

Sophie winced. "I should warn you — it's pretty tiny. My whole place would fit inside your kitchen."

"How much do you pay for it?"

"Way too much." Kim would flip if she knew she spent fifteen hundred a month on rent. "Promise you won't laugh when you see my 'kitchen.'"

"Yeah, your dad said you basically have an Easy-Bake Oven."

"Hey," Sophie asked, "how do you think he's doing? My dad?"

Kim inspected her fingernails. "I think it's tough."

"What do you mean?"

"He didn't tell you, did he?"

Sophie shook her head. Kim's face was scrunched up, so clearly pained that Sophie braced herself for news of a lump that wouldn't go away, biopsy results.

"His mortgage went up this year."

She took a deep breath and let it out. Money, she could handle.

"He has one of those, oh, what're they called—"

"A balloon?" Sophie asked.

Kim shook her head.

"An ARM?"

Kim snapped her fingers. "That's it. An ARM. The interest payments went up overnight, just like that."

"He never said anything about a reset." Finance was her *job*. Why hadn't he asked her for help?

"I'm sure he didn't want to worry you."

"How do you even know this?"

"Thanksgiving. He'd just gotten the notice."

She should've been here. He would've told her. Instead Kim had spent Thanksgiving with him. Kim had delivered his Christmas present. It was just like high school—Kim got to do all the things Sophie didn't.

"How bad is it?"

"It went up a thousand a month." Kim winced.

Her stomach did a swan dive. How was she supposed to swing another thousand dollars a month? She could eke out a hundred beyond the $250 Serena Silver already sent—maybe—but that wouldn't be enough, and she wasn't going to get her bonus for another six long months.

"And he already borrowed two thousand dollars from Lyle Rufo," Kim said.

"Shit."

Kim's eyes darted to Bryce.

So-rry, Sophie mouthed. "You know he was just trying to convince me to quit? He's giving me advice like that when he can't even pay his own bills?" She didn't even want to think about what would happen if she didn't have Sterling.

"Maybe he wanted to make sure you weren't staying there because of him." Kim said this like it was the most obvious thing in the world.

"What should I do?"

Kim smiled sympathetically and said what Sophie had when Kim found out she was pregnant. "Pretend like you can handle it until you can actually handle it?"

Her father was whittling in the living room when she got back from Kim's.

"Want to play Botticelli?" he asked. "I've been saving some that'll stump you."

She tiptoed around a sheet of newspaper covered with wood shavings. "Dad, why didn't you tell me about the mortgage?"

His shoulders pulled back.

"We can talk to the lender together," she said, "get it refinanced."

He touched the tip of his knife to his thumb. "Already tried." His voice shifted into that false-chipper mode that always irritated her. "It's going to be fine. Business is moving along. These things have a way of working themselves out."

Sophie had hoped she wouldn't have to say it. "I know about Lyle Rufo."

He sprang from his seat, tripping on the newspaper, wood shavings scattering across the floor.

"I sent Lyle a check," she said. She'd dropped it into the mail on the way home from Kim's. Once Lyle cashed it, her balance would be in the double-digits for the first time since college. Six months of spreadsheets and sleepless nights, and she was right back where she'd started — *worse* than where she'd started.

Her father turned his back to her, one hand on her mother's favorite chair, the other kneading the base of his neck.

"Dad, please. Is there anyone else you borrowed from?"

His head shook so briefly she almost missed it.

"Promise?"

His mouth twitched.

"I can't help you if you don't —"

He whirled around. "Please don't take that tone with me."

"Dad, I want to help —"

He made for the door, but Sophie placed herself between him and the exit.

"A credit card's coming in the mail, for the mortgage payments." She'd been shocked by how easy it had been. One call from Kim's kitchen to a Bangalore-accented customer-service rep who immediately approved the increase to Sophie's credit limit, insisting it was no problem at all to add a family member to her account. It was like Visa *wanted* to loan her more money. "The card should be here Tuesday —"

"Money doesn't solve everything, Sophie."

"In this case, money absolutely does solve everything."

"I'm not going to do that to you." A thin curl of wood was stuck in his beard.

"So you'll borrow from other people instead. And how will we pay them back, Dad? Do you know how hard this will be to clean up if we do it your way? If you go into default and the bank doesn't roll we'll have to —"

"We've had this place since 1972. We've always made our payments. They can't kick me out."

"Yes they can, Dad."

"It's not how the world should be."

"But it's how it is." She gripped the doorjamb, telling herself that soon, she would be back at Sterling, where people were realistic. "Look. We've got to work with the system we've got."

"So you're defending the bank? Don't you see how immoral it is?"

"It's just business, Dad. It's not immoral. It's amoral."

"Listen to yourself. Six months at that place and you talk just like them."

Talk rationally, you mean. "I'm just trying to help."

"Yeah, well. You're not."

She closed her eyes and asked herself whether money had always been one of those things you weren't supposed to talk about. "Just promise me you'll think about the credit card."

The front door slammed behind him. Sophie stared at the splintering floorboards, the dark spot on the ceiling where the second-floor bathtub had leaked, the packing tape that covered the corner of a window that hadn't been fixed. She couldn't wait to get home.

Her father flipped up the visor of his welding helmet when she appeared in his work shed later that evening.

"Listen," she said. "I'm really sorry we fought. I didn't mean to tell you what to do, I just wanted to help."

On his worktable was a schematic for a sculpture. The rectangular pillar at the center of the sketch reminded her of the Sterling building. She wished she could be there now, typing straightforward equations into tidy spreadsheets, letting Sterling feed her and drive her home.

"I know you did," he said. "I've been thinking. I really appreciate your offering to help with the house, but I'm not . . . I don't want you to take on too much. Not on my account."

"Dad, it's nothing. I want to help."

"A thousand dollars a month isn't nothing. I've been thinking. I'm going to sell the house."

"Please don't." She sank onto the bench, grateful to have something under her. "Work's going really well right now. My boss, he's really happy with me. I'm actually getting kind of good at this."

"But what if you want to leave that job of yours one day? Join the Peace Corps, or the circus, or whatever. I wouldn't want to tie you down."

"I like Sterling." Why wouldn't he see that? "I want to do this — the house."

"You're sure?"

At that moment it seemed crucial to leave no room for doubt. She drew her knees to her chest, wanting to believe there was no question that she could handle it. "Positive."

9

Thursday, December 27, 2007

Sophie Landgraf

THE MIDTOWN SKYLINE SPREAD across Sterling's floor-to-ceiling windows, open and inspiring and liberating. Sophie wouldn't have thought she could be so happy to be back at work. She dropped her duffel bag onto Vasu's spare chair.

"Welcome back," he said, in a way that didn't make her feel welcome at all.

"It's good to be back. How were your holidays?" She had no idea whether Vasu celebrated Christmas.

He shrugged. "Non-event. I was here."

She sensed there was something he wasn't telling her, but she wasn't going to push him to say more.

"Now that you're here," he said, "you're officially reassigned to Midwest Metals."

Sophie was already pulling hundred-hour weeks because of

Steelers. Now was the time to try what was already second nature to the guys she worked with: pushing back.

"I want to help out on Midwest, Vasu, but I'm at full capacity with Steelers. I really don't think —"

"We'll talk about Steelers later." He folded his arms across his desk. "Someone's got to take over Jordanne's assignments."

She couldn't believe she was getting Jordanne's scraps.

"Trust me, you're lucky you're only getting Midwest Metals. You should see the Christmas present I have for Donnigan."

"But —"

"You had four days of R&R, no? That should last you a year, at least."

Before she thought better of it, she blurted, "My dad took out an ARM."

Vasu's head snapped back, eyes wide. Part of her wished she could take it back — just because she and Vasu spent so much time together, that didn't mean they were actually friends — but only someone at Sterling would fully understand her frustration with her father's situation.

"How did he end up with an ARM?"

"He listened to a friend, said it was a good initial rate." Her father said he hadn't even read the mortgage agreement, he'd just signed it.

"How bad is it?"

"Bad." To think that just two weeks ago, she was sending off another money order from Serena Silver, thinking that another hundred dollars would be a big help.

"He's lucky he's got you."

"It's like he blames the bank for loaning him the money in the first place."

"Him and the rest of the world. Have you been reading this stuff about subprime? When is it ever a good idea to lever yourself to the hilt?"

Sophie thought of her double-digit checking account, of the Visa her father had promised to use until she got her bonus. "Well, if something's a sure thing."

"Ah, young grasshopper. You haven't been here long enough. When it comes to money, nothing is a sure thing."

She didn't want to even think about what would happen if she didn't get her bonus check. "You really think that? Literally nothing?"

"People think they deserve more than they can afford. You should go to India sometime," he said. "No one there thinks they deserve a thing. They've accepted their lots. So should you. Which reminds me: Midwest Metals is yours."

"What about Steelers? At the rate it's going —"

"Steelers is on life support."

She must have heard wrong. "What?"

"Only a matter of time before Hutchinson pulls the plug."

"But Hutch wouldn't —"

"We haven't heard a word from him. The same thing happened last summer. Hutchison went off the grid for a few days, and when he came back, the deal was gone. A deal's a living thing — it needs to be fed. Hutchinson's let this one starve for almost a week."

"Maybe he's just enjoying the holidays."

"In this business? There are no holidays. Ethan's setting up a call, to confirm what we already know."

Sophie gripped the arm of the chair, anchoring herself. She'd taken the lack of email traffic as a sign that Vasu and Ethan wanted her to enjoy her vacation. It hadn't occurred to her that no news was the worst possible news. So that was it — their deal was over? She stared at the maroon bindings of the Steelers presentations stacked on the shelves above Vasu's desk. She'd given that deal four months of her life. She'd slept under her desk, disappointed her father, gotten into this rough patch with Will. For nothing. Could she really start over with a new slate of pitches? Placing ten bets, hoping one would pay off?

"The first deal that falls apart is hard. Don't worry — you'll get used to it." He smiled. "Think of it this way: you can make plans for New Year's."

Sophie sat in her cubicle clicking through the Project Steelers models, hundreds of megabytes she'd painstakingly puzzled together, now useless. Her phone rang.

"How are you holding up?" Will asked.

"I gave my life over to that thing and I have nothing to show for it."

"What? I meant, how are you holding up with all the dad stuff. I wanted to check in, you know—"

"Sorry. I'm a little out of it." She swiveled her chair to face the windows, snow swirling to the street. "Our deal died."

"Bad week, huh?"

"It was the only stable thing."

"The house?"

"The deal."

A computer whirred.

"Oh," he said. "There'll be other deals—don't worry. You'll do a million of them."

She wanted to believe him.

"Besides," he said. "Maybe it's asking too much to conquer the corporate world and save your dad's house in the same week."

At that moment she wanted so badly to be curled against his collarbone, her cheek against his skin, warm and safe. She wanted him to scratch her scalp and pull her to the spot where she could hear the steady beat of his heart. "I love you."

"Aw, I love you too. So we'll actually see each other now?"

"Vasu said I can make plans for New Year's."

He whooped. "So what are we going to do first?"

"Whatever you want, followed by whatever you want." The snow was thicker now, fat flakes. "And then I want to go to Central Park and build a snowman and throw snowballs at it until we knock it down."

Ethan Pearce

Some bankers claimed there was a mourning period for dead deals, but as far as Ethan was concerned, that was pure self-indulgence. Ethan had already priced in the loss of the AlumiCorp merger. You make your peace and move on, fast as you can. Regret was for retired people.

Inefficiency was just as offensive. Spending an hour on the phone so Hutchinson could deliver a death sentence they all knew was coming . . .

Vasu and Sophie slumped into his office.

"Try not to look so excited, folks," Ethan said.

Vasu looked seasick, as usual. But for Sophie, hunched like a pack animal about to collapse, the piteous expression was new, and it didn't suit. She hadn't learned yet that the most important thing in this business was to look like nothing fazed you.

Vasu and Sophie were waiting for a pep talk he had no intention of giving. "Vasu, I need staffing on a few pitches I'm targeting for the first week of January. Callahan Cement, New England Waste Management, Mammoth Corp."

Vasu jotted down a note. "What's the time commitment, roughly?"

"Ten, twenty hours, max." Ethan had practically finished the books himself. After his Christmas Day punishment, he'd dusted himself off and gotten to work. Who knew if any of the pitches would get a nibble, but at least they'd keep him busy.

He'd planned to have Sophie assigned to these projects, but watching her wallow made him reconsider. Other managing directors requested certain juniors again and again, but Ethan hadn't found the right one yet. It was an efficient model: they did things your way, every time. Unlike Vasu, who lobbied to throw more resources into international diligence when Ethan had told him more than once that it was a lost cause, Sophie knew her job was to facilitate him, not the other way around. But here she was, staring at her legal pad, ready to hang herself. If she didn't know how to convert disappointment into productivity, he'd be wasting his time. Better to be a one-man shop than to have others slowing him down.

He pulled the polycom to the center of the desk. Pachelbel's Canon played while they waited for Hutchinson to join, the same piece Ethan had suggested for when Camille walked down the aisle. *Pachel-blah Canon?* she'd said. *So overplayed.* She had a strange belief that something could be too successful.

A series of beeps cascaded from the polycom.

"Jake Hutchinson. Who else is on?"

"Morning, Jake. You've got the whole team: Ethan, Vasu, and Sophie."

"Hi, all."

"Restful holidays?" Ethan asked. "Plenty of time to mull over our deal?"

"Yup."

Hutchinson wasn't going to volunteer that he was killing the deal. Fine.

"I don't want to take up too much of your time," Ethan said. "I'll get right to the —"

"Sophie," Hutchinson interrupted. "I have your piece in front of me now." He chuckled. "My wife, she's taken to calling it the Hutch-stang."

What the hell is Hutchinson talking about?

Sophie fidgeted with her pen.

Hutchinson was as chipper as Ethan had ever heard him. "I might take it into the office instead, I can't decide."

"I'm so glad you like it," Sophie said.

Ethan placed the line on mute. "What the hell is going on?"

"I sent Hutch a Christmas present made from Roll-Rite's scraps."

Ethan had sent Hutchinson the usual bottle of Johnnie Walker Blue.

"Frankly, it took me back," Hutchinson said, "Reminded me why I started doing this in the first place."

Ethan scrambled to take the line off mute. "We were hoping you'd feel that way."

"Hope you guys got plenty of rest this week. Ready to go?"

Ethan was so shocked, he almost missed his cue. "We're always ready, Jake."

"Good. Let's do it."

Ethan didn't have any idea what had just happened, but whatever it was, it had saved their deal. He'd taken Hutchinson at his word that they shouldn't reach out with business over the holidays, and Sophie sidestepped his decree with the perfect Christmas present. How did someone so green manage to get their client precisely where they wanted him?

"Carbonell and I are gonna schedule a powwow, get management and bankers together," Hutchinson said. "The other side, they're using Goldman. We're thinking January 2. Place, TBD."

Five days — not nearly enough time.

"DC would be a good choice," Ethan said. If a reporter or industry guy noticed Roll-Rite and AlumiCorp management together, he'd think the executives were in town to lobby, not to negotiate a merger.

"I'll keep that in mind," Hutchinson said. "You guys get going on the Roll-Rite forecast. I'll be in touch."

He hung up.

Sophie laughed anxiously. Ethan joined her.

"Too bad we didn't diligence the international assets while we had downtime," Vasu said.

Ethan stared Vasu down. His VP's insubordination reminded him. "Sophie, in the future, don't go over my head to the client."

She nodded. "I'm sorry, I thought —"

"It's all right — it sounds like you did some good this time. Saved our asses. But in the future, everything goes through me. No exceptions."

"Absolutely."

"You guys better get going — we're already behind schedule."

Sophie jumped up, raring to go. It was easy to underestimate her — she was young, and she led with insecurity. That was precisely her advantage: she flew stealth. Even he had bought into her lost-little-lamb exterior. The whole time she'd been orchestrating a coup he wished he could have pulled off. Ethan wasn't sure whether to be impressed or mad that he hadn't thought of it himself.

Ethan grabbed the swimming goggles from his desk drawer. When he was this excited, he couldn't sit still.

Sophie Landgraf

Sophie considered screening Will's call, but delaying their conversation would only make it worse. It was almost 6 P.M. on New Years' Eve, six hours before she'd promised the final version of her analysis of the Roll-Rite forecast to Vasu and Ethan, thirty-nine hours before the powwow with Roll-Rite, and two hours before Annabelle's party. She was alone on the floor, banging her head against her spreadsheet, her investigation complete except for a single, frustrating anomaly in the labor expense figure. She couldn't send out the analysis until she figured it out.

"You're still there," Will said, deflated. "I was hoping you'd already left."

"Yeah, me too."

He was silent. He wasn't going to make this any easier on her.

"I think I'm stuck."

She pulled the receiver away from her ear in anticipation.

"You know what?" His voice was so soft and even, it was scary. "It's my own stupid fault for actually believing you this time. I let you get my hopes up and then you stomp all over them."

"I'm really sorry—"

"Yeah? Prove it. You're not finding a cure for cancer or saving guys trapped in a mine. So explain it to me: why is this such a big deal?"

"Let's say, hypothetically speaking, that Company B sent us their forecast, and I'm supposed to —"

"Company B? Forecast? You think I even care about that?" He was yelling now. "I don't want to know why it's important to them — I want to know why it's so important *to you*."

"We can't go into the meeting and look like we haven't done our homework." She couldn't look like an idiot in front of Ethan and Hutch.

In the silence, she heard the muffled ding of the elevator on a different floor.

"Can I ask you something?" he blurted. "Are you trying to come up with reasons not to come out with me tonight? It sure sounds that way."

"You think I like being stuck in the office on New Year's?"

"Do you?"

"Please don't be mad. I really wish it were different."

"I'm not mad. I'm disappointed in you."

Which was about a million times worse.

"You know," Will said, "sometimes I think . . ."

"Say it."

"Never mind. You don't want to know."

He hung up. The floor was silent except for a printer that clicked as it powered down.

Sophie was about to start the New Year as a failure of a girlfriend. In the hours since Will had hung up on her, she'd stared at her stupid spreadsheet, and what good had it done? It was 11 P.M. and she'd made exactly zero progress. She was too upset to think straight — she wasn't going to be able to work until she patched things up with Will. She stared out the window onto the crowds heading to Times Square. What if she left now and got up early to finish the analysis with a fresh perspective? She grabbed her things. If she hurried, she could make it to Annabelle's party before midnight and surprise Will. Maybe that would be enough for him.

Annabelle answered Sophie's knock and gave her a not-quite hug. The crinoline of Annabelle's thrift-store party dress rustled as she turned away. The dining table was crammed with empty bottles of five-dollar André Champagne, boxes of Franzia, plates with congealing sauce, an impossible number of tea lights.

"Will!" Annabelle's boyfriend, Justin, shouted so loudly the couples clustered around the sofa paused their conversation to look up at Sophie, who wished she'd thought to change out of her suit. "Your woman's here!"

Judging from the chilly reception, Will had unloaded his girlfriend troubles to his friends. Sophie hadn't seen them in forever — for all Sophie knew, he'd been complaining about her for months. Mitsuko, who'd once been Sophie's biggest fan, smiled cautiously, burrowing deeper into the shoulder of a guy Sophie didn't recognize. Will's college roommate and his girlfriend were cuddling under the mosquito netting that veiled Annabelle's bed. They didn't acknowledge her presence.

Will poked his head out from the kitchen, black knit tie hanging at half-mast. Sophie knew from the hunch of his shoulders, his slit-eyed look, that Will was drunk. *Very* drunk. And when Will got drunk, he got mopey.

Sophie approached cautiously.

"Did the bank die or something?" he asked thickly. He thrust his hands into the pocket of his corduroys, making no move to touch her.

"I thought about what you said." She whispered, "I wouldn't want you to have to kiss someone else at midnight."

She waited to see if her words would have any effect. Someone turned up the music, The Strokes singing "Is This It."

Annabelle appeared with a plastic champagne flute. *"Pour vous."*

Sophie tilted her head back and drained the glass, which Annabelle promptly refilled, foam spilling over the brim.

"OK if I smoke?" Will asked.

"Just blow it out the window," Annabelle said.

Sophie swallowed her disapproval as Will pulled a pack of Kamel Red Lights out of his pocket. In college, he'd lit up every once in a while, mostly at parties and tailgates. He'd quit for good after he'd graduated, which meant the Kamels were meant to make her feel guilty. They were working.

Will ducked next to Annabelle's window and swung a leg onto the fire escape. Sophie shimmied over the windowsill after him, foot making contact with creaking metal. Fifty feet below, Ninth Avenue was bumper to bumper, clusters of revelers swerving down the sidewalk, their joy only making Sophie more miserable. She tiptoed to Will and squatted over her heels. His head was turned away from her, blowing smoke that Sophie watched twist in the wind. A halo hung over Times Square, the glow making it impossible to see any stars, only a fuzzy slice of moon.

"Has Justin busted out the shots yet?" Sophie asked, hoping rallying around a shared dislike would remind him they were on the same team.

Will shook his head.

"What do you think, twenty minutes before he brings out the Jose Cuervo?"

He hardly smiled. "Maybe Justin finally got that it *pisses Annabelle off.*"

"Maybe." She wished he'd look at her.

"She could do so much better."

Sophie was silent for a moment. "Maybe."

"You know, it's stupid, but I thought once you got here, to the city, and we were living in the same place again, things would go back to the way they were before."

She heard the television turn on inside Annabelle's apartment, an announcer going on about the size of the crowd in Times Square.

"Stupid, right?" he asked. "You're practically in a different universe."

Sophie sensed he wanted her to contradict him, but she couldn't.

"When you started at Sterling," he said, "you laughed at the banker boys. Now you're a poster child for that place."

He said this like it was an insult, but really it was a huge compliment. She'd killed herself to fit in there. But she knew that he'd meant it to hurt her, just like she knew what he wanted to hear: that Sterling was a phase she'd grow out of, rather than something she wanted to grow into.

He studied the cigarette's smoldering tip. "You know, if things were different, and we met right now, I don't know if we'd even get past hello."

She felt like he was cuing her to fight for them, to remind him of their first date, a picnic of pork buns and hard cider on top of East Rock. Of the time they'd snuck to the top of the Branford clock tower with their sleeping bags. But now that he'd said what she hadn't had the guts to admit, even to herself, she felt strangely calm. He was right.

"I know what you mean," she said.

His head snapped up. His eyes were wide and a crease ran down the center of his forehead, the same way he'd looked when he'd showed up in her dorm room after her mother's funeral, when he'd wrapped her in his arms and petted her hair and told her it was going to be OK, when it had seemed like he might really be able to keep her safe.

A chorus sounded from the apartment. "Five! Four! Three! Two! One! Happy New Year!"

She looked off toward Times Square, searching for the ball that had dropped. Roofs stretched to the horizon, neighborhoods she hadn't even visited yet, places she didn't know if she'd like but at least wanted to try.

"Maybe we shouldn't do this anymore," she said.

The fire escape creaked underneath them.

"You want to break up?"

"If you feel the way you said, then yes."

"If? Then? We're not one of your Excel formulas."

Normally this would have made her say something she'd later regret, but she didn't feel the need to defend herself — her mind felt clear for the first time in ages. "All that's keeping us together is that we've been together for four years."

"You really mean that?"

He stared at her, mouth open, so clearly shocked that she could only wince.

"I think so."

"Well, *if* you're not sure you want to be together, *then* I don't want to be together."

"Well, I guess that's it then."

His mouth opened, then shut. "I guess it is."

He climbed inside, tossing his cigarette over his shoulder. Sophie watched the orange tip of his cigarette spiral down to the street, releasing her.

She slid inside carefully, so as not to snag her suit. The others shrank from her gaze. It didn't really matter if she didn't say goodbye.

She stumbled down four flights of stairs. Standing under the anemic glow of the lobby's bare light bulb, she dialed Kim.

"Hi, you've reached the Lobells. We might be in, we might be out, but leave a message and you'll . . ."

She wanted to tell Kim that she and Will had been growing apart for so long now that they were bound to break up soon or later, that if they'd kept going, they would've ended up hating each other. If she could've said these things out loud, she would've believed them that much more herself. *If, then.* Will was right — she did say that.

The sidewalks were littered with noisemakers and deflated balloons. Partiers sipped from bottles stuffed inside paper bags, arms linked, reminding Sophie that she was on her own. Sophie told herself that independence was why she'd moved here in the first place. If her mother were here, she would have said, *people only need people and nothing else,* but her mother had never lived in New York, where people were everywhere, waiting to be met. Sophie looked down Ninth Avenue, high-rises stretching to the horizon, thousands of homes, tens of thousands of people. People needed the right people. Ones who understood you, supported you. Something else her mother used to say: *Don't sell yourself short.*

Jake Hutchinson

Tricky business, merger talks. Get noticed by the wrong person, the rumor mill would start cranking and the deal would be finished before it'd started. Some CEOs rented an airstrip in the middle of nowhere, closed it for the day, had both companies' people fly in, and negotiated right there on the tarmac. Companies more flush than AlumiCorp. So here he was, on January 2, sneaking around the Pentagon City Ritz Carlton like a guy who was cheating on his wife.

Hutch and the Sterling team took the fire stairs because you never knew who you'd meet in the elevator. The bankers lined up in order of rank outside suite 449. Ethan straightened his tie. The Indian guy scanned something on his legal pad. Sophie looked straight at Hutch, smiling as sweetly and expectantly as his daughter Darcy had on her wedding day. Gave Hutch an idea. His brother Tommy, an army man, once said overturning the expectations of your enemy was the surest way to gain the advantage early on. Hutch knocked on the door and whispered the password, "Steve McQueen." The door swung open and he motioned for Sophie to lead the way.

Made his day, watching Bruce Carbonell and the half-dozen suits rise from their seats to greet this girl who looked barely out of her teens. Hutch followed Sophie, making his way down the Roll-Rite team's receiving line, visualizing each person's name tattooed across his forehead as they shook hands, an old memory trick. Still, by the time he'd made his way around the room, he'd forgotten all the names except the two he already knew: Bruce Carbonell, Roll-Rite's CEO, and Mike Bennett, the Goldman managing director. The rest were a blur: men too young to own suits that probably cost two or three grand, who wore ties with funny little animals all over them. Even their teeth looked expensive.

The advantage of this particular suite, he'd been told, was that the living room didn't have any windows, so they wouldn't be seen. The furniture had been pushed against the walls to make room for a long conference table, but with a dozen people inside, there wasn't much space to maneuver. Hutch shimmied around a pair of armchairs to get to the conference table. The bankers flanked their respective CEOs, standing behind their chairs, two starting lineups, each player singling out the member of the opposing team he'd cover when the whistle blew. Everyone was trying not to look excited. The last meeting he'd gone to that was this important was Midwest Metals' hostile takeover attempt. AlumiCorp had been at a disadvantage then, forced to react to Midwest's moves rather than initiate their own, but here, Hutch was in the driver's seat, and he wasn't going to let anyone forget it. He made sure to sit first.

Sophie pulled a stack of presentations from her computer case and circled the table, distributing them. Usually, Hutch went into any business discussion with a list of five points he wanted to hammer home. Today, all his focus was on one thing: he was going to run the merged company. He studied Bruce Carbonell, who was leaning back on the rear legs of his chair like it was his living room. Hutch got Carbonell's message, loud and clear: I don't need you.

The seventy-year-old could posture all he wanted, but the truth was plain as could be. Carbonell needed a successor.

Hutch let Ethan lead the discussion. Pearce never got ruffled, and Hutch could save his strength for the thing that mattered most.

"Our hope for this meeting," Pearce began, "is to address each other's questions about both companies' projections and to talk through the schedule for diligence. Sound all right to everyone?"

Both CEOs nodded.

Ethan steered the discussion through growth rates and fixed costs, everything straightforward and relaxed enough until they got to capital structure. Goldman proposed increasing NewCo's debt. Bennett called it maximizing capital efficiency, Hutch would call it taking too much risk. If they piled on that much more debt, after the interest expense, they'd hardly turn a profit. He didn't want to think about what would happen if commodity prices went the wrong way.

Hutch cut in. "It'd be a challenge, running a company that levered."

Carbonell smiled. "If you're not up to it, there are others that could handle it."

The bankers looked up from their legal pads. Hutch reminded himself to stay cool. No way the seventy-year-old could handle running the new company himself. It was all a bluff. Chairs creaked as everyone leaned forward. This was it. This was where the deal would fall apart.

"Neither of our companies have ever carried that much debt," Hutch said. "NewCo'll be in the same business. Should have the same cap structure. Frankly, Bruce, anything more seems pretty darn irresponsible."

The bankers' heads spun to face Carbonell. Maybe he'd laid it on a little thick. Challenging an executive's sense of fiduciary duty was like challenging a man to a duel.

Carbonell tapped his pen against the table. "The fact is, after we cut the drag from the underperforming assets we'll let go of if we do this merger, NewCo will be a more profitable company. More profits allow for more debt. *If* the company is well run."

All eyes were on Hutchinson. Ethan had warned him that Carbonell would use succession as a bargaining tactic, that the key was not to get emotional. The heat under Hutch's cheeks told him he'd failed.

"But this is premature," Carbonell said. "Nailing down the particulars before we agree on purchase price."

Meaning: you offer us enough for our company, we'll talk about letting you run it. Well, they understood each other. AlumiCorp would have to put in a strong bid.

"Fair enough," Hutch said.

"I look forward to seeing what you come up with," Carbonell said.

A collective exhale swept through the room.

"On to forecast questions?" Ethan asked.

The squabbling continued well into what should've been the lunch hour. Hutch's stomach was grumbling by the time Sterling reached the last of their questions.

"The Indian assets aren't performing as well as we'd expect," said what's-his-name, Ethan's guy with the singsong accent. "Are there any structural impediments that account for that?"

"No," Mike Bennett said, "not that we're aware of."

A knock sounded at the door. Sophie sprang up to let in the Ritz Carlton employee wheeling in their lunch. Hutch smelled salmon. He'd hoped for beef.

"I'd like Sterling to start their work the week after next," Hutch said.

"That's fine," Bruce Carbonell said. "I'll make sure the bankers have the access they need."

If Sterling didn't turn up any skeletons during diligence, it'd all come down to whether Roll-Rite liked their bid. Hutch served himself three hunks of salmon, potato salad, and plenty of rolls. Success made him starving.

Sophie Landgraf

Sophie watched in the cab's rearview mirror as Ethan scrolled through his BlackBerry. She was dying to hear his thoughts on the powwow but she knew not to interrupt. The three of them were halfway to the DC train station, Vasu crammed against the window, Ethan's suit jacket brushing against her leg, scratchy but not unpleasant. One of the first things Sophie had learned in analyst training was that the junior guy always takes the middle seat. At the time, it had sounded like punishment.

Success suited Ethan. It made his chest seem broader, his chin stronger. He almost caught her watching him in the mirror when he looked up. He leaned closer to her as he tucked his BlackBerry into his pocket. He smelled like fresh-cut grass and cedar and something else, maybe pepper. Would it have seemed weird if she'd worn perfume today? Ethan probably wouldn't have even noticed.

"Ethan, what was your take on the meeting?" Vasu asked.

"Cautiously optimistic," Ethan said. "Roll-Rite's not going to go for cheap, but Hutchinson's excited enough to offer an attractive bid. If we manage to uncover additional sources of value. We'll have to give him every reason we can find to pay up."

"Goldman seemed awfully relaxed, don't you think?" Vasu asked. "What are they so confident about?"

"That's just their way. Sophie, try to make friends with their analyst. It'll make all our lives a lot easier."

His hand was inches from hers.

"Any observations?" Ethan asked her.

Ethan actually cared about her opinion? What would he want her to say? "I was thinking, when we were sitting across from the

Goldman team, if we were the companies getting merged, not Alu-miCorp and Roll-Rite, the Goldman guys would be the ones who got cut, they'd be the synergies."

"Congratulations," Ethan said. "You're officially a banker."

Ethan held the door to the Acela and told them to hurry.

"Bar car or business class?" he asked.

Sophie and Vasu exchanged confused looks — since when did Ethan defer on a decision?

"Whatever you think, Ethan," Vasu said.

"We'll bring the bar to us," Ethan said, leading the way to business class. "You guys sit — I'll get the drinks."

Air rushed through the door as Ethan exited to the next car.

Vasu leaned close to Sophie. "Funny, isn't it? Seeing him so worked up?"

Sophie stared at him, trying Will's trick of telling someone off without saying a word. He shouldn't insult Ethan like that. He coughed uncomfortably and pulled out a thick folder flapping with Post-its and tape flags.

"Might as well get going," he said. "You never know what's going to turn up."

"How exactly does diligence work?" Sophie asked, meaning: will I go on diligence too?

"You wouldn't put up six billion dollars based on someone else's analysis, right? So now we visit all the major plants, see if there's anything that isn't captured in the numbers."

Sophie looked out the window to a billboard advertising no-money-down auto financing. "So basically we're forming our own view about how much Roll-Rite's worth and seeing if they're hiding anything?"

"It's a big company, no? Too big for anyone to know everything that goes on inside. A lot of stuff we'll turn up, management might not even be aware of."

Vasu folded his hands, as he often did before telling a story with a lesson. Sophie wondered if Vasu had ever thought about becoming a teacher.

"Years ago, I went to West Texas on diligence for a drilling equipment manufacturer. They'd reported fourteen million in equipment in a warehouse in the middle of nowhere. It turned out the equipment was rusted over, decades out of date — scrap metal. The accountants must not have stepped inside that warehouse. *That's* why we go on dili — it saved us from a fourteen-million-dollar mistake. It would be damned embarrassing to find out something like that *after* your client signed on the dotted line."

Vasu uncapped his highlighter, and Sophie took it as a cue that she'd better take out her own work, too.

She was jotting down notes from the meeting when her Black-Berry buzzed: Kim returning her call about her and Will. She excused herself and pushed her way into the next car.

"How are you holding up?" Kim asked.

Outside the window, crumbling row houses raced by, waiting to be condemned.

"Actually I think I'm all right." Sophie squatted on her heels. "Maybe I'm going to wake up in the middle of the night one of these days totally freaking out, but I don't know. It feels right."

"I'm really sorry." Kim made it sound like Will had died or something.

"I've been through worse."

"Are you sure you're OK?"

Out of the corner of her eye, Sophie saw Ethan push through the car's far entrance, carrying a cardboard tray of tinkling beer bottles.

"Kim — I gotta go."

She smoothed her hair with her hands. It was humid out and she could feel the frizz under her fingers.

Ethan handed her a bottle of Heineken. "The look on Mike Bennett's face when you walked through that door — priceless."

She followed him back to their seats. The short hairs on the back of his neck were perfectly uniform in length.

"You've caught the bug," he said over his shoulder. "I can tell."

"The bug?"

"The rush — there's nothing like it."

She considered sliding into the empty seat next to Ethan for a moment before taking her place beside Vasu.

"A toast!" Ethan raised his beer bottle. "To our deal."

10

Thursday, January 24, 2008

Jake Hutchinson

HUTCH PULLED HIS SPEAKERPHONE closer. "Found any pigs hiding under Roll-Rite's floorboards?"

"We're only one week into diligence," Ethan said, "but I think it's safe to say we're optimistic. Vasu's making progress on the West coast, and I —"

"What about Sophie?"

"She's doing the Midwest ops, just like you asked."

"Good." Hutch's phone flashed with another call. "Ethan, excuse me a moment."

Merry spoke the words Hutch least wanted to hear. "Gene Marson's on two."

"Ethan, I'll catch up with you later."

It wasn't hard to guess why Gene was calling: someone was betting against their company. The short interest on AlumiCorp had shot up twenty percent that week, and when AlumiCorp stock traded down, someone stood to make a pretty profit. Who, exactly, Hutch couldn't say. His CFO had called their Wall Street contacts but they didn't have squat. Large shareholders had to file with the SEC. Those, Hutch could track down. But short sellers were damned near impossible to trace, unless they wanted to be found.

"Gene, what can I do for you?"

"I'll cut to the chase. We're convening a special meeting of the board. We're not happy with the direction this company is heading. We need to discuss your future."

"Short-term market fluctuations are —"

"This is no short-term fluctuation, Jake. AlumiCorp's trading at half what it was when you started as CEO."

Hutch pinched the bridge of his nose. "Look. Gene. Tell me honestly. What do you want that I'm not —"

"We'll talk about it at the meeting. March 1."

Hutch didn't have a choice. He had to play his trump. "Well, guess I won't be able to execute my latest initiative, a large strategic transaction that would vault AlumiCorp to the top of the industry."

For once, Gene Marson was silent.

"I guess the board won't be interested in that either," Hutch said.

"Who are you talking to?"

"Our friends in Pittsburgh. Sterling's kicking the tires. Didn't want to waste the board's time until I knew the deal had legs. It does, Gene."

"Fine. Bring it to us on March 1."

That'd be tight. Five weeks to complete the diligence Sterling had planned to do in nine. They'd have less information when they made their bid for Roll-Rite. But what choice did he have?

"All right. I will."

Decades ago, when Hutch had started as a plant engineer, he'd envied his boss, the plant manager. When Hutch had become plant manager, he'd envied the manager of domestic operations. And when he'd been promoted to head of domestic ops, he'd envied the CEO. He'd always hoped that as CEO, he'd finally be able to do things his own way. His board kept him on a tight leash. Today it felt like a choke chain.

As soon as Gene Marson hung up, Merry buzzed again. "Trish, line 1."

"I'll have to call her back."

"She says it's urgent."

He took a deep breath. "Put her through."

Trish's perky mood only deepened his frustration. "I'm about to buy tickets to Hawaii and I wanted to check —"

"Sugar, this really isn't a good time. I just got some bad news and —"

"What happened?"

"Loose lips sink ships." Trish was a wonderful woman, but she loved to talk.

"I can tell you're under a lot of pressure lately. That's why I thought we should get away next month, get you some rest. The Trump Waikiki has one room left and —"

He hurled his stapler at the wall. "Dammit, Trish, I said not now!" His chest heaved. Yelling at Trish was something you didn't do. Her father had been a screamer, and even the hint of a raised voice brought her to tears.

"I'm sorry, Trishy. I didn't mean —"

She didn't say good-bye. He'd really done it.

Hutch locked his door and tore into a carton of Whoppers from the cache he hid behind his books, away from the prying eyes of Merry, who'd once squealed to Trish. With the crunch of each malt ball, Hutch imagined the crack of Marson's skull. The Whoppers didn't put out the burn so he started on the Mallomars. Twenty-three years he'd given this company and this was his reward. Hutch felt sick.

Sophie Landgraf

Sophie smoothed her suit as she entered the concrete-floored reception room of the Mechanicsburg smelter, the first of her plant tours on this, the second week of diligence. A woman with tired highlights sat behind a desk with a copy of the *Pittsburgh Gazette* opened to a half-finished game of Sudoku.

"Hi," Sophie said, "Duane Heinrich's expecting me?"

While the receptionist disappeared to find the plant engineer, Sophie double-checked the contents of her bag: diligence checklist, financials for the Mechanicsburg smelter, plant employee roster, summary of Mechanicsburg's operating statistics, legal pad, calculator. She hadn't been sure what she'd need, so she'd brought everything she could think of. Luckily, this visit would be hard to screw up. Mechanicsburg was the least efficient plant in the Midwest. Sophie was here to confirm what Hutch and the bankers already understood: Mechanicsburg would be shut down if the merger went through.

A mechanical roar sounded as the door swung open. Out came a red-bearded man wearing a yellow jumpsuit, work boots, and a hard hat.

"Ms. Landgraf?"

Duane Heinrich extended his hand. The smile lines creasing the corners of his eyes reminded Sophie of her father, before her mother's accident.

"This your first time at a smelter?" Duane asked.

It was her age, wasn't it? She'd tried so hard to look professional — low ponytail, sensible shoes, pinstripe suit — but she hadn't fooled Duane Heinrich, who might well have a daughter her age.

"I've analyzed a lot of them."

He nodded slowly. "Your suit. Is it synthetic?"

She'd overdressed on purpose; a suit made her look a good five years older. Was he telling her that her best suit looked cheap?

"Can't have synthetics inside the pot room. God forbid there was a splash, the synthetic fibers, they melt, stick to your skin."

She hadn't known. "I can run back —"

He held up an index finger, turned, and wheezed. He pounded his chest. "Let me see if Penny can scrounge you up a work suit."

Sophie's BlackBerry buzzed. She'd emailed Will asking when he'd like to pick up his stuff. He'd written all of nine words: *Not up to it yet. Hope all is well.* He didn't even sign his name. She'd known he was upset when he hadn't returned her call two weeks ago, her first attempt since they'd broken up, but she hadn't realized it was this bad. She wouldn't have guessed that of the two of them, she'd be the first to recover. Sophie deleted the email and focused on the half-finished Sudoku on the receptionist's desk, the blank squares revealing their solutions to her, straightforward, no mess.

"Penny's working on it," Heinrich said, as he returned. "Corporate told me to give you free rein of the place. Where'd you like to start?"

"Maybe we can tour the floor first, then go over questions somewhere quiet."

Penny appeared with a pair of work boots. She unfurled a bolt tucked under her arm, shaking out a yellow jumpsuit like the one Duane wore.

"This here's the smallest we've got. Come on, I'll show you where you can change."

The restroom had urinals along one wall and a series of plastic drawers along another. Labels were affixed to each cubby: RUPERT, JIMENEZ, MATTISEN, VALLS. Through the clouded plastic of the one marked PERESE, Sophie saw something silver and shiny. She opened the drawer an inch before stopping herself. *Most wrongs are the result of human weakness.* No more of that.

She emerged from the restroom moments later, the jumpsuit cuffs rolled up three turns. Her ambulance corps uniform had been about two sizes too big, but this was many times worse. Lost inside the sticky fabric, how could she not be conscious of how insubstantial she was? Thankfully there weren't any mirrors in the smelter — if she caught sight of herself looking like a little boy playing dress up, no way she'd manage to convince anyone else to take her seriously.

Duane handed her earplugs, hard hat, visor, protective apron, and spats. "Ready?"

Sweat misted her forehead as they entered the pot room. Sophie knew from her research that Mechanicsburg had three hundred carbon-lined pots but her notes hadn't indicated that the steel vessels were taller than she was — five rows of witches' cauldrons stretching the length of the plant.

"Don't get too close," Duane yelled over the ventilators.

"How hot are they?"

"Seventeen hundred degrees. Have to keep the aluminum molten. It cools, you've got a pot full of frozen product. In 2003, when we had the blackouts, it took seven weeks with everyone working overtime to dig out those pots."

Duane motioned for her to follow him down the pot line toward a holding furnace. Here were all her model's inputs, lined up in the order they ran through her spreadsheets.

A man in a yellow suit stood beside a pot, scratching something on a clipboard. Sophie followed Duane along the conveyer belt that carried aluminum ingots, silver bars that seemed fit for the vault of a bank. At the end of the belt, a robotic arm lifted the ingots, stacking them into pallets, steam curling as they cooled.

Duane's chest heaved.

"Are you OK?" Sophie asked.

"It happens." He swirled a finger at the ceiling. "Fluoride or something. You got what you need?"

She gave him a thumbs-up and followed him into a hallway. Men who looked like they belonged in Stockton passed by without pausing to look at her, but after months of cubicle-spying, she could tell she was being watched. Sophie had thought that because no one here knew Roll-Rite was considering merging with AlumiCorp, she'd slip through the plant, anonymous. She could only imagine how much more attention she would have attracted in her suit, which was about as subtle as a hearse.

She heard someone say, "How bad can it be if they sent *that* little thing?"

Sophie pretended not to hear, but she knew the answer: *It'll be bad. They'll tear out the equipment and send it to China or Brazil. The smelter will be another concrete skeleton where kids drink and bums sleep.* How could the plant's employees not realize that there wasn't a future for them at Roll-Rite? Why didn't they leave, seek opportunity elsewhere? Sophie wanted to scream at them to wake up.

Of course. The employees had to see how little business was going through their plant. Even though they didn't know about the merger, they must suspect that *something* was going to happen — that Roll-Rite would shutter the plant, or sell it, or reduce staff. They would have jumped ship if they could. Maybe there was nowhere for them to go. Maybe they weren't so different from her father, too proud to admit that their lives were spinning out of their control.

Duane led her to a room with a plywood desk. She pulled out her list of questions.

"So," Duane said. "How can I help?"

He asked this so kindly that Sophie had to shift her weight to dissipate her discomfort. He was putting on a good show, just like she was. She saw his future unfurling before her: a pink slip, the rising tide of credit card bills and mortgage payments. She hoped Duane really did have a daughter her age, a responsible young woman who'd look out for her dad. She took a deep breath and stared at the list on her lap: *How many days last quarter were fewer than eighty percent of this smelter's pots running?* She uncapped her pen.

Vasu Mehta

Vasu bought some smokehouse almonds and Butterfingers at Hudson News while he waited for his flight to Delhi to board. His luggage was stuffed with perfume, flash drives, and chocolates that Aditi had stockpiled for his sister and aunties, but in his haste, he had forgotten to pack food for the plane. Now that Hutchinson was presenting the merger to his board in two weeks, international diligence was urgent. Vasu had known Ethan would not acknowledge his nastiness last month when Vasu had begged to go to India, but it took every ounce of his painstakingly cultivated subservience to remain calm when Ethan had dared say, why haven't we gotten to the international assets before now?

Vasu had planned the site visits so he would have an overnight in Delhi first, to say good-bye to his mother. He had been so focused on finding a way to get to his family, but now that he was en route, he dreaded facing Dipti and his father and seeing himself as they must: the son who arrived only at the last minute.

He was walking to the gate, passport in hand, when his BlackBerry buzzed with Aditi's call.

"They took her to Varanasi," she said. "Vasu, she's gone."

A numbness spread from his fingertips and up his limbs, froze his tongue.

"Vasu? Are you there?"

Twenty-six hours and he would have been by her side.

"Meera and I are on standby for tomorrow night's flight," Aditi said. "Dipti said they will wait for you, for the funeral. Meera and I may not get there in time but —"

"I wasn't there."

We are now boarding flight number 2749 to Delhi from gate 43.

He queued up, bumping into an elderly woman in a saffron sari who glared at him like she knew exactly what a disappointment he was.

$$$

Vasu, clad in white, head freshly shaved, bore one of the front poles of the cane bed that held his mother. The procession descended the *ghats* of Varanasi, stepping down to the wide, sludgy gray Ganges. His mother was cocooned inside gold-embroidered silk and strewn with jasmine garlands and rose petals. His father carried the left pole of the bier, his stoop worse since Vasu had seen him last, his eyes fixed on the horizon. Vasu's uncle and cousin bore the rear, respectfully silent. They paused at the entrance to the funeral ground, where Dipti and the aunties were not allowed because they might cry. Everything was backwards. His sister was the one who had been here with his mother. She should be in his place, he demoted to hers. Dipti looked at him for a moment before she left, head cocked, lips pressed thin, the same way she had looked seventeen years ago when he left for Cornell and she stayed behind.

Vasu's bare feet sank into the black mud that formed the steep slope to the river. The bier shifted forward on his shoulders, so pitifully light, his mother's shrunken body making him suspect that his absence had only prolonged her agony. A steady pulse sounded, men chopping firewood. Dark smoke rose from six pyres burning at the shore. The sun hung heavily on the horizon, a reminder that he was always late, that they had flouted custom by delaying the cremation past the first twenty-four hours so that Vasu could carry out the duties of chief mourner, as a son should. He told himself that this was the most important part: carrying his mother to the holy Ganges, breaker of the cycle of birth and rebirth.

Vasu and the other men carried his mother to the river for her final dip before lighting the pyre, touching the torch to the five points of her body. The smell of sandalwood rose to meet them. Vasu's father took one last look at the pyre, clasped his hands behind his back, and left without meeting Vasu's gaze. Vasu watched him disappear, pale scalp shiny in the sun, humped shoulders resigned. Vasu sank to a crouch. As chief mourner, he would stay here the next few hours to tend the cremation. The skin on his arms and cheeks grew hot from the flame. The shroud sucked inward as it burned, as though she was not inside at all. The last time he had seen her, she had asked what Meera wanted to be when she grew up. He had lied and said that she wanted to be a banker like him, an educated professional, not an artist. That had made her smile for a moment before she was racked by coughing — an awful, gravelly wheezing that he would never forget.

He had barely spoken with Dipti or his father, and tomorrow, he would disappoint them again when he left for Roll-Rite's Uttar Pradesh smelter. Aditi and Meera would arrive to carry out the full mourning that he could not, but their presence would not make up for his absence. It was his own fault. Delaying diligence would arouse suspicion as to why he had pushed so hard to come here last month. He was ashamed that no one at Sterling could know about his mother's death, that even in this way, he could not be properly respectful.

Rowboats carrying tourists pushed off from the shore. At sunset, the tourists would light candles and float them on the river with offerings of marigolds, as Vasu had done once, when he was newly married. He wondered if the guides pointed to him when they explained to the tourists that for Hindus a person once born never dies, that a funeral is not a time for sadness but respect, that every Hindu hopes to die in Varanasi so he can be released from the toil of reincarnation, of life. Vasu wondered if he fooled the tourists, if they thought he was a good son.

$$$

A cow blocked the entrance to the Uttar Pradesh smelter, the crown jewel of Roll-Rite's international assets. Vasu's driver exited the sedan and shooed the animal off the road. The cow trotted beside the window, sores splattered across its flank. Why Aditi wanted to move back here, he could not understand. The garbage, the disease, the crowding, they seemed to grow worse every time Vasu returned, and the funeral had only reminded him that being here would not dispel his guilt. He would be a disappointment no matter what.

His driver dropped him at the smelter compound. The grounds were devoid of any proper plant life though just a few kilometers back, the road was dotted with guava orchards and drumstick plants. Dark chunks littered the dirt, strange and stone-like. It was not until his nose ran that he realized he was staring at discarded pot liners, cyanide and fluoride, hazardous waste that in the US would be sealed and buried. No wonder nothing grew here. Pollution was to be expected, but the wasteland before him had previously existed only in his nightmares.

"Let me make sure I understand," Vasu said. The plant manager seated across from him wore a pointy collar and flared trousers straight out of *Saturday Night Fever*. "The blackouts have lasted more than four hours *three times* this quarter?"

The manager's head wobbled, the local gesture of obfuscation. The inability to elicit a direct negative answer irritated Vasu more each time he returned to India. The manager refused to deliver news he knew Vasu would not like: the constant outages left the smelter's pots without a source of electricity to keep the aluminum molten, leaving the plant with 164 pots of hardened aluminum. Digging out and repairing frozen pots took weeks, sometimes months. Between the cost to repair the pots and the lost production hours, each blackout would have eroded ten, twenty million dollars of profit. Vasu stared at the manager in disbelief.

"You have the figures, no?" Vasu asked.

The plant manager thumbed through some files and slid a few pages to Vasu.

Vasu's suspicion had been correct: the blackouts completely canceled out whatever profit the plant made. These operational issues could not be solved without building an on-site power plant to ensure a reliable source of electricity. Such a project would cost — what, half a billion? And that was before bribing the local politicians to get permission to build. Not only was there none of the upside he had told Ethan he would find, there was massive downside.

If business was this bad at the Uttar Pradesh smelter, Vasu could only imagine the dysfunction that awaited him at the twelve other sites he would visit in India, Indonesia, and Brazil. How was he, the biggest proponent of value in Roll-Rite's international operations, going to explain to Ethan that these plants were a catastrophe?

Ethan Pearce

Ethan strode off the elevator early Saturday morning, laptop case swung over his shoulder, garment bag dangling from a hooked finger. He filled his lungs with the familiar Sterling smell: stale takeout, ink cartridges, citrus cleaning solution. After seven weeks of diligence, they were finally home. What he'd seen at Roll-Rite's Pittsburgh headquarters. Fat waiting to be trimmed, hundreds of millions in cost savings. Carbonell and his management team should be ashamed.

As Ethan turned the corner, Sophie nearly walked straight into him. She blinked the same way Camille used to when he interrupted her practicing, like she hadn't quite caught up.

"Welcome back," she said, her lips tilting into a smile that was almost a dare.

"Is Vasu in yet?"

She nodded.

"Grab him and swing by, so we can all touch base."

She was a strange one, so deeply in her head that she seemed uncomfortable in her skin. As she hurried off, he found himself wondering what kind of man would go for her. Maybe a puppy-faced guy she knew from high school who wore his khakis a little too high: not bad looking, but amateurish. Yes, he thought, that was it. Fine. As long as it didn't interfere with her work.

Ethan couldn't recall a single instance during these past few months when Sophie had pushed back or made noise that someone was waiting for her at home. Vasu was the one whose commitment Ethan doubted, especially after the schlock he'd written trashing Roll-Rite's international assets. Sophie's diligence memo, on the other hand, was spot on.

Ethan ran his hand over the cool promise of his clean desktop. People said a man's home was his castle, but Ethan never felt more powerful than when he was seated at his desk. He reached into his Sterling mug, pulled out one of his favorite superfine pens, and started a to-do list. He'd filled half a page when Vasu appeared, hair shorn to a military buzz.

"Nice haircut," Ethan said.

"Thanks."

Vasu chewed on his pen. Each of the dozen times Ethan's mother had quit smoking, she'd chewed on lollipop sticks, toothpicks, anything she could find.

"Patch or gum?" Ethan asked.

Vasu looked surprised. "Patch."

"What made you quit?" Ethan's mother used to quit every year on January 2 and she'd always be smoking again by February.

"Something I saw in India."

Whatever it was, Vasu didn't want to tell him. Fine. Ethan didn't know why he'd wasted time asking in the first place. "I'm all for health. But we all need to be in top form these next few months — I can't have you losing focus."

"Of course not," Vasu said sarcastically.

Ethan glared: check that attitude at the door.

Sophie stumbled in, struggling with a stack of Redwelds. Ethan added another line to his to-do list as Vasu rose to help Sophie with her folders. Vasu dropped the stack on Ethan's desk with a thud.

"So here we are," Ethan said, "all home safe." He leaned back in his chair and regarded his troops, reunited after a month in the trenches. "First of all." He looked at Sophie. "I know everyone's been working round-the-clock. Don't think it doesn't get noticed." He drew a line through the plus sign at the top of his list: positive encouragement.

"Second thing." He locked eyes with Vasu. "I shouldn't need to remind you that our job is to give Hutchinson reasons to pay up, not to scare him off. Roll-Rite doesn't have to sell, and they're certainly not going to sell for cheap. Don't forget it."

Vasu opened his mouth, but Ethan raised his hand for silence. *That* was precisely the problem: Vasu had gotten too comfortable contradicting him. Ethan pulled out the memo Vasu had written arguing Roll-Rite's international assets were worthless, maybe even a liability.

"I'm sure there's plenty of untapped potential in the international assets. Find it. You're going to write a new memo. A positive one. When you're done, follow document retention protocol: delete the first draft." Ethan's shredder made short work of Vasu's stupidity.

Vasu wasn't even looking at him. Sophie stared at her lap.

"Got it, Vasu?"

Vasu nodded limply.

"Now get going," Ethan said. "I want a draft on my desk by ten A.M."

11

Saturday, March 1, 2008

Jake Hutchinson

Hutch sat in the alumicorp board room that Saturday morning, telling himself what he'd told his little brother Tommy the first time Tommy got beat up: don't let them see you're scared. If the directors seated around the conference table saw that they'd gotten to him, they'd only pummel him harder. Gene Marson was inching forward in his chair, shifting his weight from haunch to haunch, ready to pounce and rip a piece out of him. Hutch had told Tommy that the next time the bullies closed in, he should pick the biggest guy and pop him right between the eyes.

"Tell me, Jake." Gene Marson stared at him over the edge of thick glasses. "Do you have any idea who the bastard is who's betting against our company?"

The directors murmured, each probably thinking he would've done better than Hutch, if he were running the company. Hutch would probably feel the same way two decades from now, when he was in their position, paid six figures for showing up at four or five board meetings each year.

Hutch was sick over AlumiCorp's plummeting stock price, and he looked Marson directly in the eye so he knew it. "We don't know the identity of our short seller. Not yet."

Gene Marson leaned over to whisper to Dick Weintraub, the wattled director to his right. Wasn't hard to guess which directors were with Marson: Buddy Roche, Roberto Morales. Probably Scottie Farrell, Vince Cupertino, Mary Anne Hyde. That gave Marson half the vote, one short of what he'd need to oust Hutch. Weintraub must be Marson's best hope for swinging the vote his way. Which meant that if Hutch wanted to save his neck, he needed to sell Weintraub on his large strategic transaction.

"Gentlemen," Hutch said. "Let's focus on our agenda."

Hutch clicked his remote to advance the slides. A map of the United States fluttered onto the screen behind him, the combined operations of Roll-Rite and AlumiCorp shaded with stars and stripes — Sophie's idea. Dick Weintraub leaned forward. Mary Anne Hyde's eyes went wide. Even Gene Marson looked impressed.

"Roll-Rite and AlumiCorp might be number two and number three, but together, we'll be a force to be reckoned with. We'll surpass Midwest Metals in —"

"I have some questions," Gene Marson said.

Hutch had only reached page five of the forty-page presentation. Gene Marson wasn't going to let him finish.

Gene removed his glasses — not a good sign. "Number one. How many of our guys do you want to let go?"

The directors exchanged agitated whispers. Cheap shot, painting Hutch as the antagonist, pitting his board against him right from the get-go. Hutch could feel his underarms growing wet. He prayed sweat circles wouldn't show through his shirt.

"I don't *want* to let any guys go," Hutch said. "Look. I know this board's been reluctant to take any actions that'd lead to layoffs. Lord knows I have too. The beauty of this transaction —"

"How many, Jake?"

"The beauty of this transaction is in the cost savings. With the oversupply issues we're facing, we have no choice but to cut staff. This deal is a chance to implement the tough decisions. If we merge with Roll-Rite, we'll be able to save as many jobs as we can."

Marson smacked his open palm against the table. *"How many?"*

"Fourteen thousand, six thousand of ours, eight thousand of Roll-Rite's."

Shouts erupted.

"We can't do that to our guys!"

"The unions'll eat us alive."

"Think of the press!"

Hutch let them go at it. They wanted to protect AlumiCorp's workers. So did he. But the board had to face the facts: the layoffs were inevitable.

"I'd like to remind everyone that McKinsey recommended last year that we let go *nine thousand guys*," Hutch said. "Since they did that study, business has only gotten worse. If you think about it, this transaction's *saving* three thousand jobs."

Gene Marson raised his hand, calling order. "Gentlemen, let's not get bogged down in politics."

It made Hutch livid that Marson was taking the moral high ground. Hutch told himself to stay calm. His temper was his worst enemy.

"Question number two," Marson said. "Seventy-two a share seems awfully rich. Why would we possibly offer that much?"

All eyes were on Hutch.

He cleared his throat. "Well, Gene, I don't see how we can address purchase price without first getting into strategic rationale." He advanced the slides to page eight. "In the left-hand column, you'll see —"

Dick Weintraub jumped in. "Jake, the rationale for this deal is compelling. But what I'm trying to wrap my head around is how, when the market's been trading at historic highs — at levels close to the dot-com bubble — you can argue that the market is *under*valuing Roll-Rite stock by nearly twenty percent. Why would we do a deal that's so out of line with the market?"

Hutch could feel the noose tightening around his neck. If he hadn't sold Dick Weintraub, the deal was done for, and him with it.

$$$

The doorknob of the den rattled later that evening. Trish's muffled voice came through the locked door.

"Gene Marson's on the phone."

Hutch flipped the switch on his train table and the Pennsylvania Flyer slowed to a halt. Trish thrust the cordless through the crack, the diamond bracelet he'd bought her for their twentieth anniversary jingling against her watch. Her fingers were crossed. He kissed them for luck.

Hutch took a deep breath. "Gene."

"Jake. Good news. The directors are on board with your transaction."

Hutch could've kissed the bastard.

"We thank you for all the hard work you've put in," Gene said. "The board's not supportive at the price you were considering, but we're behind you if you decide to offer sixty-seven a share, a ten percent premium."

Sixty-seven! No way Bruce Carbonell would go for that.

"I can take it to Bruce," Hutch said, "but I gotta tell you, I don't think it'll get done at sixty-seven."

"I'm sure you'll do everything in your power to convince him. Jake, if you can pull off this deal on our terms, the board will be willing to overlook your disappointing performance."

Hutch gave the train a little push, sending it over the bridge.

Bruce Carbonell wouldn't accept sixty-seven a share unless Hutch threw something in to sweeten the deal. The only thing Hutch had to offer was himself. If he wanted to keep the deal alive, he'd have to forget about running the new company. The worst part was, Gene knew it.

Hutch pinched the bridge of his nose. "Gene, I've put decades into this company."

"And you've been well compensated for them."

If he refused to push the deal forward, he'd be ousted. But stepping down as the result of a merger, when one of the two CEOs was going to have to step down regardless — that was a graceful way to leave. He could go to future employers and sell the deal he'd brought home for AlumiCorp. He'd look like a success. But shopping around . . . He'd have to start over. Gene left him little choice. Hutch couldn't decide what killed him most: that Gene Marson had won, or that Hutch had created the noose Gene would hang him with. Since when had this deal become bigger than him?

"You let us know what Bruce says," Gene Marson said.

It took four fingers of bourbon before Hutch could call Carbonell.

Vasu Mehta

Vasu could not concentrate on the printouts spread across his desk. The skin below his right rib itched from the NicoDerm patch he had stuck there that morning, hoping he could reroute the course of his body's deterioration. In the three days since Hutchinson had submitted the bid, AlumiCorp had come to a standstill, creating empty gaps in Vasu's day that would have made perfect cigarette breaks. He reminded himself again that his mother had contracted lung cancer without smoking a day in her life. He reached for a pen to chew.

Sophie burst through his door. "Do you think his silence could be a bargaining tactic?"

It took Vasu a moment to realize she was talking about Carbonell.

"What do you think's taking him so long?" she asked.

"I think you need to *sit tight.*"

"I'll bet they're working on their counter. Seventy-two a share, where his options are in the money."

Did it even matter? Rolling mills and smelters would change their signs from "Roll-Rite" to "AlumiCorp." The lawyers would make a few million on the deal documents. The world would hardly be different.

"It's driving me crazy," Sophie said.

"I can see that."

"We have to do something."

Sophie would come to understand her impotence in her own time.

"Are you OK, Vasu?"

"Fine," he said flatly.

"You've got some ink." She touched her lips.

He tore a sheet of paper from his legal pad and wiped his lips. Sophie's mouth opened for a moment, then shut. He must have only made it worse.

"I don't get it," she said. "How are you so calm?"

Ever since the funeral, it had become increasingly difficult to spin his thoughts the way Sterling demanded. "My trip to India gave me perspective."

"I want to go there someday. Everyone says it's life changing."

He traced the outline of the NicoDerm patch under his shirt, thinking of the electrodes that must have been affixed to his mother's gaunt flesh while she was in the hospital, while he was here.

"Sophie, I'll let you know as soon as I hear anything on Alumi-Corp."

"We should call Hutch."

"That wouldn't do any good."

Her foot tapped furiously. "We say we're trying to get a head start on next steps, get him talking, see if there's news."

"If you're that bored, check in with Blumenstein. See if he needs anything on Midwest Metals."

She sprang from her chair. "I'm going to talk to Ethan."

"Sophie, it's really not a good idea —"

She was already heading off down the hall. She seemed to think that Ethan had her back. That man looked out for no one but himself. Ethan looked at people and asked, *what will you buy me?* It was a game to him, making people give him what he wanted. Vasu had played right into Ethan's hands, pushing to go to India for the wrong reasons, leaving himself no option but to write the diligence memo Ethan wanted to read. And where had it gotten him? He had been too late. That was one difference between them: Ethan succeeded in getting what he wanted, and Vasu did not. Another: Vasu regretted his mistakes.

Three years ago, Vasu was sitting in Ethan's office when an assistant knocked to say Ethan's wife was on the phone — it was urgent. Ethan was still a senior vice president then, gunning for promotion. Vasu was an associate. AlumiCorp was auctioning off its portfolio of primary aluminum assets and their lead bidder had just dropped out. Ethan picked up the phone and dispatched his wife in less than a minute. At the time, the dismissal had seemed standard enough — *Come on, Camille, how urgent can it really be? . . . Coming home now isn't an option. . . . Well, you'll just have to sit tight.*

The next morning, the office was frantic with whispers. Ethan's wife had passed away, a sudden illness. If anyone else suspected that Camille had killed herself, he kept it to himself. Vasu did not even tell Aditi. He steeled himself for Ethan's return from what he presumed would be a long leave of absence, knowing he must meet his boss's gaze without any hint of an accusation. Ethan appeared in the office the afternoon of the funeral — he did not even take the day off. He accepted Vasu's condolences with a brief nod, perfectly composed.

Vasu had met Camille once at an Industrial Group holiday party. She was so deeply inside herself that she seemed to exist on a different plane. Perhaps that was why she and Ethan were together: both were supremely self-involved. How could Camille not have regretted her choice? Sometimes Vasu wondered whether Ethan had it out for him because he knew Vasu knew that even if he was not directly responsible for his wife's death, he could have prevented it.

Vasu had made plenty of mistakes, but life's most important decision, he had gotten right. Thirteen years ago, his mother had arranged for her cousin's friends to bring their daughter over for tea. After Aditi and her parents had left, his mother had bitten into a *jalebi* and said, *that girl is a good bet.* After twelve years, Vasu was certain that whatever small happiness was his, it was because of Aditi. He wondered if she would say the same about him.

Sophie Landgraf

The floor was dead. Ethan and the rest of the senior guys had gone home hours ago. The second years in the quad next to Sophie's were eating takeout in a conference room. Still, Sophie double-checked that no one was in listening range before calling her doorman. Will still hadn't picked up the box she'd left in her apartment lobby that morning.

Of course the one night she was actually free to go home at a normal hour was the one night she couldn't — Will had finally agreed to pick up his stuff on the condition that he didn't have to see her. They'd settled it over terse emails since he still refused to talk to her on the phone. At the time, it had been cheap for Sophie to promise they wouldn't run into each other in her lobby tonight because she'd assumed she'd be at work, as usual. She couldn't have known that Steelers would be in a holding pattern.

Will thought she was the antichrist, and she'd thought they'd be friends by now. This only confirmed that they were better off apart — they occupied entirely different realities. What she cared about the most at this point was getting his stuff out of her apartment. You couldn't hide a box that size in a three-hundred-square-foot space. It was the first thing she saw when she walked through the door.

How did Ethan handle seeing constant reminders of his wife? It had taken two years before Sophie's father was able to smell lavender without falling apart. Ethan had to walk the same streets he had with his wife, maybe even sleep in the same apartment. Just like Sophie's father, Ethan avoided mentioning her — proof that he hadn't let her go. Every surface in Ethan's apartment was probably crammed with pictures of her. The perfume she'd worn probably sat on his dresser.

Someone tapped her shoulder.

"Oh my god, Donnigan. You scared me. What do you want?"

"Five million dollars and a wife who's nice to me." He sat backwards in Jordanne's old seat. "I was walking by and saw you looking all Sylvia Plath. Everything OK?"

"Donnigan, you never cease to amaze me."

"I can be perceptive once in a while. Just don't tell — wouldn't want to ruin my rep."

"I meant I'm amazed you know about Sylvia Plath."

"Spill it, Landgraf. What's wrong?"

After what had happened with Jordanne, she wasn't sure if it was wise to confide in him, but it was such a relief to have someone at Sterling — someone in New York — express any interest in her happiness. She told herself that her problems with Will were strictly personal, nothing that could be used against her in the office. She'd be more careful this time. "Promise you won't make fun?"

"Cross my heart."

"Will's decided I'm the devil."

Donnigan slapped his knees. "Come on. I'll buy you a drink."

"Oh my god, yes." She grabbed her bag off of Jordanne's old desk.

"Heard anything from that one?" he asked.

"Not really." Jordanne had sent her half a dozen emails since she'd been laid off. Sophie had deleted them. She didn't know what they'd said. "This is mean but . . . Do you know what Will said about her?"

"That she was a pretentious bitch?"

"You too, huh?" She guessed she was the last to know.

Donnigan took her to a bar where all the patrons wore suits in black, gray, or navy. Sophie blended in perfectly.

Donnigan ordered a gin and tonic. "And the lady would like a . . ."

Instead of her usual rum and Diet Coke, Sophie wanted a serious drink, like Ethan would have. "A vodka martini."

"Cheap date," Donnigan said.

"I need a new drink. I'm trying things out."

"Taste all the wines before buying a bottle."

She stared at him. "My mom used to say that."

"She's insanely proud of you, isn't she?"

Sophie peeled the corner off a paper coaster. It hadn't hit home until now that no one at Sterling — no one in New York, actually — knew about the biggest thing that had ever happened to her. "My mom's dead."

Donnigan rocked awkwardly on his stool. "Oh. Geez. I don't know what to say."

"People think you have to say something but you really don't."

Their drinks appeared, breaking the silence. Sophie raised her glass. "Cheers. To . . ."

"To that guy over there who's looking at you." He jutted his chin at a man with apish features, hairy knuckles wrapped around a scotch on the rocks.

"No, he's not."

"Well, he is now."

Sophie blushed. If she squinted, the guy could almost pass for Ethan. Something about the set of his shoulders.

"Seriously, you should get back out there," Donnigan said. "Any dates lately?"

"Right now I'm dating Steelers. He's kind of possessive."

"You gotta jump back in. What good's waiting?"

"Mmm, yeah, I don't know about that." She'd been with Will since she was eighteen — a child, really — and she wanted to get to know herself on her own terms before jumping into a new thing with a new guy. There was exactly one man who would tempt her to make an exception, and she wasn't about to get involved with her boss. Not that Ethan would ever be interested in someone like her. Maybe one day she'd meet a guy at a different bank, an Ethan version 2.0. A guy who commanded your respect.

"Just pick a guy and go for it. Which one doesn't matter much."

"How can you say that?"

"We're all looking for someone to fill the void the last person left. We find someone new, it isn't about them. It's about filling the void."

"Tell that to someone who lost the love of his life. Tell him he should substitute someone else. Tell that to Ethan."

Donnigan smiled knowingly. Sophie sipped her martini, wishing she could take it back.

"Guess what I saw today," she said. "Sinclair picking his nose at his desk. Not a fake scratch — actual full-frontal digging."

She had to be more careful. Jordanne had taught her not to let a colleague know anything she didn't want all of Sterling to know. Donnigan was a good friend, yes, but he could also be a liability.

Sophie sat in her cubicle later that evening, doing some shopping while she waited for her doorman to call and say Will had picked up the box, so she could go home. Was Gucci Envy the right thank-you present for all of the help Kim had given with her father? Thierry Mugler's Angel?

Sophie's phone rang. Her chest seized when she saw the prefix was AlumiCorp's headquarters.

"Sophie." She recognized Hutch's voice.

Her heart flew into her stomach and back again. Of all the people on Project Steelers, she couldn't believe he'd called her.

"Listen. I've got some news."

Hutch sounded so deflated—Sophie braced herself for word that their deal had died.

"Roll-Rite's board gave our bid the green light," he said flatly.

"Wait—really?" When she'd pictured this moment, she and Ethan had been sitting in his office, just the two of them. Ethan answered his phone, pumped his fist in the air, and fell on her, squeezing her tight.

"Carbonell's board listens to him. Lucky guy. They'll recommend the shareholders vote in favor when we announce. This is the final stretch."

"So why don't you sound excited?"

He chuckled. "That's what I like about you, Sophie. You still sense things." She heard paper crinkle, like Hutch was unwrapping something. "Carbonell's going to run the company."

"What? Why?"

"It's complicated," he said, his mouth full. "Let's just say, I didn't have much choice."

"But if Carbonell won't move on succession, you don't have to do the deal, right?"

"This train, Sophie, it's gonna keep moving, with or without us. Did you see where our stock closed today? Down another two points."

"We can't give too much credence to short-term market fluctuations," she said, repeating the phrase she'd heard Ethan say so many times. "This is a long-term value proposition, right?"

Hutch was silent for a moment. "Can you see the stars over there, Sophie? Make a wish for me."

Sophie peered through the glass walls of Sinclair's office. Even now, at almost nine o'clock, the sky was bright with light from Times Square. A few pinpricks shone among the haze, but Sophie couldn't tell whether they were stars, planes, or something else entirely. That was the thing about New York. So many bright things, they drowned each other out.

Ethan Pearce

Lawyers didn't understand the first thing about business. Which was why Sophie and Vasu were camped out in Ethan's office, where they were doing three separate reviews of the merger agreement to make sure the business points were intact. Sophie slid a page in front of Ethan and pointed to the second condition to closing, a good catch. He added it to his list, a document so tidy that it made him believe for a moment that all was right with the world.

Ethan's mind was one hundred percent engaged, efficient and productive, every synapse turned on. Camille used to say that sometimes, when she was playing the violin, her mind turned off, the world fell away, the self vanished, and it was just music, free-floating in space and time. *I like to think that's what it would be like to be dead.* He'd said she sounded like his mother's neighbors in North Carolina, the ones who said that the earth was about to be wiped clean and only those who adhered to the one true religion would be saved. *Beethoven Opus 132, third movement. That's my religion.*

A knock sounded against the glass.

"Grant Sinclair's on the phone," his assistant said. "He's calling from the Mort Cahn Conference."

Another conference where Sinclair got to hang out with his squash buddies. Sinclair's laziness never ceased to amaze Ethan.

"Take a message." He went back to his list. "Some of us are doing real work."

"He says it's urgent."

Ethan yanked the phone toward him and put Sinclair on speaker.

"Ethan, listen. Drew Klinghammer's about to unveil —"

"His next big call." It was all over Bloomberg. The famous short seller was announcing his next big pick at the conference, in front of a thousand members of the investment community. "I know."

He motioned for Sophie and Vasu to get back to work.

"They just handed out the slides," Sinclair said. "Ethan, it's AlumiCorp."

"What?" Hutchinson had been whining for months about a phantom short seller, but Klinghammer? How had they not known this before? Ethan couldn't imagine a worse possible answer. Klinghammer didn't make calls often, but when he did, he made them big, and he made them right. His track record was so good that when he shorted a stock, hedgie lemmings jumped onto the trade and the company's stock got decimated. When Klinghammer was through with AlumiCorp, there wouldn't be a company left to merge with Roll-Rite. "What's Klinghammer's thesis?"

"Declining orders, inflated cost base, labor issues."

"The truth," Vasu muttered.

Ethan put Sinclair on mute and told Vasu to go take a walk.

"This is *not* what we need right now," Ethan said as Vasu slumped out of his office. "I should go, Grant. I need to tell Hutchinson before someone else does."

Sophie's eyes were wide, her mouth open in a little O. "Who's Klinghammer?"

"Ever heard of Sentinel Co.?"

Sophie shook her head.

"Exactly." Sentinel was Klinghammer's big call four years ago.

Ethan shouted at his assistant to get Jake Hutchinson on the phone.

"I don't understand," Sophie said. "Can one guy shorting a stock really be that bad?"

"That's why you're calling Hutchinson with me. You're going to tell him exactly that." Why Hutchinson trusted this twenty-two-year-old more than his own judgment, Ethan didn't know and didn't care, but Hutchinson did, and Ethan would be a fool not to use it.

12

Sunday, March 16, 2008

Jake Hutchinson

TWO WEEKS AGO, WHEN HUTCH had promised to cede control of the new company to Carbonell, it had seemed like things couldn't get worse. Who would've thought that now he'd be fighting to keep his company afloat. He paced the length of the Sterling conference room, praying his bankers could deliver a miracle. Sinclair hunched in his chair, clearly exhausted. Ethan stared straight ahead, unfazed. The Indian fellow just looked bored. But Sophie, poor thing — she looked so scared, so lost. He wanted to give her a hug.

"I blame myself," Hutch said. "Got wrapped up in the merger negotiations — I should've prioritized tracking down the short seller, doing damage control."

"No amount of damage control is a match for Klinghammer." Sinclair pressed his thumb and forefinger against his eyelids. "What exactly did the rating agencies say?"

Hutch unwrapped the glazed donut he'd picked up on the way from his meeting at Standard & Poor's. "It's no good. Klinghammer's brainwashed them." The rating agencies were a bunch of ninnies. AlumiCorp paid them to evaluate their debt, spoon-feeding financial analysis, practically guaranteeing a favorable credit rating that would allow AlumiCorp to borrow on cheap terms. But Klinghammer had turned those rubber stamps into loaded guns aimed straight at Hutch's chest.

Hutch downed his donut in two bites. "They said they're lowering our credit rating unless we announce layoffs. Sorry, unless we 'drastically rationalize our cost base.' What a load of bull." The downgrade would increase AlumiCorp's interest rate to more than the company could afford. AlumiCorp would go into distress. Roll-Rite would run for the hills. AlumiCorp stock would nosedive, and Klinghammer would make a fortune. Klinghammer was doing what any short seller worth his salt would do: making the market come to him.

Ethan leaned back, relaxed. "Let's back up. The rating agencies think that if AlumiCorp remains an independent company, you need to cut costs. Fine. So does everyone here. That's the whole point of the merger. What did they say when they learned about our deal?"

"I tried to educate them, but can you believe it, they wouldn't buy it."

"What were their concerns?" Ethan asked.

"They say the cost savings aren't guaranteed."

"When are they ever? So how long do we have?"

"A week to come up with something to make them comfortable with the transaction." And when they came up with nothing, the agencies would give MergeCo such a low credit rating that the new company would be dead in the water.

"A week?" Sophie asked. "What are we supposed to do with a week?"

"Heck if I know." Hutch could feel Roll-Rite slipping away.

"Are there any assets you can sell to pay down debt?" Sinclair asked.

Ethan answered for Hutch. "We've already been down that road."

"And no additional guarantors who'd pledge to make the payments, if the company can't?" Sinclair asked.

Hutch shook his head. He wished it were that simple. He'd served as guarantor for his daughter Libby when she signed the lease on her first apartment in Chicago last fall. If Hutch hadn't pledged himself as someone legally responsible for the rent, she never would've been able to live there. But AlumiCorp didn't have a daddy to act as guarantor.

Sinclair's cheeks puffed out. "Ah, well. Jake, what can I say? I'd guaranty AlumiCorp's debt myself, if it were legal."

Wait a darn minute.

"*Is* it legal?" Hutch asked. "Can you guaranty the debt — can Sterling guaranty it?"

Ethan and Sinclair exchanged glances. Sophie leaned forward, peering around Vasu to get a look at Ethan.

"Jesus, Jake," Sinclair said. "That's quite an ask. How could our firm —"

"Look. Your firm's writing my board an opinion as we speak, swearing this merger is fairly valued."

"Yes, but —"

"How much are you charging us for that again?" Hutch asked, though everyone in that room knew the fee was two million. "Seems to me that if the deal is fair, as you're testifying, AlumiCorp would never need to rely on its guarantor. So the guaranty shouldn't be any skin off your back, right?"

Ethan looked like he was enjoying Sinclair's discomfort.

"Ethan and I will talk to our Executive Committee," Sinclair said. "I should warn you — I'm not aware of our group ever having done such a thing. But we'll see what we can do."

Sophie Landgraf

Sophie didn't understand how Ethan could be so calm. He was sitting behind his desk, shoulders thrust back, chest puffed like he enjoyed filling his lungs with everyone else's panic. Hutch had been frantic when he left their offices an hour ago. Klinghammer was on the warpath, and as far as Sophie could see, they had nothing, but here they were, the two of them, in Ethan's office, and he was acting like everything was under control. He reminded her of her crew chief on the Stockton volunteer ambulance corps, a little man who seemed to double in stature during an emergency. The difference was that her crew chief deflated after the call was finished. Ethan seemed to just grow and grow.

"We'll have to get in front of ExCom this week if we want to get Hutchinson his guaranty in time," he said. "Sinclair's going to pull some strings, try to get us on ExCom's calendar for Thursday."

She'd never been to ExCom before — none of the analysts had. Only the toughest decisions and approvals went all the way to Sterling's high council. "What do you think the chances are they'll approve it?"

"Irrelevant."

"Sorry?"

"You stop and think about the probability of success versus failure, you get used to the idea of failure. We're not going to fail."

That was the thing about Ethan. He made huge claims sound so logical and authoritative that you actually believed him. Her mother had been that way.

He swiveled to face his computer. "Holy shhh . . ."

What had Klinghammer done now? "What's wrong?"

This might be the first time she'd ever seen Ethan looked confused. "I got an email from a guy I know at Bear Stearns — *here's my personal contact information, who knows how this is going to sort out* — it's an SOS."

She didn't understand.

"You've heard the rumors about how Bear doesn't have enough liquidity?"

Not really. "Sure."

"Mark my words, Bear's going to go bust tomorrow." He squinted the same way Kim's high school boyfriend used to when the Patriots game went into overtime. "Either they'll file for bankruptcy or they'll get bought for nothing. The market will tank. If there are stocks you've been meaning to buy, tomorrow's the day."

"What does this mean for our guaranty?"

"Nobody's going to want to extend credit unless they absolutely have to. Liquidity's going to dry up — for us, for the other banks."

"So we'll have to wait?" And in the meantime, Klinghammer would destroy AlumiCorp. Their deal would be finished.

Ethan looked up from his computer, perplexed. "Why would you say that?"

"If liquidity is scarce, Sterling will have to preserve its resources, right?"

She could tell from the twitch of his lip that she'd disappointed him.

"In this environment, we'll have to fight that much harder for our fair share," he said. "Sure, resources will tighten, and that will make our jobs tougher. But if we can't secure what our clients need, we might as well pack our bags and go home. A yellow light means speed up. We have to get to ExCom tomorrow, before everyone else does."

He made it sound so simple. She had so much left to learn.

$$$

Dawn spread over the skyscrapers outside Ethan's window. Sophie, Ethan, and Vasu were huddled over Ethan's normally immaculate desk, which was littered with drafts of the ExCom memo, half-finished burritos, laptops, and wrappers from Vasu's nicotine gum. Sophie's pulse was racing from too much caffeine. They only had eight hours until their meeting with ExCom.

Ethan tapped his pen against Vasu's valuation analysis. "I told you to crib this from the valuation we gave Hutchinson for his board. How much was it again? Four —?"

"Four hundred fifty-two million," Sophie said. She didn't need to look.

Vasu chewed on his pen. "That's what Hutchinson presented to his board, yes, but my diligence makes it —"

"We're using four fifty-two," Ethan said flatly.

"How can ExCom accurately assess Sterling's risk if we don't present the assets to the best of our knowledge?" Vasu had taken that exasperated tone with her before, but never with Ethan.

Sophie glanced up from her edits. Why was Vasu getting so worked up?

"To the best of our knowledge," Ethan said, "the assets are worth what someone will pay for them. And AlumiCorp's paying four hundred fifty-two million."

"Here," Vasu handed them each a sheet of paper. "I prepared this analysis."

Ethan glanced at the page and pushed it aside. It took about half a second for Sophie to look at the numbers and see that Vasu had messed up — he'd assigned the international assets a value of zero. How could he perform such sloppy analysis? They were all running on fumes. Vasu must not be thinking clearly.

"Um, Vasu?" She tried not to sound too critical. "I think there's a mistake on here." She slid his page under her chair.

Vasu handed the page back to her. "There's no mistake. That's the cost of two new power plants, one for the Uttar Pradesh smelter, one for the Indonesian smelter."

"Two new power plants?" What was he talking about? She waited to see if Ethan would correct Vasu, or at least look up from his markup. "That's not what's in the model, Vasu."

"I know." Vasu glared at Ethan.

Ethan scratched changes onto his draft, unperturbed. She shouldn't be the one grilling Vasu, but his numbers were wrong, and if Ethan wasn't going to correct him . . .

"Why would AlumiCorp need two new power plants?" she asked.

Vasu took a deep breath, as if he was about to tell her something he'd told her a million times. "Because you can't get any upside out of those smelters unless you solve the power outages."

Power outages? Normally, she wouldn't let on that she didn't understand Vasu, but this was too important to let go. "I don't get it. We would've found a problem like that in diligence."

"We did." The corner of Vasu's lip twitched. "Ethan remembers."

She thought back to diligence, when the three of them had met in this office, and Ethan told Vasu to rewrite a memo — yes, on the international assets. She remembered Ethan shredding the first draft. She hadn't paid any attention to it at the time.

She took another look at the analysis. If Vasu was right about the outages, the cost of building two new power plants would cancel out the $452 million of upside that they'd modeled. Or AlumiCorp could decide not to build the power plants, and the international assets would continue to lose money. Which meant the international assets were worthless.

"Ethan?" He didn't look up. "I think Vasu's right. We need to show ExCom —"

"The market's spoken," Ethan said flatly. "The assets are worth what someone's willing to pay for them: four hundred fifty-two million. That's what goes in the memo."

That didn't make sense. Yes, AlumiCorp valued the international assets at $452 million, but that was only because they, Sterling, had told AlumiCorp that there was $452 million to be gained from improving the plants. If that couldn't be done . . .

"We should at least show both," she said. "We could show ExCom a range, so they can —"

"That's not how it works." Ethan stood. "We're not going to get what we need out of ExCom if we don't put our best foot forward." He handed Sophie his edits. "Get me the revised draft by 10 A.M."

Ethan grabbed his swimming goggles and strode off. Vasu followed, slamming the door behind him. Sophie was left staring at the analysis with the big, fat zero next to the international assets. AlumiCorp never would have done the deal at this price if they'd thought the international assets were worthless. They probably wouldn't have done the deal at all. What had they done?

It was all her fault — she'd built the model supporting the $452 million valuation. She stared out Ethan's window at the midtown skyscrapers, building after building filled with people who didn't make mistakes. Could she really be to blame if she hadn't known her model was wrong? When they'd sent their valuation recommendation to Hutch, she'd been sure her numbers were one-hundred-percent right. If you thought about it, a model's results were only true at the moment they were calculated. New economic data was constantly being released, forcing you to revisit assumptions, changing your result. Her job was to build a model that was accurate at the time it was built. She'd done that. If anyone was to blame, it was Vasu. He'd checked her model, blessed her assumptions.

She looked at Ethan's edits sitting on her lap. Ethan must have his reasons for not including Vasu's analysis — he couldn't be asking them to just forget about what Vasu had seen during diligence, could he? There had to be something she didn't understand.

She had to talk to Vasu. She tried his office but it was empty, just harsh fluorescent lights. He wasn't by the coffee machine or the printer. She waited outside the men's room for ten minutes before it occurred to her to check the corner outside where Sterling smokers took cigarette breaks.

It was freezing out — Sophie wished she'd brought her coat. Vasu was leaning against Sterling, head tilted back, eyes half-closed, the same way Will looked when he smoked. Vasu didn't see her until she was right in front of him.

"You should've explained the outages to me," she said. "Before."

"Well, now you know." He gave a little bow. She couldn't tell whether he was mocking her for being so slow to figure it out.

She stamped her feet, to warm up. "What are we going to do?"

He offered her a cigarette, which she refused. "It's Ethan's call."

She scanned the sidewalk to confirm Ethan wasn't in earshot. "I get that the asset's worth what someone's willing to pay for it, but what's the harm in showing it both ways?"

Vasu motioned for her to follow him. He led her down the block, past vendors setting up food carts, the first shift of commuters. The fact that Vasu didn't want to be overheard only confirmed her suspicion that what Ethan was asking of them wasn't right.

Vasu stopped at a corporate plaza that she hadn't known existed, a windswept courtyard with concrete benches and an absurd amount of pigeons. A couple in sandals and socks inspected a map — why anyone would choose to get up this early, Sophie had no idea. Vasu picked the table farthest away from the tourists and shooed the birds.

She sat on the ice-cold bench. "We showed bad numbers to Hutch."

"You think Hutch is blameless?" He lit a fresh cigarette. "Why do you think we're here? Ethan needs the fees. Carbonell wants to maximize shareholder value. And Hutchinson?" Vasu blew his smoke away from her. "Hutchinson chose not to look at the numbers too closely. You've seen how badly he wants this deal. I guarantee you that if you got inside his head, you'd find an incentive to do this merger. Either that or he's an idiot, and someone who's been in this business that long can't be an idiot."

This must be how her father had felt at Christmas, when he'd said this wasn't how the world should be. "I guess I want to think they're better than that."

Vasu shrugged. "Worse deals have gotten done — can't think of one off the top of my head, but they have. What's surprising isn't that we are where we are, what's surprising is that it doesn't happen more often."

"We could write our own memo — Ethan wouldn't have to know. Or we could explain it to ExCom in the meeting . . ."

"You think ExCom cares what we think?" He pressed his index finger against the table. "Let me tell you how this meeting will go: The committee will say hello without looking up from their memos. Ethan will do all the talking. You and I will sit there like a pair of deaf mutes. It will be like we weren't even there."

"What about all shit flowing downhill? Don't we have to make sure ExCom knows?"

Vasu ground his cigarette into the concrete bench. "Everyone's selling something — ExCom knows that better than anyone."

She wanted to believe him.

He patted her shoulder and walked off.

The wind cut through Sophie's thin suit. The last thing she wanted right then was to head back to Sterling, so she stayed there, hugging herself against the cold.

Sophie sat in her cubicle, staring at Ethan's markup. The ExCom memo was due in four hours. Just last night, Ethan had seemed so calm, so rational, like he had everything under control. She wanted to think that he knew what he was doing, that he must have his reasons. Her brain was fuzzy from lack of sleep — there was almost surely something she was too slow to understand, something that would make it all make sense.

She wanted to talk to someone, but there weren't many people at Sterling she trusted. Besides, she had a sneaking suspicion that she should keep this between her, Ethan, and Vasu. Calling her father was out of the question — she had no intention of fueling his hatred of Sterling. Kim's phone went straight to voicemail. Maybe . . .

Nancy Cho's assistant said Nancy had gone down to the cafeteria to pick up some breakfast. Sophie headed for the elevator. She wasn't sure what she would say to Nancy. Even if she told her what was happening — which she absolutely couldn't, not under any circumstances — she already knew what Nancy would say: *don't go all Pollyanna on me.*

Sophie raced past cashiers, platters of bagels, pyramids of yogurts, fruit salad stations, cereal dispensers. In the back of the cafeteria, where the chefs made omelets to order, stood Nancy Cho, reading the paper. Sophie had to say hello twice before Nancy looked up.

Nancy cleared her throat and read, "*The Fed stated that it stepped in to avert the 'expected contagion' that would have followed the 'immediate failure' of Bear Stearns.* Christ."

Sophie craned her neck for a better view of the front page. "Bear? It blew up?"

"Whirlwind deal with J.P. Morgan. We're in for a rough ride. Sentiment's shifting against us."

"And I thought I was having a bad morning."

"*Only 6,500 of Bear's 13,500 employees will be retained.*"

"Half?"

"All the banks are going to have to defend themselves or else get taken over. It's our Pearl Harbor." Nancy stared at something behind Sophie's head. "Who do you think will be the next bank to lay people off?"

Sophie thought back to the December layoffs: Donnigan hiding under his desk with his vodka. Vasu squeezing her so tight when she'd told him they'd made it. Jordanne staring into her drawers, knowing there wasn't anything to take with her, just like Sophie would have been if Ethan hadn't protected her.

The chef slid Nancy a Styrofoam container.

"Can you imagine the fights over at Bear right now?" Nancy asked. "Everyone stepping on each other to save themselves?"

"Bosses lobbying to save their favorites?"

Nancy tapped Sophie's lapel. "Exactly."

· · ·

Sophie spread Ethan's edits across her desk. Vasu had said this was Ethan's call. And if things were about to get ugly, like Nancy said, now more than ever she needed to keep Ethan happy. Unless she wanted to follow Jordanne and half of Bear Stearns out the door.

Of all the people involved with the deal, people who had infinitely more experience than she did, who was she to say that something wasn't good enough for her when it was obviously good enough for everyone else? There was probably something she didn't understand. Ethan had been at the bank for seventeen years, with unbelievable success. He wouldn't have gotten this far at Sterling if he'd been doing anything the bank didn't want him to do.

She looked at the changes Ethan had made for the millionth time. Under the section titled "Risk Factors," Vasu's original version said, *the target's international assets are plagued by systemic outages due to local electricity constraints.* Instead, Ethan had written, *the acquirer's plans to bring the target's international assets up to industry best practices are subject to operational risk.* Both versions were true, if you thought about it. Like Ethan said, Alumi-Corp *was* planning to improve the assets, and he flagged the possibility that they wouldn't be able to.

Her cursor hovered over the line item for the international assets. Ethan had crossed out Vasu's $0 and written $452. Ethan knew what was best. She typed: 4-5-2. Like Ethan had said, an asset was worth whatever someone was willing to pay for it.

Ethan Pearce

It was a Sterling tradition that before meeting with ExCom, you rubbed the shiny nose of the Jeff Koons stag sculpture sitting outside Chip Masey's office. Ethan wasn't a superstitious man, but he gave the stag a good rub all the same. Masey's office door was open — their division head and the other dinosaurs were waiting for them. Ethan had presented to the division's high council only once before, when it wasn't clear whether the fees on the Relia-Run restructuring were worth the reputational hit of advising a company that had been found guilty of accounting fraud. The Alumi-Corp guaranty was nothing by comparison.

"Ready, folks?" Ethan asked.

Vasu and Sophie nodded weakly. Sophie's fingers were shaking. Only a rookie would let ExCom see her nerves. She noticed him looking at her hands and stuffed them into her pockets. Ethan was going to have to carry this thing, as usual.

Chip Masey and the four other committee members didn't look up from their seats at the far end of the glass conference table. Masey pulled their memo from a stack of papers. His freckle tan and broad blue eyes made him look more like a Little League coach than a division head, but his unthreatening exterior didn't fool Ethan. Not for a second.

"Great," Masey said. "Another credit request."

"You got any others with these kinds of fees attached?" Ethan asked.

"Here's the issue. In this environment, we're not taking on any more risk unless it's a matter of absolute necessity."

This wasn't anything Ethan hadn't predicted. "We understand that. On page four, you'll see the fees we expect to bring in as a result of AlumiCorp's merger with Roll-Rite. A hundred twenty million in advisory fees, plus another ten when we do the acquisition financing. And of course, we'll charge the client a fee for providing the guaranty. This is a money-making proposition for our firm."

Carl Sheehan, a raisined man who served as Sterling's Chief Risk Officer, folded his arms. "If we threw credit at every money-making proposition, we'd be out of jobs."

"This merger is a huge win for the Sterling franchise — it's the biggest aluminum merger in history," Ethan said. "This has been our number-one priority in the Industrial Group. And frankly," — Sinclair wasn't here, he might as well go for the kill — "it's the only live deal the group's been engaged on this year."

"You know, people out there are searching for reasons to vilify us. Consumers ask us for loans they can't afford, then they blame us for making them," Masey said, with a chuckle of disbelief. "They're sharpening their pitchforks, waiting for us to fuck up. Now is not the time to overextend ourselves."

Ethan hadn't pegged Masey as the paranoid type. Sure, Americans had cried Wall Street greed before — what difference had it made? Sterling was as solid as ever. Had they gotten that way by bowing to public opinion? No. Sterling survived by taking smart risks.

"This isn't one of those deals," Ethan said. "The strategic rationale is solid, the —"

Chip Masey raised a hand. "The deal makes strategic sense. But at this price, the valuation for Roll-Rite looks awfully high."

"It's in line with historical premiums paid," Ethan said quickly.

He glared at Sophie to quit fidgeting under the table. Nothing undermined credibility like a nervous analyst.

Masey continued, "What I want to know is, would *you* pay sixty-seven dollars a share of your own money for this company?"

The committee members leaned forward.

"Absolutely," Ethan said. "All day long."

Sophie nodded, not quite as vigorously as he would've liked.

All eyes were on Vasu, who chewed on his pen, taking his sweet time.

"What do you think, Vashoo?" Masey asked.

Vasu looked from Ethan to Masey and back again. Ethan wanted to shake him: *hurry up and spit it out!*

"Sixty-seven is a little rich," Vasu said.

Ethan was about to jump out of his chair, pull Vasu by his tie, and string him up from the ceiling.

"And why is that?" Masey asked.

"The domestic ops are fairly valued," Vasu said. "But the international assets are a bit challenged."

Ethan stared Vasu down. "I think what Vasu means is, there's plenty of room for upside. AlumiCorp wants to invest the time and money to make sure those assets live up to their potential."

Vasu held Ethan's gaze. "I meant the international assets are crap."

Ethan could barely sit still. Was Vasu *trying* to get them fired? If this deal didn't go through because of Vasu's renegade bullshit, Ethan would have zilch to show for 2008. He'd get forced out, and he'd sure as hell take Vasu down with him.

Masey pointed at Vasu. "Keep that one around. He's got a clear head on his shoulders."

Now he'd never get that subversive bastard off his team.

Masey leaned back, relaxed. "Now that we're being honest with ourselves, let's take another look. The international assets. If they're worth zero, then . . ."

Ethan exhaled. "If the international assets are worthless, our guaranty's covered, no question. Any risk on the international assets is in the equity." Meaning: they're the AlumiCorp stockholders' problem, not ours.

"Can't argue with that."

Carl Sheehan removed his glasses. "Why is AlumiCorp willing to overpay?"

"Irrelevant," Ethan said.

Masey glanced at his watch. "Agreed. Carl, why don't you guys discuss that offline? It doesn't bear on our guaranty."

Thank god. Masey was finally being reasonable. "If AlumiCorp can't keep their credit rating, they can't do the deal. And if they don't do the deal . . ." Ethan raised his empty palms. "As I see it, we provide a guaranty that's practically risk free in order to secure over one hundred twenty million in banking fees. Awfully good risk-reward, if you ask me."

"Give us a minute, folks," Masey said.

Ethan flew at Vasu as soon as they reached the hall. "Do you have a death wish? Is that it?"

Vasu didn't flinch. Ethan threw his hands in the air. He was surrounded by idiots.

"Good job on the memo," he said to Sophie, the only one who had her priorities straight. "It would be a shame if all your hard work came to nothing because someone undermined our deal." Ethan spoke loudly enough for Vasu to hear, but the VP didn't react.

She stared up at him. "They're not going to vote it down, are they? What would we —"

Carl Sheehan opened the door and summoned them back inside.

"The deal's overvalued, no question," Chip Masey said. "But like you said, Ethan, that doesn't affect the guaranty, just the Alumi-Corp shareholders. AlumiCorp's board's approved it, the market's blessed it. We'll get paid."

Come on, Masey, say the magic words.

"Your guaranty is approved. Now get the hell out of here." Masey flashed them a benevolent smile.

Ethan clapped Sophie on the back. She blushed, clearly as thrilled as he was. Vasu hurried out of Masey's office. By the time Ethan and Sophie reached the hall, Vasu was gone, the fire door swinging closed.

"Don't let him take you down with him." Ethan told Sophie.

She didn't skip a beat. "Can I call Hutch? Tell him the good news?"

Letting Sophie make the call would allow him to get to the Sterling gym that much faster. After Vasu's mutiny, Ethan needed to feel the capability of his muscles.

13

―――――
―――――

Thursday, April 17, 2008

Jake Hutchinson

HUTCH'S HOUSE WAS DARK when he pulled into the driveway. When he'd started as CEO, Gwen had been in high school. She always forgot to turn off the lights, leaving a trail of electricity bills in each room she entered. Drove Trish crazy. Hutch didn't mind though because it meant that no matter the hour he came home, the entire place would be lit up. Maybe he'd ask Trish to start leaving the lights on, now that he'd be coming home at a decent hour. Twenty-three years you worked for a company and then one day they didn't need you. Tomorrow the merger would announce, and a few months later, he'd leave Alumi-Corp for good. It was all outlined in the deal timeline, a four-page document that seemed to dictate the rest of his life: a half-hearted attempt at finding another company he could believe in, an early retirement, the first broken hip.

Trish had taken over the kitchen table with her scrapbooking.

Stacks of photos, pressed petals from Darcy's wedding. A brown flake — maybe a dried rose — stuck to the front of Trish's sweater. A cup of tea sat beside her, the Wash U mug Gwen had brought home during Thanksgiving. She peered over the rims of her reading glasses, "Seven thirty? To what do I owe this honor?"

He came up behind her and rested his head on her shoulder, soft and welcoming. One of her hairs tickled his nose. She still wore her hair the way she had when he'd married her, short and curled around her cheeks.

"Have you eaten?"

He'd wolfed down turkey tetrazzini with the bankers an hour ago, as he'd done most nights this month. Tomorrow the bankers would fly back to New York, probably have a big steak dinner to celebrate the deal that was his downfall. The tetrazzini would normally have been plenty, but tonight, no amount of food seemed like enough. "Would it be too much trouble?"

She patted the chair beside her and inspected the fridge. "Pork loin?"

"Patrycja Hutchinson, you're a wonderful wife — you know that?"

"And you're easy to please." She lit the range. "One of the many reasons I married you."

"Trishy, I've got news."

She leaned against the stove, arms crossed, spatula dangling from her hand, the same way she'd stood when Darcy had announced that she and her husband were moving to San Diego but promised to visit at least twice a year.

"The thing that's been keeping me so busy —"

"The big secret." She pressed the spatula into her palm hard enough for the skin around it to turn white.

"We're merging with Roll-Rite. The Pittsburgh company? It'll announce tomorrow."

Her forehead creased. "What does this mean for us?"

"I'll be leaving. Maybe four months, maybe six — depends on how long the regulators take. I wanted to tell you sooner, but —"

"Loose lips sink ships." When she was annoyed, her right dimple twitched.

"And I didn't have a choice. If I'd had a choice, we would've made it together, but this one was made for me."

She turned off the stove. Wood screeched against tile as she pulled out the chair that was farthest away from him.

"I'm sorry, Trishy. It's a generous exit package. We'll have plenty of room to plan our next step." He reached for her hand. "We can take that cruise now, if you want. And visit Gwen in Warsaw next semester?"

If Trish was taking it this bad, he could only imagine what was in store for him tomorrow. What he'd give to stay here with Trish and avoid the speech to his employees. There would be plenty of time between the press release and the meeting for everyone in Alumi-Corp's headquarters to get worked up.

Years ago, he and Trish were going through a rough patch, and night after night Hutch dreamed they'd decided to split up, and it was up to him to tell the girls. In the dream, he took Gwen and Darcy to Friendly's and they sat in a booth, splitting one of those clown sundaes where the cone looked like a dunce cap. Gwen and Darcy fought over the whipped cream. When he told the girls they were going to have two homes now, they stared up at him, too scared to blink, chocolate sauce on the corners of their mouths, trying to look brave but failing.

That was what he dreaded: seeing his employees need reassurance he couldn't give them. His investor relations team had spent weeks on the script for tomorrow's meeting, but no amount of practice could prepare him for that.

$$$

In the twenty-three years Hutch had worked at AlumiCorp, he'd never seen their auditorium full. He must have stood at this podium for dozens of annual meetings and investor days. Those times, he was lucky if half of the olive-drab seats were taken. People would be typing on their phones, talking to the person next to them. A hundred folks, at most, would be paying attention. Today, not only were there not enough seats for everybody, but the whole crowd was staring right at him. People were pressed against the railing of the balcony normally reserved for management. The aisles were so thick with employees that Hutch couldn't see the speckled lino-leum floor. Aerial photos of AlumiCorp's factories lined the walls — the Ashland extrusion plant, the Chambersburg rolling mill where Hutch had started off as a plant engineer twenty-three years ago, reminding him of all the plant workers and regional employees huddled in their break rooms, listening in on this meeting via live feed. Hutch wasn't an anxious guy, but standing in front of a thousand panicked faces would've put anyone on edge. The only people who didn't look scared half to death were the bankers sitting in the second row, solemn but calm. Sophie met his gaze and smiled.

As Hutch gave the speech his investor relations staff had written for him, he wondered if this was how political puppets felt: pathetic, powerless, false. "This transaction'll create value for you, our employees, and also for our shareholders. Now, you may've read that there'll be changes to this company's management. After the transaction closes, I'll be stepping down as CEO. Bruce Carbonell, Roll-Rite's CEO, will be heading this company."

When he'd practiced the speech, he'd paused here for a collective sigh from the audience. None came.

"Bruce Carbonell is an excellent leader — the best — and though I regret to be leaving you —" He cleared his throat. "Though I regret to be leaving you after twenty-three years, I know you'll be in the best of hands."

Hutch's voice cracked on the second page of empty promises. His investor relations team had instructed him to finish the speech, answer four questions, and conclude the meeting. Didn't feel right.

"Look. I could keep going. But I'm sure you all have lots of questions. I'm gonna open up the floor."

Hands shot up, fifty or so at first, more once folks saw they weren't alone. Hutch called on a bearded gentleman who squared his chest.

"How many of us are going to lose our jobs?"

Murmurs rippled through the crowd. A sideburned employee leaning against the photograph of the Ashland extrusion plant folded his arms and scowled at Hutch. An older woman on the balcony leaned so far over the railing that Hutch almost put out a hand to stop her.

Hutch gave the answer he'd rehearsed to death. "I assure you — we've fought to keep every last job we can. Truth is, this transaction's saving jobs — combining operations with Roll-Rite means a healthier top line, and a healthier top line means more jobs —"

"Screw your top line!" Someone shouted from the back.

Hutch motioned for quiet. "Look, I don't want to diminish the misfortune that some AlumiCorp employees will face. A man's job is his dignity. We have to have faith . . ." He knew how hollow his words sounded.

"Faith isn't going to feed my kids!" Back center.

Soles squeaked, people springing to their feet.

"Screw you!" Balcony.

"Answer the freaking question!" Left aisle.

"Ever been sued, asshole?" Left . . .

The shouts were coming so fast now, he couldn't catch where they came from. Bodies tilted toward the stage. Hutch raised his hands to bring everyone to order. There, off the tip of his index finger, he saw it: the slim, stainless steel barrel of a double-stack pistol, aimed straight at him.

Sophie Landgraf

There was a woman across the aisle in the AlumiCorp auditorium who in a parallel universe could have been Sophie's mother. The kids at Stockton Elementary used to call Sophie's mother Morticia because she wore her dark hair long and severely parted down the middle. The woman across the aisle was bobbed and cardiganed, basically the definition of normal, the way Sophie used to wish her mother would be. Sophie tried not to stare, but by the time Hutch solicited questions from the audience, the woman had noticed her looking over so many times that she'd stopped smiling back.

When the shouts erupted, Sophie was staring at the freckles on the woman's wrist and wondering if they were a sign that the woman kept a vegetable garden, like Sophie's mother. People yelled that layoffs were un-American — how could Hutch live with himself? Employees stood, clasping the seats in front of them, blocking Sophie's view of the cardiganed woman. She leaned forward, craning her neck, trying to see past Vasu and Ethan. She was sure the woman's face would be creased with frown lines, reproaching Sophie for being part of this merger, making her feel so young, so inadequate, so fake. Ethan snapped his fingers in front of Sophie's face and jutted his chin toward the stage.

Someone right behind her shouted, "Ever been sued, asshole?"

Sophie swiveled around. Ethan didn't stop her this time. The whole audience was on their feet, dark open mouths and clenched fists.

A shriek rose above the shouts, shrill and urgent. A cluster of people jumped back from something, shouldering each other to get out of the way.

Pops sounded. Vasu's hand shot across her chest. Sophie turned to see Hutch's leg buckle.

People were screaming. Vasu yanked her down so hard, her wrist burned. Footsteps sounded behind her. Sophie's face was pressed against the cold metal seat — she couldn't see whether Hutch was all right. She squeezed her eyes shut and counted Ramanujan primes. *2, 11, 17, 29, 41, 47, 59* . . . People were grunting, shouting, *Move! Call the police! Get out of my way!* She lost count and started again. *2, 11, 17* . . . *2, 11, 17, 29* . . . *2, 11* . . .

Vasu grabbed her hand. "We need to get out of here." He was

trembling. His eyes seemed darker right then, deep ellipses, perfect. He jerked her to the aisle. She felt his other hand on her back, telling her to stay down.

The current of bodies tugged her to the back of the auditorium. She was crushed against a man's corduroy jacket when something snapped against her fingertips. She'd lost Vasu's hand.

She turned to see Hutch lying on the stage, legs splayed, right arm reaching out. He could be bleeding to death. Alone.

People slammed against her shoulder, pushing past her, frantic. She shouted Hutch's name. Shoes scuffed against the floor.

Deep inside her, something switched on. She shoved her way to the stage, past open palms, sharp elbows.

Blood was spurting from Hutch's thigh, pooling underneath him. He was pale, blue-lipped. His eyes fixed onto her. She shouted at him. Nothing.

She thought back to EMT training. ABCs. Airway Breathing Circulation.

A: Turn his head to the side so he won't choke.

B: Make sure he's breathing.

C: Stop the bleeding. She pulled off her jacket, thumbed fabric into the wound, pressed down as hard as she could. Blood spurted around her hands. Her jacket was already soaked, red streaked across her fingers. She put all her weight onto Hutch's leg but blood kept gushing out.

Pressure points, between the wound and the heart. She lined her shin across Hutch's thigh, shifted her weight onto him. The bleeding wouldn't stop.

She needed a tourniquet. Her eyes darted around the empty stage for anything she could use. Her shirtsleeve wouldn't be long enough. Maybe Hutch's jacket, or ... She fumbled to unknot his tie, her fingers shaking, too slow. Fabric whooshed and the tie came free, red fingerprints across Hutch's throat.

She tied the first knot. The spurting slowed. She stumbled to the podium, grabbed a pen, tied the second knot around it and twisted once, twice, until the bleeding stopped. She took Hutch's hand. Cold and clammy—not a good sign. If any small part of her had once wondered if there was a god, it had stopped wondering when her mother died, but still, she closed her eyes and prayed.

The emergency room staff whisked Hutch behind a curtain. Sophie watched the dark soles of his shoes disappear. The halls were lined with stretchers, a man with an oxygen mask, a girl cradling an arm that was bent at an unnatural angle. A nurse appeared from behind the curtain and asked Sophie if she was family—only family could stay in the ER.

"Is he going to be OK?"

"We're doing everything we can."

Not encouraging. Sophie had said the same thing during her sixth and final call for the Stockton volunteer ambulance corps, when a ninety-two-year-old woman suffered what probably wasn't her first stroke. It was what she'd been told to say when she genuinely wasn't sure.

"We called in vascular," the nurse said. "He'll go into surgery as soon as they arrive."

Behind the curtain, someone shouted that Hutch was coding. He must be in shock, he must have stopped breathing. Why hadn't she thought to find something to keep him warm?

"Did I do the right thing, with the tourniquet?" Sophie asked. "I didn't know—"

The nurse had disappeared behind the curtain.

Sophie weaved between IV stands and heart monitors, past an old man with a nasal cannula and cracked lips.

The waiting room wasn't busy, a dozen or so people huddled on every third vinyl seat. No windows, bare walls painted blue. One of the fluorescent lights on the ceiling was on the fritz, blinking and erratic. At Sterling, if a light went out, an unobtrusive maintenance man swooped in and fixed it within ten minutes. In one corner, a television hung precariously from the ceiling, playing a shaky, low-resolution video of a man slumping behind a podium. A news anchor reported, "In Cincinnati earlier this afternoon, a disgruntled AlumiCorp employee shot and seriously wounded the company's CEO, Jake Hutchinson, then killed himself before a SWAT team entered the building. Leonard Bergmuller, a forty-two-year-old employee in AlumiCorp's accounts payable department, pulled out a Ruger SR9 handgun at an employee meeting following AlumiCorp's announcement of a merger with competitor Roll-Rite. Authorities believe Bergmuller retrieved the licensed gun from his vehicle after hearing the morning's . . ."

Someone touched Sophie's shoulder. A hen of a woman asked, "Are you all right?"

Sophie hadn't realized she was shaking.

The woman whispered, "Would you like one of my Ativan?"

Sophie shook her head. She noticed the woman looking at the bloodstains across the front of her shirt.

A young family huddled in one corner, the toddler clutching his Elmo doll. A girl who looked about eighteen sat with her knees pulled to her chest, Ohio U sweatshirt tugged down over her shins, chin on stacked fists. The girl chewed on her lip, probably trying to convince herself that her mother or boyfriend or father would be all right. Hutch had said he had two daughters, one a few years older than Sophie, married with a kid on the way, the other still in college. Sophie dropped her head between her knees, imagining Hutch's younger daughter hearing about her father's death over the phone when she was alone in her dorm, miles away with no way to get home fast enough — the same way Sophie had heard about her mother.

Her father didn't answer his phone, and at that moment Sophie was unbelievably furious at him and the completely irrational principles that said he was too good for an answering machine. Kim didn't pick up. Was it out of bounds to call Will? Did this count as an exception to his very clear wish not to talk to her?

Someone called her name. Vasu squatted in front of her. "How are you holding up?"

If she'd learned anything these past months, it was not to let colleagues see her at anything but her best. "I'm fine." She wanted this to be true, but she could tell that Vasu didn't buy it.

"You did a brave thing back there."

Sophie shook her head. "They're not sure he's going to make it. I didn't do enough."

A nurse came into the waiting room and glanced at her clipboard. Everyone grew quiet until the nurse summoned the woman who'd offered Sophie the Ativan.

"Is everyone else OK?" Sophie asked. "Where's Ethan?"

"The police are still there." He sank into the chair next to her. "You know, one of the reasons we left India was to avoid the bombings, the train burnings. Nine years we've been here — first 9/11, now this."

Sophie didn't know what to say. She looked up at the television, a commercial for Papa John's, cheese stretching impossibly long. The toddler in the corner cried for his mother.

"Where's Ethan?" she asked.

"Trying to spin this thing."

Six months ago, she might have been naïve enough to think that today's events would slow down their deal, slow down Ethan. It was so predictable, it was almost comforting: the world could be falling apart and still Ethan would be plugged in and moving the ball forward, like nothing had changed.

"Is it actually possible to spin something like this?" she asked.

"Ethan and Amanda, the investor relations woman, they already sent out something about how it 'fosters sympathy' and 'marginalizes the opposition.'"

Sophie hadn't even thought to check her BlackBerry. Just a few hours ago, after the merger announcement, her inbox had been brimming with emails. Backenroth, the head of the Energy Group, had written: *huge win for the STL franchise.* Nancy Cho had said: *welcome to the majors.* Jordanne had written to congratulate her, and to let Sophie know she'd gotten into Northwestern's B-school off cycle.

"Fosters sympathy?" she asked.

"Have I told you about Aditi's uncle Kaushik?"

Sophie couldn't remember Vasu ever telling her anything even remotely personal.

"Aditi's uncle is a little bit . . . off. When Aditi was pregnant, she read books like *How to Raise an Empathetic Child,* studies that said avoiding wheat decreased behavior problems in children — she was so terrified of ending up with a child like her uncle —"

"Meera's OK, right?"

"Perfect."

It was the first time she'd seen Vasu smile in months.

"When Aditi's father was a boy, he was playing in the courtyard and sliced his arm on some broken pottery — right above the wrist, a terrible cut. His mother heard him screaming and came running. His brother, Kaushik, was sitting not ten feet away, playing with his toy truck, perfectly calm. You can see why Aditi was worried, no? If you met her uncle, he's so charming, you would think nothing was wrong. But never once has he shown any regret, any concern. It's inhuman."

"Are you trying to say Ethan's like that?" Ethan had been concerned enough to protect her from the layoffs that winter. He might not be perfect, but he definitely wasn't inhuman. Jordanne had taught her that when a colleague said something nasty about another colleague, you had to question his motives. "You can't just judge someone like that. You can't just—"

"Why not?" Vasu snapped. His lips were peeling. "You think people aren't judging us?"

The Ohio U girl glared at them and burrowed further into her sweatshirt.

This had to be about ExCom — both Vasu and Ethan were still fuming. Ethan had told her to steer clear of Vasu, that Vasu would take her down with him. Now Vasu was trying to vilify Ethan. It was like watching her parents fight. "You need to smooth things over with Ethan. I know you're pissed about the international assets. But look, it all worked out. You got to tell ExCom you thought the assets were worthless — they even agreed with you — and they approved the guaranty anyway. We couldn't have planned it better. Now you and Ethan have to put it behind you. You need Ethan, we both do. Don't you remember what you told me when I was new? *Align yourself with a senior guy who's a machine.*"

"He's a machine, that's for sure," he muttered.

"What?"

He took a deep breath. "Never mind. Forgive me."

"No." The last time she'd seen Vasu this exasperated was that day in Ethan's office, when she'd learned the truth about the international assets. "Tell me."

His eyes darted around the waiting room, as though Ethan might appear at any moment. "Did you see how quickly he ran out of the auditorium?"

She hadn't. He just suddenly wasn't there. "So he panicked. Like the rest of us."

Vasu chewed on the corner of his thumb.

"What did you see?"

Vasu edged closer, his face inches from hers. "The man beside the aisle froze, he wouldn't get out of Ethan's way. Ethan stomped on his foot. He shoved the man onto the floor so he could get through."

Sophie pulled her knees to her chest. She wanted to believe that Vasu had it out for Ethan, that he was exaggerating. "No one behaves their best in a crisis."

"You did."

It was the only thing she'd done right all year. "Ethan lost his wife. The poor guy's traumatized. Maybe he was scared —"

"You think he's the only person who's lost someone?"

Sophie stared at him. He couldn't know about her mother, could he? "No. I don't."

He ran his teeth over his lips until they bled. "Do you think action and inaction are moral equivalents?"

It sounded like a cryptic quip of her mother's, something Sophie once would have taken as truth because it was said with authority, something that on closer inspection would only be hollow words.

"Vasu, you're not making any sense."

"If something bad happens—not something sudden like the shooting, but something long and drawn out, a downward spiral. Let's say it might have happened without you, that you weren't directly responsible, but you fed it, perhaps even pushed it over the edge. You should blame yourself, you should regret it, no?"

"No!" She wasn't going to sit there and let Vasu pin this disaster on her, on them. The merger would have happened with or without them. People were going to be laid off—it was a fact. Even if the merger hadn't happened, AlumiCorp was such a mess that it couldn't have avoided downsizing for long. Leonard Bergmuller would still have gone off the deep end. Hutch would still have gotten shot. Like Hutch had said, this thing was bigger than any of them. If she had made any small difference, it was that Hutch wouldn't have stood a chance today if no one had stopped the bleeding.

Vasu raised his hands in surrender. "Forget it. I'll go see if the nurses have an update."

Someone tapped Sophie's shoulder. She must have fallen asleep. The ceiling lights were off again, the television in the corner the only bright thing in the waiting room. An ample middle-aged blonde hovered over her, short permed hair, soft blue sweater over pendulous breasts—the sort of woman a kid would ask for help if he got lost. At first Sophie thought the woman must be a hospital administrator, but then she noticed the balled up tissues in the woman's fist.

"You're Sophie Landgraf, right? They said I could find you out here. I'm Trish Hutchinson."

Sophie scrambled to her feet. "How is he?"

"Surgery's finished. Four hours — they couldn't get it closed. But it's done. He's out of the woods."

Sophie took in a long breath and let it out.

"Thank you for what you did." Twin creases ran down Trish Hutchinson's forehead, like it pained her to say this. "They said he was lucky you were there."

The television was playing a commercial for LendingTree, *when banks compete, you win.*

"Can I see him?" Sophie asked.

"They said he needs his rest." Trish rose. "Tomorrow, maybe."

"I'm so sorry this happened."

Trish Hutchinson disappeared into a dark hallway. Sophie had promised her father she'd call him back the second there was any news. She assured him that no, he didn't need to fly out to be with her after all. Really.

Dancing with the Stars played on the television, couples smiling and perfect. The Ohio U girl was gone, so was the young family. A woman in exercise gear sat in the corner, tilting a bottle of water to her lips but not sipping any.

Sophie called Ethan on her way out.

"Glad to hear Hutchinson's all right," he said. "When will he be awake?"

"I'm not sure. I'll ask."

"You do that. Listen, I need to get back to New York ASAP. You should too. I'm on the 1 A.M. —"

"Tonight?" Was he kidding? "I want to see Hutch tomorrow when he wakes up. I can't just leave and —"

"Trust me. If you don't get back to New York soon, you'll regret it."

How could he be so indifferent? Hutch had almost *died.*

"I'm not leaving," she said firmly. "Not until I see Hutch."

"Suit yourself."

He hung up without saying good-bye.

Ethan Pearce

By the time the market closed the afternoon of the shooting, damage control was complete, no thanks to the AlumiCorp investor relations team. It never ceased to amaze Ethan how blithely people accepted incompetence. It was only four o'clock and the whole investor relations staff was packing up to go home for the weekend. If Ethan were running AlumiCorp, he'd scrap the whole team and start from scratch, merger or no.

Ethan was the only one left in the conference room when he got the call from Grant Sinclair.

"I was sorry to hear about Hutchinson," Sinclair said.

"Aren't we all."

"Thank god our people are all right. I was impressed—" A click sounded. "Ethan, hang on a minute."

Sinclair put him on hold. The guy probably got off on making him wait. Ethan cleaned out his inbox in the meantime. Citigroup had laid off nine thousand that morning, which meant that he'd received about a dozen good-bye emails. *I've attached my permanent contact information. It's been a great twelve years. I count myself lucky to have worked with each and every one of you.* Blood was running on the Street.

"Sorry about that, Ethan. I know you have your hands full at the moment, but I've been asked to present the higher-ups with our group's pending transactions. I need you to write up your clients by 9 A.M."

"You're kidding. I just announced the biggest transaction this group has ever done. I just spent the afternoon spinning a goddamn *shooting* and you're asking me to do *paperwork?*"

"I don't disagree with you, Ethan. Really I don't. It's not my call."

"Can it want till Monday at least?"

"It can't."

If Chip Masey needed updates over the weekend, something big was brewing. At the least, massive layoffs, like Citi. At worst, Sterling was the next Bear Stearns.

"Grant, what's going on?"

"I know as little as you."

Ethan didn't buy that for a second. "OK. Let me ask you this — would you advise me against making some calls, soliciting interest from other shops?"

"I'm not in a position to give advice."

Good enough for him.

"Ethan, we need to keep this under wraps for as long as we can, understand?"

Perfectly. Sinclair didn't want to risk a stampede. In this, their interests were aligned. Ethan couldn't afford to have Sophie or Vasu fall apart on him. Even if Sinclair hadn't asked, Ethan wouldn't have told Vasu — he had every intention of sending that subversive bastard down with the ship. Sophie, he might have told. If he'd had any doubts about her before now, it was her ability to stay calm under pressure. After what happened today, he was that much more certain of her worth. He'd like to keep her with him, if it didn't cost too much. Maybe, despite Sinclair's wishes, he should give Sophie a head start in launching her campaign for continued employment.

He pulled out a blank legal pad. He'd have to deal with Sophie later. There was much to do.

In every crisis, there was opportunity. Turnover separated the good from the excellent, and if you were excellent, you used the event to your advantage. Every Sterling employee was about to be marked to market. Ethan had long been undervalued at Sterling, and with the announcement of the biggest aluminum deal of the century, his stock had shot through the roof. He'd engineer a competitive situation. Uncertainty at Sterling gave him the perfect opening to capture his value: it gave him a story as to why he was looking around. He had no allegiance to Sterling — he just worked for them.

Ethan called J.P. Morgan first. Their Industrial Group was the weakest of the top-tier banks — they needed him the most, maybe they'd pay the most.

By 9 P.M., the auction was in full swing. He'd booked a flight back to New York. He'd scheduled meetings for Saturday with the top prospects, conference calls with the rest. By Monday, when whatever was going on at Sterling hit the tape, he'd have everything lined up. He'd auction himself off to the highest bidder. Monday evening, he and Clara Schumann would feast on steak.

He was wrapping up Sinclair's write-up when Sophie called. She sounded so composed, so professional in spite of all that had happened that for a moment he considered telling her about the trouble at Sterling. But what was to be gained from telling her now? The earliest he might need her was during his meetings tomorrow, if it became clear that one of the banks he was auditioning was low on junior talent. If so, he'd want to advertise that he had a team of all-stars he could slot right in, so he could hit the ground running. Otherwise, he wouldn't need her until Monday, when the news hit. Best not to tell her yet. Still, he should get her back to New York. That way, if she proved useful, she'd be positioned close by.

"Listen," he said. "I need to get back to New York ASAP. You should too. I'm on the 1 A.M. —"

"Tonight?" she asked. "I want to see Hutch tomorrow when he wakes up. I can't just leave and —"

"Trust me. If you don't get back to New York soon, you'll regret it." He was as clear as he could be.

"I'm not leaving," she said. "Not until I see Hutch."

He could only help her so much. She'd have to duke it out on Sunday or whenever the rumor mill got cranking. Some sparring would probably do her good.

14

Saturday, April 19, 2008

Vasu Mehta

L ATE SATURDAY EVENING, Vasu bounded up the stairs
to his apartment building two at a time. Yesterday's shooting, Ethan, ExCom — he would put everything behind
him. After months of traveling on diligence and going back and
forth to AlumiCorp's headquarters in Cincinnati, he was finally
home for good. He paused outside the front door, picking off the
bruised outer petals from the bouquet he had bought in an airport
shop, the best to be found when he had landed at 1 A.M. Why was it
that flights were always delayed on the way home, never the other
way around?

The apartment smelled of onion and cumin. The lights were
off, the glow of a street lamp illuminating the couch where he had
hoped Aditi would be waiting for him. A note on the kitchen table
told him to heat up the plate in the fridge, which he did though he

was not hungry, finishing all the *dhansak* and serving himself second scoops of rice and dal. His BlackBerry buzzed. Sophie emailed from Cincinnati to say that Hutch was improving, she'd booked a return flight for tomorrow, Sunday. And wasn't it kind of strange, she wrote, that they hadn't heard anything from Ethan since he'd left Ohio yesterday? Vasu hit delete. He was not about to be drawn into speculating about Ethan or any other such time waste. From now on, he would only do what was absolutely necessary to close the Steelers deal, nothing more. He had neglected his family long enough. Tomorrow, he would take Meera to Coney Island. He would book his family a proper vacation, a resort in Bali where Aditi would get a massage while he took Meera snorkeling, where their most difficult decision would be SPF 15 or 30, mango juice or guava.

Vasu put the roses into a vase and eased open the bedroom door. Aditi lay in the middle of the mattress, hugging a pillow, sheets tangled at her feet. He tried to be quiet though he hoped she would hear him, sit up in bed, and reach for him. He set the flowers on her nightstand and the BlackBerry on his. As he lifted the sheets, she pulled her knees to her chest, the same way Meera slept. Her eyes snapped open when he lay down. She patted her chest, inviting him to curl up in her arms. She kissed the top of his head and he closed his eyes, breathing in the smell of the coconut oil she rubbed into her hair.

$$$

Vasu's BlackBerry buzzed at 5 A.M. Sunday morning. He silently cursed Ethan as he reached to turn it off. It was his friend Raj Naranjan — Raj would only wake Vasu if it were an absolute emergency.

Vasu scurried into the hall so as not to wake Aditi.

"Thank goodness I caught you," Raj said. In the four months since Raj had been laid off, he and Vasu had spoken once a week. In four months, Raj had not yet found a new job. He had had dozens of interviews, but as they said in India, apply, apply, no reply.

If not for his marriage to Priyanka, an American citizen, he would be back in India by now. Before Vasu could ask Raj how he was holding up, Raj said, "I talked to the head of my old desk today. Sterling's counterparties, they're spooked. Friday, they refused to take the other side of Sterling's overnight trades."

"What?" Such investments were as safe as they came at an investment bank, practically risk free. Vasu had to sit down. "It's like —"

"Bear. Precisely."

Aditi waded into the hall, squinting against the light, hair mussed. *Sterling's in trouble,* he mouthed. She cocked her head, looking more curious than worried. He pulled her closer until their foreheads were touching, so they both could listen.

"They don't trust that we have the cash."

The market had decided that Sterling had taken on too much debt — from subprime, from the AlumiCorp guaranty. Investment banking was a business based on confidence. If the market doubted they would get their money back, they would stop doing business with Sterling. It was a death sentence.

"No one wants to be the one holding the bag when the music stops," Raj said. "They're saying that by Monday, Sterling will be bankrupt or bought, like Bear. Either way, they're fucked. I thought you'd want as much time as possible to . . ."

To try to save his job. Aditi's brow creased with concern. Vasu knew that half of Bear's workforce had been let go when the bank blew up. Already Sterling's employees would be en route to midtown, hoping to convince their superiors they were indispensible. Sterling would probably announce the news Monday morning, which meant they had twenty-six hours. After ExCom, Ethan would make sure Vasu was the first person Sinclair cut. He would be out of a job come Monday. For years, he had worried about receiving a call like this, for his end to appear, fully formed and nonnegotiable. But now, he felt strangely calm. Perhaps he was in shock.

He thanked Raj abruptly and hung up. He and Aditi sat in silence, her head in the crook of his shoulder, his hand absentmindedly petting her hair. If only they could stay in New York until Meera finished high school. Perhaps he could start his own business. Something that did not require too much capital. Something that took advantage of his financial background. A microlending fund, perhaps. They could make loans to families in Gujarat. They could be based here, in Brooklyn. They would be able to stay.

He struck four matches before he managed to light his cigarette. Even if he risked their own money to seed the venture, their savings would not be enough. And still there was the problem of the visa. The microlending fund was the ill-thought-out dream of a teenager who thought working at a bank meant scanning stock prices and smoking cigars, who was not yet familiar with the world's constraints, and his own.

In this job market, post-Bear, the only positions Vasu would find would be steps down the ladder. Even if he fought his way up again, it would be the same thing: massaging the numbers to give Pearce or his equivalent the ammunition he needed, being shunned for telling the truth as he had at ExCom. For seven years he had told himself that if he was part of a transaction like Steelers, it would all be worth it, but here he was, his life still hopelessly out of sync. Vasu was thirty-six, but in banker years, he was sixty-five at least. Inside the office, time slowed so that each workday felt like three. Outside Sterling, seasons changed without him, Meera celebrated birthdays when he could have sworn the last one had passed only a month before. He needed to true up time.

In all the nightmares Vasu had had about losing his job, none had ended like this. Never could he have imagined that he would be *ready* to leave.

He crushed his cigarette into the ashtray.

"Perhaps it's time to go home," Vasu whispered.

Aditi blinked, as though she was not sure she was awake. "How soon can we leave?" She curled tighter into him and closed her eyes.

He wondered whether when the sun rose, she would think she had dreamt it.

Sophie Landgraf

Seven voicemails about Sterling's crisis were waiting for Sophie when she landed in LaGuardia late Sunday morning — four from Vasu, three from Donnigan, none from Ethan. As her cab sped across the Triborough Bridge into Manhattan, she couldn't help fixating on the fact that Ethan had to have known Sterling was in trouble, and he didn't call. Vasu had phoned for the first time early that morning, Donnigan a few hours later. If Vasu and Donnigan had known by Sunday morning, then Ethan must have known by sometime last night, at least. Maybe even Friday, the day of the shooting. He might even have known Friday night, when she'd called to tell him that Hutch was OK, when Ethan had said he was flying back to New York. After all she'd done for him, she didn't deserve a heads-up? She'd come up with the Roll-Rite idea in the first place, she'd saved their deal at Christmas, she'd backed up Ethan at ExCom, and *nothing?* Vasu was right: Ethan had a piece missing. Not only had he not called to tell her that Sterling was on the rocks, he hadn't even returned the messages she'd left since she'd learned the news. She couldn't believe she'd ever been even remotely interested in anyone so selfish.

Her cab zoomed down the FDR but she couldn't get to Sterling fast enough. Donnigan said that everyone had come into the office that morning, in case. In case what, no one knew, but theories abounded: Ira Blumenstein said that Warren Buffett was going to buy them for a penny. Greg Liden thought that J.P. Morgan was going to swallow them up like they'd swallowed Bear Stearns. Nancy Cho speculated that they'd be split up into pieces and sold to Blackstone. Vasu thought they'd be nationalized to prevent Singapore's sovereign wealth fund buying them instead.

She told herself that now was not the time to panic — she needed to show Ethan and everyone else how professional she was, that she wasn't the same person who'd done those idiotic things her first few months. Looking calm wasn't going to be easy. She'd missed breakfast, her neck was killing her from the plane, and she hadn't been able to sleep since the shooting.

If you thought about it coolly and rationally, the odds were in her favor: the government wouldn't let an institution as big as Sterling fail, so the probability of a true collapse was near zero. Sterling would get bought, which meant that half of the workforce would be let go, like they were at Bear Stearns. Whoever bought them would have to preserve the bank's fees, like AlumiCorp, which meant that she, Ethan, and Vasu were safe. The numbers said she'd make it to the other side.

Stock prices crawled around Sterling's glass façade calmly, reliably, like the bank had everything under control. The stag mounted atop the building's entrance was as inscrutable as ever. Two extra maroon-clad security guards flanked the entrance, but everything else was the same. No one passing by would have guessed that inside, Sterling was in crisis.

Sophie was halfway to the entrance when her BlackBerry buzzed. Will's number was the last she'd expected to see. The fact that he was calling her now after ignoring her for four months made her wonder if the Sterling rumors had hit the press. She ducked around the corner, out of sight.

"Are you OK?" Will asked.

"Trying not to panic but so far —"

"I saw this video on the weekend review. The shooting in Cincinnati — was that you?"

It took her a second to catch up. Sterling's crisis had forced Friday's events into the back of her mind. It seemed impossible that the shooting had only been two days ago. "Unfortunately, yes."

"Are you *insane?* Jumping up there when someone crazy has a gun?"

"He didn't want to shoot *me.*"

A woman pushing a stroller cast her a sideways glance and hurried up.

"So this is what was keeping you so busy?" he asked. "This . . . merger?"

In the silence, Sophie could picture his eyebrows lifting in that judgmental way of his. She wouldn't have answered if she'd known this was where he was headed. "Thanks for calling, Will. It's good to talk to you. If you want to talk for real, can we do it later?"

She hung up that much more glad that she hadn't told Kim or her father about the rumors. Only after knowing her fate could she talk to them. Now, it was useless — like Will, they wouldn't get it, and that would only make her feel that much more alone. Jobs were like a religion: the only people who understood were the ones on the inside with you.

She pushed back her shoulders, to make herself feel stronger more than anything else. She'd never noticed before that one of the Sterling security guards kind of looked like Will — probing eyes and sloppy hair.

Footsteps echoed through the marble lobby. Inside the elevator, people spoke the way relatives did when visiting the infirm: too loudly, too cheerily, skirting around the one thing everyone was thinking.

On the twenty-sixth floor, Donnigan and a few of the second years were tossing a NERF football down the corridor, trying to blow off steam.

"Go long!" one shouted.

Sophie flattened herself against the wall as he sprinted past.

"Get hit by any falling bodies on your way in?" Donnigan asked.

She motioned for him to follow her to Ethan's office. "Any news?"

"Zilch. Silly Sterling. Took down too much subprime product. It's like that dude at the Vending Machine Challenge — swallow too much too fast, you throw up."

"So we're Sterling's vomit?"

"If the shoe fits . . . I've been updating my resume to say 'Wall Street Casualty,' former peon."

Sophie's first thought on seeing Ethan's bare office was that he'd already abandoned them. She told herself that she was being paranoid — Ethan's desk was always empty. "Have you seen him?"

"Nope. I was starting to wonder if you were off together in some hotel room —"

If he'd made the same comment yesterday, she might have blushed. "Fuck off, Donnigan. You're going to get yourself sued one day."

He whistled. "Blumenstein ordered pizza if you want some. Fattening us up for the slaughter."

She'd lost her appetite.

"It's funny," he said. "All those nights I was stuck here till 4 A.M., doing something totally worthless, I'd pray that someone would blow this place up. This isn't what I meant."

"Getting awfully philosophical, Donnigan. They're not going to let Sterling fail. And when we get bought, they won't fire all of us — they need some of us to keep the franchise going." They'd need AlumiCorp. They'd need her.

"We all need backup plans. I'm thinking used-car sales — I've got a ton of experience that'll translate nicely. After your heroic efforts in the field, you should try the secret service."

Why couldn't Will have seen it that way? "Mr. Liberal Guilt said I was crazy for doing that."

Donnigan waved this away. "In this world, there are watchers and there are doers."

She wanted to believe him, but by that logic, the shooter was a doer, same as her. Which reminded her of what she'd discovered on the plane. She'd munched on honey-roasted peanuts while digging through the synergies analysis. She'd found the page Hutch's team at AlumiCorp had prepared that identified the company's employees by seven-digit numbers rather than names. AlumiCorp had marked whether each employee would be optimized — let go — as a result of the merger, and Sophie had fed the savings from their salaries into her model along with the other cost-cutting initiatives: property taxes, alumina, electricity. Leonard Bergmuller's employee ID number — 2387149 — was right there in her model. The whole time, the shooter's job was safe. They weren't going to let him go.

Vasu looked up at her knock. "How's Hutchinson?" He stood behind his desk, dropping files into a Sterling duffel bag. All of his drawers were open.

"They're putting in a rod tomorrow. He'll probably limp, but other than that . . . Thank god we got our guaranty through, right?"

"Sorry?"

"Can you imagine where we'd be if we'd let the deal fall apart? No fees to save us?"

"That's one way to look at it." He sounded surprisingly calm. "Another way to look at it is that the AlumiCorp guaranty was among the last credit the bank extended before the gate closed. Perhaps, if ExCom had not granted the guaranty . . ."

Nancy Cho would have said *don't go all Pollyanna on me.* "This is an old-fashioned bank run. The market's decided our collateral isn't worth what we say it is, and now no one will do business with us — it's a self-fulfilling prophecy."

"After what you've seen these past few months, do *you* believe Sterling's collateral is worth what they say it is? After we went to ExCom with that—" His eyes darted to the hallway. "With that absurd valuation? Claiming AlumiCorp's international assets are worth four hundred fifty-two million?"

Did he want her to say that he'd been right to undermine their deal in ExCom, when AlumiCorp was the only thing between them and a pink slip? "The firm had finite resources —"

"And plenty of other groups needed the credit — yes, Ethan's right about that. But what happens when every group at Sterling does the same thing? We all present lopsided valuations, we all withhold risks. How can ExCom accurately value the bank's collateral if its employees don't?"

Ethan's way of doing things might not have been in the bank's best interests, but she wasn't going to let Vasu pin this on her. "What do we do now?"

"Not much *to* do, no? Pack your box in case they don't let us back in tomorrow. Print anything you can't live without in case we get locked out of our systems. They've already disabled the flash drives."

"The models, you mean?"

"Your address book, telephone numbers, all your contacts. If we blow up on Monday, that's what you'll need."

He was right. Her entire life was sitting on a computer that wasn't even hers.

15

Monday, April 21, 2008

Ethan Pearce

TODAY, THE GOOD WOULD BE SEPARATED from the excellent. The bank hadn't made an announcement over the weekend, which meant the news would hit in a few hours, when the markets opened for the week. Ethan was doubling his workout, so he'd be doubly ready. At 4 A.M. on a normal Monday, Ethan would have had the Sterling pool to himself, but today four others were doing laps. Everyone had plenty of anxiety to burn.

The whole point of swimming was to clear his head, which was impossible when he was sharing the pool with anyone, let alone another banker who saw everything as a competition. The other swimmers broadcasted their presence, pulling him back into reality when the goal was to leave his body. When he'd explained this to Camille, she'd said it was the same with music. She avoided conservatory practice rooms at all costs — too many people sharing the same muse.

"Not the same," he'd said. "You're bringing things to you, I'm pushing them out."

"Things like . . ." It was fall, and the trees along the Champs Élysées were losing their leaves. Ethan was uncomfortably aware of the three and a half carats in his pocket. Alain Ducasse had set aside a bottle of 1995 Châteaux Margaux for dinner, and one of Dom Perignon, for after she said yes. "Give me an example of these things you must push out."

"Couldn't tell you — they're in the land of the forgotten."

"Oh, I see." Camille and Clara Schumann had the same way of squinting when they were about to pounce. "Survival by selective amnesia."

Ethan pulled himself out of the water, puddles forming at his feet. This was what happened when you were forced to share the pool. The demons crept into your brain.

Showered and shaved, Ethan swiped onto the twenty-sixth floor. He hadn't expected to find the floor empty. It didn't surprise him that Sinclair and Vasu were getting their beauty sleep, but the bankers who were actually hungry should have been there, manning the fort, in case an opportunity presented itself. The second he walked through that door, Sophie should've ambushed him, asked about his next steps, and convinced him to take her with him.

Ethan surveyed his office for anything that needed to be salvaged. His swimming goggles and spare tie. The mug with the Sterling slogan — *where dreams get built* — if the bank went bust, it would soon be a collector's item. The CD of the Sibelius Concerto, a man's tribute, as Camille used to say, to the person he wished he'd been. Life seemed so complicated to her. You decided who you wanted to be and then you became that person. Simple.

Ethan's BlackBerry buzzed. He didn't recognize the number.

"Ethan, Zach McNutt here."

Ethan hadn't spoken to McNutt since he'd left DLJ for Bain Capital, the private equity firm where he'd been a partner for the past eight years.

"Still sipping shit through a straw, huh?" Zach asked.

"Still in the strip mining business, huh?"

"My sources say you might be looking around."

"Your sources are correct." A cold call — today was going to be even better than he'd thought.

"I have a proposition for you."

Let the bidding begin.

Sophie Landgraf

Sophie stopped pretending to sleep around five on Monday morning. Every time her BlackBerry buzzed she felt a punch between her third and fourth ribs. She'd tried silencing it, but that only meant she checked it every five seconds. Yesterday she'd been able to believe in the low probability of the bank blowing up, the high probability of the bank getting bought and AlumiCorp saving her, but the numbers weren't enough anymore because still, there was a non-zero chance that the bank would fail, and then she'd be one hundred percent out of a job. She had a monster headache — she never got headaches — and she'd already taken six Advil, which hadn't done a thing.

Every light in her apartment was on because being alone in the dark with nothing but your thoughts was a recipe for losing your mind. Putting on her suit and seeing a self-possessed professional reflected in the mirror hardly helped at all. Part of her wanted to go to Sterling and be at her desk when the news hit, but she couldn't let her colleagues see her this worked up. Today of all days, she needed to broadcast calm and competence.

Why hadn't she gotten a dog? With the hours she worked, a pet was out of the question, but at that moment she'd have given anything for a wet nose, a furry lump at her feet, anything to remind her that there was a world outside her head.

She tried Kim for the fifth time, but Kim's cell phone still went to voicemail. Kim must have turned off her phone for the night. Sophie cursed Kim for not having a land line, though of course Sophie didn't have one either. She tried counting Chen primes. *2, 3, 5 . . . 7, 11 . . . 13 . . . 17 . . .* She couldn't concentrate. She tried reciting them out loud. *2, 3 . . . 5, 7 . . .* Maybe if she wrote them down . . . *2 . . . 3 . . . 5 . . . 7 . . .* Her hand shook, reminding her that she had every reason to be freaked out.

She was about to give up and head to Sterling when she thought of her mother's yarn. She'd let it stay as a scarf for almost two years now. The scarf unraveled easily. She looped the yarn around the knobs of her kitchen cabinet to form a skein, but the wool scratching against her palm wasn't as comforting as she'd remembered. Even the click of her knitting needles, the mathematical repetition of knit one, purl two, failed to calm her. What she wanted was to follow the trail of yarn back to the way things had been on Thursday.

If her mother were here, she would have said that Sophie had a way of letting her imagination get the best of her, and she would have been right, but that didn't help one bit. Her mother wasn't here. No one was here to scratch her scalp in the way both Will and her mother knew would calm her. This was what Sophie had wanted, sort of: to be on her own in New York City. Why was it that when you actually got what you wanted, it didn't look the way you'd thought it would?

She almost called her dad, but she knew what he'd say: good riddance. Not only would he not even begin to understand, she'd only fuel his conviction that Sterling was the land of Stepford sleepwalkers. If everything turned out fine, which in all probability it would, she'd never live this down.

The press release from Mickey Wright, Sterling's CEO, hit Sophie's BlackBerry right before the markets opened. Her fingers went numb as she raced through the text: *insolvency . . . support of the Fed . . . maximize value . . . Goldman Sachs*. There, halfway down, was the only word that mattered: *merger*. She was safe.

Sophie flew off the subway thirty minutes later, pushing past people with their papers open, like it was a normal Monday morning. Cameras flashed at suits streaming from Sterling's headquarters. Reporters shouted questions about financial weapons of mass destruction. One man balanced two of the cardboard boxes the bank used to archive files, one stacked on top of the other, chin clamped over the top lid, lips squeezed tight. Another grimaced as he struggled to negotiate a pair of stag-embroidered duffle bags so full their zippers wouldn't close. Those men didn't have AlumiCorp to save them.

A CNBC anchorwoman was interviewing a man who stared at the microphone, unable to speak. Sophie had seen eyes like that once, years ago, when a young ewe named Antigone had escaped from their barn. The sheep wandered into town where it froze in place right in the middle of the intersection outside IHOP. The police tased her. Sophie went down to the station with her mother to claim Antigone. The ewe's eyes had that same look, like she was beyond fear.

Sophie charged through the gauntlet of reporters. As she raised her ID badge for the Sterling security guards, someone shouted at her, "So how does it feel to get booted out of Wall Street and onto Main Street?" She turned away from the voice only to have someone thrust a business card in front of her face. "At Tillet Partners, we have clients who are hiring financial professionals. Send us your résumé."

The twenty-sixth floor stank of alcohol and sweat. Since she'd left the night before, the place had been destroyed — papers scattered across the carpet, trashcans turned on their sides, chairs stranded in the middle of the hall. Somebody had stacked empty cardboard boxes against the wall, the same kind she'd seen people carrying out of Sterling. A shattered picture frame lay outside the conference room, shards of glass glittering against the carpet. Sophie tiptoed around them. Sinclair's photos were stripped from his credenza, his computer screen black: an evacuation zone.

She told herself not to panic. Ethan knew how essential she was to AlumiCorp. That was all that mattered. Ethan had saved her from the ax in December, and he'd save her now. When she didn't find him in his office, she headed straight for Vasu's.

Sophie stood in the hall, watching Vasu drop papers into a cardboard box. Why would he be clearing out now, when they knew about the merger? Had they fired him because of ExCom? Vasu hollered for her to come in.

"Have you heard from Ethan on AlumiCorp?" she asked.

Vasu dropped a thick copy of *Mining and Refining Aluminum* into the trash. He paused, dug it out, and placed it in the cardboard box. "We're all gone."

"*What?*" There must be a mistake. She waited for him to say that their group was gone but the AlumiCorp team was moving to . . . "What about AlumiCorp?"

He laughed. "Wake up, Sophie. We've been bought by *Goldman*. Remember who's advising Roll-Rite? Having the same bank on both sides of a merger would be a conflict of interest, no? AlumiCorp isn't ours anymore."

Goldman. She'd been so focused on the fact that the bank hadn't blown up, that Sterling had only announced a merger . . . how had she not put the pieces together? If the whole group was gone, then Ethan couldn't fight on her behalf, and if Ethan couldn't fight on her behalf . . . Was that it? She had no job? What was she supposed to do now? She couldn't think straight.

"Goldman's Industrial Group is better than Sterling's. AlumiCorp was the only client Sterling had a line into that Goldman didn't. And now, that's irrelevant. We're not worth anything to them."

Something inside her collapsed, telling her to sit down. She was nothing to Sterling but a number to be manipulated, maximized, deleted. "We're synergies."

"Congratulations. You win the prize: two months' severance, like the rest of us."

He laid Meera's crayon drawings in the box. Three stick figures in a field of red flowers, a world where there weren't student loans or mortgages to pay, where you could sit and make daisy chains under a giant sun, where you'd never be alone and have no idea what to do next.

"What am I going to do?"

Vasu perched on his desk. "Sublet your apartment. Or better yet, get out of your lease, if you can. Move home. Take advantage of the fact that nobody depends on you. Look for a new job. Or go back to school."

More school: more debt. "That's it?"

"Be glad you're a citizen."

Her mind was so fuzzy, that hadn't even occurred to her. "Oh, Vasu, I'm so sorry. I hadn't realized —"

"It's fine. Aditi wants to move back to India anyway. Perhaps one day Meera will earn enough to bring her old man back to the States." He didn't sound as put out as she would have expected. "You'll get through this, Sophie. Let's hope it's the worst the Street deals you."

She had to find Ethan. He'd already have a plan. So what if she wasn't sure how much she respected him. So what if he only looked out for himself. So what if she couldn't trust him, not one cent. He was her best shot. Her only shot.

Vasu reached into his pocket and pulled out a flask that glinted in the fluorescent light. "STL" was etched into its face. She tipped her head back and closed her eyes, thankful for the burn.

"Keep it," he said. "It's a good-bye present."

"Thanks, Vasu. For everything."

He extended his hand. "It's been a pleasure working with you."

"You too."

"Keep in touch."

Sophie wondered if he meant it. He'd probably spent more time with her this year than his family, and still, they hardly knew each other. He smiled for a moment before returning to his packing.

"Door open or closed?" she asked.

He didn't look up. "What's the difference?"

Sophie lapped the floor, asking everyone if they'd seen Ethan. Rich Angstrom told her to quit asking, he'd already told her twice that he hadn't. The only other place she could think to look was the Sterling gym. The pool was empty. So was the exercise room. Ethan wasn't on the treadmill. He wasn't lifting weights. Sophie stood there, staring at the polished barbells and carefully rolled towels, unable to move or speak.

The door to the men's locker room swung open and out stepped Ethan, smoothing his jacket. He walked to the front desk and scribbled on the sign-in sheet, calm and at ease, like he didn't have a care in the world. She cleared her throat. His hair was wet and he'd nicked his chin from shaving, a tiny bead of blood.

"Oh, Sophie. Hi." He looked through her, like she was nothing.

"Are you on your way out?"

He glanced at his watch. "What is it?"

She got the feeling that she was already failing some test. "Are you leaving Sterling?"

"I had a good run here." He buttoned his coat. "But yes. I'm joining Lehman — as the head of their Industrial Group."

"Congratulations."

He nodded grandly. "It's going to be interesting."

She stared at his square shoulders, hating the way he stood so straight, hating the downy hairs on his wrist, hating the crisp crease of his pants and the perfect points of his collar, but mostly hating herself for needing him to get her out of this mess.

"Take me with you." In her head, it hadn't sounded so desperate.

"I already signed my contract," he said flatly. "No more negotiating leverage. Sorry."

"The analysts over there — they don't know the way you like to do things, right? Your transition would be so much smoother if I —"

"You're a good professional, Sophie." He said "good" like it was an insult. "I have every confidence you'll land somewhere decent."

She wanted so badly to slap him, hard and fast, to leave a mark across his cheek.

"Getting laid off isn't personal. Sterling only sees you — sees any of us — as a number."

"Do you think I'll find something in two months, before severance runs out?"

He leaned against an exercise bike, folding his arms, like nothing was wrong. "Be thankful for credit. People out there want to hate us for extending it in the first place, but consider the alternative."

This comforted her for about half a second, until she thought of the credit card she'd maxed out with her father's mortgage payments. She looked around at the elliptical machines, the treadmills, wondering how Ethan had managed to exercise when there was so much to worry about.

"Don't let panic get the best of you. We've been here before. Friday the 13th, 1989. Black Wednesday, 1992. The dot-com bubble. 9/11. Trust me, the dusts always settles, and after it does, things won't look so different. Banks might have different names, people might have swapped seats, but that's cosmetics. The market has peaks and crashes, but Wall Street itself — the players, the rules — Wall Street's always the same."

He was out the door, his footsteps so loud they were almost a brag.

"Wait!" she shouted after him. "So should I move back home?"

He called over his shoulder, "You don't win big by playing safe."

Sophie's ID didn't open the twenty-sixth floor. She swiped it again, resulting in the same flashing red light. They'd locked her out. She knocked on the glass until a security guard appeared, the one who looked like Will — shoulders bent bashfully, hair falling over his forehead.

"I can't let you back in," he said sheepishly. "And I need to take your BlackBerry and ID badge." He pointed to an empty pizza box on the ground, BlackBerries tossed on top of grease-stained waxed paper.

She stared through the glass wall. The gray carpet stretched to meet the sky, an alternate horizon in a world where she no longer belonged. From where she stood, the honeycomb of cubicles almost looked cozy. By Wednesday, some Goldman guy would be sitting in her seat — if they didn't decide to move the Plexiglas walls and eliminate her cubicle entirely. The contents of her desk drawers would be shredded. Her folder on the networked drive would be deleted, her hard drive erased. One day, a Goldman analyst would open a model she'd worked on and see her initials buried in the cell comments, but he might think "STL" stood for Sterling rather than for her, and with the rest of the Industrial Group gone, no one would correct him. All that would remain of her would be a thin file in HR: *Sophie Landgraf. Start Date 7/16/07. Terminated 4/21/08.* As far as Sterling was concerned, it would almost be like she'd never existed.

The security guard's eyebrows knit. "Do you want me to call someone for you?"

Everything she wanted was on the other side of the glass, out of reach. "There's no one."

A ding announced the elevator. She stepped inside, illuminated numbers sinking slowly from twenty-six to one.

Vasu Mehta

Vasu waited under the Nathan's sign with a cardboard box. He flipped the lapels of his suit jacket around his ears to keep off the chill from the ocean breeze.

Before leaving Sterling an hour earlier, Vasu had made one final call from his office. Aditi had agreed to do as he asked: she would get Meera out of school, take the F train to Coney Island's Stillwell Avenue, and they would all meet at Nathan's.

Now, here he was, with a cardboard box that held seven years of his life: primers on shipping containers and lean production and aluminum refining, textbooks on GAAP accounting and valuation techniques, Meera's crayon drawings, a 2001 edition of the *Dictionary of Finance and Investment Terms*, a framed photo of him and Aditi in their wedding garlands circling the fire to take their first steps as man and wife, a half-empty box of NicoDerm CQ Stop Smoking Patches, and two Hewlett-Packard 12C calculators. He could not believe seven years fit in such a small space.

Vasu pulled out a cigarette. He turned to the subway station, hoping to see his wife and daughter rushing toward him. The station entrance was quiet. In fact, everything here at Coney Island was quieter than he had expected. Neon signs flashed along Surf Avenue: *Visit Deno's Wonder Wheel, See the Great Spectacularium, Sink our dwarf!* Vasu had stopped noticing the bright lights of Times Square years ago. Here, he stared like the tourist he was.

Seven years they had lived in New York, and there were still so many sights they had not visited together. Aditi and Meera had walked the Brooklyn Bridge, but he had not been with them. The three of them had not gone to the monkey house at the Bronx Zoo or the unicorn tapestries at the Cloisters. They had not been to the Metropolitan Museum of Art to walk among relics of the great fallen empires. That was how they would spend the next few weeks, before they returned to Delhi to live with his father and sister in their family home.

His father had a friend at Tata Motors who said there might be a place for Vasu in their comptroller's office. Aditi had written her old lab to see if they would take her back. They had gotten in touch with the international school about enrolling Meera. They had not yet heard back. He would have thought these plans would depress him, but the decision to move brought a lightness he had not felt in years, making him wonder why they had not done this sooner.

He looked off toward the Cyclone roller coaster, tracks undulating like the spines of the dinosaur skeletons at the Natural History Museum, Meera's favorite. Tomorrow, he would take her there himself. They would visit the dinosaurs, the Gem Room, the Planetarium.

Feet slapped behind him and Meera was wrapped around his leg, squeezing off all feeling below his knee. "Can we ride the Ferris wheel?"

Aditi hung back, smiling tentatively, patient. He whispered in Meera's ear, "Ask your mother what she wants."

16

<hr>

Thursday, August 21, 2008

Sophie Landgraf

THE WEIRDEST THING about being back in Stockton these past four months was that no one asked Sophie about work. When she ran into Dolores Carson at IHOP or Natalie Tibirski at the Food Lion, they didn't ask if she'd had any luck with interviews — they wanted to know how her dad was doing, if she'd heard that Merle had to close the Donut Kitchen, if their house had made it through the storm OK because you know the Schuylers' oak came down and missed their roof by about *that much*. If Sophie had still had a job, this might have bothered her, but honestly, with the way everyone was dragging Wall Street through the mud, it was probably for the best.

Merle Lockhardt, who was closing the Donut Kitchen after twenty-two years because Berkshire Savings had foreclosed on her mortgage, wouldn't understand that yes, Sophie had worked at a bank, but first of all, it was an investment bank, not a retail bank like Berkshire Savings, and second of all, Sophie's job had absolutely nothing to do with mortgages or people losing their homes. Anna Maletz, a single mom who taught second grade and waitressed on the weekends, wouldn't have much sympathy for the bills from Sophie's father's bank and the student loan agency because come on, how was it possible to work for ten months at a $55,000 salary and not save a cent? If Sophie told Dolores Carson how the dozens of banks and hedge funds she'd interviewed with hadn't offered her a job, Dolores would say that if Sophie needed work, she should drive down to Shady Pines Nursing Home, which was good enough for Dolores and should be good enough for Sophie.

Subletting her apartment and putting the few things she owned into storage had been the right decision — it had helped her stretch out her severance for four months — but the two tutoring gigs she'd found hardly brought in anything, and if she didn't land a real job soon, the jig would be up. It killed her that Blumenstein had brought Donnigan along to J.P. Morgan, the way she'd hoped Ethan would take care of her. She couldn't help fixating on the fact that if Sterling had still existed, she would've gotten her first bonus three weeks ago, and tonight she'd be out with Donnigan, martini in hand.

Sophie grabbed a case of Diet Coke from Kim's trunk and followed her to the back door.

"Thanks for watching Bryce," Kim said, as she had every weekday afternoon for the past four months. It still sounded strange to Sophie — during eight months at Sterling, she'd probably been thanked about twice.

"I brought him something." Sophie presented the beige hat and mittens she'd knit with the last of her mother's yarn. "Do you think he'll mind the color?"

"He'll love them." Kim tugged at the pom-pom. "But are you sure?"

"Positive." Sometimes it felt good to leave things behind. It made it seem like you were moving forward.

Kim dropped the last of the grocery bags onto the kitchen table and motioned for Sophie to sit while she put things away. "So tomorrow's the big trip to New York? Your meeting with Ethan?"

"If this doesn't work . . ." She couldn't believe she'd been stupid enough to beg Ethan for a job the day Sterling collapsed — she should have known that looking desperate would only disgust him. The odds of success were in her favor then and she'd squandered her chance. Now she had one last shot to convince Ethan to give her a job, and she had no real leverage. If she failed, she'd have to stop telling herself that she didn't belong in Stockton.

Kim's head disappeared into the refrigerator. "What does your dad think?"

"Haven't told him." When she'd arrived here in April with a half-full duffel bag and four suits, her father had wanted to know why she was even considering going back to a place where people only looked out for themselves. Ever since, she'd been rehearsing the reply that she hadn't been able to articulate in the moment: the only difference between Wall Street and everywhere else was that on Wall Street, people were up front about their self-interest, and in the rest of the world, people did everything possible to hide it.

Sophie hopped up to shelve cans of minestrone. "What bugs me the most is that he refuses to acknowledge the reality of the situation — like the fact that I've been paying his mortgage for eight months is only reason number two hundred and twelve to go back."

"You're not going to say that, are you?"

Sophie consolidated grocery bags. "Course not."

"So what does Chuck think, you're knitting all day?" Kim stopped loading pears into the crisper. "Oh. I get it. He thinks you're still considering the premed postbac thing." In so many ways, Kim was the smartest person Sophie knew. "So are you?"

"To want to be a doctor, I think you have to actually believe one person can make a difference."

Kim pressed her lips as she always did before telling Sophie to open her eyes, it was perfectly obvious what was going on. Sophie waited for her friend's insight. Kim peered out the window toward the corner where the school bus would stop.

"So are you going to do anything else while you're in New York?" Kim asked.

"You mean, am I going to see Will? No." Sophie hadn't spoken to him in months but she had a feeling that he was dating someone, a publishing intern who called in sick every Thursday so she could lie in bed and work on the novel she'd never finish, who did yoga on a pier in the mornings and thought the self was something you could perfect — someone who was right for him. "I don't want to do anything that'll distract me from my meeting with Ethan."

"I wonder what would happen if your dad met Ethan."

That was a scary thought. "I kind of think the world would blow up. Like it couldn't handle that many different realities or something."

Kim cocked her head. "I don't get it."

Kim was right, it didn't make sense. Sophie picked at her nail polish. "I have to get out of this place. My brain is turning to mush."

"Let's check you into Shady Pines."

If nothing came of her meeting tomorrow, she'd be working at Shady Pines until she gave up on finance and took the LSAT like all the other twenty-three-year-olds who didn't know what to do with the rest of their lives. She still hoped that something would work out with Brasilia Aluminum, where Hutchinson was now CEO, but the company was under a hiring freeze. Hutch said that when they'd appointed him CEO last month, they'd made him swear that he wouldn't parachute in a new team of foreigners — if she could hang on for six months, a year at the most, he'd find something for her, he promised. Brasilia Aluminum wasn't Wall Street, she spoke zero Portuguese, and São Paolo was way too far from her father and Kim, but she wasn't in a position to be choosy.

Kim ripped open a bag of pretzels. "Are you sure you want to get back in with Ethan? You've spent the past four months telling me how awful he is."

"As a human being. I'm just talking about working for him." Outside, a kid shouted *tag you're it*. Bryce whizzed across the Maletzes' lawn, bangs flopping, arms spread, joyful and eager and trusting. "With Ethan, it's strictly transactional. I let it get personal last time — of course I got burned. I have to look at Ethan and say, how can he get me what I need?"

"That's the master plan you've been working on all these weeks? To use him?"

"More like play him. The way he played me."

Kim's squint betrayed a hint of judgment. That was probably how Sophie had looked to Vasu that night in the Cincinnati ER when he'd said that Ethan had a piece missing. If she ever saw Vasu again, she'd apologize. Sometimes you needed someone who was on the inside with you to reassure you that you weren't imagining things.

$$$

When Sophie reached Fiftieth Street, she strode half a block toward what used to be the Sterling building before catching herself and heading to Lehman Brothers. She weaved around a tour group in matching red T-shirts, their obvious foreignness prompting her to remove the Band-Aids from the back of her ankles so she wouldn't remind Ethan that she'd hardly worn these heels in four months. Since Sterling's collapse, she'd read every issue of *The Wall Street Journal*, the *Financial Times*, *Barron's*, and *The Economist*, cover to cover. She'd kept current on AlumiCorp and the rest of the industrial companies, and she'd gotten up to speed on the energy, financial, and healthcare sectors, in case. Still, she couldn't help worrying that as soon as Ethan shook her hand, he'd take in her freckle tan and the lack of circles under her eyes, he'd decide that if she was that well rested she must have gone soft, that there was a reason he hadn't taken her with him to Lehman in the first place.

She gazed up at Lehman's gray-green façade — forty stories, ten thousand people, and that was only one bank. Between everyone working at Morgan Stanley, UBS, J.P. Morgan, and all the rest, Wall Street chose to protect hundreds of thousands of people instead of her. The day Sterling had blown up, the last time she'd seen Ethan, he'd told her not to take getting laid off personally, but how could she not? Only someone who had a piece missing would be able to forget that inside Lehman and Goldman, bankers were prepping for meetings and populating spreadsheets, like nothing had changed.

Lehman's seventeenth floor was eerily similar to Sterling, glass walls and an open floor plan, the smell of metallic printer cartridges and greasy takeout. A maze of cubicles wound from the elevators to the offices ringing the perimeter, computer screens glowing with spreadsheets, hunched heads unaware of how lucky they were. The gleaming glass and fluorescent lights made the floor seem brighter and cleaner than the rest of the world. Everything in sight was monochrome except the carpet, whose shade would forever remind her of crouching on the floor of the AlumiCorp auditorium with her cheek pressed against an olive-drab seat.

The receptionist pointed her toward Ethan's office. Sophie could see through the glass that Ethan was waiting for her, squared shoulders a boast, hands folded across an empty desktop. Sophie told herself to slow down, relax her shoulders, raise her chin — she needed Ethan to think that she had something he wanted, not the other way around. Nine months working under Ethan had taught her that you could make people believe what you wanted them to.

Ethan glanced at his computer screen as she walked in, reminding her that he was barely tolerating her. He had a corner office now, large enough to fit four guest chairs instead of two. The glass room seemed to float over Seventh Avenue, hermetically sealed to keep out the rest of the world. His floor-to-ceiling windows looked onto the building across the street — empty cubicles, track lighting, drooping plants — not nearly as good a view as he'd had at Sterling.

She extended her hand. "Good to see you, Ethan." She hoped that would be the only thing she told him today that wasn't even partially true.

She made sure to sit first, to tell Ethan that this was her meeting, her agenda.

He didn't waste any time. "Your email said you had an opportunity for me."

"Have you talked to Hutchinson lately?" Hutch had told her he hadn't spoken to Ethan since he'd moved.

"How's he liking São Paolo?" He made no effort to conceal the gloating in his voice. "Gotten carjacked yet?"

"Hutch tells me Brasilia Aluminum is in the market to do a debt deal."

Ethan sat up straighter, the way he did when he wanted to conceal a weakness. He must hate that she knew something he didn't. Which was exactly what she wanted.

"Look, I don't have much time," he said. "I'll write you a recommendation for B-school, but I should warn you, there are people on the Street who see an MBA as proof that nobody in the real world would hire you."

Sophie opened her mouth, then shut it, reminding herself that it was all a game to him. He was trying to put her in her place for showing him up about Hutch. If anything, she should be encouraged that he'd gone on the offensive — it was proof that she was on the right track.

"I'm not applying to business school."

Ethan glanced at his computer monitor. "Then why are you here?"

She'd planned to present her proposal by now, but with Ethan, you needed to fight fire with fire. She needed a weakness to exploit. "I'm here because your group is behind budget." It was a reasonable guess. Industrial companies hadn't announced transactions in the past few months, and with the markets as panicked as they were, they wouldn't anytime soon.

Ethan crossed his arms. His lack of a denial told her she'd guessed correctly.

"The Brasilia Aluminum deal would bring in a few million in fees — *if* you managed to get it." A year ago, Ethan would have scoffed at a transaction so small, but for the first time in his career, he was running a group, and if she knew Ethan, he'd want to be certain that he not only delivered what was expected of him, but exceeded it.

"And?"

"And Hutch hasn't tapped a shop yet." This was technically correct, though Hutch had told her that he planned to hire Ethan — Hutch said he hated the bastard, but Ethan was the best in the business. As a favor to her, Hutch had promised not to tell Ethan this for another week. "He'll go wherever I land."

Ethan folded his hands, perfectly calm, like her proposal was the least compelling thing he'd heard all year. She told herself that if he really wasn't interested, he would have already said no.

"Who else have you talked to?" he asked.

"Citigroup. J.P. Morgan. Goldman. To name a few." Yes, she'd had meetings with each of those banks. Nancy Cho had put her in touch with an MD in the Industrial Group at Citigroup, where Nancy now worked, but Sophie's informational interview had been three months ago and they hadn't called her back. Same with Donnigan and J.P. Morgan. Ben Backenroth, who was still at Goldman after the Sterling merger, had put in a good word for her there, but nothing had come of it. She'd emailed Vasu asking him if there was anyone he recommended she speak to, but when he replied two weeks later, all he said was that he hoped she was well, India was India, and Aditi was pregnant — a boy. Ethan was Sophie's only shot.

Ethan smiled the same slow, scary smile she remembered from the time she'd told Hutch that he shouldn't give up on succession, not without a fight. "What's your ask?"

She would have settled for anything—first-year analyst salary of $55,000 with no bonus, half that, anything—but obviously she couldn't say that. She needed him to think she was in a position of strength. She'd considered overshooting as a negotiating tactic, asking for a guaranteed bonus of $100K. She'd even toyed with asking for a promotion on the grounds that normally only vice presidents and above brought in clients. But if she aimed too high, Ethan would scoff, and if she aimed too low, he'd see through her ruse and her chance of employment on Wall Street would officially be zero. There was one answer she knew Ethan wouldn't disagree with. "Whatever the market will pay. Bidding ends at 5 P.M."

His lip twitched, maybe a smile, maybe an itch. "I'll ask around, but I should warn you, we don't have much appetite for new hires these days."

"Of course." She got up and left, like nothing he'd said had fazed her one bit.

Sophie managed to appear calm until she was inside the Lehman ladies' room. She leaned against the wall, stone cool against her back.

A weak-chinned young woman with a perfect ponytail looked up from the sink and smiled. "Hi. I'm Naomi." She wore a dove gray suit that looked wrong on her though it was probably the right size. "I just started in the Tech Group?"

Naomi extended her hand in a quick jerk. Good handshake.

"Sophie Landgraf. I'm just here for a meeting—I don't work here."

"But you're a banker, right?"

This shouldn't have meant as much to Sophie as it did. "I am."

"Sorry to bother you."

"Don't be. You did it just right." Sophie applied a coat of Blood Diamond lipstick. "Free advice?" She watched Naomi in the mirror to see if it would be welcome. "Say your last name — they all do."

Naomi shrank an inch. Sophie blotted her lipstick, opened her mouth with a pop. She wanted to tell Naomi that she needed to hide how much she doubted herself because it was so painfully obvious. She wanted to tell her that you couldn't have doubters on your team, and that had to start with you. She wanted to tell her that it might seem like what mattered in this job was getting the numbers one hundred percent right, but really, building models was the easiest part. She wasn't going to survive unless she puffed herself up the way they did, because as much as people said that you should just be yourself, in banking, it was the exact opposite: you needed to save yourself for the outside, and in here, you needed to be what they wanted to see.

The security guards flanking the old Sterling building wore Goldman uniforms now but Sophie was pretty sure they were the same guys. Tourists strolled by, hands in pockets, like it didn't matter if they got wherever they were going. The Sterling stag still hung over the building's entrance, imposing and inscrutable, nothing like the deer she'd seen last week. She'd been hiking Mount Greylock with her father when she'd seen a stag among the trees, antlers bowed, neck bare, scared and vulnerable. Soon hunting season would start, and that deer would be fighting for its life.

Her phone vibrated in her pocket. "Sophie Landgraf." Her voice sounded so steady she almost didn't recognize it.

"You start as an analyst," Ethan said. "We promote you if the Brasilia deal closes . . ."

She stared up, the tops of skyscrapers reflecting the sky, clear and open and forgiving. Ethan was explaining that she'd only earn a bonus if the Brasilia deal closed, but Sophie couldn't focus on the details. All that mattered was that she had a seat at the table. She'd sold Ethan. She was back.

" . . . and you only work for me." He paused, probably checking his inbox. "So, are you in?"

Sophie Landgraf, Lehman Brothers. It sounded right. She wasn't about to accept on the spot like she had her senior year of college, when she'd worried that Sterling's job offer might disappear overnight. She wanted to extend this moment as long as possible. In a week, she'd be under Ethan's thumb again, and she wanted both of them to remember that there had been a time when she hadn't been a subordinate but an adversary who had the upper hand.

"I'll let you know on Monday."

Ethan hung up. No *nicely played*, no *welcome back*, no *I should have taken you with me months ago*, no *I knew you were still hungry*. It was useless to expect encouragement from Ethan, just like it was useless to wonder whether her mother would have been proud of her for beating him at his own game.

There was much to do. She needed to break the news to her father. She needed to find an apartment. She needed to banish four months' worth of doubt that she could fight her way back — when she started at Lehman next week, she needed to be ready for anything. The television screens wrapped around the old Sterling building glowed with impossibly beautiful skies and suspiciously perfect white clouds, as if the bank dealt in hope, not dollars and cents. Bankers pushed through the revolving door, collars askew, probably already dreading their morning alarms. Sophie fell into step with them, knowing that for now, she didn't owe anybody a thing.

ACKNOWLEDGMENTS

I would like to thank my agent, Binky Urban, for her superb guidance. This book benefited from two phenomenal editors: Liz Egan, who significantly improved the novel's final form, and Carmen Johnson, who brought it into the world. Thank you to Julia Cheiffetz, Alicia Criner, Courtney Dodson, Carly Hoffman, Larry Kirshbaum, Justin Renard, Maggie Sivon, Alexandra Woodworth, and everyone else at Amazon Publishing and Houghton Mifflin Harcourt for taking such excellent care of this book.

Alexandra Shelley was the first person who believed in this project, and I am grateful for her advice and friendship.

I am indebted to many friends and peers whose generosity and intelligence I've leaned on heavily these past few years. Jenny Halper is the best writing buddy a girl could ask for, not only because she read and reread multiple drafts of this book along the way. Lisa Sklar lent her keen eye, contagious warmth, and sensitive spirit. I am deeply grateful to Lisa Rosman for her honesty and generosity. Anne Elliot, Mihal Gartenberg, Violet Elizabeth Grayson, Jane Hoppen, Diya Gullapalli Iyer, Melissa Sarver, and Luke Sirinides provided invaluable comments on early drafts. For their encouragement and support, thank you to Bonnie Ernst, Itzhak Gartenberg, Chris Herbert, Bert Huang, Nancy Mauro, Priya Naidu, Aaron Poochigian, Joanna Smith Rakoff, Suzzy Roche, Jim Stewart, Laura Strausfeld, Jeannie Suk, Tim Wu, and Ginny Yang.

Meg Wolitzer, Sigrid Nunez, and the participants of their workshops at the 92nd Street Y and Southampton provided excellent advice, as did the Jane Street Workshop. The writers at Paragraph saved me from insanity.

Thank you to my family, especially my mother and my brother. Most of all, thank you to my husband, Scott, for encouraging me to take a risk, holding my hand, and keeping the faith.